Joyce through Lacan and Žižek

NEW DIRECTIONS IN IRISH AND IRISH AMERICAN LITERATURE
Claire A. Culleton, Kent State University, Series Editor

Contemporary Irish Republican Prison Writing: Writing and Resistance
by Lachlan Whalen (December 2007)

Narratives of Class in New Irish and Scottish Literature: From Joyce to Kelman, Doyle, Galloway, and McNamee
by Mary M. McGlynn (April 2008)

Irish Periodical Culture, 1937–1972: Genre in Ireland, Wales, and Scotland
by Malcolm Ballin (August 2008)

Joyce through Lacan and Žižek: Explorations
by Shelly Brivic (October 2008)

Joyce through Lacan and Žižek

Explorations

Shelly Brivic

palgrave
macmillan

JOYCE THROUGH LACAN AND ŽIŽEK

First published in 2008 by
PALGRAVE MACMILLAN®
in the United States—a division of St. Martin's Press LLC,
175 Fifth Avenue, New York, NY 10010.

Where this book is distributed in the UK, Europe and the rest of the world, this is by Palgrave Macmillan, a division of Macmillan Publishers Limited, registered in England, company number 785998, of Houndmills, Basingstoke, Hampshire RG21 6XS.

Palgrave Macmillan is the global academic imprint of the above companies and has companies and representatives throughout the world.

ISBN-13: 978–0–230–60330–1
ISBN-10: 0–230–60330–0

Library of Congress Cataloging-in-Publication Data

Brivic, Sheldon, 1943–
Joyce through Lacan and Žižek : explorations / Shelly Brivic.
p. cm.—(New directions in Irish and Irish American literature)
Includes bibliographical references.
ISBN 0–230–60330–0 (alk. paper)
1. Joyce, James, 1882–1941—Criticism and interpretation.
2. Psychological fiction, English—History and criticism. 3. Lacan, Jacques, 1901–1981. 4. Žižek, Slavoj. 5. Psychoanalysis and literature—Ireland. I. Title.

PR6019.O9Z5263175 2008
823′.912—dc22 2008007171

A catalogue record of the book is available from the British Library.

Design by Newgen Imaging Systems (P) Ltd., Chennai, India.

First edition: October 2008

10 9 8 7 6 5 4 3 2 1

Printed in the United States of America.

for David
u. s. w.

Contents

Figures

Preface

My primary purpose in *Joyce through Lacan and Žižek* is to bring out the basic theories of Lacan's seminars on Joyce (*Seminar XXIII: Le sinthome*) so as to illuminate Joyce's novels. These seminars may be one of the major works of literary criticism of their age, yet they are difficult and they have been described as incoherent. Having studied them for years and benefited from recent advances in their explanation by others, I try to present their main principles in clear, comprehensible terms while reaching out to the complexity of their implications. The central concept here is the *sinthome,* which Lacan derived from Joyce's writing and made central to the latest phase of Lacanian analysis. I interpret the *sinthome* as a voluntary symptom that aims at the unknown to discover new possibilities.

For Lacan, consciousness is made up of language that aims at an object it can never reach, while Joyce developed as a model for life the idea of the writer projecting words into a world he can never occupy. The disparity between our language and what it reaches toward causes the symptom, but the recognition that the world is a fiction makes the symptom voluntary. Because words can never connect with the world, they are driven to move from one object to another, and this produces an exhilarating freedom, yet no version of the goal of language can attain reality. Although Lacan deploys the *sinthome* as a model for psychoanalysis, both writers see this ongoing reattachment as a model for art, life, politics, language, human relations, and philosophy. And in fact Lacan even sees Joyce's works as carrying out a process of Lacanian analysis.

In every field progress is made by realizing that there is a further level and this is continually reprojected as a goal whose value is proportional to its distance, so that the process of exploration articulates the activity of the *sinthome*. My original subtitle for this book was "Exploring in Language," and the book still centers on the idea of exploration. This procedure in Joyce, as revealed by Lacan, shapes the fundamental model of writing, the nature of agency, the interface between the genders within each individual, the activity of truth, the use of Homer, the techniques that structure *Ulysses*, the operation of social economy, the framing of injustice as patriarchal authority, the understanding of other races, and the ability to extend consciousness toward the majority of the population of the planet.

To help me to unfold the implications of Lacan's thinking in social, cultural, and political areas, I make much use of the works of Slavoj Žižek, who has a gift for explaining and applying Lacan's theories and adds striking insights of his own. And to help explain Joyce's insights into gender and feminism, I refer to the ideas of Judith Butler, Luce Irigaray, and other feminists.

Because I took a decade off from writing books on Joyce to write one on American literature (*Tears of Rage: The Racial Interface of Modern American Fiction: Faulkner, Wright, Pynchon, Morrison* took longer than I expected), I gather material here from a dozen years. I hope that the range of outlooks involving language, subjectivity, sexuality, politics, colonialism, narrative structure, and so forth will operate to show the scope of Joyce's, Lacan's, and Žižek's thoughts, and their tendencies to link the most diverse subjects to open up new perspectives. In fact, I hope that this study will have the effect of ten books in one. By arranging *Joyce through Lacan and Žižek* in a large number of short chapters, I seek to minimize intellectual overload. The ideas of the three thinkers can be complex, so I mean to allow readers access to their conceptual interplay in manageable doses without getting bogged down in technicalities.

Joyce, Lacan, and Žižek all see the world as made up of language and they all focus relentlessly on departure, transition, and discovery. Joyce began his career in fiction by writing stories without endings in *Dubliners* and ended up writing endings without stories in *Finnegans Wake*. In between he perfected a series of techniques for jumping away from the frame of language into its peripheral possibilities. Lacan is known for abruptly stopping analytic sessions so as to create new boundaries of reverberation. He was continually mapping out diagrams of the unconscious as a structure of language, and in the last phase of his work that I focus on here, the lines of these diagrams began to move, to expand, to grasp, and to release each other, and to wander into ever more diversified configurations. Žižek is a contrarian who generally reverses what is expected. The word *paradox* tends to be superfluous in his work because virtually everything is paradoxical. His tone is illustrated in such contradictory titles as *Enjoy Your Symptom, The Plague of Fantasies,* and *The Fragile Absolute*. To write about such thinkers in an orderly way risks reducing some of their most dynamic qualities. They all work by mixing levels that seem too distant to connect and by deriving new modes of thinking from their interplay. The tendency of my book to bound from one area to another should serve to evoke such interplay, and to create a conceptual amalgam that approaches self-multiplication.

In pursuing exploration and discovery, I mean to indicate that there is virtually no end to it. I have only read a fraction of Lacan's twenty-five seminars, but whenever I dip into them, I find my mind stirred and revitalized, confronted with new worlds. As for Žižek, I have no fear of using him up because he writes faster than I can read. But my main subject is Joyce. If I can discover in the twenty-first century such elements as the primary model of writing in his work, the nature of his concept of truth, a central pattern linking him to Homer, and the leading role of the third world in the *Wake*, this should demonstrate that Joyce criticism is only beginning.

My book *The Veil of Signs: Joyce, Lacan, and Perception* (1991) may be the first Lacanian book on Joyce, though other books had already used Lacan prominently. That book centered on Lacan's theory of the gaze in *Seminar XI*. Here I concentrate on a later phase of Lacan's career, and Lacan's works may inspire any number of books on Joyce, as they have already generated some eight. At the time of the earlier book, I had made efforts to get through the seminars on Joyce, but found only flashes of insight. The person to whom I am most grateful for my increased knowledge of *Seminar XXIII* is Luke Thurston. He translated Roberto Harari's study of these seminars, *How James Joyce Made His Name* (1995). Thurston also provided me with his unpublished translation of *Le sinthome*, which enabled me to get through the French with a degree of perception, and he critiqued my first chapter.

My friend David Bloom, went over every chapter of this book with me in detail and helped to write most pages.

My Korean American colleague Sue-Im Lee read the Asia chapter and suggested that I was too admiring of Japanese imperialism; Eishiro Ito read the chapter and suggested that my criticism of Japan might be overdone. I have tried to steer between them, but they both have been helpful, and Ito, an accomplished Joycean, has provided me with many valuable details.

Kevin Z. Moore translated Lacan's essay "Joyce *le symptôme* II" for me. I refer to his translation and hope that it will be published.

I am indebted to many other Joyceans who appeared on Lacanian or feminist panels that I organized at Joyce Symposia over the years: John Bishop, Christine van Boheemen, Barbara Cole, Marian Eide, Christine Froula, Dominique Groenevild, Jeff Hibbert, Colleen Lamos, Gina MacKenzie, Vicki Mahaffey, Nick Miller, Margot Norris, Dan O'Hara, Jean-Michel Rabaté, Frances Restuccia, Charles Shepherdson, Tony Thwaites, and Joe Valente.

My friendship with Tony has been especially enriching.

Other Joyceans who have given me support include Dick Beckman, Kim Devlin, Böbel Goldschmit, Brandy Kershner, Gunter Knust, Barbara Lonnquist, Tim Martin, Claus Melchior, Mike O'Shea, and Aida Yared.

Gina Masucci MacKenzie wrote a dissertation for my colleague Dan O'Hara on the theater of the Real, and I was on her committee. Although the idea of approaching the Real was already developed in my work, the strength of Gina's vision was encouraging. O'Hara has given me reinforcement by being a dedicated Lacanian.

Jean-Michel Rabaté has provided advice, help, and information on things Lacanian. His wife Patricia Gherovici runs a Lacanian discussion group that I have visited with profit.

My wife Barbara gave me continual editorial advice on the book. Since I met her forty-seven years ago, my symptoms have been voluntary.

Peter Hanley and Rick Moffat of Temple's computer lab gave me technical assistance, especially with drawing the Lacanian diagrams.

Students who have helped me include Phil Mahoney, Brian Reece, and Joanne Stearns. Joanne indexed the book.

Thanks to University of Florida Press, *James Joyce Quarterly, European Joyce Studies,* and *Joyce Studies Annual* for allowing me to reprint material from articles, all of which were extensively revised. I am also grateful to Temple University for giving me a Study Leave and a Research Grant to work on this project.

Abbreviations

The following abbreviations refer to the corresponding books, for which bibliographical data appears in my "Works Cited."

CW	James Joyce, *Critical Writings*
D	Joyce, *Dubliners*
E	Joyce, *Exiles*
Encore	Jacques Lacan, *Seminar XX: On Feminine Sexuality, The Limits of Love and Knowledge*
FW	Joyce, *Finnegans Wake*
JJ	Richard Ellmann, *James Joyce*
Letters I, II, III	*Letters of James Joyce, Vols. I, II, and III*
P	*A Portrait of the Artist as a Young Man,* Anderson edition
PV	Slavoj Žižek, *The Parallax View*
SE	*The Standard Edition of the Complete Psychological Works of Sigmund Freud*
SL	*Selected Letters of James Joyce*
U	Joyce, *Ulysses*

Chapter 1

Introduction: Exploring Freedom through Language

Re-volitionary Explorations

Jorge Luis Borges's parable "Of Exactitude in Science" tells of an empire in which "the craft of cartography had attained such perfection" that maps increased in size until one finally covered the entire area it described (*Universal* 141). Joyce's fiction unfolded a map of the operation of language that expanded so far that it went beyond the world it por-trayed or drew forth, adding perspectives to that world. Joyce here anticipated Jacques Lacan's idea that the perceivable world, the only one we can ever know, is made of language (*Écrits* 344), an idea that Joyce may have influenced.[1] The Joycean world of language is one in which we can live and grow because of the teeming of its truths. To expand beyond what is known is to explore, and the idea of exploration is linked at the root to the idea of giving language to the unknown, for the Latin *explorare* literally means "to cry out" (*plorare* is "to cry or lament"). Language initiates itself as a cry of discovery.

My primary theoretical source for this book is the work of Lacan, especially his twenty-third volume of seminars, *Le sinthome*, which he devoted to Joyce in 1975–76. *Seminar XXIII*, Lacan's longest and most profound statement on literature, modifies his theories by developing a new function, the *sinthome*, which is based on Joyce's relation to his writing, and which becomes a key term for Lacan. In the first of these seminars, Lacan announces "what this year will be my interrogation of art" (22), and I see the *sinthome* as a symptom cultivated as an artistic activity. This lecture also describes the *sinthome* as a mode of exploration, and Joyce's fiction was always exploring the unknown—externally and internally, what was distant and what was denied.

In using language as a means of exploration, Joyce was guided into the unknown by censorship. As Katherine Mullin points out, Joyce's works generally sought to provoke censorship, starting with his 1901 essay "The Day of the Rabblement," which was omitted from *St. Stephen's Magazine* because it discussed Gabriele D'Annunzio's novel *Il Fuoco* ("The Flame"), a work on the Papal Index (Mullin 11–18). Mullin says that the vigilantes of social purity determined "the shape of Joyce's writing" (18). Censorship not only provides a cachet for each of his volumes of fiction, but also generates them. In focusing on what was forbidden or denied, Joyce delineated a margin that combined creativity with revolution: he explored the roots of oppression to reveal how those who are socially excluded—including women and non-Westerners—constituted the creative edge of world civilization. Revolutionary thinking brings to consciousness what has been suppressed so as to recreate the world through the forbidden knowledge of the downtrodden.

I attended "Joyce *le symptôme*," a lecture that Lacan gave at the Sorbonne on June 16, 1975 to Joyce scholars attending the Fifth International Joyce Symposium.[2] Though it did not appear in the printed abridgement of this prelude to his seminars (Aubert 21–29), I heard Lacan say, "*l'orbe est sur* Joyce" ("the orb or sphere is about Joyce, or on or out of Joyce").[3] This suggests that Joyce's work encompasses the orbit of the world, both its movement through space and the process of going around it—as well as two activities that form the world, circulating in the chain of signifiers and gaining freedom through increasing knowledge. Uttered in an awestruck tone, it finds Joyce's power as creator astonishing: rather than his works being about the world, the world seems to be about them. For it activates itself intellectually, artistically, and ethically through such works. Joyce discovered the modern world, and so this world can be explored in his works by means of his relation to those works, the *sinthome*.

Like Joyce, Lacan saw the human subject as an interaction of fields of language, and they both studied the operation of words to explore an inwardness that extends outwardly. Both had fundamental tendencies to see their works in terms of voyages. In his 1932 doctoral thesis, "On Paranoid Psychosis in Its Relations to Personality...," Lacan saw the interior in a characteristic way as foreign and unexplored: "narcissism appears in...psychoanalytic doctrine as a *terra incognita*...whose interior remains mythical and unknown." Jean-Michel Rabaté, in citing this passage, says that it "maps out the terrain that Lacan would keep on exploring over the next decade via the mirror stage" (*Cambridge* 15). Many writers use images of travel, which may range from incidental to crucial. They seem important in Lacan's work, especially in *Le sinthome*, for one primary function of the *sinthome* is to travel as far as possible—or more so—from what is known. Lacan added a spatial level to his theories by using diagrams, and then he added movement and tension to this space by turning to knots. We will see that a key purpose of the knot is to untie or slip away. An advantage of the ubiquitous idea of exploration is that insofar as it shifts from a topic to a method, it applies widely to reveal new areas.

In the seminar of February 17, 1976, Lacan says, "It's necessary that we continue to make the tour" (*Le sinthome* 85), and the word *tour* here, as "turn," means not only "tour," but "revolution." One recalls that in Joyce's fiction intellectual activity, such as Stephen Dedalus' esthetics theory in *A Portrait of the Artist*, tends to be peripatetic. At the end of this seminar, Lacan expresses consolation ("*soulagement*") "to have traveled this road today" (89). Between these two quotes, he indicates that all travel traverses language: "There is no real space. It's a pure verbal construction that one spells out in three dimensions..." (86). This indicates that exploration works through signifiers. On April 13, 1976, Lacan makes a transition to a new conceptual field by saying, "Let's change our place" ("*Changeons de place.*"133). In the final talk of May 11, he says that perhaps one of his notions should not be taken seriously because others have said similar things, so it "doesn't go so far away" ("*ne va pas tellement loin,*" 152). This suggests that he values his ideas insofar as they reach into the distance.

As for Joyce, the titles of all of his novels refer to a movement toward realization, for to *portray* something means to draw it forth (Latin "*protrahere*"), and the title of the *Wake* refers to a sea voyage, as does the title of *Ulysses.* The *Wake* was originally called "Work in Progress," and to progress is to step forward. In his article on *Ulysses*, Borges says, "Joyce is as bold as the prow of a ship, and as universal as a mariner's compass" (*Non-Fictions* 14). The appearance of this article, "Joyce's *Ulysses*," in Argentina in 1925 means that Joyce has begun to ship his message to the other side of the planet, where it will flourish.

Joyce's modernist map never simply covers its area, as realism claims to do: it always supports an awareness that as art it expresses an individualism consisting of metaphors or symptoms. (One is individual insofar as one does not behave rationally, for rationality follows an impersonal logic.) For Fredric Jameson, "not only is desire for Lacan a function of metonymy, the symptom is a product of metaphor ("Imaginary" 367). The symptom/metaphor transforms established reality to create new levels, multiple fields we inhabit, such as the terms of Joyce's structural diagram of *Ulysses.* As a product of society, the symptom maps out flaws in the social structure, and Slavoj Žižek argues that society is organized around such flaws, so structure can discover the critical tensions of politics.

A map tells us how to get somewhere, and two of my concerns that intertwine are with how language is deployed and observed in Joyce's work first to explore or expand the field of reality, and second to articulate the changing of the mind, the creation of a new will. To see a new reality, one must take on a new mind, and vice versa. Such re-volition has political value because the ability to change one's mind is the key to freedom. Freedom is misused if it is an indulgence in a privileged area, but such freedom is not really free; true freedom aims at the largest, most inclusive context of knowledge and humanity, so it is progressive and should be supported. And the world Joyce explores through the revolutionary unfolding of language is a world of injustice as a linguistic entrapment that he carries us beyond. Sean P. Murphy argues in *James Joyce and Victims: Reading the Logic of Exclusion* that all of Joyce's fiction is concerned with attacking and passing beyond the binary thinking that divides people into winners and losers, and that Joyce sides with the excluded.

Stephen already follows a paradigm for exploration through language when he is about twelve in *A Portrait*: "Words which he did not understand he said over and over to himself till he had learned them by heart: and through them he had glimpses of the real world about him" (*P* 62). In post-structuralist terms, he recognizes here that the world can only be seen through language; but the Lacanian point of view emphasizes that his purpose is to reach through to the real world extending outward "about him." Deconstruction as philosophical critique aims to take apart the language construct of the world, while Lacan's therapeutic aim as an analyst committed him to approaching what is real. Yet what is real for Lacan is outside the constraint of language, so the approach to it leads away from what is known. And deconstruction, which Derrida partly derived from Lacan, as Barbara Johnson argues in "The Frame of Reference" (465–66), remains a powerful part of the Lacanian procedure, which is committed to the purpose of helping people through the opening up of linguistic reality. This is Lacan's version of the exploratory imperative. And Lacan believes that to reach the real is to reach the source of history that shows through the gaps of language as a social construction.

Rather than taking language apart merely to critique it, Lacan wants to recognize the subject as a split formed by conflicts in society. In this area the explanation of Lacan by his leading commentator, Žižek, illuminates the social operation of the subject in Joyce's work. Žižek emphasizes that subjectivity is based on a sense of loss. As Leopold Bloom puts it, "Thou lost one. All songs on that theme" (*U* 11.802). Žižek says that it is when one realizes that one does not possess the contents of one's mind that one is human (*Tarrying* 41). As long as one believes that one possesses those contents, one is dominated by language that is external to one; in Žižek's Marxist terms, one is controlled by ideology. This is why Joyce's epiphanies are confrontations with what cannot be understood, or stood under. It is because self-consciousness is based on realizing what one does not know that psychoanalysis has played such a central role in modern criticism: to realize what one does not know is to confront the unconscious.

The commitment to the unconscious makes analysis so necessary for literary criticism that critics often use its ideas (such as ambivalence, a word introduced by Freud)[4] while denouncing it. Decisions in which one choice is logically better than another are not significant decisions for criticism; in fact, they are not decisions. Human decisions grow important insofar as they are not explainable. The major choices in life—such as mates, careers, and ideologies—cannot be adequately explained. Supposedly if one knows the truth, one will operate rationally; but Lacan points out that the truth can only be known in part (*Encore* 92), and the part that one does not know is generally what motivates a person insofar as one has power to decide. Žižek observes that we avoid realizing the impossibility of reaching the whole truth by making up stories in which our separation from the truth is an accident that we can overcome by moving toward a goal (*Plague* 10). Joyce exposes this by turning Odysseus' exile into Bloom's alienation from his wife by his own fantasies, his "love" for Gerty MacDowell. This alienation cannot be solved by going home: it is built into the social arrangement of sexuality in genders, which attaches male desire to fantasy.

Psychoanalysis is hard for criticism to avoid not only because deep motivations cannot be explained rationally but also because art focuses on the limitation of the existing world that makes the creation of another one by art necessary. To believe in the reality of one's representation of the world is ideology, but art predicates a world that is nonexistent (or exists elsewhere) so as to reveal the artificiality with which the world is constructed. The supplementary art world is built in the gap between reality and meaning. As Žižek maintains, the effect of transcendence is always based on deprivation (*Tarrying* 37), so that as Stephen puts it, the universe is "founded... upon on the void" (*U* 9.841–42).

Rational psychology, insofar as it derives meaningful insights from literature, is obliged to focus on missing information and the irrational behavior that analysis sees as conflict. The latest literary version of this is possible worlds theory, which explains motivation usefully by dividing it into a number of channels. The interaction between these channels has the potential to capture the conflictual nature of human motivation in rational terms. The value of this theory would be enhanced if it could see each channel dynamically.[5] The main other system to explain motivation conflictually is religion, but that may entail more questionable assumptions and a more authoritarian framework than analysis.

Some of the problematic claims of analysis about inner depths, energy flow, and ubiquitous sexuality, as well as its tendency to normalize, are not crucial to Lacanian analysis, which explains mental conflicts by the fact that consciousness takes the form of language aiming at meaning it can never reach. Thus the subject depends on the unconscious as a word depends on the extensive field of all the other words by which it is defined. That Joyce focuses on subjectivity as a complicated linguistic network is a key reason that there have been so many Lacanian studies of Joyce's fiction.[6] Moreover, both thinkers map out the complexities in which we are entangled in order to liberate us.

Charles Shepherdson argues in *Vital Signs* that while a conflict has long gone on over whether behavior is caused by nature or nurture, neither concept is in itself adequate to explain mental life; and psychoanalysis goes beyond this polarity by showing the origin of behavior in language as a field of interchange, including the exchange between circumstances and our wills (2–4).[7] He says that the radical dependence of the analytic project on reaching out to the Other makes it an ethical relation (46), one in which the totality of language in the big Other is approached by deep contact with other individuals. This matches Marian Eide's definition of ethics in Joyce's work as "an engagement with radical alterity, or difference" in *Ethical Joyce* (3). If ethics consists of extending oneself toward the other, then the more different the others are that one gives voice to, the greater the extent of the ethical action, and I will argue that one of the ultimate objects of Joyce's ethical drive is the other side of the planet.

By advancing his world of language into what is denied, Joyce augments ethics by expanding freedom. In *Seminar VII* (1959–60), Lacan emphasizes the connection between ethics and the extremity or excess of freedom that transgresses and goes beyond all barriers (*Ethics* 218–83). His major example is Antigone, and he says that Sophocles' tragedy is a turning point in the field of ethics because it goes against the law (243). Alenka Zupancic clarifies what this means in "Ethics and Tragedy in Lacan," when she says that the ethical purpose of tragedy for Lacan is to go beyond the limits of the law to approach the Real, what is beyond language, and that this purpose matches the aim of analysis (Rabaté, *Cambridge* 175).

By further extensions in this direction, Lacan studies in the twenty-first century has often shifted emphasis onto the later Lacan of the 1970s, with its focus on the shock of the Real, on the feminine sexuality that goes beyond knowledge, on passing beyond the law of the father, and on the eccentricity of the *sinthome*; and I will be dwelling on these concepts, which match late developments in Joyce's fiction. They increase concentration in the works of both writers on the activity of calling everything fundamental into question.

I aim to build theoretical links between the internal or subjective aspect of Joyce's works, exemplified by the narcissistic focus of *Portrait,* and the public world of historical discourse that expands in *Ulysses.* Jameson argues that Lacan's orders of language, as cultural products that constitute the subject, have great value in connecting desire to the social ("Imaginary" 349, 394). At the same time, I hope to show that the esthetic can support political progress by facilitating freedom. My view is that exploration of the "inner" world enhances our perception of the outer one by defining the submerged language devices that shape our exterior observation.

In *The Four Fundamental Concepts of Psycho-analysis,* Lacan says that "the locus where…the unconscious is played out" is in the optical layers "between perception and consciousness" (45). Yet this mechanism that defines vision must be seen in the distance: "the form of the unconscious—must, once again, be apprehended" through "the idea of another locality, another space, another scene, *the between perception and consciousness*" (56, Lacan's italics). What controls our thoughts must be discovered elsewhere, as Stephen indicates by saying that he must leave Ireland to connect with it: "the shortest way to Tara was via Holyhead" (*P* 250).

Freud's epigraph from Virgil for *The Interpretation of Dreams* expresses the idea that if one cannot change the higher realm, one will work on the infernal or buried regions ("*Flectere si nequeo superos, Acheronta movebo,*" *SE* V.608). Thus by acting on the submerged level, we may ultimately bring change to the visible or public one. Žižek interprets this to mean that to change society, we must confront the obscene supplement that is concealed under every social order (*PV* 366). As Dominic Manganiello has shown in *Joyce's Politics*, Joyce's orientation was to the left, toward anarchism and socialism (67–114). His absorption in esthetic techniques was meant to see the intricacy of life clearly in order to surpass it, to free humanity. My book moves from examining the mental operations that Joyce revealed to showing the range of social vision that those operations allowed him. In this way, his esthetics and politics continued to serve a unified purpose through all of his changes.

In a 1930 interview with Adolf Hoffmeister, Joyce said, "My work is a whole and cannot be divided by book titles" (Potts 129). Then he expanded on this: "My work, from *Dubliners* on, goes in a straight line of development. It is almost indivisible, only the scale of expressiveness and writing technique rises somewhat steeply" (Potts 131). The increase in complexity has to constitute movement toward a goal, though this goal may be one of maximum questioning rather than resolution, a goal of dispersal. One perceptive account of the continuity that Joyce affirms here is developed by Colin MacCabe, who uses Lacan's ideas to trace a progressive destabilization of language through Joyce's career. MacCabe shows how from *Dubliners* to the *Wake*, the meaning of Joyce's words tends to grow less and less clear while the subject—both the matter dealt with and Lacan's term for the signifying mechanism of the mind—grows more and more diffuse. MacCabe finds in Joyce a Marxist critique of the consolidation of the established order by definite language and identity.

I argue that Joyce's steep rise in expressiveness serves to liberate humanity by multiplying its linguistic and figural resources. The scale of expressiveness includes the widest range of interpretations reaching in all directions from any point, an enlarging incorporation of more areas of life that makes the canon exploratory. By multiplying the mobilities of consciousness, Joyce unfolds a new kind of exploration that moves in many directions at once. To do so, he must abandon the attainability of the goal.

Luke Thurston's work sees both Joyce and Lacan moving from an early phase in which what they wrote about seemed to be reducible to definite terms to a later one in which the main effect of each phrase is to defeat definition,[8] The clarity that goes with conventional authority is avoided by both men so as to approach a wider authority that speaks for the vastness of the suppressed parts of human consciousness. The increasing playfulness with language that advances through their careers leads both to a final emphasis on the perceptiveness of misdirection and even folly. Lacan's Seminar *XXI*, for example, is called *Les non-dupes errent, 1973–74*, which means "people who are not fools are mistaken." Such people are authoritarian, as shown by the pun on *Le nom du père*, "the name of the Father," which sounds alike in French. Joyce, Lacan, and Žižek are rarely without a humorous level that serves to undercut certainty.

All three, with their grounding in the improper side of life represented by sexuality, speak whenever possible for those who are called indecent and attack those who claim legitimacy; and I hope to show that they carry forward a psychological and linguistic groundwork for social reform. The *Wake*, which is the second half of Joyce's canon, gives voices of opposition and positions of creative leadership to the subordinated groups who make up the great majority of humanity, women and non-white people.

The enhancement of writing techniques in Joyce's work serves an increase in expressiveness. The technique is a snowballing, a constant adding of new words, new figures, constructions, levels, and modes of interpretation. It changes identity all the time, continuous mainly in its changingness. The new effects are brought into what Rabaté calls Joyce's word machine ("Lapsus" 80–81) by a process of negation. As the Joycean artist develops each new term, he sees through it and uses it up, realizing how the escape it promised is accommodated by the system.[9] This is why Joyce's canon grows more complicated from each book of fiction to the next and in the course of each book, until a dizzy plateau is reached with the virtually endless complications of the *Wake*.

The progression of Joyce's oeuvre is parallel to that of Lacanian analysis as described by Bruce Fink. He speaks of it as the forging of new metaphors, each of which is used up and replaced. The concluding metaphor is an identification of the analysand with the Other, or with otherness in general, as the source of all signifiers (*Lacanian* 70), an extension of the subject into all of language. Because the *Wake* attempts to speak for all of humanity, this is a major progression in Joyce's writings that indicates why Lacan sees Joyce's works as parallel to analysis in "Joyce *le symptôme II*": "The extraordinary thing is that Joyce arrives there... without recourse to the experience of analysis..." (Aubert 36, see also *Encore* 37).

Itinerary

Chapter 2 of my unfolding of Joyce's canon as an expanding linguistic apparatus finds the primary model of writing in Joyce's work on the first page of *A Portrait of the Artist*—an obscene, incomprehensible expression that is constantly spreading and taking on different qualities, what Žižek calls the stain of the Real (*Tarrying* 65–68): "When you wet the bed first it is warm and then it gets cold" (*P* 7). I show how Stephen's message calling his mother to change him anticipates many features of Joyce's writing as an impure act of rebellion. And whenever one of Joyce's characters changes, he imagines a woman changing him, while Joyce's transformations of language involve "liquid letters" (*P* 223) and consciousness as a stream that becomes his ultimate heroine.

My third chapter tells how Stephen, who is obsessed with changes in words, is engaged from childhood in systematically running through every verbal structure and figure of speech. He keeps trying to put these language structures into a system, but he learns most when they fail to cohere. I emphasize Stephen's confrontation with the figure of metaphor during the Christmas dinner scene in Chapter 1 of *Portrait*, where he defines his subjectivity by seeing politics as a series of irreconcilable metaphors. His uneasy sense that the sides cannot be reconciled is the basis for movement toward what Žižek, using a term Joyce uses, calls the parallax view, a realization that central concerns can only take the form of incommensurable oppositions (*PV* 4).

Perhaps the most elaborate and fundamental language constructs into which Stephen is inserted are those of gender, and my next chapter uses Judith Butler's ideas to show how he moves back and forth between male and female positions in each chapter of *Portrait*. Although he is not usually aware of this gender shift, he does grow aware toward the end of the novel of the constructedness of his gender role—and the falseness of his misogyny.

Chapter 5 points out the Lacanian significance of one phase in the cycle of transformation that Stephen—as Hugh Kenner first observed (*P* 435)—goes through in each chapter of *Portrait*. It is a phase of disillusionment that he enters after he has been deflected from the identity that he was ensconced in at the start of the chapter, whether as a sinner or a saint. This phase of being emptied of fantasy, which Žižek calls "subjective destitution" (*Looking* 140), corresponds to one goal of Lacanian analysis, freeing the subject to reassemble itself by "traversing the fantasy" or passing through and beyond it (Fink 65–68). The steps by which Stephen's subjectivity keeps changing map out Lacan's late conception of the truth as circulation. In this schema (*Encore* 90), truth never exists at any one point, but is constructed by a series of stages, each of which is false in itself and pertains to truth only by being en route. The dynamic imperative that puts the greatest value on moving beyond carries us from the displacements of the signifier and the subject toward the idea of exploration, or moving as far away as possible from what is known both linguistically and geographically.

From this perspective, Joycean narrative goes against existing theories of narratology because it does not aim at any goal. What it aims at unconsciously is missing the goal in order to release new possibilities. Eide sees ethical value in the sense that the reader gets from Joyce's work of not being able to arrive at an epistemological destination (32). The thesis of chapter 6 is that one of the main reasons that the *Odyssey* is a model for *Ulysses* is that Odysseus' major objective—from a modern point of view that works deeply in the *Odyssey*—is to get lost. I argue that his maximum point of disoriented destitution is his greatest achievement because it leads to his most radical insight. A parallel point of desolation in *Ulysses* is presented in similar language.

The movement away from established bearings is embodied and reiterated in *Ulysses* by the continually proliferating techniques, arts, and symbols of Joyce's structural diagrams. These extra dimensions, which I discuss in chapter 7, increasingly deflect the linear narrative toward alternative realities. Lacan was particularly impressed by these added Joycean levels, such as rhetoric and theology, because he defined the *sinthome* as a temporary splicing of the functions of ordinary consciousness onto further levels that allowed them to reconstitute themselves. The *sinthome* as a splicing of conflicting levels corresponds to Žižek's parallax gap. It also evokes hidden levels of relationship between the characters.

Odysseus is described in the *Odyssey* as suffering more than any other human and therefore being more poetic. He spends much of his time in exile as a suppliant or beggar, and Joyce's characters in *Ulysses* are personally dispossessed inhabitants of a dispossessed nation. Joyce generally focuses on feelings that are excluded because they are embarrassing (a word that includes being in doubt), and in *Ulysses* he reveals an economy of shame—the subject of chapter 8—a ubiquitous practice in which shame is the real object of social exchange. For example, the hardest part of Bloom's job is the humiliation that he has to endure from his clients, so this is what he actually does for a living. In revealing such a network of shame, Joyce uses his focus on what is unmentionable to develop a penetrating analysis of all levels of oppression. The major industry of the world is the production of pride and the phallic power to signify for a small number through the imposition of shame on the great majority.

Joyce's conception of signification as a power that is taken from the powerless is built into the *Wake* through one of the main founding myths of the *Wake* world, the scene with HCE (Humphrey Chimpden Earwicker) and the two women in the Phoenix Park. This repeating scene of the Fall represents the establishment of the paternal principle in terms of fetishism as a man taking the power to signify from women. In Freud's essay "Fetishism," the need for the fetish is based on the notion that women are castrated, while in Marx's *Capital*, all commodities tend to be fetishes (71–83). My ninth chapter uses their theories of fetishism and Lacan's to demonstrate that reality and history are made out of fetishes in the *Wake*. The supreme fetish is phallic identity. The pattern of identity as a fetish leads to stereotypes, and my final two chapters on the *Wake* deal with Joyce's attack on racism.

As a global work, the *Wake* reaches out to the farthest extremes of the earth, extending exploration to its limit, and extending Joyce's sympathy with the oppressed to include the majority of people on the planet. Chapter 10 examines the ways in which the creative members of the *Wake*'s family are extensively identified as African. Joyce's insistence on the cultural importance of the continent that gave birth to civilization led to his great influence, as a pioneer of postcolonial writing, on such figures aligned with the Third World as Borges, Richard Wright, and DerekWalcott.

My final chapter, "The Rising Sun," concerns the last chapter of the *Wake*, which expands on the idea of sunrise to portray Asia as rising to a central position of world power. Joyce could already see this prospect in Japan's advance, which impressed him as early as 1906. But Japan's ascent was accompanied by atrocities, and Joyce developed his last section in 1938 to include references to the Rape of Nanking late in 1937. The Joycean idea that the rise to power generally involves brutality is especially prominent in the *Wake*'s last book. Yet it is counterbalanced by the hope at the end that the downtrodden groups of women and Asians can free themselves to carry humanity to a higher level, though this hope must remain threatened.

My conclusion takes up the question of the relation between changing one's volition, opening up multiple meaning in language, and moving to a different area. The three are inseparable aspects of carrying consciousness to a new level or increasing one's awareness of otherness. They may be described by analogy with Lacan's three linguistic registers: the Imaginary (changing one's mind), the Symbolic (expanding language), and the Real (confronting something outside one's language). The *sinthome*, which Lacan equated with Joyce's talent, is the ability to shift these registers, which it does by confronting the parallax gap of internal conflict. But now we have encountered terminology that will require more explanation.

Le sinthome

From November of 1975 to May of 1976, Lacan delivered a series of ten seminars on Joyce that make up his twenty-third volume of seminars, *Le sinthome.* Most of these seminars soon became available individually, and the whole volume was published in French, edited by Jacques-Alain Miller in 2005. This book uses knot diagrams to develop the concept of the *sinthome*, which Lacan derives from Joyce and makes central to his theories. In the prefatory lecture "Joyce *Le Symptôme*" (I), Lacan says that he met Joyce when Lacan was seventeen, attended a lecture on *Ulysses* (by Valery Larbaud) at which Joyce was present late in 1921, and always carried Joyce's books with him (*Le sinthome* 162–63). While Joyce did not reach Paris until 1920, so that Lacan probably meant nineteen when he said seventeen, this indicates a considerable fifty-five-year interest in Joyce.[10]

Colette Soler points out that in his later seminars, Lacan used "the knot as an operator, to think differently about clinical issues previously formulated in terms of language..." ("paradoxes of the symptom," Rabaté, *Cambridge* 94), and Lacan's elaboration of knot topology increased enormously his ability to talk about how forces interact.[11] Up to this stage of his teachings, Lacan had emphasized three registers that made up the subject, the Imaginary, the Symbolic, and the Real.[12] In the "preliminary" terms of Roberto Harari, the major interpreter of *Le sinthome*, the Imaginary is the self-reflecting, "captivating" image of feeling and the body, while the Symbolic "refers to the place of speech and language" (7). The Imaginary is often seen as the earliest immediate link to mother that father interrupts by introducing the Symbolic.[13] The Real, which Lacan emphasized in his last phase, is located outside any law or language, and can only be expressed through contradiction (Harari 7). Hard to define, the Real is what is posited before language; but because we cannot perceive without language, the Real can only appear to us when language goes wrong, so it cannot be said to actually exist. Outside any order, the Real is the opposite of reality in the sense that reality makes (illusory) sense, while the Real is incomprehensible and provokes anxiety (Harari 7). The Real is not foundational or substantial.

The link between the registers may be suggested by saying that in order to sustain consciousness, we must be capable of feeling (Imaginary), using language (Symbolic), and encountering surprise (Real). But the three functions are not commensurate with or convertible to each other, so they must be seen as separate registers. Lacan envisions them as three rings of a Borromean knot, looping into each other in such a way that if any one is opened, the other two will come apart (figure 1.1). This indicates that they depend on each other: language would not mean much without feeling, feeling needs language to articulate itself, and neither could last without the ability to handle the surprise through which we make contact with what is active outside ourselves.

In *Le sinthome*, Lacan says, "it would be in the imaginary that I would put the support of what is consistency; likewise I would make the essential

Figure 1.1 The Borromean Knot

constituent of the symbolic the hole, and what especially supports the real I call ex-sistence [*l'ex-sistence*]" (50).[14] This means that the Imaginary as feeling holds things together and the Symbolic as language operates in the space between words; while the Real, being beyond the reality of feeling or language, always causes displacement or exists outside. The quest for a more real reality is an endless exploration.

The *sinthome*, the new term added to this trio, is identified with Joyce's talent and involves a series of puns, such as the tome of sin and the saint of man. It takes the topological form of a splice between the rings that allows the Borromean knot to be temporarily rearranged (Harari 163), unloosing the bonds between the three orders (figure 1.2). As a symptom that is voluntary or accepted, the *sinthome* matches the Lacanian motto of Žižek's title *Enjoy Your Symptom!* Thus, Harari argues that the pathological elements in Joyce's works serve the purpose of art. So Joyce should not be seen as, say, psychotic in the bizarre distortions of the *Wake*, but as someone working with the exploration of psychotic patterns for a liberating purpose (Harari 46).

The first definition of the action of the *sinthome* that Lacan presents in *Seminar XXIII* describes it as a mode of exploration. In the first

Figure 1.2 The *Sinthome*

section of the first seminar in the book, which is dated November 18, 1975 and entitled "*DE L'USAGE LOGIQUE DU SINTHOME*, *OU* FREUD *AVEC* JOYCE," Lacan says

> it is a fact that Joyce chooses, in which he is like me, a heretic, for *haeresis* [Greek "ability to choose"] is exactly what defines the heretic. One must choose the path ["*la voie*"] by which to grasp the truth; although once the choice is made, there's nothing to prevent one from subjecting it to confirmation…
>
> …having recognized the nature of the *sinthome*, not depriving oneself of using it logically, which is to say, until it reaches its Real, beyond which it has no thirst. (15)[15]

So Joyce's *sinthome* was to choose a path and follow it until halted by the Real, what is surprising and incomprehensible, which is how Lacan sees the Joycean epiphany. This decidedly matches the way Stephen takes off on a new path—one whose goal is unknown to him—as the defining action of each chapter of *Portrait*. In *Ulysses,* both he and Bloom embark on unknown paths, and Michael Seidel's *Epic Geography* develops parallels between their peregrinations and the voyages of Odysseus in the epic of exploration on which *Ulysses* is based. As for the *Wake*, the nautical word *wake* is based on Old Scandinavian words for a hole or opening in ice, and the *Wake* provides more choices of paths than any other book—though it could be said to choose them all at once: "we go out in all directions" (*FW* 618.19).[16] The path of a wake widens and diffuses.

I see the *sinthome* as deranging language and subjectivity in order to create new possibilities. It allows one to change volition by apprehending one's identity as a construction. It is promoted by writing as the entrance into a self-created world in which one produces the subject. The epiphany at the end of Joyce's story "Araby" may serve as an example: "I saw myself as a creature driven and derided by vanity..." (*D* 28). At this point the boy in the story sees himself as a boy in a story with faulty motivation, a creation that he had never seen before. A founding move of the *sinthome* is to see one's life as a fiction, a synthetic home. One's life is always a fiction (especially when it is written), and to see it as fictional is the way to become free, to unfold an alternate route, to change roles. As soon as one sees one's role, one is outside it, ex-sistent.

The potential of the *sinthome* to enlarge humanity is linked in *Seminar XXIII* to the concept of *nomination*, which refers to making up new words and language formations. This activity is obvious in the *Wake*, with its thousands of invented words. Lacan sees Joyce as passing beyond the dependence of language and reality on established authority (Harari 301–5, 346–47). Lacan concludes "that the Name-of-the-Father can very well be by-passed as long as use is made of it" ("*le Nom-du-Père, on peut aussi bien s'en passer... a condition de s'en servir*," *Le sinthome* 136). This implies that one can do without God by assuming his role. Harari says that Lacan learned from Joyce that one can make up one's own words that do not depend on authority: "by foreclosing meaning that is congealed or frozen, I am able to engender new, unprecedented meanings..." (Harari's words 301). Language is thus placed in a specialized oppositional role that is not responsible or stable, but this role may be salutary, liberating, exhilarating.

Earlier in Lacan's work, the Name-of-the-Father was the inevitable center of power, as a result of which Lacan was criticized as patriarchal. As Harari puts it, "*any metaphor only functions on the basis of an effectively working paternal metaphor*" (240, his italics). But in the last phase of Lacan's work, as in the *Wake*, metaphor no longer *functions* or can be clearly defined. The paternal center against which everything can be measured has, like HCE, the central figure of the *Wake*, collapsed. It is replaced by forms of nomination that create language detached from conventional sense so as to multiply new circuits of quasi-reality. If this language lacks completion, it may reflect the fact that the completion of the language we live in is only Imaginary.

The artist does without God by playing the role of God himself, making his own verbal universe. This corresponds to Joyce's insistence, from *Portrait* on, that the artist plays the role of "the God of the creation" (*P* 215). In *Seminar XXIII*, Lacan says, "It wasn't God who perpetrated this trick we call the universe. What we impute to God is the artist's affair..." ("*C'est pas Dieu qui a commi ce truc qu'on appelle l'Univers. On impute àDieu ce qui est l'affaire de l'artiste...*" *Le sinthome* 64). This statement rests on the fact that we can only see what we have language for, and the creators of this language were by definition artists. Their symptom was that their signs could not reach reality, and they accepted that symptom to make it a *sinthome* by creating a new reality.

These lines claim to clear God of the charge of perpetrating (committing) a trick, the vulgar use of *truc,* "gadget." There is a parallel passage in the *Wake* that explains the disappearance of God or the sacred ancestor by saying "he thought of a better one" (*FW* 24.8). That is to say, God worked for our ancestors, so if He hasn't been around lately, it must be because He thought of an even more ludicrous joke than the universe to amuse Himself with. This might imply that God has passed into the absurd activities of artists.

Le sinthome supplements Lacan's familiar position that we are spoken or constrained by language, for he now holds that "one creates a language inasmuch as at every instant one gives it a meaning, one gives it a little prod, without which it would not be living" (*Le sinthome* 133).[17] Humans now carry their language beyond authority. Instead of replacement by metaphor, there is now suppletion, a process of adding to the language one speaks by invention (Harrari 305). These activities match the conclusion of Joyce's career in the *Wake*, in which a seemingly endless number of idiolects or individual languages keep generating new word forms to approach a state in which (while serviceable words have to recur) virtually no strongly active word is repeated.

The term Lacan emphasizes to indicate how Joyce can keep generating new language beyond authority is *savoir faire* (Harari 114–18; *sinthome* 61); but a problem arises as to how savoir faire—knowing how to do things—can exist without the Law of the Father to establish standards by which expertise can be measured. Fink, for example, says that should the Name-of-the-Father be missing, "none of the other signifiers represents anything at all" (*Lacanian* 74). Neither Harari nor Thurston seem to solve this problem.

I believe that the savoir faire of invention through the *sinthome* enters into and depends upon a feminine economy that corresponds to the dominance of ALP (Anna Livia Plurabelle) in the *Wake*. Anna tends to substitute a shifting authority with an undefined boundary for the static

Name-of-the-Father: "In the name of Annah the Allmaziful, the Everliving, the Bringer of Plurabilities, haloed be her eve, her singtime sung, her rill be run, unhemmed as it is uneven!" (*FW* 104.1–3). This was preceded in *Ulysses* by Bloom's faith in Mother Nature and his painful servitude to his wife's adultery. Such projected feminine economy matches Lacan's arguments in *Seminars XX* and *XXIII* that woman effectively plays the role of God (*Encore* 77, 89): "The woman in question is another name for God, which is why she doesn't exist, as I have said many times" (*Le sinthome* 14). Even the skeptical Žižek sees the *objet a*—the object of desire that often appears as woman's sex organ—as the cause of the multiplicity of the universe: "*objet petit a* is the very cause of the parallax gap, that unfathomable X which forever eludes the symbolic grasp, and thus causes the multiplicity of symbolic perspectives" (*PV* 18), bringing plurabilities.

D. W. Winnicott, whose work Lacan accepted as important (*Écrits* 511), presents the feminine creative field in *Playing and Reality*.[18] He argues that the mother creates a protective space in which the child can feel free to expand its feelings because nothing can hurt it. In this field, the boundary between the self and the outside world is repealed, and one returns to this maternal space (the muse) during dreaming and creative activity when one expands one's mind beyond the boundary of oneself (12–16, 40–43). This is a basic support of the ability to explore, which depends on an assumption of an image that resonates at the end of *Ulysses*, the earth as mother.

Similar maternal powers appear in Shepherdson's presentation of Michele Montrelay's account of the process by which a woman becomes a symbolic mother. The baby's mother leads him to project or emit an object—Montrelay's example is the cry—"that can only signify itself" and this becomes "an index, not an object of need such as the breast... but a mark... a first signifier..." (Shepherdson, Vital 27–28). Mother gives the infant the ability to express itself, to press itself beyond itself, and on this basis it acquires the power to signify, which is phallic for Lacan. In Stephen's case, the object is urine, which signifies because its stirs his mother's feelings and his own.

Thurston identifies the *sinthome* with writing itself, or entering into the incomprehensibility of the language event (*James* 166). I would say that writing is entering into the mother because language for Lacan aims to enter a lost (m)Other from whom one has become separated (Fink 58–59), and dreaming is going back into the womb where one's mind can flow freely. Soler says, "every partner, insofar as he, she or it is an object of jouissance [dreadful pleasure], is determined by the unconscious, by an element of unconscious language. Thus Lacan could call both a woman and the literary use of letters a symptom" ("paradoxes of the symptom,"

Cambridge 93). So writing as enjoying feeling (with dread) is like connecting with a woman.

Le sinthome says that a woman is a *sinthome* for all men ("...*une femme est un sinthome pour tout homme*..." 101). She renders his symptom voluntary by appreciating it: he may tend to blink, but if she likes him, his blinking could be cute, or sympathetic. Likewise, bedwetting is a symptom, but it becomes voluntary if it aims to bring the mother to handle the child's body. As *sinthome* she allows him to expand, to encounter the unsettling Real, the point where language slips out of focus so that a new word can be invented, instead of maintaining the male defensive attitude of sheltering oneself behind the walls of existing words (the phallic signifier). Therefore, it was understood for millennia that when a man thinks of a new idea, he must imagine contact with a woman, the muse of an art or a science. In this sense, the idea comes from her.

The recognition of the dependance on the mother in Joyce's work has advantages and disadvantages from feminist perspectives. On one hand, the need to be regenerated by contact with stereotypical maternal women means that women have to be used to serve man's subjective development. To state the grievance bluntly, they have to take shit from him, and if men sometimes take similar maculation from women, it is less often, and this is due to the structure of gender. On the other hand, Joyce's worship of women has projected images of their power and freedom that have inspired feminists such as Hélène Cixous and Julia Kristeva, both ardent admirers of Joyce's for decades. As in Montrelay's analysis, the mother generates the Symbolic. But the disturbing factor is that she generates it for the use of the child, whom Montrelay refers to as masculine. If this pattern exists, feminism should acknowledge it rather than eliding it.

Joyce's analysis of the dependence of men on women reveals patterns that cannot readily be obviated. To affirm that men need not depend on women is like affirming that the upper classes need not depend on labor. So it serves feminism to be aware—insofar as it is possible—of the depth of this dependence. People for whom no one (male or female) plays the part of mother are unlikely to survive. Thus to pretend that the Law of the Father can be left behind without depending on feminine activity is to conceal the use, exploitation, and exaltation of women. As I stated, the later Lacan insists on the use of woman as *sinthome*, and he may have derived this insight from Joyce, whose two great novels end with a deep concentration on woman.

Shepherdson explains how for Luce Irigaray, the value of women's viewpoint is not based on some essence that they contain as women, but on their exclusion from the Symbolic order (*Vital* 45–47). This position enables them to recognize the contradictions in this order as it has been built up on a patriarchal basis. Similar insight based on exclusion may be found in the so-called minorities featured in the *Wake*.

Alternative Theories? Lacan and Žižek

Among the theorists I use to supplement Lacan, Judith Butler is the least related to him. The other theorists, Freud and Žižek, are Lacan's predecessor and likely successor. Butler, in fact relies on Lacan for her conception of gender as subjectivity in language, and she gives him credit for recognizing phallic authority as an artificial construction dependent on female subordination (*Gender* 44–46). But she condemns him for suggesting that lesbianism is based on disappointed heterosexuality, as if the latter were primary (48–49). I use Butler's ideas to extend Lacan's insights into agency and gender theory. I also use Luce Irigaray and others to fill out feminist views of Joyce's work.

In the sequence Freud-Lacan-Žižek, the latter two begin by following their predecessors and end by taking off in their own directions. Lacan starts with an immense dedication to explaining Freud's work and an insistence that he is only clarifying what is revealed by recognizing that Freud's unconscious always operates through language. Žižek's work is based on his wonderful talent for explaining and extending Lacan's ideas in entertaining yet complex yet clear terms; and he continues to insist as recently as the 2005 film *Žižek!* that he is a "card-carrying Lacanian" (Taylor). There is a rich accomplishment in Žižek's unfolding of Lacan's analytic abstractions into the concrete worlds of society, history, and culture, and into larger systems of philosophy. But both Lacan and Žižek go beyond their masters to become theorists rather than mere explicators.

Thurston develops a key advance of Lacan's on Freud: whereas Freud strove to resolve issues in order to provide clear formulations for therapy and teaching, Lacan, under the influence of Joyce, moved toward the position that the subject of the unconscious had to remain perpetually untranslatable and unspeakable (*James* 27–103). For Thurston, the procedure of enclosing either life or Joyce's language in clearly defined terms always falsifies what is crucial. The rejection of clarity in Lacan and Joyce leads to the radical liberation of inventing one's own words.

The multiplicity of Joyce's meanings, which generates depth, and the uniqueness of his language, combined with his predilection for autobiography, mean that critical taboos against connecting biography to the text do not apply well to Joyce. In *Le sinthome*, Lacan often connects Joyce's life to his works, sometimes excessively: "I have said that Joyce was the symptom. All of his work is one long testimony to this"("*J'ai dit que* Joyce *était le symptôme. Toute son oeuvre en est un long témoignage,*" 70). Although it is important to be cautious about assuming that an author's life explains the writing, this is because such assumption is inevitable. It is useful to avoid eating too much, but not to stop all eating. Stanley Fish faces the fact: "...the efforts of readers are always efforts to discern and therefore to realize (in the sense of becoming) an author's intention" (182). This remains true though such efforts can never quite succeed.[19] Joyce had little sense of the Jamesian separation of author from text. In the Hoffmeister interviews, he says, "In the first story in *Dubliners,* I wrote that the word 'paralysis' filled me with horror and fear....I loved this word and would whisper it to myself..." (132). Here he simply presents the narrator of "The Sisters" as himself ("me"); and this is consistent with his 1905 letter to his brother Stanislaus describing the order of the stories, in which he refers to the first three as "stories of my childhood" (SL 77).

Of course the self that Joyce shared with the autobiographical characters in all of his books changes through the process of writing and takes its vitality from being indefinable. It extends into the social field in the text, which only appears as it passes through the author, though (s)he may be unconscious of or opposed to areas of it. In the *Wake,* Joyce expanded the author to include the world, but this was because *he decided* to bring in things such as African languages and future developments. In his receptivity to discourse that was outside himself, he originated indefinite authorship, opening a far-flung field of language that would be theorized by Lacan.

The value of Lacan's denial of definite formulation is appreciated by Žižek at the start of *Tarrying with the Negative* (1993), when he speaks of the importance of maintaining "a distance toward every reigning Master-Signifier" (2). But then he says that he will describe Lacan as a philosopher even though this "blatantly contradicts Lacan's repeated statements which explicitly dismiss philosophy as a version of the 'discourse of the Master'" (3). Tarrying is a temporary activity, and in the last decade, impelled by political forces, Žižek has found it necessary to assert the dominant signifier. He sees the need for a center to support the Symbolic system even though that center be empty, so he values revolutionary zealots such as Stalin and St. Paul.[20] The advantage of this is that Žižek stands up for radical political positions, seeing the need for forceful attitudes to resist the seductions of late capitalism. Yet Žižek's political program often seems impractical, as with his idea of "good terror" in *The Ticklish Subject* (378). This assumes that the aim of history must be seen clearly enough to distinguish good terrorism from bad. I would not deny that such an assumption may be necessary for strong action, but it places an emphasis that is more prominent in Žižek than it is in Joyce, or Lacan.

Joseph Valente presents a sharp critique of the political value of Žižek and Lacan in "Lacan's Marxism, Marxism's Lacan," arguing that while Marx saw the symptoms of capitalism as afflictions pressing toward change, Lacan and Žižek believe in working with one's symptom. Moreover Žižek sees capitalism as advancing through reverses, and he finds that most rebellious attitudes are accommodated by the system (Rabaté, *Cambridge*

155–56). Valente, however, in dismissing Žižek, minimizes the value of recognizing the system's insidious grip, and he does not consider Žižek's advocacy of the revolutionary act. This advocacy is forceful: "What is needed is the assertion of a Real which…(re)introduces the dimension of the impossibility that shatters the Imaginary; in short, what is needed is an *act* as opposed to mere activity—the authentic act that involves disturbing ('traversing') the fantasy" (*Ticklish* 374, his italics). This terrible act must shake us loose from ideology. For Joyce, it is generally an act of departure, of voyaging.

Žižek's affirmation of the need for an active subject is always framed by awareness that the subject is built on negation and that real action is almost impossible. He says in *Tarrying* that if the act succeeds "wholly," it enters a realm in which subject and object are equal, and that is a "catastrophe," leading to either suicide or madness (31–32). In this sense, the action he urges remains as distant as any goal in Joyce's world, so Žižek never stops tarrying with the negative. Since Žižek avoids dogmatism, or makes it a joke, his playful attitude should be supported for allowing us to confront difficult truths.

Žižek's commitment to a progressive view of history attaches him to German idealist philosophy. At one point in *Tarrying with the Negative*, he notes that in his later work, Lacan turned against Hegel, but Žižek insists that what Lacan was saying at this point can still be seen as Hegelian (121). Žižek's divergence from Lacan is aware of itself here, and even laughs at itself. Shepherdson argues that Lacanians have to move beyond the nineteenth century ideology that history is marching forward (*Vital* 45). Yet Žižek, while he realizes the difficulties of such a position, may be justified in arguing that it must be engaged in order to motivate radical action.

Žižek was first educated in a communist country (Yugoslavia), and his work carries forward the culture of actual (rather than academic) socialism. By articulating the concrete political effects of ideas within the social field of interacting forces, Žižek helps us to discern the progressive thrust of Joyce's works. Despite the fact that he has hardly written about Joyce,[21] he delineates an important Joycean configuration by showing how the politics of the Real can be valid in its opposition to reality. For Žižek, the Real is what is excluded from the Symbolic because it is "the traumatic core of some social antagonism" (*PV* 26). On this level, Joyce's focusing of his writing on what was censored was homing in on the Real. Among the Žižekian features that illuminate Joyce, Žižek's missionary aspect works better in its exploration than in its conversion, and his extensions of Lacan are more useful than the areas in which he leaves Lacan behind.

Žižek's recent book *The Parallax View* (2006) aims to surpass his authoritarian tendencies by seeing the central focus of all important issues as divided into two incommensurable sides that can never be resolved, enacting *parallax* as the displacement of an object seen from two points of view (*PV* 4, 20). This corresponds to the *sinthome*, which is always divided between two levels, and like the *sinthome*, the parallax requires movement (two points of view).[22] That this matches Joyce's concerns is indicated by *Ulysses*, where the term *parallax* occurs eight times, referring among other things to a world seen through the irreconcilable viewpoints of Stephen and Bloom.[23] The parallax view detaches Žižek from the Master Signifier by dividing that signifier into opposites. Yet Žižek may not escape the Master Signifier as well as Joyce does, for Joyce sees the parallax as divided between two outlooks, whereas Žižek insists that it is "inherent to the One" (*PV* 38) so as to lend it the centrality of authority.[24] Žižek insists on separating the purposive, therapeutic aim of Lacanism from post-structuralism's open-ended freeplay of all possibilities ("Why Lacan…"). Yet the acceptance of every alternative in Derrida's dissemination may be closer than Žižek's teleology both to Joyce and to Lacan. In fact, Žižek expresses reconciliation with Derrida in *The Parallax View*, linking the parallax gap to Derrida's *différance* (11, 39).

Lacan constructed a late model for truth that is dynamic and includes as stages of its movement both Derrida's receptivity to difference and Žižek's focus on action, and I will describe this model in chapter 5 as it operates in Joyce. I am inclined to accept Christine van Boheemen-Saaf's argument in *Joyce, Derrida, Lacan*…that Joyce's vision of the contradictory totality of life is often more advanced than the philosopher and the analyst and includes them (195). Derrida says that his early works were dialogues with Joyce ("Two Words" 150–51), just as we have seen that Lacan insists that Joyce was a pervasive influence on him. Joyce also contributed to the work of Julia Kristeva and Hélène Cixous.[25] The thinkers whom he inspired have proven fruitful in expanding his exploratory comprehension into new territories. Perhaps the reason Joyce's vision could extend so far is that are allowed it to recognize itself as a voluntary symptom rather than an actual engagement with reality.

Part I

The Revolitionary Portrait of the Artist

Chapter 2

Stephen Dedalus Gets Changed

Creating the Real

Lacan's concept of the Real works in the twenty-third seminar to describe how writing operates in Joyce's fiction to embody the changing of people's minds as they enact freedom and creativity. Here Lacan's late turn toward the Real leads him to emphasize its positive potential, though it does not lose its frightening incomprehensibility. *Le sinthome* says that we enter the Real "through little bits of writing" ("*par des petits bouts d'écriture,*" 68). Here writing as a concrete object is the basis of a sense of changing reality. Later, Lacan says that in these lectures he wants to give us "a bit of the real" (119). Lacan's Real is outside language, so it is "always a bit" ("*toujours un bout*" 123), a separated point before language reknits itself. Therefore the "little moments of historical emergence" ("*petites émergences historiques*" 123) that he speaks of here appear as details that make no sense. Likewise the focal points of Joyce's writing are words whose meaning cannot be specified. An innovation of Lacan's is to see language as creating reality not by representing it directly as something established, but by projecting words as unclear bits; the Real works to supplement reality by calling into question these mysterious signifiers. The prime example of a little bit of the Real that Lacan cites—the apple that puzzled Newton by falling (123)—is an excrescence, cast off from the whole: the whole of the tree and the whole of causality.

In *Looking Awry*, Žižek sees the emergence of the Real as a spot or stain that he explains through the anamorphosis, a distorted figure that must be seen from the side to become comprehensible. Lacan focuses on a famous anamorphosis in his *Four Fundamental Concepts* (85–92), the puzzling wraith at the bottom of Hans Holbein's painting *The Ambassadors* (1533). Here two prosperous men stand proudly beside a group of symbols of accomplishment, but at the bottom of the painting is an abstract white smear. This elongated streak makes no sense until one looks at it awry or sideways, at which point it can be seen as a skull, a reminder of mortality intended to shock one into wisdom. Like a sex organ, it may be an embarrassing excretory blot when seen directly, but becomes attractive, threatening, and significant when looked at through the bias of desire. So the lifting bar shape on the painting enacts the Lacanian phallus as the power to signify mysteriously.

Lacan's influential theory of the gaze holds that in order to see an object, I must imagine that it looks back at me.[1] Žižek speaks of the hidden power that this theory sees in every visual field or artistic object. In doing so, he describes a "search for meaning" that animates Joyce's work, though Žižek does not refer to Joyce here: "The 'phallic' element of a picture is a meaningless stain that 'denatures' it, rendering all its constituents 'suspicious,' and thus opens up the abyss of the search for a meaning—nothing is what it seems to be, everything is to be interpreted, everything is supposed to possess some supplementary meaning" (*Looking* 91). This writing as stain matches Margot Norris's method of "suspicious" reading of Joyce (*Suspicious* 6–8.). At crucial moments, the Joycean text only makes sense when looked at awry or uneasily. Žižek sees "looking awry"—an apprehensive phrase from Shakespeare's *Richard II* (II.ii. 21)—as the procedure for analyzing the subject because the unconscious is visible only through distortion (*Looking* 10–12). It is the perspective of leaving something behind or departing from it.

Later Žižek expands on the idea that the subject is constituted by the stain, "citing" a hypothetical statement by Lacan: "as Lacan would put it, there is no I without the stain" (*Tarrying* 66). To realize itself, the subject must project itself as a blot that cannot be understood, the gap in discourse that expresses the unconscious source of consciousness. So it is only by setting forth something incoherent that I can become aware of the Real of my self: "*self-consciousness as such is literally decentered*: the slip—the stain—bears witness to the ex-sistence of a certain decentered, external place where I *do* arrive at self-consciousness" (66, Žižek's italics).

We have seen that in *Le sinthome*, ex-sistence is what supports the Real, which can never be reached (50). To approach the difficult object of self-awareness, I must see myself as hopelessly incomprehensible, so I must pass beyond or depart from myself. If I express myself as a symptom when I depart from rationality, then I express more of myself by assuming it as a sinthome, by not explaining or resolving the symptom: "the symptom qua ciphered message waits to be dissolved by way of its interpretation , whereas the 'sinthome' is a stain correlative to the very (non) being of the subject" (*Tarrying* 67).

If the first seminar of volume XXIII describes the "logical usage of the *sinthome*" (11) as choosing a path toward its Real ("*jusqu'à atteindre son réel*" 15), and if the support or basis of the Real is "*l'ex-sistence*," then the *sinthome* is a techniques for reaching outside language to create the subject. Lacan begins the section of *Le sinthome* called "The Track of Joyce" (59) by defining the knowledge characteristic of Joyce the *sinthome* as "*savoir faire*," which he refers to as the artifice that gives art its remarkable value (61). Savoir faire can mean not only "knowing how to do," but "knowing how to make"; in fact, it can mean "to make knowledge." In *Seminar XVII*, Lacan says that savoir faire belongs to slaves, the artisans who know how to make things, though philosophy has always translated this real knowledge into an artificial form of knowledge supposed to belong to the masters (21). Therefore the knowledge Joyce aims at in the Real is the knowledge of the oppressed, who know the tough truth about how the world is organized.

The movement toward the Real creates the subject, and this is why all of Joyce's novels focus on voyages into the unknown, such as the new path that Stephen sets out on in each chapter of *Portrait*, or the wanderings of Ulysses, or the wake of a ship that cuts a path in the ocean. Žižek argues in *The Ticklish Subject* that the subject must be seen in its complexity as the basis of political action (2–3, 374–76). In this sense consciousness in itself is revolutionary in releasing what is stifled, so that to bring into literature an area that has been excluded as improper is to strike a blow for freedom. What is explored is not only what is far away geographically, but what is denied politically, so the subject learns about itself by moving toward what has been suppressed, as Odysseus moves toward contact with the lives of servants.

The First Inscription of Freedom

Joyce's writing takes the form of a Lacanian stain of the Real from its first traces in *Portrait*, which fit one of Lacan's definitions of the Real by being a direct expression of the metabolism of the body. Fink says that the Real is "an infant's body 'before' it comes under the sway of the symbolic order, before it is subjected to toilet training and instructed in the ways of the world" (*Lacanian* 24). "Before" is in quotes because this infantile body can only be recovered by imagining it retroactively. Žižek's "accidentally produced 'little bit of the real'" (*Looking* 31), which is fragmentary because it cannot be connected to the system of language, tends to be figuratively excremental, a part broken off or detritus. We have seen it as a falling apple and a skull, and in this line from Žižek, it is the dead body in Alfred Hitchcock's film *The Trouble with Harry*.[2]

It is well known that Stephen invents his first original image, the green rose, on the first page of *Portrait*, but it has not been realized that his first writing appears here. This is because writing is for Stephen from the start an obscene activity belabored and in fact generated by censorship in the form of control on bodily urges.[3] Moreover, it is a kind of writing that has never been recognized, original beyond description. That originality is the key feature of *Portrait* is implied by the book's epigraph, Ovid's "*et ignotas animum dimittit in artes*. Daedalus "gave himself over to *unknown* arts" in the *Metamorphoses* in order to make wings to fly with. The next words after the Latin quoted are "*naturamque novat*," 'and renewed nature' (Ovid VIII.188). Daedalus changed the laws of nature by allowing men to fly, and Joyce intends to change these supposedly fixed laws by creating new kinds of writing. After Joyce, the human mind is different because, to give the readiest example, it has a stream of consciousness.[4] This term, invented by William James, but made famous by Joyce, is a liquid image partly because Joyce is a specialist in the fluidity of language, or "liquid letters" (*P* 223). As Maud Ellmann demonstrates, "Everything that passes through Stephen's mind or body liquefies" (160). Lacan speaks of "the fluid, flowing rhythm, the model of which is enuresis" (*Other* 96).

The account of this innovative writing reads as follows: "When you wet the bed first it is warm then it gets cold. His mother put on the oilsheet. That had the queer smell" (*P* 7). Bedwetting is a symptom shared by all human infants. Like most symptoms, it does not become pathological until it passes a limit. But in the field of Stephen's desire for his mother, or insofar as it is meant to summon her intimacy, as it does, it becomes voluntary—a *sinthome* and possibly the primary model for all *sinthomes*.[5] As a *sinthome*, it is a symptom whose meaning can never be known because the meaning of intimate attachment to mother is unbearable: "What did that mean, to kiss?" (*P* 15).[6] This field is the locus of Stephen's art, for both of his poems in *Portrait* are oriented toward his mother.

After writing the first one, he stares into her mirror (*P* 71). Here he enacts Lacan's theory that the subject forms itself by being reflected ("The Mirror Stage," *Ecrits* 75–81)—to which *Le sinthome* adds that it may be reflected by art. Stephen's second poem, the villanelle of the Temptress, is a feminist poem that calls upon women to give up the lures of sexual mythology, as its ending makes clear: "*Are you not weary of ardent ways? / Tell no more of enchanted days*" (*P* 224). Although this is ostensibly directed at Emma Clery, it is also parallel to Stephen's effort to wean his mother away from the church and traditional values (*P* 164, 248), to seduce her into impropriety. Admittedly, his feminist aspirations are compromised by being linked to a plea to the woman to stop teasing. But while there is falseness in his reuniting with her in an egotistical Eucharist after condemning her (*P* 221), this may be overcome by the way he calls upon her to renew herself, to become "the loveliness which has not yet come into the world" (*P* 251).

If the power to reshape the structure of perception is the invention of language free from authority, then to go beyond the law of the Father, one must uproot the fundamental traditional basis of language. As Stephen goes beyond the law by breaking the rules to secure his mother's intimacy, the *sinthome* performs this exploratory delving into infancy through Stephen's childhood regression on the first page of *Portrait*.

When Stephen wets his bed, he is turning the Imaginary into the Symbolic by inscribing his feeling, and turning the Symbolic into the Real by writing something that has to be unremembered, for he omits the action of his mother changing him, which has to be inferred from the fact that she changes the sheet.[7] This shift in registers is the action of the *sinthome* in forming the subject through the activity of writing or producing a signifier. Judith Butler says that the formation of the subject is the first work of art (*Power* 67), and she sees it as preceding the division into genders.

The import of Stephen's regression to before linguistic distinctions—a typical pattern in the stylistic experiments of *Ulysses* and moreso of the *Wake*—is developed in a passage from the seminar of January 20, 1976. Here Lacan presents the division between genders as an artificial construction built into the thinking that gives form to the world we live in:

> It is clear that the very first sketch of what we call thinking, of all that makes sense as soon as it shows itself on the tip of your nose, comprises a reference, a gravitation to the sex act, however little evident that act may be. The very word act implies the polarity active-passive, which is already to entangle oneself in a false sense. (*Le sinthome* 64)[8]

The primary polarity that makes signifying possible is grounded on sexual opposition, for the concept of activity here depends on the division between active and passive. Yet this division is false because these abstract poles never exist except in combination with each other; and the treatment of people as if they were either active or passive has been central to the hierarchical injustices of history, with their men and women, masters and slaves. Shepherdson's argument that the original unity never existed (*Vital* 34, 61–62) and Žižek's claim that rebellion is part of the system (*Plague* 21–27), while valid, should not obliterate the insistence of Joyce and Lacan that the idea of freedom springs from imagining a prior state that allows one to see through the polarity. Although we should be aware of the difficulties of claiming freedom, we should not lose track of its value. Murphy describes all of Joyce's fiction as moving progressively beyond binary thinking.

The oppressive gender polarity active (male)-passive (female) is called into question by Stephen's first writing, which seeks to be mastered by a woman, though it also uses her to serve. This resembles a pattern of male masochists, who seek to be dominated by women, but may really be using them. It is evident that what Stephen inscribes on his sheet with his personal pen is a message calling his mother to change the bed, and it is virtually certain, though concealed, that he is calling her to change him. Like any manifestation of the Real, the stain that is a message looks meaningless when seen directly, but takes on meaning when analysis looks awry at it.

My daughter Elisabeth said of her infant son Matthew that he just loved to be changed, especially having his sex organ wiped off. In fact, Otto Fenichel, in his Freudian compendium, *The Psychoanalytic Theory of Neurosis* (1945) cites ten sources to support his claim that bedwetting is "the most frequent masturbatory equivalent in children" (232). What psychoanalysis may have repressed is that the mother—insofar as her hygienic procedure shows care—tends to initiate the infant into a masturbatory ritual. Winnicott heads in this direction when he speaks of the child "claiming special attention through bedwetting" (*Therapeutic* 217).

The Parallax View cites a passage in which Hegel uses the male sex organ to illustrate the idea that Reason is "essentially . . . sundered into itself and its opposite" because this organ combines the lowest and highest functions (*Phenomenology* 210). Žižek says that Hegel's point is not that the vulgar see urination and the speculative should see insemination: "The paradox is that the direct choice of insemination is the infallible way of missing it: it is not possible to choose the 'true meaning' directly, one has to begin by making the 'wrong' choice (of urination)—the true speculative meaning emerges only through the repeated reading, as the after-effect . . . of the first 'wrong' reading" (*PV* 33). Therefore the confusion that every child makes between the urge to pee and sexual excitation is a model of the foundation of logical progression.

When Stephen writes his message of excitement to his mother, he is no longer using diapers (a term that appeared late in the nineteenth century), but he is trying by his writing to return to the pleasure of being changed. It is clear that if May Dedalus changes his sheet, she must wipe him off, for one would not leave a dirty child on a clean sheet. Since he gets her to minister to him, this is a successful piece of writing, and he may be referred to here as showing *savoir faire pipi* by knowing how to make water effectively.

Making water also means voyaging over the sea, and *l'eau* means a wake, so the title of the *Wake* refers to the history of humanity written in water. Exploration is a powerful factor in Stephen's bedwetting because he is seeing *how far he can go* to break the rules in order to get his mother to handle his body. This is an inquiry into the limits of possible action in securing the desire of the Other, so it is basic to the expansion of the subject through writing as exploration of the Real, the source of the world created by language. We cannot perceive what we do not have images for, and anyone who creates an image is an artist, so Joyce and Lacan agree that the world created by the savoir faire of the artist is the only world, founded on the void of the Real.

Bedwetting is the primary model of writing as exploration, but when Stephen is formally taught writing by the Church, the emphasis is on *denying* his ability to explore. The sentence he is supposed (but unable) to write in his writing class at Clongowes is "*Zeal without prudence is like a ship adrift*" (*P* 46, his italics). This is the kind of writing that controls the world, a clear, stabilized, factual statement that rejects the unknown of the Real. Stephen, Joyce, and Lacan move toward inventing a language of the Real or unknown, but the restrictive regime in control of language prevents Stephen from describing the actual contact with his mother through which he expands his subject, the area of meeting or coitus that is neither his nor hers.

Of course, information on how mothers handled incontinence at this time and place is hard to come by, or to attach to May in particular. Yet Daniel Beekman, in his history of child care, says, "Once [Joseph] Lister had demonstrated the relationship between antisepsis and contagion (1867), cleanliness became not only a social preoccupation but an obsession" (117). The treatment of babies remained unhygienic by our standards until the mid-twentieth century, but efforts toward cleanliness grew far more frequent in the late nineteenth.

From a mother's point of view, changing baby may derive a certain romantic quality from the fact that it is a relationship that must be given up. As with Isolde bathing Tristan, it is a connection whose erotic overtones are enhanced by being forbidden. Yet Stephen in *Ulysses* calls mother love "the only true thing in life" (9.843). Evidence exists that Stephen and May are absorbed in the sensuality of her wiping him off. For their mutual satisfaction in cleansing is so deep that they cannot stop doing it for years after they know that they should stop. This is emphasized in a graphic scene in the last chapter of the novel, where she complains that their hygienic bond is wrong:

> When the enamel basin had been fitted...and the old washingglove flung on the side of it he allowed his mother to scrub his neck and root into the folds of his ears and into the interstices at the wings of his nose.
>
> —Well it's a poor case, she said, when a university student is so dirty that his mother has to wash him.
>
> —But it gives you pleasure, said Stephen calmly. (*P* 175)

The extensive history behind this ritual is indicated by "the old washingglove."[9] A dozen years after the opening overture, Stephen still needs to feel that May enjoys the embarrassment of wiping off his orifices and rooting into the folds of his protuberances, delineating him as a Lacanian signifier. The answering gaze or attention of mother gives meaning, transforming a meaningless stain into a meaningful sign by cleansing him, absorbing it. He encourages her by not washing himself, a pattern that Stephen never gives up.

The scrubbing scene shows that May is aggressive in scouring her children, and there is evidence that May Joyce was similarly aggressive when her children were small. Eileen Vance, who appears under her own name in the first chapter of *Portrait*, is paraphrased by Harry J. Pollock as saying in 1966, "If any of the Joyce brood misbehaved Mrs. Joyce would hold the miscreant head downward in the toilet and pull the chain" (Pollock). "Jimmie" may have enjoyed telling about this procedure. In any case, even if May Dedalus barely touched the middle of Stephen's body or only changed his bed, it might still stir a sensuality that would remain in-fluential.

The *eaubscene* of Writing

If writing creates the Real, which Lacan described as always coming back (*Four* 49), then the initial scene of writing to cause change in the novel's overture lays down a series of patterns related to writing and sexuality that repeat with changes throughout Stephen's life and Joyce's works. In "Circe" Stephen uses the medical term "Uropoetic" (*U* 15. 4388), which refers to food that produces or makes urine. In fact, writing and urination blend with each other throughout Joyce's canon from beginning to end: from *Chamber Music* (1907)—the title of which refers to tinkling in a chamber pot as musical composition—to the *Wake*, in which Shem the Penman makes with the solvent of his own urine the ink with which the book is written (*FW* 185). Later I will examine the recurring park scene in the *Wake*, which presents two women urinating as the origin of signification. In fact, ALP, who is a river, is understood to be the primary author of the *Wake*, so that every syllable of the book from the first to the last may be equated with the sound of female running water, of which Shem's urine is an extension.

References to writing as urination in Joyce's works are too numerous to list, in the hundreds. Some entail extensive associations. For example, Buck Mulligan links making water to the Eucharist in the "Telemachus" episode of *Ulysses*, when Mulligan sings of Jesus turning wine into water (1.590–92; compare 1.357–62)—a model for *Ulysses*, which transforms the sacred into a voyage—so that all references to the Eucharist are woven into a signifying water motif. Many examples are direct. For instance, when Mulligan claims in "Scylla and Charybdis" that Stephen peed on John Millington Synge's door, Stephen replies that this was "your contribution to literature" (*U* 9.572). The scene in which Stephen and Bloom urinate together on parting in "Ithaca" sums up their meeting in terms of two parallel streams of "sibilant" discourse that never touch, wielded by two men avoiding the homosexual implications of what they are doing as they stand there holding their organs (17.1186–1209). In "Proteus," the voice of Stephen's urine—"seesoo, hrss, rsseeiss"—[10] tends to be on a similar wavelength to his attempts to capture in language the primal sound before language: "ooeeehah" (3.457, 403).

In Joyce's development of Stephen's use of the stain of the Real for writing, the primary features may be the radical originality and emphasis on fluidity that I have cited. Then the uropoetic motif may be the third of some sixteen significant features of Stephen's writing and Joyce's that are established in the initial scene of writing as bedwetting. (I started with eight and kept finding more.) The fourth is that they write with the body, expressing physical feelings excluded by polite discourse. This pattern matches what Elizabeth and Edmond Wright, in their introduction to *The Žižek Reader*, refer to as "the Real of the body" (3), which is never captured by the language that aims at it.

The focus on the excluded leads to a fifth point about content: what the Joycean artist writes about is forbidden and shameful. To a great extent, the writing, like the wetting, would not be significant if it were not forbidden. And this extends to a sixth point, that such writing is a protest against restrictive rules; Stephen is being forced to do without diapers, to control himself. And he later derives mirth from Mulligan's literary effusion on Synge's door. The link between rebellion and shame is the basis of some of Joyce's most penetrating social critique, as I hope to show. It is parallel to a link between revolution and the Real as a shocking confrontation with a reality that clashes with the system.

Lacan's twentieth volume of seminars, *Encore* (1972–73), refers to Copernicus's writing as "grounded in the real—of revolution" (43). Lacan is always attacking authority and imperialism, and therefore a profoundly revolutionary writer, even if he saw the student radicals of 1968 as unreal.[11] An indication of why the Real is revolutionary may be found in a definition later in this volume: "The real can only be described on the basis of an impasse of formalization" (93). The Real appears as a formless blot because as what is outside language, it can only be visualized as the space between two existing words that disagree with each other. This aspect of the Real resembles Jean-François Lyotard's political definition of the *differend*. Based on a conflict between terms that cannot be resolved in existing language, the "differend is the unstable state and instant of language wherein something which must be able to be put into phrases cannot yet be" (Lyotard 13). The application to Joyce's revolutionary language has been discussed:[12] for Joyce every excluded term manifests social injustice.

Moreover, the shameful nature of the initial intimacy with the mother works against idealizing it. However Stephen may wax rhapsodic about future contacts with symbolic women, the priority of the changing scenes underlines the fact that the women play a servile role. In the field of communication between himself and his mother, he receives physical information about her subservient situation even though he rarely listens to her. As I mentioned in *Joyce's Waking Women* (10), Joyce wrote a powerful letter to Nora Barnacle in 1904 in which he told how he had looked on his mother's dead body and "cursed the system that had made her a victim" (SL 25).

The seventh feature of Joyce's writings predicted is that they are addressed primarily to his mother, and here some explanation is needed. Joyce's father was very far from appreciating his son's work. Richard Ellmann gives John's reaction to *Ulysses*, which does not seem to have changed: "John Joyce, after staring at parts of the book through his monocle, observed without rancor to his daughter Eva, 'He's a nice sort of blackguard' " (*James* 530). On the other hand, while May Joyce did not live to see her son's books, he was active about involving her in his intellectual life. Stephen Daedalus tries to convert his mother to Ibsenism (which is linked to feminism) in *Stephen Hero*: he gets her to read *The Wild Duck* and praise it (84–87). And here he remarks about his father, "I know he doesn't care a jack straw about what I think or what I write" (85). It is likely that Joyce arranged his writing not only to address mom, but to alienate dad. In 1916, Joyce's sister May, hearing that *Portrait* was about to be published, recalled that Joyce had read chapters of the novel to his mother even though she died in 1903: "You have rewritten it since we lived in St. Peters Terrace when we used to be all put out of the room when you were reading each new chapter to mother" (*Letters II* 383).[13] In March 20 of that year, Joyce wrote his mother from Paris a list of three books he planned to write, ending with the italicized line "This *must* interest you!" (*Letters II* 38).

The extent to which Joyce's writings remained focused on his mother despite her death, and despite the fact that the literary world he lived in was run by men, may be traced back to the fact that his mother was at the root of his writing. Here we recall Montrelay's claim that the mother elicits from the child the objects that become the first signifiers. As Shepherdson notes, the popular Lacanism whereby the father introduces the Symbolic must be modified to show the mother initiating writing (*Vital* 28–29, 73–74).

In *Portrait,* as I mentioned, after writing his first poem, Stephen gazes "at his face for a long time in the mirror" of his mother's dressingtable or vanity (*P* 71). The poem, which is not given, but described as idealized and imaginary, is his image of himself through her eyes. Later he writes his villanelle in bed with a "dewy wet" soul in a compositional process accompanied by lustful feelings (*P* 217–23). Using the second person, the poem that originates in this bed of dampness invokes a maternal "Temptress," urging her to liberate herself from the traditional female role of collusion.[14]

The idea that Joyce's works are aimed at his mother may be confirmed by the way they move toward a final focus on emotionally entering the mind of a woman who is a mother, such as Gretta Conroy, Molly Bloom, and Anna Livia Plurabelle. Even the egocentric *Portrait* speaks poignantly for Stephen's mother in its last page, where she announces one of the possible scenarios for *Ulysses*: "She prays now, she says, that I may learn in my own life and away from home and friends what the heart is and what it feels. Amen. So be it" (*P* 252). In aiming at his mother, Stephen aims at change, for in his world, there is little possibility of change except through her. If we see *Ulysses* as an extension of *Portrait*, which at one time was supposed to extend to June 16, 1904 (Litz 3, 132–39), it may be argued that each stage of every Joyce novel brings it closer to a maternal goal linked to uncertainty and freedom. This perspective appears in Norris's "The Last Chapter of 'Finnegans Wake': Stephen Finds His Mother," which focuses on the childlike St. Kevin washing himself in Book IV of the *Wake* as part of a return to mother that finally involves Stephen in ALP's rebellious soliloquy (Norris 21–28).

The eighth quality of Joyce's writing anticipated by Stephen's wetting is that it is incomprehensible and upsetting in its effects. Thurston argues that the central function of Joyce's works is to confront readers with an incomprehensible text that undermines their theoretical apparatus (*James* 12, 71, 149). This pattern may be related to a remarkable ninth feature, that the inscription changes its nature as soon as it is produced, so that the bedwetting immediately begins to shift from warm to cold. Any attempt to fix the text's meaning-in-progress must always be incomplete and instantaneously erroneous. Henry Staten describes this aspect in "The Decomposing Form of Joyce's *Ulysses*." His model for the novel accords with the stain of the Real by being excremental or external to form: "What *Ulysses* as a whole imitates... is not any phenomenal form but rather its making and unmaking at the limit where imitative form becomes indiscernible from deconstruction" (382). In following the changes of mood that run through experience, the book takes apart its own coherence.

The combination of cold and hot is linked by Bella/o Cohen in the "Circe" episode of *Ulysses* to bisexuality when (s)he says to Bloom, "No more blow hot and cold" (15. 2964). This means that Bloom, having formerly been ambivalent, will now be subordinated to the position of woman. So the warm-cold shift indicates the tenth feature of the bedwetting. It is androgynous, as Rabaté says that the narrator of the *Wake* is (*Void* 154–80). In fact, men generally urinate standing, while women do it sitting, as Bello emphasizes (*U* 15.3015–23), but bedwetters do not distinguish. For Melanie Klein, wetting starts as a feminine activity, but gets more masculine and aggressive as it develops (291–92). Klein emphasizes the destructive disruption involved in enuresis. The androgyny of bedwetting establishes Stephen's writing on a level prior to the hierarchical polarity that Lacan critiques. Yet its shameful nature precludes imagining it as a lost ideal, making shame a critical tool against essentialism.

The eleventh attribute of Stephen's uropoesis is that it compels his mother to act. Just as Stephen tried to convert his mother to progressive ideas in *Stephen Hero,* so in the last chapter of *Portrait*, the new Stephen expresses a determination to influence the daughters of Ireland so "that they might breed a race less ignoble than their own" (*P* 238). In this affirmation of nurture over nature, his art still aims at maternal action. Joyce's works always have the purpose of reforming society, though he finds that for him, the best way to do so is through art, and artistic concerns may distract him from social ones. His most elaborate written explanations of what he wrote were his many long letters to Harriet Shaw Weaver on the *Wake* from 1923 to 1933, enlisting the support of an older woman.

The call for progressive action (reform as cleaning up) is related to the twelfth trait of the wetting: it aims at freedom through release, a physical relief that frees the mind. Letting out bodily tension lowers defenses and allows one to see the stain of the Real that liberates the subject by calling all assumptions in doubt. I quoted *Seminar XX* earlier on the revolutionary implications of the Real, and the Wrights say, "freedom involves the impossible Real, a hard kernel resisting symbolization" (*Reader* 4). The thirteenth feature may be covered quickly: bedwetting and Joycean writing are funny.

The final aspects of Stephen's writing that I want to consider extend from the word *obscene*, which carries an elaborate superstructure of implications. Being past diapers, Stephen is aware of the obscenity of his bedwetting, which involves a heavy atmosphere of shame that generates a special intimacy with his mother. This atmosphere is made concrete by smell—and Joyce is generally regarded as one of the most olfactory of writers—so as to actualize a different scene, a different field. The *American Heritage Dictionary* connects the prefix *ob-* to "opposite," and I argue that obscenity creates an opposing scene, a different stage setting filled with subversive undertones. This opposing level corresponds to the secondary level created by writing and also to the unconscious. Lacan says, "...Freud called the locus of the unconscious *ein anderer Schauplatz*, another scene...' (*Écrits* 458), and Lacan sees this as the place of the Other where the chains of language reside (*Écrits* 525, 578). When Stephen writes by projecting his drive as an object or stain, he opens the alternative field of language as object.

Now the word *obscene* does not appear in the bedwetting passage, but it is implied by that passage as surely as the word *urine*, though Stephen may not know either word at the time that he remembers through Joyce. By expressing himself as the unknown signifier *urine*, Stephen sees himself as a *you* that is *in* his action, a subject as object. Levels of language between the character and the author are important to Joyce's emphasis on the fact that we are written by language. To a great extent they are where the action is. Freedom is the freedom to be aware of all of one's implications, to take responsibility for one's authorship, whereas ideology is what encloses one in fixed language. Joyce's reaching toward the ultimate horizons of language relates to the social field and to Lacan's chain of signifiers. David Bloom pointed out in conversation that the *Wake* consists largely of words that are not present. The words that are present are often tangential to the ones implied.

The two levels on which this writing takes place, scene and ob-scene or conscious and unconscious, manifest an implication of the way it turns from warm to cold. It includes in itself opposing forces and therefore the Joycean artist's initial signature contains within itself elements that contradict each other. One consequence of this is that at any point in Joyce's work opposing intentions are expressed, a pattern that is defined in sexual terms by Colleen Lamos (124–25) and in political terms by Valente ("Between Resistance and Complicity"). What allows these elements to coexist involves liquidity and obscurity.

In "Joyce *le symptôme II*," Lacan writes in an obscure syntax of fluid puns, so that as with the *Wake*, translation is conjectural or only one possibility. Here he seems to say that the formation of manhood for Joyce involves the "*eaubscene*," A pun on the French *eau*, "water": "*. . . l'eaubscene. Écrivez ça eaub . . . Pour rappeler que le beau n'est pas autre chose*" (Aubert 31, second ellipsis Lacan's). "The *eaubscene*. Write this *eaub* to recall that the beautiful [*beau*] is nothing else." Since *eaub* reverses *beau*, this implies that the beautiful is the reflection of water, or that Joyce's obscenity is the reverse of beauty, or is beauty itself. It is most unlikely, but not entirely impossible that this refers to the bedwetting scene as the *eaubscene* of writing, of the subject as a reverse inscription of beauty as water.[15] Urine may be described as water in reverse, going out instead of coming "in you," something like a photographic negative of water; and this may be connected to fiction as a photo of life, an inanimate extension filled with vitality.

Winnicott emphasizes that the mother creates a protective field that allows the child to expand (*Playing* 62–66). Stephen's reaching out through his wetting is an expansion that he can be conscious of because it reaches toward her and is shared with her, made significant by her. By expressing himself with a signifier, in Montrelay's terms, he becomes conscious of himself. And becoming conscious of oneself is a mode of exploration, a spatial displacement of seeing oneself from outside. Žižek presents this strongly with regard to the idea that one exists by thinking: "Upon reaching the point of absolute certainty in *cogito ergo sum*, Descartes does not yet conceive of the *cogito* as correlative to the whole of reality, i. e., as the point external to reality, exempted from it, which delineates reality's horizon . . ." (*Tarrying* 13). Self-consciousness claims a perspective that takes one beyond what is known to define the limits of the world. It is so alienating that for Joyce, it may only be done by projecting something that plays the role of a mother. In giving Stephen writing, his mother gives him exploration, the drawing-forth of portrayal.

Of course Joyce's writings involve literary principles as well as submerged forces. To say that imitative form builds on the body's writing, symbolism is sexual, impressionism is subjective, and the stream of consciousness depends on liquidity, is quite reductive. Other perspectives extend the meaning of such techniques far beyond such emphasis. But the fundamental patterns that I list play profound shaping roles in form and content.

Being Changed

Stephen returns to the situation of being changed whenever he enacts freedom, progress, or creativity. His most elaborate vision of such transformation appears when he daydreams as a pre-adolescent about "the unsubstantial image which his soul so constantly beheld" (*P* 65). This image of the ideal soon turns out to be female and maternal: "He would fade into something impalpable under her eyes and then, in a moment, he would be transfigured. Weakness and timidity and inexperience would fall from him in that magic moment." Change is exalted to transfiguration here, yet it retains its underlying configuration of being changed. This process—in which a woman removes weakness and impurity from Stephen so that he feels renewed—is repeated at the end of each succeeding chapter with the prostitute, the church embodied by the Virgin Mother, and the bird girl on the beach. In the prostitute's "arms he felt that he had suddenly become strong and fearless and sure of himself" (*P* 101). Embracing the Church, which he can address only as Mary (his mother's name, while God is in the third person), he is "conscious of an invisible grace pervading and making light his limbs" (145), And on the beach that leads to the bird girl, "the body he knew was purified in a breath and delivered of incertitude" (169). Colleen Jaurretche remarked to me that the feeling of being uplifted, which is enacted in all of these passages and reaches its height in the "soaring" on the beach (169), may be based on the mother holding up the changed child to separate it from its mess and to celebrate its renewal, implying an exclamation like "Aren't we clean!" The transfiguration afforded by the maternal image is a change of figures that reties the knot of subjectivity, carrying out the operation of the *sinthome*. It involves a new language in each case as Stephen becomes a whoremonger, then a pious person, and then a revolutionary artist. Maternal changing grants an originality that creates a different world by a process so unheard of or repressed that it took ninety years to be discovered.

The inspiring maternal image at the end of the novel is not obvious, but in fact Stephen's mother emerges vividly in the last ten lines because he is leaving her decisively for the first time. On one level, he is killing her by departing, and he blames himself dreadfully in *Ulysses* for her death, however conscious he may be of the suspicion that she died because he left her. But parting brings closeness, and indeed, she *is* presented at the end as changing his garments: "Mother is putting my new secondhand clothes in order" (*P* 252). He could not take a new form without her making the old clothes new.

Elizabeth Sheffield, in *Joyce's Abandoned Female Costumes, Gratefully Received*, presents a keen feminist analysis of how Joyce uses women as objects to realize Stephen and himself. She says that woman is a figure of the space of writing in Joyce's texts, a space he always approaches with trepidation (11). This is true, but Joyce did not turn away from writing or women: he continued to approach them eagerly as sources of development. And his woman characters are more than objects: they are among the most vital women in literature. The Joycean male cannot change without being changed by them, so freedom is something that women are in charge of, though they do not possess it themselves. As Shepherdson points out, the enforced position of women outside the Symbolic means that through their alterity, one can intellectually reshape the structure of reality (*Vital* 45–47).

The need to be changed extends into every area of Stephen's life. For example, Joyce tells us that the only smell Stephen dislikes is "like that of longstanding urine" (*P* 151). This may bring him back to the grievous state in which his mother withholds her attention. When E__. C__. fails to appear after he strives to impress her by playing the role of the "farcical pedagogue (*P* 73)—a role that marriage to her might put him into—he is disappointed that she has not come to transform him into a star. So he exposes himself to a "rank heavy air" of "horse piss and rotted straw" (*P* 86) to punish his pride.

One branch of the pattern of changing is the image of molting, which shows how Stephen's need to use women to free himself is built into his body: whenever Stephen feels strong emotion, it falls away from him like peel dropping from a fruit. Lacan treats this image extensively, focusing on the scene in which it is established, the one in which Stephen is assaulted by Heron and his friends for defending his artistic values (*P* 80–82). While Lacan gets some facts of the scene wrong, his interpretation has reach (*Le sinthome* 148–52). He argues that Stephen's Imaginary or ego is displaced from the knot of his subjectivity by this brutal confrontation with the Real: this results in Stephen's splicing his knot with a temporary correction (152). Lacan says that this new detached relation to the ego explains the displacement of Joyce's writings from conventional feelings, which makes them productively "*illisible*" (151) because they do not sustain Imaginary satisfaction. While Lacan does not use the term here, his most elaborate examination of a scene from Joyce is his most concrete account of the formation of the *sinthome*, the splice that allows the knot to be retied. Lacan sees the power of paternal aggression, as embodied by Heron, in forcing the alienation of the *sinthome* (150), but he does not consider that Stephen could not react to this violence so impassively without drawing on the comfort (*soulagement*) of May Dedalus.

In Joyce's view, Stephen's body seems not to belong to him, but to his mother. For in the account of his molting, an unnamed power is in charge: "some power was divesting him of that suddenwoven anger as easily as a fruit is divested of its soft ripe peel" (*P* 82, compare 86 and 149), another image of being changed. Stephen is uneasy about giving power over his body to a man, and I think that this power that removes the peel or waste matter of agitation is the maternal one that generally wipes away weakness. By allowing him to let go of his grievance (or ego) like a rind—or as Lacan puts it, *lâcher comme une pelure* (149)—this power allows him to free his body to change its formation rather than being enclosed. Such permutability is granted by a mother who wipes away shame, and this is a crucial function of woman for Joyce. The *Wake* refers to a wife as a "wip" (465.8), and *Ulysses* repeats the image of a woman giving a man a bath (3.234–38), which appeals to Bloom in "Lotus Eaters" (5.503).[16]

Erotic scenes in Joyce's fiction often place emphasis on the process of being wiped off, so that to a certain degree the aim of the male sex organ is not a woman's body, but the woman's fabric, as when Bloom gazes at Gerty McDowell's stockings (*U* 13.716, 929, 1261–62). This corresponds to Joyce's 1930 witticism to Frank Budgen: "now I don't care a damn about their bodies. I am only interested in their clothes" (Ellmann, *JJ* 631). For this reason, the earliest sex scene that Molly Bloom remembers may be seen not as deprived, but as fetishistically privileged. She thinks of Lieutenant Mulvey, "I pulled him off into my handkerchief…I wouldn't let him touch me inside my petticoat" (18.809–11). On one level of Joyce's conception, Mulvey's contact with Molly is not less direct, but more so, because the fabric he reaches is the real object of desire, linked to the weaving of language, so it secures primacy. In fact, this evinces the Lacanian Real because it marks the sex act as unrealizable. After Bloom's scene with Gerty in "Nausicaa," he feels "stuck" (*U* 13.979, an expression of affection) to his underwear; and in Joyce's first sexual scene with Nora Barnacle, he did not remove his trousers (Maddox 27). Again the object of ejaculation is cloth.

In *Reauthorizing Joyce*, Vicki Mahaffey develops the connection in Joyce's work between textuality and textiles (141–65), and in a 2004 conference paper, "Those Dirty Sheets: Paper and Linen, Ink and Soil," she connects bed sheets to sheets of paper as fields of inscription. On several occasions when Bloom sees Molly erotically, she is covered with a veil (5.494, 8.914, 15.300); and in the first of these, the veil is actually a bed sheet held up to her eyes.[17] The villanelle scene is not the only one in which Stephen gushes with erotic feeling for his womb of cloth: "It would be lovely in a few minutes. He felt a warm glow creeping up from the cold shivering sheets, warmer and warmer till he felt warm all over, ever so warm..." (*P* 17).

The sexual contact between the Joycean male and fabric corresponds to the way Joyce's writing presents an impenetrable veil of textuality. Whatever is behind language can only be invoked by the veil itself, as an effect of the stirring of the signifying threads, the changing within words. This depends on a function coded as womanly, for the uncertainty that Molly as Penelope weaves (Penelope's dilatory weaving is in Book II of the *Odyssey*) is what attracts and energizes Bloom. He cannot bear either to be rejected or to be fully accepted, so he is caught in a vacillation that he sees her as controlling as he thinks about her infidelity throughout the day. She directs him by having the power to change, which operates in both of them at once.

Washing Wishes

One of the central functions of women in the *Wake* is washing clothes, an activity that runs through the ALP chapter (196–216). Traditionally woman never stops washing man's soil, and even if a man does his laundry (a rarity!), her cleansing function remains. This process stands among other things for the way a woman cleanses a man through sex. A man's fantasies may be perverse, and Žižek sees fantasy as being very close to perversion (*Plague* 14). Indeed, fantasies that are not fulfilled (the rule) are perverse in the sense of enjoying what is not actually done. But as soon as someone reciprocates, the "perversion" expresses love—which Thomas Mann describes in *The Magic Mountain* as made up of a series of perversions (127). Kissing is a perversion (oral fixation). So the dirty is made clean and beautiful, the little bit of the Real given the illusion of being shared. The filthiest thought a man can have can grow radiant when he enacts it with a mate, and this is one of the strongest senses in which women are washers. But there are others: their social skills may often smooth over the awkwardness of egotistical men.

The ultimate passage on the washers, in Book IV of the *Wake*, returns to the image of washing babies' nappies, emphasizing the wet penises of the twins: "one chap googling the holyboy's thingabib and this lad wetting his widdle" (620.23). Joyce apparently invented the verb *google*. The "Annone wishwashwhose" (*FW* 614.2)—or washinghouse of wishes—may be equated with the "vicocyclometer" lower on the same page, which stands for the entire *Wake* as a machine of Viconian recycling. This refers not only to digestion, but to an electric washing machine, a device invented in 1910. The process by which women constantly cleanse men makes the ongoing changes of life possible.

Because of the progress in "the emancipation of women," which Joyce described in 1923 as "the greatest revolution in our time" (Power 35), we hope that the servile roles that women play in washing men will be better distributed between the sexes. Devlin holds that archetypes are stereotypes (*James* 83–84), and Joyce portrays the archetypes or stereotypes of male and female partly to expose them as forms of paralysis, to critique their persistence. In *Joyce's Waking Women*, I see a strong current of feminism in the *Wake* that leads to ALP's decision to leave her husband at the end (81–131; *FW* 627). Norris points out that the portrayal of the washerwomen in the ALP chapter emphasizes the hardships of female labor (*Joyce's Web* 139–63), and Joyce's insistence on the prevalence of this form of servitude helps us to see why it should be modified. The great Irish bard Van Morrison pays tribute to Blake's male ability to cleanse perception, and to a workingman, in his song "Cleaning Windows."

Yet maternal cleansing persists because it has been a source of strength to women. On this level, Joyce celebrates heroinism, a word that, if it existed, would differentiate the heroism of women. The "Annone wishwashwhose" (614.2) is also "the noneknown worrier" (596.10), so it refers to Anna as the Unknown Warrioress. She is unknown because women's productive bravery—often through worry—has not been appreciated. Insofar as women use their power as women actively, it transforms their hidden sex organ into the possession ("whose") of every wish of washing. So it appears as a hose that will wash one off thoroughly, in accord with Lacan's idea that woman can possess the phallus as the power to signify (*Ecrits* 579). The powers of the wishwashing hose may be linked to Stephen's phrase about Ann Hathaway, "woman's invisible weapon" (*U* 9.461). Man has access to the creative process only through a version of her (a muse), and this gives her great power that may work better if it is unknown, or if she says no.

Moreover, she can wash away his wishes and make him wonder "whose" they are. For her power to cleanse is the power to transform, and what comes back from her house is what is fit to survive her washing: "the fittest surviva lives that blued, iorn and storridge ["bluing, ironing, and starch"] can make them" (614.12–13). This indicates something tough or ruthless about the opposition she subjects him to ("blood, iron, and starch"). She confronts him with the Real that dislodges his fantasies and makes him refigure them in polished (dapper) roles: "each rinse results in a dapperant rolle…" (614.5–6). Her difference changes him over and over, for contact with her involves her denial insofar as she differs from him, or is really there.

So Joyce has to return, at the ends of "The Dead" and his novels to the power a woman has to deny a man: Gretta's love for another, May Dedalus's insistence on the falseness of her son's position, Molly's infidelity, and ALP's decision to leave HCE. All erupt as the Real to upset the male protagonist's self-possession, so all illustrate the power women can have through their control of the shock of the Real, the surprise that does not fit, that rearranges assumptions. If Joyce's symptom led him to impersonate women, he used it as a *sinthome* to deliver a new understanding of womanly resistance that could carry humanity forward.

If a woman's denial is what ultimately draws the narrative ahead, this is because it is by exploring the point of interchange with otherness that the text approaches the reality of woman outside of what is known, and this is the margin from which the apparatus of knowledge can be renewed, for Joyce's sinthomatic attachment to woman is not fixed, but a splice that can be transformed. So Joyce returned at the end of his last novel to the Real overlap between mother and child that appeared at the start of his first. And so we spin full cycle from the mother who changes Stephen to the text that changes us. Having indicated a fundamental basis for the changing of the mind in Joyce's fiction, I will examine in the next chapter how such re-volition works through language in *Portrait*.

Chapter 3

Freedom through Figuration in A Portrait

The action of *Portrait* consists of a process of changing identity that Stephen goes through in each chapter, a sequence of stages that works by reconstituting the linguistic formations that make up the shifting interplay of his volitions. At the start of each chapter, Stephen settles into a new role and believes that he fills the phrase that describes him: "*Stephen Dedalus/Class of Elements…*" (P 15). But he soon grows aware that he does not fit this phrase, so a threat arises that embodies the limitation of identity as the oppressive authority that defines roles. This paternal threat forces him to be displaced from the phrase that he has occupied and to set out in a new direction.

As Stephen shifts into new identity at the end of each chapter, his triumphant sense of having found his true meaning projects the image of a new mother nursing and changing him, yet this wonderful new identity will prove inadequate in the next chapter. His real goal is not identity, but displacement or ex-sistence,[1] for his individuality is the activity that changes what he has been to what he will be. This activity occurs whenever he encounters a phrase that he does not understand (the Real), so that he is required to take on a new construction of language. I aim to show how figures of speech assemble his subject as a site of resistance as he first *sees* through them and then sees *through* them.

Stephen's vital core is the contradiction between disparate roles that he assumes. In Chapter I he tries to fit in or hide until he is driven by brutality to protest. This protest leaves him quite a different person in II, a rebel who imitates the Count of Monte Cristo and Napoleon, rejects the "hollow sounding " (*P* 83) voices of convention presented by parents and schoolmates (80–84), and moves toward seeking himself in sin or deviation. The debauchee of Chapter III, the devout Christian of IV, and the artist who shifts from domesticity to exile in V—all of these figures remain active in Stephen; and his ability to modulate between them is learned through language, through learning how words can change meanings in different contexts.

In "The *Portrait* in Perspective," the most influential essay on the novel, Hugh Kenner first pointed out that "the action of each of the five chapters is really the same action. Each chapter closes with a synthesis of triumph which the next destroys" (*P* 435).[2] Kenner's emphasis on how unrealizable Stephen's aims are established the idea that *Portrait* is mainly censorious toward Stephen, that he will not become Joyce. The great critic Kenner was politically conservative, and it may be that he sees Stephen as "indigestibly Byronic" (*P* 439) out of opposition to the idea of changing the world.

The negative view of Stephen may be the most prevalent one among critics today, yet many still hold that Stephen may be a portrait of the artist as a young man.[3] Valente presents a balanced perspective, seeing an oscillating "tonal shifting from sympathetic identification to ironic distance in *A Portrait*" (*James* 45). For many readers, Stephen is usually more sympathetic after the middle of each chapter, when he is needy and disoriented, than he is at the start, when he thinks that he knows who he is. Neither of these two states can identify him, for he is made up of the shift between them. Lacan says that it is in the initial (or initiating) link between one signifier and another that "it is possible for this fault we call the subject to open" (*Other* 88).

I hold that Stephen moves toward becoming Joyce precisely when he is deflected from his aim. As Žižek states, the subject is formed when its Symbolic support falls away (*Tarrying* 42). Moreover, Žižek says that one thesis of Lacan's Seminar *Le sinthome* is that *jouissance* "arises when its movement repeatedly misses its goal, a pleasure that is generated by the repeated failure itself" (*PV* 96). This is the *sinthome* as a voluntary symptom of alienation. Stephen becomes the Joycean artist by detaching himself from his object, tasting "the joy of his loneliness" (*P* 68) as he turns the world to a series of incomprehensible epiphanies of himself and "testing its mortifying flavour in secret" (*P* 67). As the world withholds itself from him as if in scorn, he sees it and himself as they really are, focusing on what cannot be understood rather than imposing on it.

One reason that Stephen's future should not be decried is that Joyce probably supports Stephen's assertion that pity and terror are necessary not only to tragedy, but to the dramatic form (*P* 204–5). Insofar as Stephen serves largely to illustrate wrong attitudes, pity and terror disappear. Yet our pity and terror grow stronger toward Stephen in *Ulysses* after he loses his mother. And he moves closer to Joyce in *Ulysses* by improvising a story, "*A Pisgah Sight of Palestine or The Parable of the Plums*" (*U* 7.923–1058), which resembles stories in *Dubliners*, and which is preceded by Stephen thinking to himself as a complete paragraph, "Dubliners" (7.922). *Portrait* has been the bestselling novel of all time (until Harry Potter) partly because people derive a sense of liberation from Stephen's attacks on church and state. To build up the condemnation of Stephen is to weaken this progressive effect.

While there are differences between Joyce and Stephen linked to the differences between author and character and between youth and maturity, the idea that Joyce sees Stephen as another person who is hopelessly wrong is badly undercut by the Hoffmeister interview. Here Joyce says, "*Portrait* was the picture of my spiritual self'" (Potts 132). He may underestimate the distance between himself and his creation, as Lacan sometimes does in his discussion of Joyce in *Le sinthome*, but this quote indicates an intention that is realized to a remarkable degree.[4]

Stephen achieves freedom by perceiving how the changes in his identity work through the oppositions in language. The semantic conflicts in words that Stephen focuses on draw him out so as to serve as a key to his evolution and to the structure of the novel. To portray something is to draw it forward (Latin *pro-trahere*), and Stephen is drawn forward to realize himself (rather than being contained by the past) when he encounters language that he does not understand. Answers can be destructive to questions, and this may be a theme of the "Ithaca" episode of *Ulysses*. Every time Stephen confronts a question that cannot be answered, such as whether it is wrong to kiss one's mother in one's mind before going to sleep at Clongowes (*P* 14) or what smugging is (42), he is forced to confront a division within himself. This outer/inner exploration is parallel to the epiphanies and is the Joycean way to grow.

The central action of each chapter takes place when Stephen is attacked by a father figure who forces him to turn in a new direction. This figure represents repressive authority (church and state), as is obvious in the case of Fathers Dolan and Arnall in chapters I and III. Vincent Heron in II follows this pattern by being an Irish youth who imitates the English. He keeps using British phrases like "what a lark," "ripping" (twice), "your governor," and "deucedly" (*P* 75–77). He also insists that the chauvinistic Tennyson is the greatest poet, accuses Stephen of heresy, and forces him to confess (*P* 78–82). The father-attackers grow more subtle, from Dolan, who beats Stephen seriously, to Heron, who beats him in play, to Arnall, who terrorizes Stephen verbally with the sermons on hell, to the Jesuit director, who merely offers Stephen a vocation, to Cranly, who is only reasonable about conforming externally instead of tormenting one's mother. This advance in subtlety shows how Stephen moves toward increasing freedom. Yet in every case the attack, like all threats, generates unanswered questions and forces Stephen to rearrange the figuration of his identity. His acceptance of this shock of the Real—which corresponds to the falling-away of anger like a peel—is the *sinthome* that allows him to change through an act of movement that makes the symptom of injury voluntary.

Reversed Figures

Joyce shares with Judith Butler a focus on how the individual can evade the constraints mapped out by social language. The subject subjects itself by deriving existence from terms and categories designed to control it. But it resists subordination by transforming the terms of power as it internalizes them. This adds specificity to Lacan's idea that one invents one's own language (*sinthome* 133). Butler sees the transformation of the power imposed on one into the power one exerts as working through turns or tropes (*Power* 3–17). Law works by requiring the meaning of every word to be certain. If one is subjected to external power or called to account every time one knows what a word means in the system, one internalizes this power by making the meaning slide.[5] The movement of the meaning gives the effect of interior space, and this extends perception further, for external vision depends on internal scope.

In Lacanian terms, just as the subject consists of an interaction between signifiers (Fink 70), the sense of what is between signifiers allows one to see such movement in the outside world.[6] In the passage from Chapter 2 about seeing the world "about him" through words (*P* 62, cited), Stephen is developing language techniques to make him more responsive to what is out there, increasing his vocabulary. This will increase the range of his action by making him more uncertain and divided. If volition is the power to choose, it increases with the number of choices.

Butler says that agency "is to be located within the possibility of a variation on" the repetition that compels discourse (*Gender* 145). So the ability to decide increases when one changes the meaning of a phrase; but it expands even more powerfully when the structure that produces meaning comes into play. Butler cites Quintillian's distinction that a trope is a change of meaning, but a figure is a change of form (*Power* 201, n.1). Stephen increases consciousness when he does not know what a word means, when he holds back from the ordinary or official meaning. He continually wonders about the meanings of words; but he goes even further to add to the resistance of his subject when he encounters a new form of verbal obscurity. Here he realizes himself by realizing that he expresses himself incompletely or inaccurately in a new figure. This is his abiding objective even before he grows aware of it, a quest for misdirection.

In his ongoing construction of subjectivity, Stephen is struck frequently and forcefully by new figures of incomprehension, new ways in which the meanings of words are called into question. Each of these new terms amounts to a paternal attack, an ambush planted in language by previous generations. This is how he adds to the elaboration of the Joycean subject. Butler says, "If the subject is understood as a kind of necessary fiction, then it is also one of the first artistic accomplishments" (*Power* 67). The subject as artifice is the symptom as *sinthome*. Every skewed figure added to the artifice of the Joycean subject gives it access to new patterns of agency. This corresponds to Lacanian analysis, which Fink describes as proceeding by adding metaphors: "each new metaphor brings with it a precipitation of subjectivity which can alter the subject's position"

(*Lacanian* 70). On this page, Fink says, "there is no subjectification without metaphorization."

The first figure to express Stephen directly is an identification that comes from his father: "He was baby tuckoo" (*P* 7). While this says who he is straightforwardly, it is fictional, and does not seem to fit him any better than most identities that parents impose on children. Yet its fictional status may be its most valuable function: it appeals to Stephen because it posits his identity as an object he is outside of , an ambiguous figure that lets him see a version of himself without losing his distance or committing himself. In this way, it could be the origin of his truest identity, just as Joyce's literary persona was in many ways more real to him than his ostensible life. Stephen begins to fabricate such a persona by turning his father's identification of him around and making it his in its implausibility. The pattern is here established that every phrase that comes from language tradition and tries to enclose his consciousness is an attack from the father that must be reversed. This is why Joyce moves relentlessly toward creating his own language, which becomes obvious in the *Wake*.

Of course Stephen's personal language violated propriety from the start. The next figure to represent him is "O, the geen wothe botheth" (*P* 7).[7] This is closer to Stephen's identity because whereas Baby Tuckoo was his father's creation, this is his first original poetic image. Yet it is incoherent, a mistake, a term that never existed, formed by splicing the rose and the green place of the song. It barely emerges from outside legibility as a result of Stephen's desire to bring language into *his* space: "That was his song" (*P* 7). His infantile ambition to go beyond limits causes his words to flow beyond knowledge like an excrescence. One reason that he is satisfied with his words without knowing why is that he has changed the voice of authority to his own voice by making it incomprehensible; and in fact most of his words are orthographically new.

A green rose is an oxymoron that confounds categories, and before long Stephen takes such recombination of words as his leading principle. Yet in doing so, he puts himself in conflict, as indicated by two sentences starting with "But": "But you could not have a green rose. But perhaps somewhere in the world you could" (24). His devotion to what he knows to be impossible makes him of two minds, and Butler says that the subject is always founded on conflict with itself. Joyce first encountered this pattern through the idea of sin, and he also found it in Blake: "Without contraries, is no progression" (Blake 34). Without conflict there is no originality, and therefore no agency.

Though impressed with the Church's system, Joyce countered it with his own anti-system. The Church depends on iteration, urging followers to repeat phrases and images that should in-form their souls with virtue. Foucault says that confession played a great role in the formation of subjectivity, and that the desire to confess is so deeply ingrained in us that we don't see it as an effect of power (*History* 61). To confess is to change one's personal language to that of the Church by classifying one's actions as sins. Catholicism specifies the meaning of every term and attaches figures of speech to a rational order that reaches back to the First Cause. The subtitle of Loyola's *Spiritual Exercises* calls it *A Well-Ordered and Logically Connected System*. This system charges Stephen with the power that he uses to turn against it, and its logical rigor is reversed by his rigorous illogic. Unlike the Church, Joyce strove to make each figure a new kind of configuration that does not fit into a rational order. What is speaking in Joyce is generally a conflict between languages. For example, the two sentences beginning with "But" in my last paragraph break a rule of good writing (never begin two sentences in a row with *but*) in order to express a secondary language of psychological conflict. This double writing corresponds to Lyotard's *differend*, the difference between two points of view that needs to be put into phrases and cannot yet be (13).

Of course, Stephen's thoughts about words generally try to fit them into a comprehensive system, to eliminate conflicting elements, but they never succeed. It is the breakdown of coherence that provides the real productivity of these musings, because it makes them *his*, and calls the existing order into question. An example of Stephen's systematic aim appears when he sees a scullion wearing a white apron: "He wondered whether all white things were cold and damp" (*P* 13). The theory is ridiculous. An advantage of the Church's systematic outlook is that it reveals that every term depends on a larger framework. The more complicated the system, the more readily it can fall into contradiction, and Stephen relentlessly pursues the anomalies of Church doctrine at the same time that he pursues sin, which undermines that doctrine (*P* 105–6).

Words impact on Stephen when they slip from their meanings. For example, a word can have two entirely opposed meanings, as *belt* stands for either a snug enclosure or a violent attack (*P* 9). Or several words can have the same meaning, as *Dieu* and *God* do (*P* 16). For Stephen to affirm that *Dieu* equals God is to lay the basis for questions about how different versions of God can be reconciled. Every metaphor that links two terms into one meaning also divides that meaning into ambiguity. If the same words have different meanings and different words have the same one, then the subject as signifier is liberated from the constraints of identity.

The subject is created as a figure of speech, but this figure must be denied to maintain the subject's solidity. Lacan holds that the subject can only ever appear as a signifier, and that in the relation of the signifier to the Other, the totality of language from which it is derived, "this point from which it emerges that there is signifier (*du signifiant*) is the one which in a way can't be signified" (*Anxiety* 118). Lacan's objective, like Joyce's and Butler's, is to return to this point of figuration that is concealed. As Nietzsche explains in

"'On Truth and Lie in an Extra-Moral Sense," the subject and its unities and realities are all deeply based on metaphors: "The thing in itself'...Is quite incomprehensible to the creators of language and not at all worth aiming for. One designates only the relation of things to man, and to express them, one calls on the boldest metaphors. A nerve stimulus, first transposed into an image—first metaphor. The image in turn, imitated by a sound—second metaphor" (45–46). Perception and language are based on invisible metaphors. To call attention to these metaphors in rather Lacanian terms is to deconstruct the appearance of unmediated reality that they fabricate.

Butler critiques the revolutionary value of figures of speech after she questions some of Louis Althusser's arguments by pointing out that he depends on religious imagery. She says, "I do not mean to suggest that the 'truth' of Althusser's text can be discovered in how the figural disrupts 'rigorous' conceptualization. Such an approach romanticizes the figural as essentially disruptive, whereas figures may well compound and intensify conceptual claims" (Butler, *Power* 114). So figures can support ideology as well as questioning it. The crucial distinction here seems to be between the aspect of the metaphor that brings terms together by saying that a woman is ivory and the aspect that takes them apart by revealing that what is being described is neither woman nor ivory. This process of division constitutes Lyotard's *differend*, which points toward what has to be said by indicating the inadequacy of what can be said. What is really there in such disputes is neither what one side says nor what the other says, but something that cannot be defined because both sides are partial. Fink gives a key role in Lacanian theory to a version of this distinction between aspects of metaphor. On one hand, a metaphor can be a precipitate that combines signifiers, or on the other, it can be a breach that opens the distance between signifiers. These two aspects correspond to the subject as metaphor, for people can be defined either as sediments who fit into society or as breaches who create openings into new possibilities (*Lacanian* 69).

The fitting in or enclosure of language is caused by fear organized by authority, which is a system for distributing fear. This harnessing of language to the fear system is countered by Lacan's analysis of anxiety in *Seminar X* (*L'Angoisse, 1962–63*). Here he builds on Freud's statement that while anxiety is fear without an object, nevertheless, it is about something (*Etwas*).[8] Lacan says that this something, the impalpable object of anxiety, is the Real, what is outside language, and this is why "among all the signals, anxiety is the one which does not deceive" (Lacan, *Anxiety* 142). He equates the Real with the mathematical operation of division (142) because to confront the unknown is to be divided by not knowing, to confront the figurative basis of the self rather than maintaining unity.

The sermons on hell in *Portrait* insist that one must stay enclosed by the Law or one will be subject to the endless multiplication of Eternity, which is expanded on as the most dreadful aspect of hell (*P* 131–32). To step outside the Law's frame is to enter into the anxiety of losing one's bearings. So the fear of anxiety drives us to enclose ourselves in the terms of the establishment. Yet as Eide emphasizes, it is only by freeing oneself that one can hope to do justice to the other rather than subjecting it to one's terms. So the ethical imperative is to break down the cohesiveness of metaphor.

Dining on Metaphors

Stephen sees metaphors from the outside in the Christmas dinner scene. Terry Eagleton says that the aim of Marxism should be to work back to the perception of a child who sees through the ideological constructions and emotional associations conditioned into adults ("Brecht" 170), and so one can detect the real operations of power. At the age of eight or so, Stephen is in a very early stage of learning what metaphors are. So he is struck by the enigmatic parade of metaphors passing before him, and puzzled by them in ways that reach outside the ordinary. Remembering how a butcher had called a turkey "the real Ally Daly" makes Stephen wonder, "Why did Mr Barrett in Clongowes call his pandybat a turkey?" (30). Generally a figure or nickname applied to an instrument of torture adds to its erotic charge, something that Stephen may sense because he cannot process the metaphor normally. He suspects the violence that its fitness would conceal.

Simon Dedalus calls the turkey's tail "the pope's nose" (32), an image with an anticlerical undertone. Many intense metaphors in the scene are political, as when Simon refers to a Bishop as a "tub of guts" (33) or to priests as "Sons of bitches!" (34). Mr. Casey says the Church has turned "*the house of God into a polling booth*" (31), and Dante Riordan says that Simon's discourse spits on religion (34). So if the turkey is garnished with metaphors, the bird may have political import.

Stephen smiles when Mr. Casey taps the gland of his neck because Stephen now realizes that it is not true that Casey has a purse of silver in his throat (*P* 28). But Stephen does not seem to recognize, nor have his critics, a buried political metaphor here by which Casey must have been said to have a silver throat as a powerful orator. Yet Stephen has heard of Casey making speeches (*P* 37). Casey himself has reduced the metaphor to a literalized joke that he shares with the child, and Casey's Parnellite rhetoric is bitterly defeated by Dante in this scene. So the metaphor, whatever inkling Stephen may have of it, is stripped of its positive force. As Derek Attridge puts it, Joyce's use of language in *Portrait* is "the opposite of metaphorical" (*Joyce* 72).

During the dinner, Stephen is preoccupied by the question of how the Virgin Mary can be a tower of ivory and a house of gold. He has heard these metaphors from her Litany mocked by Protestants. Now he recalls that when Eileen Vance put her hands over his eyes, they were cold and white like ivory: "That was the meaning of *Tower of Ivory*" (36). In a later scene, he will remember her hair as gold: "*House of Gold*. By thinking of things you could understand them" (43). Here he sees the world by readjusting the arrangement of his mental language in order to re-cognize how perception is constructed. His sensory impressions of Eileen are far from capturing the full meaning of the Virgin figure, as he must realize; but he is excavating the substructure of belief, demythologizing Mary. His misdirected meditation on the Virgin is sharply focused on the analysis of metaphor because the intense cultural and political framework of the dinner scene gives metaphor weight. This is the most dramatic scene in the book because it is the one in which ideology is taken most seriously, most destructively as a symptom. It is dawning on Stephen that the world of politics is attached to those of religion, gender, and desire, and that the whole complex consists of a series of buried metaphors.

These metaphors are highlighted for Stephen because they are powerful but incomprehensible. For example, Dante Riordan insists that priests should be exempt from criticism because they are "the apple of God's eye" (38). The metaphor that the priests are God's treasure and gaze (the pupil of his eye) is quite beyond Stephen's ken, but he can see that it has great force because Dante wins the argument. Žižek points out that the notions people believe in most are least examined (*Metastases* 58), and for Dante, any questioning of the clear metaphor of the priests as treasure is impious. She takes on the phallic ability to signify through the authority of the Church. To make one's metaphor count as an equation is generally to occupy the masculine position of dominance; whereas to see the disjunction in the metaphor is to occupy the subaltern or feminine position. At dinner Simon Dedalus says, "It is true for them" (37), and Seamus Deane glosses this as a saying from the Irish meaning "They (the clergy) are in control, have the upper hand" (Deane edition of *Portrait* 286, n. 65). Here the Irish can see through the level of truth maintained by the authorities.

The dinner scene is explicitly presented as a conflict between two languages. Dante derides the words of Simon Dedalus and Casey as "Nice language for any Catholic to use!" (31), and they refer to her discourse as "the language with which the priests and the priests' pawns broke Parnell's heart and hounded him into his grave" (33–34). The word *language* is used judgmentally seven times in this scene. It is repeatedly made obvious to Stephen that any given element can be described by two mutually exclusive sets of terms, each coming from a different metaphorical framework. The women, being religious, think of Parnell as a sinner, while the men, as anticlerical nationalists, think of him as their uncrowned king. Neither of these warring metaphors for Parnell, sinner or king, fits him better than baby tuckoo fit Stephen, insofar as Parnell is human.

They represent stories into which Parnell is inserted, and they also operate in Lacan's terms as master signifiers around which all other language is organized for each group (Fink 75).

In the dinner scene Stephen lays the groundwork for personal freedom by seeing how completely the world of political power is one of metaphors, and how arbitrary, metonymic, and contingent the metaphors are. He approaches postmodernism insofar as the significance of these figures for him lies not in their appropriateness (a modernist aim), but in their inappropriateness.[9] Barrett's calling the pandybat a turkey is an ugly, sinister distortion. Casey does not have silver in his throat: colonialism finally breaks his voice. Eileen only resembles ivory at certain accidental, glancing moments. Stephen must be puzzled by the apple of God's eye. And Parnell cannot be both of the things that he is supposed to be; in fact, the world will not allow him to be either one. His historical actuality is an unresolved conflict, like the ambivalence at the heart of psychoanalysis. Everyone else at the dinner is on one side or another to varying degrees. Only Stephen can see the *differend*, how the two sides negate each other, the dissonance of the Real.

Stephen's initial view of such dichotomies was naïve: on the second page, he thought, "Rody Kickham was a decent fellow but Nasty Roche was a stink" (8). But then he thought of the differences in words, and now one person is divided into two poles—or carved into drumsticks, each beating a different drum. Just as Parnell cannot simply be a hero or a devil, Stephen's feeling that the rebels are right is undercut by their self-defeating attitude, the hysteria with which Casey cries, "No God for Ireland!" (39). Stephen's realization that the two opposed languages have to coexist lays the basis for Joyce's later view of Ireland as what Valente calls "the charged intersection" of opposed transnational ideologies ("Joyce's Politics" 87).

Insofar as he realizes that the two implacable sides cannot be reconciled, Stephen moves beyond the potentially solvable linguistic conflict of the *differend* toward the more radical division of the parallax gap. He begins to suspect that every point of focus is a metaphor and that the two sides of the metaphor can only be attached to each other firmly or stabilized by falsifying one. The more intensely people focus on the object of concern, the clearer it becomes that the object changes with each point of view (parallax) and so it can only exist as an unresolved metaphor

If Stephen advances by seeing through metaphors, he can only do so within the space created by the mother, which allows him release from the rigid male attachment to the signifier. He can see through the metaphors of ivory and gold by seeing that Eileen is not captured by them. So the real goal of the Joycean protagonist is to see that a woman goes beyond the efforts of language to contain her. In the scene in which Stephen completes his analysis of the metaphors from the liturgy, he remembers that Eileen puts her hand in his pocket so that he can feel it, but only within the ambivalent container of the pocket. Then she passes beyond his containment: "She had said that pockets were funny things to have: and then all of a sudden she had broken away and had run laughing down the sloping curve of the path. Her fair hair had streamed out behind her like gold in the sun" (*P* 43). Though he uses her hair to "solve" the metaphor, she is receding from him when he does so, just as he loses contact with her hand. The effort of language to reach its object works through a disintegrating connection, just as his original intimacy with his mother worked through separation. When Eileen puts her hand in his pocket, he plays the female role, so that their link has a side that he must repress.[10] She hints at this when she says that pocket are funny things to have. This indicates the absurdity of all containers for feeling and the difficulty of the female role, with its built-in pockets. The freedom of a woman to escape Stephen, to resist his linguistic enclosure, is what allows him to move forward to further exploration of the otherness of woman and language.

Later, when Stephen is on the tram with E__. C__., he remembers the scene with Eileen as one in which he failed to connect with her, as he fails to connect with Emma (but now he's aware of it). In both cases, he imagines that the girl desires him, and that his masculinity falls short: "She too wants me to catch hold of her, he thought" (*P* 70). Each defeat of his masculinity or failure to reach the goal is an accession to new literary power. When Eileen ran away, he saw her hair in the sun and comprehended the "*House of Gold*" metaphor (*P* 43).[11] After failing with E__. C__., he writes a poem. Here again, failure to reach the goal constitutes subjectivity. It also gives the girls power to make an impression on him that he will never forget, as if they punished him by evading him.

Using memories of Eileen to expand his analysis, Stephen confronts political language at the dinner to create himself as a split subject able to see the parallax view. At the first Christmas in which he joins the adults, he becomes a public subject. Lacan says in "The Position of the Unconscious" that "The effect of language is to introduce the cause into the subject." This can be a political cause like Valente's intersection of ideologies. Lacan goes on, "Through this effect, he is not the cause of himself; he bears within himself the worm of the cause that splits him" (*Écrits* 708).

The Word or *Logos*, the subject as split signifier, is born through this Nativity communion. The grotesque, buried central metaphor of the scene is Christ as Parnell transfigured into a turkey that everyone eats a different part of, having roasted him, a totem animal like HCE in the *Wake* (7.6–19). Language liberates Stephen from ideology by teaching him that politics can never exist except in this divided form. If Parnell, who, as a leader, might be called "the boss," has to die for Stephen to become a subject in language, just as Simon must be reduced to tears, it is fitting that the first description of Stephen at the Christmas scene presents him sitting in front of the fire with "his feet resting on the toasted boss" (27).

The Endless Equation

Stephen has already embarked on the scorched-earth policy that will cause Joyce's works to differ from each other so radically, making his canon a voyage to the end of language.[12] Once an artist has seen an image, it is not possible for him to see it again, so *Dubliners* is a very different kind of book from *Portrait*, which differs greatly from *Exiles*, and so forth. By the fifth chapter of *Portrait*, Stephen will engage in emptying words of their "instantaneous sense" (179), which is the immediate sense that they are supposed to have before they drift into other possibilities. Here Stephen advances his perception of *ivory* by deciding that the material word and the language structures that define it are the sources of the external referent that they define and control. At the same time, he realizes the absurd inadequacy of the language frame and pushes restlessly toward further levels to expand the referent as the only way to approach material reality.

As a child Stephen already runs assiduously through every frame of meaning, driven by his demand for comprehension to find the limitation and artificiality of every figure. The double colonial apparatus of Rome and England impels him to create a personal space of displacement that will allow him to give play to his own version of reality rather than having it imposed on him. The validity of this personal vision rests or rides on the fact that it shifts constantly. When Stephen refers to his soul early in the third chapter as "unfolding itself sin by sin," he means that every time he loses his bearings, the space in which he can destabilize language expands. His soul as what is created by the breakdown of language in the Real is much like the Lacanian subject as the signifier of the barred Other, personality as a word that stands for the unknowable.

I focus on metaphor, but Stephen passes through numerous figures as he proliferates his repertory of verbal formations. Many of these figures involve following the jump of associations: "Sorry because he was afraid. Afraid that it was some disease. Canker was a disease of plants and cancer one of animals..." (*P* 21). As Stephen follows his linking thoughts about the bully Wells here, he notices that two words for feeling can work in different modes (the emotional "sorry" and the strategic "afraid"), and that one can negate the other (he isn't really sorry if he is afraid). Moreover, changing a single letter can turn something minor to something terrible (cancer). Other figures mix different languages or levels of discourse; "*Ivory, ivoire, avorio, ebur*" (179); "A decollated precursor trying to pick the lock" (248). The latter example contrasts the high diction of its first half with the low diction of its second to underscore the difficulty of conceiving sacred concepts in earthly terms and to mock Cranly's compromise. There are too many figures to list here, for Joyce aims at a new figure on virtually every page. As in these examples, they tend to involve a sense of proximity, of moving outward.

When Stephen speaks to the English dean of studies, he thinks, "The language in which we are speaking is his before it is mine" (*P* 189). Because English is the alien language of his conquerors, it threatens to enclose Stephen, so he strives to move beyond its discrete meanings into peripheral extensions, alternative meanings, symbolic or foreign equivalents, etymological substrata, and so forth. His colonial noninheritance, as a version of paternal imposition, drives him toward freedom and exploration in language.

One productive way to move beyond metaphor is to use several at once. The equation scene that speaks of Stephen as unfolding his soul uses four metaphors simultaneously: "another equation began to unfold itself slowly and to spread abroad its widening tail. It was his own soul going forth to experience, unfolding itself sin by sin, spreading abroad the balefire of its burning stars..." (103). He sees his soul as an equation that is also a rhythmic alternation through time, a series of sins, a peacock's tail, and a group of stars being born and fading. The most insistent image may be that of expansion, for "unfold itself' and "spread abroad" both repeat. Though Stephen is far from going to Europe, this vision of "going forth" suggests geographical exploration ("abroad") as a stainful spreading of selves.

Multiplying metaphors can also be a sophisticated way to undermine them, to present metaphors encased in metaphors encased in others, like fish being eaten by bigger ones. The swarming of perspectives is visionary, as analysis that delves into ordinary reality often is. Earlier, at Clongowes, it "pained" Stephen that he did not know what politics meant or where the universe ended. He imagined that the older students knew and thought of gaining such knowledge over the years in terms of a complex chain of similes in which vacations and terms were compared to a train going into and out of tunnels, which was compared to the noise he heard when he uncovered his ears. As in the equation scene, the distance in time of the approach to knowledge is seen as distance in space: "That was very far away.... How far away it was!" (*P* 17). Even before the equation scene, Stephen sees his life as an alternation leading to a great distance. In the *Wake*, the artistic brother Shem is linked to time, the internal dimension, while the authoritarian brother Shaun occupies space. Here the Shem side of Stephen thinks of time, but the Shaun side turns it to a spatial image, a postman's image of traveling.

Lyotard says that each phrase has its own universe of linguistic attachments (*Differend* 70). Just as the images of Parnell as devil or hero were linked to different languages, so Stephen's four figurative levels in the scene at Clongowes (knowledge, time, train, ears), and even moreso the four or five levels of the equation scene (equation, progress, sins, peacock tail, stars) imply four different worlds. Because Stephen has access to several universes at critical moments, he can switch from one level to another as he accumulates different alternate selves. This corresponds to the value of possible worlds theory.

The ability to recognize multiple selves and to move among them may be the best method for reaching freedom. For example, at the end of the novel, Stephen realizes the falseness of his earlier irony about women and his hostility to Emma: "I liked her and it seems a new feeling to me. Then, in that case, all the rest, all that I thought I thought and all that I felt I felt..." (*P* 252). He realizes that his misogyny was not what he really thought or felt, but a level of discourse and an identity imposed on him by his society. He had noticed the artificiality of his sexual cynicism earlier: "It was not even the way in which he thought of her" (*P* 233).

In his diary Stephen critiques his attitude toward love by quoting Blake's "William Bond." in which William is bound in sickness by repression ("an Angel of Providence at his Head," Blake 497) until he stops being bound by accepting love as connection:

> Seek Love in the Pity of others Woe
> In the gentle relief of anothers care
> In the darkness of night & the winters snow
> In the naked & outcast Seek Love There
> (Blake 498)

Stephen quotes the earlier lines "I wonder if William Bond will die / For assuredly he is very ill" (*P* 249), and then says, "Alas, poor William!" Here Stephen ironically realizes that he is bound by repression and needs to realize what love is.

The subject of the equation is Stephen becoming equal to himself, becoming more of what he could be. He does so, however, not by consolidating a discrete identity, but by multiplying differences. He sees the expansion of the equation as more positive than its coming together, which he sees as "fading...quenching" (103). He seeks not reduction to unity, but expansion toward infinity: "What was after the universe?" (*P* 16). The course of development that Stephen projects for himself matches Fink's account of Lacanian analysis, which consists of moving through a series of metaphors, each of which reconfigures the subject (Fink 69–70). The goal of analysis is for the subject to articulate and therefore identify with a metaphor that signifies the subject's cause, or the imaginary totality of language called the Other (Fink 65–66). Stephen moves toward this position when his awareness of the multiplying of metaphors places him between or beyond metaphors, in the place where new metaphors are generated. Žižek says that the remainder that keeps the metaphor from being equal to itself is the Real (*Tarrying* 43). Insofar as the tenor and vehicle are interchangeable, as they are for Dante Riordan (the priests are the apple), we experience reality; but the excess of the Real deflects us from accepting the metaphor as actual, impelling us toward further possibilities. The multiplying of metaphors indicates that the extra margin is the intervention of another metaphor on the chain. The Real is the source of the metaphor because it compels us toward new ones.

Stephen's identification with his cause is brought out most forcefully by his blasphemous identification with "the God of the creation" (*P* 215), and by his intention of becoming the artist who writes his own story. The Other is also social, and Stephen's expansion is grounded on expressing the cultural and political forces that cause him by shaping him: the phrase "all that I felt I felt" claims the power of extension that allows him to see the vast historical structure that has controlled him. To realize that all he thought and felt was shaped by the system takes him beyond the system and the totality of his thought, going beyond the horizon.

He divides himself by engaging in interaction with what is beyond knowledge, and the unresolvability of this extension is the drive toward future exploration that he seeks. The disparity and the sense of multiple meanings with which Stephen seeks to equate himself enacts personal conflict as social conflict. The building of information in Joyce's fiction leads to a final uncertainty that poses a question searching enough, exploratory enough, to open up the complex depth of history and selfhood. The more Stephen commits himself to art as self-formation, forging in the smithy of his soul, the more his drive toward the unknown becomes the artist who shapes him. As his language becomes more literary with each chapter, he is increasingly living in art or taking responsibility for writing himself until he finally takes over in the incoherence of the final diary.

The diary carries on conflicts between social control and freedom that Stephen has struggled with throughout the book. If the diary emphasizes departure toward "the future" and "the loveliness which has not yet come into the world" (*P* 251), nevertheless as Michael Levenson points out in "Stephen's Diary: The Shape of Life," it also repeats patterns of the past. Stephen must focus on these patterns to articulate what he has to struggle against. Levenson's conservative view that Stephen is caught in the past is not only opposed to Stephen, but opposed to Joyce's innovative aspect. Stephen's dilemma is defined by Cranly's conundrum about the crocodile. This apologue appears after Stephen has two dreams: the first about weary kings of stone and the second about stunted men who "seem to ask me something" (*P* 250). The dreams may represent oppressed Ireland or humanity in need of answers to go beyond exhausted authorities. When Stephen speaks of creating conscience or consciousness for his "race" on the last page, this refers both to the Irish and to humanity.

In Cranly's tale, a crocodile seizes a child whose mother let it fall into the Nile: "Mother asked it back. Crocodile said all right if she told him what he was going to do with the child, eat it or not eat it" (250). If she says he will eat it, she will be right, but the child will be lost; if she says he will not, he can make her wrong and the child will still be lost. The point of the story may be that the Irish and humanity can only free themselves by realizing that the establishment will devour them no matter what they do, or even if they obey, so they may as well resist. Half a page later, Stephen's father urges him to take up rowing and become a lawyer. Here Stephen thinks, "More mud, more crocodiles" (*P* 250), meaning that these respectable activities will only support the dominant order.

If the subject is between signifiers, as Fink states (*Lacanian* 64), then Stephen should focus on unresolvable dilemmas to develop himself and his grasp of the complexity of history. Many critical terms can be linked to this insoluble dichotomy, such as Lyotard's *differend* and Jameson's absent cause of history (based on Althusser), which, as the entire system of relationships that causes history, is too complex to be specified (Jameson, *Political* 34–36). It corresponds to Thurston's argument that the main activity of Joyce's texts is to confront the incomprehensible and to Shepherdson's insistence that the crucial feature of psychoanalysis is that it abrogates polarities by showing that they are made up of interaction.

Finally, Žižek's parallax view perceives that if all crucial facts are between alternatives, one grows aware that one cannot reach the true point, and takes pleasure and insight from the alternation, turning symptom into *sinthome*: "the very failure to reach its goal, the repetition of this failure, the endless circulation around the object, generates a satisfaction of its own" (*PV* 63). For Žižek, the true object is loss (62), and to see this is to traverse or see through the human condition of constantly seeking more. Stephen's sequence of equations prefigures the fact that as he claims each new identity and turns against it, he sees his subject in ongoing division.

Insofar as Stephen's aim is to unfold the complexity of language, he aims to elaborate the richness of the subject. His guiding principle parallels Lacan's idea that the structure of the unconscious is the structure of language (Fink 8). The two most massive and powerful language systems that Stephen must combine within himself are masculine and feminine. Their opposition defines many of the main limitations of consciousness, and insofar as their synthesis can be approached, it indicates the fullness of consciousness. Joyce advances toward combining genders in *Ulysses*, which features "the new womanly man" Bloom (15. 1798–99), but he is already combining them actively in *Portrait*.

Chapter 4

Entwined Genders in A Portrait

Juliet Mitchell states in her "Introduction-I" to *Feminine Sexuality*, the Lacanian collection that she edited with Jacqeline Rose, that "no human being can become a subject outside the division into two sexes" (6). So for Lacan, one has to take a sexual position to attain subjectivity, but Mitchell later adds that Lacan always sees subjectivity as a fiction (30). My point is that because one starts, as Freud observed, with the potential for both genders and represses one's opposite (*SE* VII. 140), one's sexual position is always accompanied by the other side: so one becomes a subject *inside* the gender division. This view is developed by Judith Butler, but it is already operative in *Portrait*. And it applies to every parallactic division that constitutes the subject.

In *Le sinthome*, Lacan, as we have seen, argues that language, action, and knowledge are themselves based on sexual division from the start, and that this division is illusory. He says that from the beginning of thought, sexual division is posited: "The word *act* itself implies the polarity active-passive, which is already to become involved in a false sense" (64). Here the foundation of thought, the polar separation between active and passive, is an arbitrary maneuver with no clear basis in reality; but because it defines the code of gender, it dictates the most fundamental categories into which people are inserted. If the opposition between sexes is at the root of consciousness through language, then the most deep-reaching way to undermine systematic authority is to show that these poles are not separate but intertwined in each subject. Joyce arranges the connection between gender codes to demonstrate this in *Portrait* by showing how both genders enact each other as false positions within Stephen Dedalus. I have argued that Joyce develops his primary uropoetic model of writing as prior to the active-passive, male-female division; and on this basis he moves toward the invention of a language free of authority that *Le sinthome* finds in his work. Joyce is also able to a great extent to anticipate Butler's advocacy of transgenderation as passing from one gender to another (*Undoing* 6–12), and her theories provide useful tools for delineating this development.

Gender as Pathology

All of Joyce's major units of fiction (those over twenty-five pages long) begin with a male figure maintaining a masculine identity, proceed to indicate that this masculinity is insolubly conflicted, and end up seeking release through the assumption of a feminine mentality. Thus, the action of Joycean narrative shows masculinity being overwhelmed by femininity to open up alternative possibilities. So it consists not of movement toward a goal, but of displacement from one movement toward another, and the subject involved is neither masculine nor feminine, but an interaction of the two. The main point is not to move from masculine to feminine, but from a discrete gender to a mixture. This complementary compromise of genders enacts Butler's theories, which see the genders distorting and displacing each other in all active, significant sexual practice.

It may be argued that *Portrait* moves toward the goal of Stephen's becoming an artist (Lawrence 32), but this goal has to be constructed retrospectively for the first three chapters. It does not exist as a goal until Chapter IV, and he is far from reaching it at the end. He changes his aim radically in V when he decides that his art will be practiced overseas; and for Joyce, none of whose books resemble each other in form, the position of the artist involves constant change. Moreover, it has become common in recent years for critics to see Stephen's ideas as wrong, and such arguments reflect an ambiguity that counteracts any attempt to see Stephen as reaching a goal. The equivocality of Joyce's plots participates in the same bifurcation that permutes his genders.

I first noticed the pattern of shifting gender consciousness in each chapter of *Portrait,* but it is also found in "The Dead," *Exiles*, *Ulysses*, and *Finnegans Wake*. In "The Dead," Gabriel Conroy realizes that the masculine role he has played is a sham, and he ends up focused on the mind of his wife, Gretta. Riquelme argues that she is the speaker in the last paragraph of the story ("Joyce's" 125). In *Exiles*, Richard Rowan, locked in conflict with Robert Hand, chooses to suspend himself from his uncertainty about Bertha, whose voice is the last one heard. At the end of *Ulysses*, Molly Bloom's soliloquy seems to provide relief from the perplexed relation between Stephen and Bloom. And in the *Wake*, the Shem and Shaun aspects of HCE lead to a conclusion in which a woman's mind strives to escape male dominance. In every case, perpetual male conflict renders the power system that supports masculinity unbearable; yet femininity is also untenable to the protagonist who starts as a male. So the goal that is reached is not really female, but suspended between genders.

Though Joyce supported what he called "the emancipation of women, . . . the greatest revolution in our time" (Power 35), feminists have criticized him because his female figures remain informed by male thinking;

but for Butler, the mixing of the two genders so that one modifies the other is the most progressive gender practice insofar as it is intentional. She argues in *Gender Trouble* that the stereotypes of male and female cannot be abolished by fiat, but they can be proven false by showing that the violation of these codes is fundamental to sexed beings (148).

Nancy Chodorow has argued that in order to overcome the deep-rooted sense of natural maleness and femaleness, with its powerful tendency to subordinate the female, it is important to see our ideas of both genders as pathological formations.[1] Shepherdson explains that Lacan's schema of sexuation in *Seminar XX* (*Encore* 78) sees both genders as formed by the threat of castration (*Vital* 74–78). In Joyce's subversion of genders, the masculine and feminine that interact to make up his narrative dynamics appear not as natural identities, but as pathological extremes between which his characters move.

Effective terms to describe the two polarized genders as unhealthy social formations already exist in Freud's two main categories of neurosis, obsession and hysteria. As products of modern European culture (Freud's cases were generally middle-class Viennese), obsession and hysteria may be seen as symptoms of the strict division of people into the familiar codes of masculine and feminine. Freud says that the two neuroses generally occur combined with each other (*SE* II.259), but that the predominance of obsession is the most common form of neurosis in men, while hysteria tends to be the dominant affliction in women: "there is no doubt that hysteria has a strong affinity with femininity, just as obsessional neurosis has with masculinity..." (*SE* XX: 143). Žižek audaciously takes it as evident that the neuroses fit the genders when he speaks of "a male (obsessional), not feminine (hysterical) fantasy" (*Fragile* 24).

Butler insists that masculinity and femininity do not exist outside of patriarchal construction (*Gender* 23–30). Within such construction, obsessive-compulsive behavior is the condition that drives masculinity, while hysteria (which is named for the womb) is the affliction that defines the limits of femininity. Joyce differentiates these stereotypes from biological gender by showing that they are both active in a male. Of course both genders are found in the "womanly" Bloom, but Stephen may be more indicative because he is less evidently passive. Elaine Showalter explains how for centuries men separated themselves from symptoms identified as female by using other names for male hysteria, such as melancholy and shell shock (290–91).[2] Yet Joyce manifests through his imagery that Stephen's conversion of thoughts into ungovernable physical states is feminine.

The obsessive is driven by rationalized ideas isolated from feelings and tends to be obsessed with sexuality as control. Obsession converts feelings into ideas, while hysteria converts ideas into feelings. Obsession is organized by denying the threat posed by one's feminine side, while hysteria is an intensification of the feeling of someone threatened by masculinity. As Showalter puts it, not enough attention has been paid to "hysterical symptoms as a response to powerlessness" (305).

The terms *obsessive* and *hysterical* are used not only for illness, but for normal patterns of behavior, and the overlap between the pathological and the ordinary is extensive. As Shepherdson remarks, Freud generally calls into question the distinction between normal and abnormal (*Vital* 86). For example, when one laughs or cries hard, one really is hysterical in the sense of being temporarily dysfunctional. Monique David-Ménard says that for Freud, "affective states in general are understood as hysterical attacks" (10). In fact, obsession and hysteria may be sources of strength, strength often linked to gender. A man who is successful is expected to be obsessed with his specialty: he may not succeed if he isn't driven. And traditionally one of woman's stereotypical weapons in the battle between the sexes has been hysteria, which can be formidable.

Freud notes that the central obsessional technique of isolation avoids emotion by suppressing "associative connections," so that it is an exaggeration of rational concentration on what is important (*SE* XX; 120–21). Showalter cites Paul Chodoff's description of hysteria as "a caricature of femininity," and she calls it "an exaggeration of the cognitive and personal styles that women are encouraged to develop as attractively 'feminine' (287). In fact, though men may be linked to driving rationality, while women are defined by sensitivity to feelings, it seems rather that obsession and hysteria are *aspects of the same condition*, the cultural polarization of genders. Everyone of either sex in patriarchal society is defined by some opposition between the two that causes a continual shift from rationality to emotion and back. Neither rationality nor emotion is a "normal" state, and likewise masculinity and femininity can be seen as abnormal configurations that are designated as normal by society, just as a fairly insane belief in the supernatural may be regarded as normal in some religious societies. The unhealthy effects of normality are developed in Butler's *Undoing Gender* (2–3).

Seeing how the gender/neuroses depend on each other, one can recognize the extremes of masculine rationality and feminine sensitivity as virtual positions, occupied through fantasy, colonial structures of imposition in which no one is really at home. Having grown up in a colony, Joyce recognized imperialism as a determining model for many systems of control. In the *Wake*, masculinity is associated with colonialism by identifying HCE with a series of empires. The dominant culture of patriarchy installs every subject in a gender identity and activates it to think that it can stay within that gender. The subject must filter off many impulses that come from outside its bounds by insisting that it really is a man or a woman. No one fits into pure masculinity or femininity without a vital part being left out. Likewise, colonial codes are hybrids, neither native nor imperial, but they insist on dividing everyone onto one side or another. This is parallel to the division that allows men to colonize women.

While hysteria has been linked to women since the ancient Greeks, Foucault says that a "hysterization of women's bodies" that caused them to be "thoroughly saturated with sexuality" accelerated in the West in the eighteenth century, implanting a supposed "pathology intrinsic" to women (104). But if the intense expression of womanhood is pathological, it is also progressive in its opposition. Valente connects the laughter and pain of Joyce's women to Lyotard's *differend*, what needs to be spoken and cannot be (*James* 8–10, 230–37). And Cixous and Catherine Clément, in *The Newly Born Woman*, call hysteria the "nuclear example of woman's power to protest" (154). This suggests that the rejection of the term *hysteria* by academic psychologists has political implications. The reformative force of hysteria can operate in a man insofar as its impetus is recognized.

Obsession, Hysteria, and Power

Whether hysteria or obsession is emphasized depends on political factors. The obsessive focus on rational control is the attitude of the oppressor: it calculates how to secure power through an abstract system that avoids feelings. This remains true even though most severe obsessives lose the ability to control others and end up controlling only themselves. Freud's term for obsession, *der Zwang*, means "coercion, force, compulsion." It is the neurosis of the drive toward power. The hysterical omission of consciousness, on the other hand, is the reaction of the oppressed, who cannot bear the awareness of their unjust situation. Traditionally, men were conscious of the logical system that controlled power, while women, children, and the colonized were not. Yet Lacan argues in *Seminar XVII* that knowledge comes from the oppressed (21). The rationale for depriving these groups of power is that they are not logical, but maybe they are not logical because they do not have power. Not to understand the system that subjects one to abuse fills one with unfocusable anxiety so that one cannot sustain consciousness.

We see Stephen in such a situation, for example, when he returns to Clongowes after the Christmas dinner scene in Chapter I. At the end of that scene he saw his father reduced to tears and Casey sobbing (*P* 39) because they had had their Parnell cut off. The scene implies that any Irishman who tries to assert his manhood will have it taken away by the colonial system of church and state. Stephen insists in both *Stephen Hero* (53) and *Ulysses* (1.638) that both Britain and Rome are foreign powers occupying Ireland. Having seen the hysteria of the men, Stephen is susceptible to threats when he returns to school. He hears that some boys are to be beaten for committing a crime, but the nature of the crime, though it seems to be "queer," is unknown. Among other possibilities, Stephen wonders if it might be writing graffiti: "Perhaps . . . Because it was a place where some fellows wrote things for a cod" (*P* 43). If the crime is rebellious joking with language, Stephen is inclined toward it, so the unknown nature of the crime means that he cannot be sure if he is guilty. Now "He looked with the others in silence across the playground and began to feel afraid." They are all implicated in the crime because the vital inclinations of the subordinate tend toward freedom. They are in Kafka's minority situation of never knowing that they are not guilty. The elaborate, secret codes of the Church make it virtually impossible to keep track of all the rules, while an incomprehensible God is supposed to know one better than one knows oneself. The subaltern is held incapable of understanding the power that controls him. Stephen struggles to build systematic knowledge to control his position, but the system keeps knocking him back into hysterical gaps of knowledge. Fortunately for him, this hysteria represents a new kind of knowledge through which he makes important advances.

The plot of *Portrait* involves an alternation of these subject positions. Stephen starts each chapter with a masculine identity, whether as student, adolescent, whoremonger, pious youth, or artist. His manhood consists of his thrusting himself toward a particular goal defined by his new identity; and he always measures his progress by accumulating signs of his mastery of the latest order of discourse. Early in Chapter I, he tries to assemble the words and images that he meditates on—such as *belt, suck, God,* and white—into a system that will explain the world of Clongowes. At the start of II, the terms he analyzes are meant to prepare for "the great part which he felt awaited him" in the world (*P* 65). In III and IV he accumulates money for prostitutes and moments of grace for salvation, In the last chapter, he is storing poetic images of the Dublin world he lives in.

It later turns out that the images he stores amount to reasons to leave Dublin, and the meaning of the objects he accumulates is always reversed when he is deflected from his initial male identity. Thus, though he seems to be putting signs together into a system in the first two chapters, the real value of these meditations on language for his development lies in taking apart the conventional codes to allow awareness of alternative possibilities. Similarly, his pursuits of vice and virtue end up having the effects of using up those proclivities. The process always leads outside of known territory, so it is fundamentally exploratory, just as political revolution is a quest for new possibilities.

Lacan explains why accumulation tends not to reach its goal when he says that the force of infantile desire that is expressed in the accumulation of libido depends on the fact that because of immaturity, the object-cause of desire cannot be reached. This is parallel to the way that the accumulation of surplus jouissance in capitalism tends to exclude the actual jouissance of copulation (*Other* 98). Thus the saving up of details is deflected from its goal by the inherent structure of the process that enacts the disparity between the aim of the saver and the altogether different sense of satisfaction.

Moreover, the renewal of Stephen's identity in each chapter results from his discovery that the male position is not viable because of the threats that it entails. Lacan argues that masculinity is only assumed through a threat (*Écrits* 575), and Stephen's sense that he is colonized is an awareness of how the threat of authority, because it is internally imposed, negates the subject it constitutes. Every assertion of conscious identity searches for the limit of authority represented by the paternal threat that attacks Stephen in the middle of each chapter. Not to go far enough to find this threat is not to advance.

Such authority deflects him from the narrative framework that he has been following into another one that is unknown to him. The agitated state that derails his identity is hysterical, and the new identity that he reaches is articulated through femininity, though it assumes masculinity. Stephen appropriates womanhood as a medium through which he exchanges one version of himself for another, but by so doing, he enhances femininity as his own component, perhaps no less authentic than those of masquerading women.

In Joyce's vision, femininity is the ability to shift frames of reference, whereas masculinity is a fixed position, as suggested by ALP's being a river in the *Wake*, while HCE is a tower. Stephen's devotion to transformation and to the future (*P* 251) means that he accepts the feminine within himself as his leading principle. It is his feminine side, his "virgin womb of the imagination" (*P* 217), for which the paternal principle is always attacking him. When Wells, for example, asks Stephen, "Do you kiss your mother before you go to bed?" (14), the question, in the present, is not about the past, but about what Stephen does now at Clongowes. He imagines kissing his mother, having to pass through maternal shelter to reach the inner world of sleep.[3] So he is attacked not merely for being a mama's boy, but for his imagination as a feminine aspect. Discovery lies in the direction of mixing genders, and what is discovered is that the imposition of masculinity covers up what is most deeply felt: "While his mind had been pursuing its intangible phantoms...He had heard about him the constant voices of his fathers and of his masters, urging him to be a gentleman....These voices had now come to be hollowsounding..." (*P* 83).

Gender as Genre

The title of the novel indicates that gender is a disguise: "*as a Young Man*." A young man is not quite a man, and Stephen retains the gender ambivalence of infancy throughout the book as part of the baggage of genius. His first original line is in homosexual dialect partly because he has not yet been conditioned to pretend that he is all male: "O the geen wothe botheth" (Gabler text 3). Male babies are allowed to be feminine. Later Stephen feels "For one rare moment he seemed to be clothed in the real apparel of boyhood" (*P* 85), but even at this unique point of authenticity, he is wearing a costume.

Freud argued in *Three Essays on the Theory of Sexuality* that everyone starts with a bisexual disposition and has to learn in early childhood to repress shis (to use Joyce's bisexual pronoun)[4] homosexual side (*SE* VII.140). I pointed out in 1980 that Stephen reveals a residue of repressed homosexuality at the age of six to eight when he remembers being in the bathroom with his father and the words *queer*, *suck*, and *cocks* keep repeating themselves (*Joyce between* 24; *P* 11).

The overture that opens the novel harks back to a pre-gendered state in which Stephen has not built up masculinity and obsession to control femininity and hysteria. Here he cannot sustain a continuous narrative, so he presents six or seven scenes in less than two pages. It is hard to tell where scenes end here and there is no salient present from which episodes may be identified as recollected. The reader is afloat, without the cause-and-effect that Aristotle defined as the basis of continuity in plot. Stephen's education has yet to instill in him the system of logic that sutures impressions into narrative. The Scholastic system of causality that will make Stephen a rational male subject (and teach him that women are not rational) has affinities with obsession. The first entry in Paul L. Adams's "Notes toward a Psychiatric Chronology of Obsession" (1973) begins, "1522–23: Ignatius Loyola produced…the 'Spiritual Exercises to Conquer Self and Regulate One's Life…" (251). Dr. Adams sees the modern concept of obsession starting with the Jesuit text that dictated cognitive patterns in all of Joyce's schools.

The force that works against such regulation from the overture onward can be defined as hysteria, though its basis lies before definition in the Real. Attridge points out that the breakdown of continuity in the overture makes it a radically new kind of modernist writing (*Joyce* 73). This disconnectedness corresponds to the desultory mode of cognition attributed to hysterics by David Shapiro (111–16), and Showalter calls hysterical narrative "fragmentary and discontinuous" (318). Such cognition strays from the linear thrust of male logic because it shifts from one line of reasoning to another. Hysterics are displaced from power, as women, children, and the colonized are, so they do not solidly fill a logical path.

The shift from one line of discourse to another can only take place—or lose place—through the disorientation of hysteria.

The goal of Joycean narrative is never something that is aimed at; it is always a deflection that rearranges perception. On a line-by-line level, this shifting of perspective is the basis of the stream-of-consciousness method. which reveals immediate mental activity as dissonance, slipping off the track. Without such hysterical delirium, no one could be alive. As long as the mind follows a path laid down for it by established or imposed patterns, it is not actively conscious. One becomes actively aware of oneself as a sense of disparity between possibilities—whether of action, perception, identity, or gender—and it is at this juncture that one makes original observations. This matches Lacan's notion of the subject as a circuit between signifiers.

The newly perceived connections are between levels of cognition, each with its own framework of masculine identity. The hysteric is thus able to see power relations concealed by the consistent logic of male subject positions. This is why the hysteric "Dora" was able to outwit Freud. She saw that he was participating in making her an object of homosocial exchange: her father wanted to give her to Herr K. in exchange for Herr K.'s wife (*SE* VII.37). When she told Freud of this, he was so busy with his theories that he missed the importance of what she said, so she sent him packing. As Lacan points out, she used Freud to make known the facts about how she was being used, so she got satisfaction from him before dismissing him (*Other* 97).

The first scene of the six or more in the overture shifts hysterically and strategically through three levels of discourse. First Stephen's father tells the story of the moocow, then Stephen sees him speaking, and then Stephen sees himself in the story: "He was baby tuckoo. The moocow came down along the road where Betty Byrne lived: she sold lemon platt" (*P* 7). He is able to shift out of his position and recognize his father's imposition by becoming Baby Tuckoo. By entering the story, he undermines it; for he gives it his own setting, transferring it from the realm of fable that his father has in mind to his own more realistic magic place, a nearby candy store: "she sold lemon platt." The claim of the paternal narrative is negated by mixing discourses and taking it over.

By following his feelings as they change, Stephen realizes that the meaning of the signifier shifts continually, as the hysterical overflow of his bedwetting is first warm and then cold (7). The stain prefigures the way Joyce's writing changes as the speaking consciousness changes gender positions. The change in temperature, which recurs in the scene with his father in the bathroom with the cold and hot cocks (11), may be associated with sexual excitement. For the child with no idea what sexuality is, the alternation of cold and hot is a hysterical way of expressing a thrill. Since cold and hot are linked to masculine and feminine in

"Circe," (*U* 15.2964), Stephen's first version of sexual excitement slides between genders.

After the bedwetting scene in the overture—or scenes, as it is impossible to tell how many times it recurs—Stephen turns toward his mother, who has a nicer smell than father and plays music that he dances to. Whereas father's discourse imposes on Stephen, mother's is wordless; and he seems to fantasize fusing with her music, for we cannot tell whether the lines "*Tralala lala/Tralala tralaladdy*" (*P* 7) are sung by him or her. Christine Froula argues in *Modernism's Body* that Stephen's art is based on his repressed identification with his mother (37–43), and that it is the maternal substratum of his subjectivity that gives him a basis by which to defy the Law of the Father (17). For Froula, Stephen's "virgin womb of the imagination" (*P* 217) expresses a "transsexual annunciation" (34). What she may not consider is how far the conflicted nature of Stephen's maternal identification keeps it from being natural or viable.

Controlling Hysteria

When we join Stephen at Clongowes to begin the main narrative of Chapter I, he is inserted into the male position, but cannot feel at home in it. The boys play football, an English game in which they develop their manhood by banging each other around as much as possible, confronting each other with paternal threats. He can only escape the dominance of masculinity through temporary outbreaks of hysteria such as his fear of playing. In this chapter, he will use the sobbing hysteria that results from his beating to transfigure himself, shunting himself in a new direction so effectively that by the end of the chapter, the boys he dreaded will hail him as a hero.

As a man, Stephen should control his hysteria, as he ultimately does by using it to advance his power; but this use makes him seek it more voluntarily and depend on it more as the chapters revolve. In Chapter I, he is assailed by a need to leave the path the other boys are on and turn onto an unknown and frightening path. But when he turns aside toward vice at the end of II or confession at the end of III, there is more of a sense of his choosing something for his own development; and by the time he turns toward the beach late in IV or to Europe at the end, the anxious aspect of his hysterical excitement is subordinated to its exultant aspect. Volition increases as he recognizes the usefulness of his agitation by seeing beyond it, making his agitation voluntary, a *sinthome*.

The question of whether Stephen uses his feeling to support his advancement (hysteria to support obsession) or uses his rationality to support his feminine imagination can be answered differently depending on one's viewpoint. I once thought that the term *obsessive* covered Stephen's case, but it now appears that the two sides exchange with and influence each other. The pattern of controlling feelings is linked to the English side of Stephen's cultural complex as well as the masculine, whereas the loss of control is associated with the Irish side as feminine. This is suggested when Stephen twice describes the "type" of his "race" as "a batlike soul" whose self-consciousness is repressed and who gives herself as a woman to strangers (*P* 183, 221).

Just as Stephen later takes ideas from the Church for subversive artistic aims, so he uses the English rationality of the high-class schools he goes to (which study English literature, not Irish) to develop an Irish consciousness. It is on this oppositional level that he uses masculine reason to support feminine imagination. He soon starts to notice that the masculine position that he claims at the end of each chapter turns out to be a limiting reification that leads to subsequent discontent; that what is really valuable is the unrest and discontent that precede the new identity. At the end of Chapter I, as the boys carry him, toss their caps, and shout "Hurroo," Stephen seems to be in the position of an English hero; but his heart is not in it and he struggles "to get free" of them (58).

Joyce indicates that the masculine obsessive is reacting against a feminine hysteric within him. Both compulsion and hysteria are reactions to gender ambivalence, but the compulsive keeps trying to deny this ambivalence, to maintain authority; whereas the hysteric, caught in a shameful position, has to seek independence by building ambivalence. This is why hysteria is so creative. After all, the hysterical woman is asserting herself with a kind of violence by refusing the feminine role of compliance. Freud argues that hysteria performs two gender identities, citing the case of a woman whose right hand tore off her clothing while her left clutched it on (*SE* IX.163). Claire Kahane says that the questions hysteria asks are "Am I a man? Am I a woman? How is sexual identity assumed?" (Bernheimer and Kahane 22). If obsession aims to maintain the authority of masculinity by controlling hysteria, then the compulsive is constituted by containing hysteria. The hysteric, striving for release from a compulsion that is felt as an external threat, cannot exist without an external authority that (s)he opposes, dreads, appropriates, and projects. So the hysteric is contained by obsession.

Stephen passes into his hysterical phase on being confronted by male threats representing the church/state that dispossesses him of manhood, forcing him to set out in a new direction. Here he feels the compulsive repetition of established identity as a constriction from which he must burst free, so there is always emphasis on repetition at this stage: Father Dolan says, "Tomorrow and tomorrow and tomorrow" (*P* 49), and Heron threatens Stephen in two parallel scenes that are juxtaposed (*P* 77–82). The hell of Chapter 3 is an endless cycle, as is the Jesuit life offered Stephen in IV, and the only sample of classroom experience presented in V: "The droning voice of the professor continued to wind itself slowly round and round..." (*P* 194).

Hysterical features that proliferate after these threats, usually near the end of the chapter, include fear of one's own body, screams or outcries, uncontrollable excitement or movement through the body, inability to speak or act, weeping, and loss of awareness of the goal of action. The last is necessary for Stephen to reach a new level, and he is increasingly intentional about cultivating such disorientation, a pattern that tends to corrupt the hysteria with obsession. At the end of Chapter I, for example, Stephen is not only reduced to hysteria by being beaten, but after his confrontation with the rector, his body is overwhelmed with energy: "Faster and faster he hurried on through the gloom excitedly...running quicker and quicker..." (*P* 58). Insofar as he chooses a violent exertion that will seize and transform his body, his drive for power uses his hysteria here. He is celebrating the fact that he did not give in because his hysteria urged him to keep resisting Conmee's milder offers. Conmee's generosity threatens to subordinate Stephen, for concessions may be lures to a machinery of entrapment for the colonized. Showalter cites a passage from W. E. B. Du Bois that sees hysteria as a condition to which Afro-Americans are often driven (334–35).

I have pointed out that as Stephen approaches losing his virginity in Chapter II, he has a sense of being raped by his own desire (*Waking* 17–18). "His hands clenched convulsively and his teeth set together as he suffered the agony of its penetration" (100). Since male desire is driven by fear of not being a man, Joyce sees manhood as based on an unconscious fear of being sodomized that indicates extreme hysteria. Traditionally, both women and the colonized are psychologically or physically violated by their masters. Joyce sees masculinity as subject to the same persecution, as is indicated, for example by Bloom's being haunted by Blazes Boylan.

Freud speaks of hysteria as operating like an active person that invades the body, in effect, an incubus: "the memory of the trauma—acts like a foreign body which long after its entry must continue to be regarded as an agent that is still at work" (*SE* II.6). Hysteria is an imaginary invasion by the father. A man has the option of associating with the invader as superego and controlling his hysteria by obsession, assuming a patriarchal position, as Stephen does by using British money to subjugate the prostitute. But a woman is not empowered either to use symbols of self-control to deny the invasion, or to unleash her hysteria by violence. She must contain the paternal implant by burying it in her body, which then issues strange voices, hysterical symptoms spoken by the body to complain of how she is besieged by her womanhood. In *Seminar XVII*, Lacan says that when man imposes his phallic jouissance on woman, he subjects her to a deprivation, a hysterical non-satisfaction that longs for something further (*Other* 73–74).

Hysterical Knowledge

Joyce recognizes a hysterical force behind the drive toward manhood. In the first nighttown scene, Stephen's "agony of penetration" leads to a "wail" or "cry for an iniquitous abandonment" (*P* 100); and when he is with the prostitute, we are told that he "all but burst into hysterical weeping" (101). The activation of his sexuality involves features coded as feminine that pass through a male body. In Butler's analysis of transvestites, focus on such mixtures reveals that desire is neither masculine nor feminine, but a "dissonant juxtaposition" that transfigures both genders, creating a composite gender formation without a name (*Gender* 123).

The gender arrangement in which Stephen is situated as he moves toward losing his virginity may be Joyce's model of male motivation, one in which the subject is pushed from behind by a paternal force and drawn from before by a maternal one. The father that sodomizes him corresponds to the feeling that he must push ahead to prove his masculinity or be reduced to a feminine role, just as his interest in E__. C__. followed his being mistaken for a woman (*P* 68–69). Bloom is haunted by Blazes Boylan as he yearns for Molly, and I will show in chapter 8 that one of the most frequent motifs in the *Wake* is the image of HCE with threatening men behind him and attractive women in front. Žižek holds that the modern superego often takes the form of an injunction to pleasure.[5]

The hysterical stages at the ends of the last three chapters are, like Stephen's tears of relief with the prostitute, reactions to oppression. Stephen's agitation at going to confession is a response to the sermons on hell, his rapturous artistic vocation is a response to the threat of a priestly calling, and his excitement about going to Europe is a reaction to the blighted world of colonized Ireland. He will carry with him the irrevocable implant of the authority he opposes, but he also makes discoveries. Hysteria is the phase of his mind that moves toward new possibilities, the medium that carries history forward intellectually. Obsession, which is linked to (almost another name for) repetition compulsion, cannot let go of what it knows because it cannot lose control; but hysteria focuses on what is not known, continually taking off in new directions.

Butler points out that identity is constituted by repetition, which defines the subject, but agency comes from variation, which generates "alternative domains of cultural intelligibility, i. e. , new possibilities for gender that contest the rigid codes of hierarchical binarisms" (*Gender* 145). Obsession, then, provides a framework from which hysteria departs. The active part of signification, its agency, depends on the displacement of hysteria to find new forms. Ongoing hysterical departure constitutes what Butler calls the rearticulating of the subject, which calls norms into question (*Bodies* 2).

Lacan connects Joyce's creative symptom to hysteria in "Joyce *le Symptôme* II ," the extension of his talk of June, 16 1975. Here he says that Socrates, who recognized that all men have rights, was a "*parfait hysterique,*" and that this led him to practice "*une sorte de préfiguration de l'analyze.*" In fact, if he had only charged people, he would have been a psychoanalyst, so that he was a genius. Then Lacan says that all he has been saying is only to specify where Joyce has his place ("*tout ça n'est que pour spécifier de* Joyce *de sa place*") (Aubert 35). Here he adds that when Joyce realizes himself as a symptom, he holds himself to be a woman ("Joyce *ne se tient pour femme à l'occasion que de s'accomplir en tant que symptôme*").

In *The Four Fundamental Concepts of Psycho-Analysis* (*Seminar XI*), Lacan says that the hysteric's desire can only be sustained as unsatisfied (12), and that Freud would have become an idealist if he hadn't devoted himself to the Other in the form of the hysteric (28). That is, he would humanistically have settled for a particular form of truth if the unclassifiable minds of hysterics had not drawn him to other possibilities beyond any that he could reach, to the principle of otherness. Shoshana Felman finds in Lacan the argument that Freud developed psychoanalysis by listening receptively to the discourse of female hysterics (59–61; see *Seminar XVII* 74).

David-Ménard's analysis of Freud's treatment of hysteria brings out its exploratory function in the case of Elisabeth von R., in which he used her "pain like a compass" (David-Ménard 28). When Freud realized that he should consider not just the place in her body that speaks to him, but the position she is in when the symptom appears, he finds a new organization in her body that constitutes "a different scene, a new breeding ground for the illness" (David-Ménard 40; *SE* 2: 150) as he repeatedly revises the map of her symbolic body.

Freud's inability to settle for any particular truth, which is reflected by his continual modification of his theories, matches Joyce's endless innovations; and Robert Spoo states that the idea of history leading to a goal is left behind by Joyce in the changing directions of *Portrait* (63). "Joyce *le Symptome* II" seems to recognize the tendency of Joycean narrative to aim at deflection, at a kind of "hystery":

> Joyce denies himself anything that passes according to what the history of the historians is supposed to take as a purpose (*objet*) He is right, history is nothing other than a flight [or evasion], of which we recount only episodes of exodus. (Aubert 34)

This is typical of Lacan's extreme sensitivity to the mobility of history. As Fink observes, he came to equate the discourse of the hysteric with that of the scientist because the hysteric keeps pushing to the point where knowledge is lacking. For the hysteric, as for the scientist, the hidden motor force is the Real (Fink 134–35). The Real is the world before language, so we can never reach it, and it appears only in whatever doesn't work, when language doesn't work in what cannot be explained. The mistrustfulness of the hysteric is such that it will accept no answer, and ALP is referred to as "Livia Noanswa," (*FW* 23.20). This is a version of Victoria Nyanza, the unreachable source of the Nile that explorers searched for through the nineteenth century. The exploratory nature of hysteria is indicated in lines that Juan-David Nasio, in his book on hysteria, quotes from Lacan, who says that the libido extends beyond the body and that "the hysteric plays at testing its elasticity to the utmost" (Nasio 138). So in the flight of history, the hysteric aims to extend the field of desire to the widest territory.

By dividing its loyalties, hysteria tries to embrace Althusser and Jameson's "absent cause of history," which both equate with Lacan's Real (Jameson, *Political* 82). This absent cause is the overall set of relations that ultimately causes history and that is too complex to be captured by any system. The key feature of hysteria that engages the absent cause is its inability to be resolved, which avoids settling on a solution. Richard Pearce explains why the absent cause appears in gaps in the text's continuity: the *h*ole expresses the *w*hole because the hiatuses in speech speak for those who have been silenced, the majority of humanity excluded by the dominant (male, imperialist) tradition (*Politics* 13, 139). These gaps represent the speechlessness of hysteria, so they speak for the powerless, for those in the position of being violated. Their voices must be muted if the patriarchal system is to maintain that it is motivated by logic rather than by a craving for superiority. The obsessive nature of the dominator is revealed by the hysteria of the dominated, both creating each other.

Joyce's inverted epistemology pursues not knowledge, but points where language and knowledge break down to reconstitute themselves for further comprehension. In the second chapter, Stephen begins registering epiphanies, which lay the basis for Joyce's art because Joyce replaces the movement of plot toward a goal—which imposes ideology—with a narrative activity of finding a hidden meaning that cannot quite be understood, or actively missing that meaning. Lacan says in *Le sinthome* that Joyce's epiphanies always show the result "of an error in the knot, namely that the unconscious is joined to the Real" ("*de l'erreur dans le noeud, à savoir que l'inconscient est lié au réel*" 154). The perceiver of the Real is forced to rearrange the knot of shis subjectivity by encountering the Real beyond language. This is central to Thurston's book, with its emphasis on how Joyce confronts the subject with the incomprehensible.

Joyce introduces Stephen's three epiphanies as follows: "He chronicled with patience what he saw, detaching himself from it and tasting its mortifying flavour in secret" (*P* 67). Why does Stephen make mortification, an intellectual version of the sense of being violated or defiled, essential to pre-esthetic perception? Because the pride of entitled coherence must be cast off to see the Real that expresses what is denied or suppressed. In each of the scenes that follows this statement, an event becomes embarrassing as it is sundered from meaning. One meaning of embarrass is 'to place in doubt or perplexity.' In each scene Stephen encounters a question he cannot answer, a question of gender and power. Thus he is dislodged from the active/passive polarity by losing his grip on the basis of activity.

In the kitchen, why is there such a gap between the crude boy and the picture of "The beautiful Mabel Hunter" (*P* 67)? In the high room, why is Stephen so struck by being mistaken for Josephine (68)? At the party, why does he "taste the joy of his loneliness" (68)? And in the tram scene that is an extension of the party, why can't he take hold of E__. C__. (69–70)? Could it be that desire cannot connect with beauty, just as his urge to approach the girl is driven by an uncertainty about his manhood that is spurred by being mistaken for a woman? The mortification of not being able to comprehend forces Stephen to see things in a new way. The church/state attaches Stephen to a manhood that is in doubt and a desire that is unrealizable. Seeing through these illusions displaces him from the enclosure of known identity, forcing him to see himself in the hysterical form of a question without an answer.

Freud says that hysteria results from the effect of a trauma that cannot find release in action or words. He adds that language recognizes this effect by referring to "an injury that has been suffered in silence as 'a mortification' ['*Krankung*,' lit. 'making ill']" (*SE* II. 8, Strachey's brackets). Stephen values mortification because it delineates his oppression, and he already senses that this is the way to be free. The unconscious shaped by Irish history can only be reached through mortification, just as the Irish feel the need to rebel when they realize how they have been injured. Sexual repression is linked to economic oppression in this world because there was little Puritanism in Ireland before Rome and England took over.

The mortification of not understanding reveals Stephen's colonial status as defined by hysteria, and Stephen cultivates this mortification because it is only through hysteria that his narrative moves forward into the unknown, the potential for freedom outside the existing order. The feminine emotion that Joyce builds toward liberates the forward movement of history as a breakdown of the clearly defined limits of masculine boundaries. Creativity is outside the civilized world. The artist who focuses on embarrassment, the subject who realizes the unfairness of the (gender) system, and the colonized person who insists on injustice are all grasping their affliction to make it a voluntary symptom, a *sinthome*.

Taking on Mother

Although the concentration on feminine mentality at the end of Joyce's other works is clear, it is not so apparent at the end of *Portrait.* But Stephen does gravitate toward the feminine at the end in such a way as to actively compromise his masculinity. This process moves through three stages on the last six pages of the book. At the end of the novel's action, while speaking to Cranly, he renounces his masculine position. And on the last page of the diary that follows, he first realizes that he was all wrong about E__. C__., and then is transfixed by his mother's opposition.

In the debate with Cranly, he abandons his position as a man in relation to his family and his society, saying that he does not want the protection of the law and he will not stay in Ireland. He also gives up his claim to Emma, the most attractive woman in his life. He shows here an uneasy sense of gender ambivalence that Valente calls homosexual panic ("Thrilled" 185–88): imagining that Cranly is acting erotically with both Emma and himself, Stephen refuses roles of male competitor and homosexual lover that were probably not offered. For a man to refuse to compete for a woman in whom he has an intense interest has to involve at least a touch of abjection, especially when the competition (as he must suspect) may not even be there. Abjection is related to mortification, and Butler sees Kristeva's function of abjection (Kristeva, *Powers* 4–13) as passing outside the bounds of what is expressible (*Gender 133*). In his resolute rejection of Irish colonial citizenship and Victorian manhood, Stephen positions himself, as Froula puts it, "outside the name and law of the father" (19). Passage outside the manly role may help him to see Emma sympathetically when he last meets her (*P* 252). He repeatedly realizes in the last chapter that his ideas of her as sex object and conniver do not fit her and do not even fit his own mind (*P* 222, 233). His awareness of how he distorts her allows him to see his mind invaded by discourses of dominance.

The idea of return to the maternal principle, which Froula sees as central to Joyce's gender critique, may seem to be contradicted by the fact that Stephen is leaving his mother in Chapter V, having rejected her piety in IV (*P* 164–65). Yet he is probably as close to her at the end as he has been since the first page, but negatively close. The moment at which one parts from someone to whom one is attached is a highly emotional moment of concentrated intimacy. In the last chapter (although Joyce returned to Dublin and went to Paris again before his mother's illness appeared), Stephen will not see his mother again within the fiction until she is dying.

Freud says that one forms one's ego by a series of identifications and that it is at the moments when one separates from them that one identifies with or *introjects* (ingests) those who go into making one up (*SE* XIX.29), so every part of one's subject is a parting. The last words of Stephen's mother at the end of the novel are deeply inscribed in his mind: "She prays now, she says, that I may learn in my own life and away from home and friends what the heart is and what it feels" (*P* 252). Stephen's conflicted—far from entirely ironic—response is "Amen. So be it. Welcome, O life! I go to encounter for the millionth time the reality of experience and to forge in the smithy of my soul the uncreated conscience of my race" (252–53). His rejection of her view wrenches him: it is the Real that reties his knot.

Lacan sees Joyce's art as charged with the father ("*chargé de père*") so as to make his family subsist as illustrious ("*fait non seulement subsister sa famille mais l'illustre*...," *Le sinthome* 22), the paternal function of making his family immortal. This is only part of the truth. The lines that precede Stephen's announcement of his mission make it clear that he is also charged with his mother. The reality of experience that she enjoins him to find may be equated with Lacan' s Real, the point at which the otherness of the world surprises one; and the Real is crucial to love, which Lacan describes in *Encore* as a relationship on an unconscious level (144), but Stephen contracts this Real from his mother.

May Dedalus's injunction to find love ("what the heart is and what it feels") is intensely remembered in *Ulysses*, though it does not seem to be realized directly. The third page of *Ulysses* says, "Pain, that was not yet the pain of love, fretted his heart" (1.102); and soon Stephen's inward thoughts ask his internal mother for the word known to all men (*U* 3.435), which he later identifies with "love" (*U* 9.429). This maternal component of the mind, "*amor matris*," is not only his love for her or hers for him, but his love that comes from his mother, the reproduction of mothering in male sensitivity. Her hope for him reaches back to what they shared before the division of categories and forward to the hope that love can overcome those boundaries. It has theoretical value as an image of the impossibility of the Real, the maximum disparity between his irony and what his irony denies.

For this action of internalizing the feminine, which causes Stephen to bear his mother's ghost with him throughout *Ulysses*, is also brutally masculine: she haunts him to the extent that he has killed her. In Joyce's 1904 letter to Nora about standing over his mother's body and seeing her as a victim of the system, one of the causes of her death that he lists is "my cynical frankness of conduct" (*Letters II* 48). As Eide points out, this letter is an announcement of his mission to attack the system (2), but Stephen realizes that the primary field in which he must attack the system is in himself, hammering at the smithy of his soul.

May's hope that Stephen will learn what the heart is accuses him by implying that he has no heart. The partings from his mother that begin and end *Portrait* are models for Stephen's relationships with women, which always have as their primary goal relinquishment, "a sadly proud gesture of refusal" (*P* 63) that extends to Molly. Willful parting is a common macho way of dealing with the threat of women, and this maneuver is conveyed to Stephen by his father. Simon never makes Stephen happier than he does by singing "a sadhappy air" at the Victoria Hotel in Cork when Stephen is about thirteen. Although Stephen will soon be disillusioned by his father's weakness, they seem here to share the exhilaration of being boys away from female supervision:

'Tis youth and folly
Makes young men marry,
So here my love, I'll
No longer stay.
(*P* 88)

Leaving his love because she is too attractive (tempting to marriage), the singer is both hypermasculine and cowardly. He at once both separates himself from her and plants her in his mind (still addressing her), showing the femininity in masculinity, a womanly deposit to which he will have to return.

Leaving is the way to get closest to mother because staying with her keeps her at a distance. But once one goes, once she is gone, one can write poignant letters, or fiction which, insofar as it is moving (and it is), approaches her spirit. The restlessness generated by the absolute unattainability of the mother drives consciousness into new possibilities, so that one comes to approach her through the unattainable itself.

Thus, at the conclusion of *Portrait*, Stephen is absorbed in his projection of a feminine mentality, yet denies that mentality—he insistently though indirectly renounces his mother throughout Chapter V: "Ireland is the old sow that eats her farrow" (203). Part of him strives to secure his manhood by pretending that his feminine side does not exist. He ends up hailing Daedalus as his father though this puts him in the position of Icarus, underlining the delusory nature of masculinity. His denial of his attachment to his mother's body reflects the depth and intensity of that attachment. She thus becomes a means to expand his subject into the utmost Real of disparity, which may be a precondition to encountering the actuality of woman in her opposition.

In "The Last Chapter of *Finnegans Wake*: Stephen Finds His Mother," Norris sees Stephen's parting from his mother reverberating through Joyce's work, culminating in the death of the mother at the end of the *Wake*. ALP is identified as the author of the *Wake*, and she formally contains the book; for her last word leads to its first, making her death its point of origin. The intimacy with which ALP is portrayed is the final point of an escalating drive toward imagined intimacy with a woman's soul through all of Joyce's canon, and is so close as to impoverish superlatives. He may be as close to her at the end as any man has ever been to a woman in literature, with particular emphasis on aspects of women that were little known previously, their defiance and terror toward the male and the depth of their lesbian impulses. In "Joyce and Gender," Mahaffey argues that a key ethical criterion of Joyce's work is whether people have the mental freedom to imagine what is impossible, and that a strong case of this is Stephen's participation in the opposite gender (134–35). Thus, Joyce's sinthomatic goal becomes a moral one.

The extraordinary fusion of the Joycean artist's soul with the projected woman's soul is the affective goal of Joyce's work and is a maximum development of the return to the shared liquid margin of interchange between mother and child. This appears at the end of the *Wake* when ALP senses her daughter Issy "Swimming in my hindmoist" (627.3). Insofar as Joyce approaches this intermingling, it generates the power to reshape human consciousness by an expansion of the space before the active-passive polarity. Lacan may have been led by reading ALP's book to a clearer sense of the illusory status of active and passive.

Stephen's final position is neither masculine nor feminine, as it is neither Irish nor European, neither character nor author as a text Stephen is writing. He rejects his placement in gender, social identity, and created reality in order to seek what Butler calls "alternative domains of cultural intelligibility." This stepping outside of bounds leads to the feminization of manhood, the internationalization of Irish culture, and the idea of each individual creating hris own identity. It embodies the forward movement of history (insofar as it can move forward) into gender dissonance, hybrid civilization, and the improvisation of self-invention. In gender, as in nationality and in personality, the Joycean "position" is one of exile and improvisation. And if he sees through the unity of identity, then he sees also through that of truth in constructing a subject that includes all sides.

Chapter 5

Žižek, Fantasy, and Truth

Fantasy as Reality

Žižek argues in *The Plague of Fantasies* that fantasy is the primordial form of narrative and that it serves to hide an original and insuperable deadlock, such as the impossibility of the fulfillment of desire because its actual object cannot match the one it imagines.[1] Such contradictions indicate the Real beyond language. People tell stories to resolve a fundamental antinomy by rearranging its terms in temporal succession, making the answer a goal to be reached; but this does not solve the problem because the goal cannot be reached (Žižek, *Plague* 10). Columbus believed that he had reached India, and so Native Americans were called Indians. What one reaches (the Real) can never be articulated to match what one aims at (the Imaginary). The psychoanalytic nature of truth, discovered by Freud and shared by Joyce, Lacan, and Žižek, means that what one explores always remains in doubt, and that what one discovers is not what one expected. So the object can never match desire, and truth can never satisfy what summons it. The active importance of this level of Joyce's narrative has not been recognized.

For Žižek, fantasy, even when rebellious, supports ideology by serving as its inherent transgression, a level of imaginary misbehavior that allows us to accept the limits of "reality." Žižek says that true art consists of manipulating censorship of the underlying fantasy of a representation so "as to reveal the radical falsity of this fantasy" (*Plague* 20). On a continuous and sharply-defined level, Joyce's *Portrait* keeps demonstrating the illusion of fantasies, primarily because the new identity Stephen seizes at the end of each chapter turns out in the next one to be hardly *more* than a fantasy. Thus Joyce maps out the fantasmatic machinery that every claim to reality is based on. Žižek argues that one can traverse or pass beyond the fantasy by realizing that the real object is loss (*PV* 61–63).

Žižek's conception allows us to see Joyce's works as a progressive disassembly of narrative leading to the virtual abolition of temporal continuity in the *Wake*. It also allows us to see Stephen in *Portrait* growing aware of a fundamental fantasy of truth that makes up his various realities. A crucial accomplishment of his esthetic theory may be to realize that the esthetic object is part of a sequence. This reveals the change that is always implicit in the goal. To see the object as "that thing which it is and no other thing" (*P* 213) seems to accept existing reality, but Stephen's desire to do so is undercut by his relentless critique of reality. In Chapter V he finds himself in a degraded world that he will have to leave, as he did in all of the previous chapters. The truth of the butcher boy's basket (*P* 212) is the Real of oppression that hangs over his head; and the "enchantment of the heart" is the shock of the Real, a phrase that Luigi Galvani, whom Stephen cites, used to describe "the momentary cessation of a frog's heartbeat when a needle is inserted in its spinal cord" (Gifford 254).

When Stephen finds an "enchantment of the heart" (*P* 217), the formula for radiance (*P* 213), in the villanelle section of V that follows the esthetics theory, what he focuses on is the weariness of woman (*P* 217, 222, 223), her need to leave behind the "*ardent ways*" that presently define her. The beauty of woman evokes a need to change that can take her beyond being the lure of the fallen. That Stephen reaches this enchantment without focusing on a concrete object undercuts his claim on a theory that apprehends static actuality. The goal Stephen reaches at the end of V is that of departure. The goals of the first three chapters, the triumph over the Church's authority, the sinful kiss, and the Eucharist, stay in place though they bring change. The goal of IV, the flight of Dedalus, envisions departure, but that of V assumes it fully.

The end of *Portrait* displaces the idea of radiance as the revelation of what the object actually is by realizing that the strongest truth of the object is what it can become, and this corresponds to Stephen's insistence in V that "the present is living only because it brings forth the future" (*P* 251). The object inclined toward change is incomplete, so Stephen's changing of Aquinas's transcendental object into a factual or made one is a step toward conceiving the object as displacement, an idea expressed in *Ulysses* when Stephen speaks of the errors of the genius as portals of discovery (9.228–29). To see the object as erroneous is to see it as the need for change, and this perception has grown through the epiphanies of *Portrait*, and leads to the "Proteus" episode of *Ulysses*. "[T]hat thing which it is" is finally the object's Real or revolutionary potential as opposed to what it has been assumed to be.

The formation of fantasy constitutes a situation in which satisfaction lies at a further level, in the hands of an unreachable other (Žižek, *Plague* 32). It is this ideal figure who is imagined to complete fulfillment, not oneself. Stephen analyzes from the first chapter how he approaches reality through surrogates and a mental construction of stages. This appears in his quadruple metaphor of approaching the truth, when he'll be like the older fellows and know what politics means and where the universe ends (*P* 17). By comparing stages of the future to changes in sound on a train in a tunnel, and to closing his ears, Stephen sees progress toward his goal as a ritual he controls.

That the goal is illusory (the upper-class men do not know these things) is underscored by Stephen's need to approach it through ritual. Ritual gives him a form to study that can lead him to realize that the goal is fantasy and the ritual is the source of satisfaction, so it can free him from ideology—the belief in reaching truth.

If the goals Stephen reaches at the end of each chapter—to be a hero of Clongowes, to embrace a prostitute or to embrace the church—turn out to be unreal in the succeeding chapter, this contributes to Stephen's analysis of the steps he goes through. Such analysis leads him to see beauty as the enactment of a sequential structure in his esthetics theory, which emphasizes by comparing beauty to "a fading coal" (*P* 213) that it begins to dwindle as soon as it is perceived. The steps that reveal the structure are not the ones that seem to reach the goal, but those that fail, exposing the fantasmatic level.

Žižek says that fantasy is on the side of reality because something only seems real insofar as it answers our fundamental fantasy: "when the fantasmatic frame disintegrates, the subject undergoes a 'loss of reality' and starts to perceive reality as an 'irreal' nightmarish universe with no firm ontological foundation..." (*Plague* 66). Stephen passes through a phase of feeling unreal in each chapter as he gives up a familiar fantasy framework. This is a stage at which language loses its meaning, as described by R. Brandon Kershner: "At each significant stage of the development of Stephen's consciousness, he undergoes a period of painful sensitivity to 'raw' language, language that seems in some respects to lack denotation" ("The Artist" 883). The missing focus that would give language meaning is for Žižek fantastic.

The breakdown of the father at the Christmas dinner weakens the fantasy of unified authority to present Stephen with a parallax of two sides, neither of which can be ascertained as right: Dante is on the side of God, but she is unpleasant, while the men are uneasily against the Church, but attractive. The falseness each imposes on the other reveals them to be fantasies. Resolution is impossible, and the father is left in tears, an image of broken authority. After this scene, Stephen is insecure and vulnerable back at Clongowes. His sense of unreality is manifested by broken eyeglasses that deprive him of a frame: "the fellows seemed to him smaller and farther away and the goalposts so thin and far and the soft grey sky so high up" (*P* 41). His field of vision has been emptied out.

In the next chapter, Simon loses his property, disillusioning Stephen—"in the manner of his own dispossession, he felt the world give the lie rudely to his fantasy" (*P* 87)—as he sees that his romantic dreams are dependent on patriarchal status and property. The exposure of fantasy devastates Stephen as his fantasies grow increasingly sexual. Seeing everything in lurid terms makes the other frames of reference hollow, rendering everything fantastic: "By his monstrous way of life he seemed to have put himself beyond the limits of reality. Nothing moved him or spoke to him from the real world unless he heard in it an echo of the infuriated cries within him...He could scarcely recognize as his his own thoughts" (*P* 92). Passing through this "subjective destitution" allows Stephen to examine how his sense of reality depends on fantasy; and he explores this further when he heads for the red light district, where pure fantasies are detached from human beings.

The prostitute Stephen visits is emblematized as inanimate: "A huge doll sat with her legs apart in the copious easy chair" (*P* 100). Thus Joyce indicates that vice is a puppet show; but Stephen, though he notices this, takes this arrangement for reality while he is absorbed in it, showing that fantasy can be deeply satisfying. At the start of Chapter III, it pulsates through all of his senses (*P* 102), and it establishes "a dark peace" between his body and his soul (*P* 103). Yet it remains puppetry, so it can be swept away by the terrifying sermons on hell: "the jewelleyed harlots of his imagination, fled before the hurricane, squeaking like mice..." (*P* 115). This returns Stephen to radical alienation from himself: "One soul was lost; a tiny soul: his. It flickered once and went out, forgotten, lost. The end: black cold void waste" (*P* 141). Only by emptying himself of Imaginary identity can he separate himself from his fundamental fantasy in order to see its outline in the equation of self-fulfillment.

Religion delineates the structure of fantasy clearly through a totalizing system that affirms the distance between physical reality and another reality. The acts of priesthood please Stephen "by reason of their semblance of reality and of their distance from it" (*P* 158). The Church helps Stephen to see that the only way he has ever connected with reality or action is through fantasy constructions: "In vague sacrificial or sacramental acts alone his will seemed drawn to go forth to encounter reality: and it was partly the absence of an appointed rite which had always constrained him to inaction" (*P* 159). The rite turns an impasse (the Real) into a sequence, and it leads to the stages of esthetic perception, which turn the conflicted element of beauty to a narrative. But the realization that he can only approach reality through ritual exposes the structure of his fundamental fantasy.

Stephen's phrase "drawn to go forth to encounter reality" shows that ritual affords him contact with reality only by generating desire. It defines the action of the novel as drawing forth or portrayal, both the access to the effect of inherence and an artificial production. Here he anticipates Žižek's view that the closer one gets to reality, the more one is involved in fantasy. Žižek argues that we are inclined to say, "No matter what unknown mechanism governs my acts, perceptions and thoughts, nobody can take from me what I see and feel now" (*Fragile* 84). So if someone explains my passion to me in, say, chemical terms, I still believe that this intense experience is my own. Yet what makes the experience immediate and intense is absorption in fantasy, which never belongs to me because it is enjoyed by an ideal other.

Stephen is usually most absorbed in his fantasies at the ends of his chapters, and these endings feature extremely close or microscopic focus, an intense immediacy. Yet this closeness is always undercut by ambivalent self-consciousness, for Stephen is always in the process of turning into someone else or taking on a new fantasy as the chapter ends. The first chapter ends with Stephen hearing "the sound of the cricket bats: pick, pack, pock, puck: like drops of water in a fountain..." (59). This background noise sounded like water the first time Stephen heard it (41), but the next two times, it sounded like boys being beaten (44, 45). Now that Stephen is victorious at Clongowes, he can hear it as the attractive sound of a "brimming bowl" (59). But in this chapter, Stephen ponders the different meanings that the same word can have, as with *belt* and *Parnell*. So he must be aware that the sound of the bats changes with different contexts; and every cycle of repetition is likely to make him more aware of inconsistencies that dislodge his recurring images from their authority and reveal them as fantasies—in this case, two fantasies for the same sound. These two fantasies suggest that his subject is suspended between a male threat and a female attraction. The Joycean use of motifs shows how these phrases change every time they recur. No matter how closely Stephen focuses on the most minute subsurface details of "reality," he never stops moving toward fantasy. Yet seeing how one fantasy succeeds another calls their ideological power into doubt.

The prostitute's kiss at the end of the second chapter dissolves boundaries between inner and outer and, through synesthesia, between one sense and another. Between her lips, he feels an "unknown" pressure "darker than the swoon of sin, softer than sound or odour" (101). He later refers to "sound and shape and colour" as "the prison gates of the soul" (*P* 207). The containment of the senses by convention is a bondage, so whatever breaks down the boundaries between the senses is liberating, another figure of freedom. The end of Chapter III is closely parallel to that of II, with Stephen about to receive the Eucharist in his mouth as he was about to receive the prostitute's tongue. Both initiate him into a new world, but by the time of the second gift of tongue—which has to be partly a parody of the first—Stephen is already thinking in comparative terms. This makes him insist in a way that runs into irony: "Another life! A life of grace and virtue and happiness! It was true. It was not a dream from which he would wake The past was past" (*P* 146). To deny repeatedly that it is an illusion, using two exclamation marks, is to inscribe a desperation behind the claims of release. In fact the line 'It was not a dream from which he would awake" refers to a passage half-a-page above: "In a dream he fell asleep. In a dream he rose and saw that it was morning. In a waking dream..." (*P 146*). So the later line cannot deny that it is a dream, but only that he will wake.

For Stephen to know that he is living in a dream is to realize that his perceptions are shaped by unconscious forces, and such a realization paradoxically leads to a more perceptive awakening. Stephen's ability to see that his life is controlled by fantasies that come from outside has roots in his religious education, which emphasized from the start that every true word he spoke was spoken through him by God: "*O Lord, open our lips/ and our mouth shall announce thy praise*" (*P* 17). Central to his use of the Church's ideas against its ideology is his mapping out of the fantasy constructs into which it has inserted him. In fact, Christianity tells him that his thinking is always fantastic unless it is religious, the unreal real of Scholasticism: Frederick Copleston, S. J. says that in medieval Scholastic doctrine, "the human intellect...in this life, depends on the phantasm" (213).

Just as in his early life of vice Stephen continually condemned himself theologically ("he knew that his soul lusted after its own destruction," *P* 103–4), so in his life of piety, he keeps criticizing himself skeptically, observing, for example, that he is reducing life to a transcendent abstraction: "The world for all its solid substance and complexity no longer existed for his soul save as a theorem of divine power and love and universality" (*P* 150). The typical violence of self-criticism here works against the idea of Stephen as self-righteous. Later Stephen will describe his love of God as the closest he ever came to love in his life (*P* 240), and *Ulysses* does not make it clear that this is ever surpassed. Stephen never gets rid of the fundamental fantasy that his words and perceptions belong to a higher power (Other), but he now claims them by seeing them as aimed at the artist he will become. So if earlier his best phrases belonged to God, now these phrases move toward writing his story definitively and becoming the God who creates Himself. Like any fantasy of full attainment, this is impossible; but it is creative insofar as it brings him into contact with the Real of his own division.

Art may be the most effective way to isolate fantasies from actuality since it is more detached from reality than lust, religion or even philosophy, which believes in its connection to reality, while art accepts its fantastic status. Art as *sinthome* has the advantage of accepting its relation to reality as symptomatic. Stephen's assumption of his artistic vocation in Chapter IV leads him to focus on the process by which he controls his perceptions. So he brings his eyelids together and observes how the light between them dances to form the greatest variety of shapes: "His eyelids trembled.... A world, a glimmer or a flower?" (*P* 172). He learns how to be an artist by watching how his perceptual system creates through distortion, ranging from a glimmer to a world. If whatever he sees is projected, it approaches infinite changeability.

At his final fantasy discovery of a deeper reality that can only be reached by going overseas, Stephen says, "I go to encounter for the millionth time the reality of experience ... " (253). This implies an endless series of realities that differ from each other. It corresponds to his esthetics theory, which reiterates its three-stage process to make each object of beauty, positing a radiance that begins to fade as soon as it appears. The reality Stephen encounters through his esthetic is a projection of fantasy in which beauty consists of structures in the mind. His theory is true insofar as beauty could not exist without being constructed. As soon as it is made, it begins to lose its glow and another object must be sought; for the same object of beauty cannot be perceived as such twice.

Žižek says that the progressive aim of analysis is to traverse the fantasy, to go through the fantasy so as to leave it behind and confront the impossibility of the Real, the unbearable conflict that the fantasy of reality smoothes over (Žižek, *Plague* 29, 33). Such a confrontation would be spurred by increasing awareness of the multiple and contradictory nature of one's fantasies. The Real of the object as conflict can only be approached by dividing it into the relationship of its parts.

The process of going through fantasy may not be incompatible with Mahaffey's claim in "Joyce and Gender" that Joyce's characters liberate themselves by having vital fantasies that transgress the limits on their freedom by imagining what is impossible (124–26). This argument suggests the Real, but it may overlook how such unlikely fantasies use themselves up in a rhythm that requires renewal through denial. The richer one's fantasy life, the better one may be able to distinguish the Real, provided that the fantasy is perceived as fantastic or impossible.

Fantasy shapes reality at its foundation, so that the nascent aspect of fantasy is the source of creative vitality and even of strength itself as the ability to go further. Thus even though fantasy is a delusion, it makes it possible to see more; but the key to the additional vision it provides is the recognition of its delusory nature. Therefore Joyce insists on his critical side that fantasy has to be seen through at all times, even when it is being enjoyed, expanded, or commiserated with. The separation of fantasies from reality does not keep them from being funny or penetrating or poignant: it can help them to do so, as the "Circe" or "Penelope" episodes of *Ulysses* make manifest. The technique of each episode of *Ulysses* gives a different flavor of fantasy for each hour of the day.

Fantasies infiltrate reality and importune so plaguily to be taken for it that they tend to make up reality insofar as it is not interrupted by the conflict of the Real. Joyce's works are a series of interruptions of reality that grow more interruptive as the canon proceeds. For Tony Thwaites, Joyce's work is increasingly structured by an "*arrest* that ... sends any point elsewhere" (74). The breakdowns of narrative and discourse in the *Wake* are meant to give birth to new frameworks and languages in cascades. The new frames themselves are less important than the displacement of the ability to frame, which confronts the impossible so as to change reality endlessly.

In *Tarrying with the Negative*, Žižek builds his argument that there is no sense of reality that does not depend on fantasy. He cites Jeremy Bentham's theory of fictions, which holds that it is not possible to speak without making use of fictitious entities, things that cannot be specified to exist, such as the flow of water or the weight of a table (*Tarrying* 88). Being outside of the ability of language to explain them, these fictions lie in Lacan's Real, the incomprehensible foundation of reality. Bentham is especially insistent about thought: "Of nothing, therefore, that has place, or passes in our mind, can we speak, or so much as think, otherwise than in the way of *fiction*" (Bentham, "Fragment" 199, cited in *Tarrying* 88, Žižek's italics).

Žižek also refers to Kant's *Critique of Pure Reason*, which argues that we have to use transcendental Ideas that are beyond perception in order to give shape to experience, so that illusion is "inseparable from human reason" (Kant A 298, cited in *Tarrying* 88). Moreover, Žižek points out that the things we believe in most strongly, such as ethnicity and ideology, do not depend on content, but on gestures of identification that are fantasies (*Tarrying* 78). So that he concludes that "if we renounce fictions, reality itself dissolves" (91). This is the inquiry that Stephen has been pursuing through his relentless questioning of words and figures, essentially seeing all language as bedwetting. And here we see how difficult his fantasmic deprivation is and how it leads to a quest for truth, but not for the fantasy-based truth of reality as we usually know it. By revealing that reality is made up of a series of fantasies and that it is only through their displacement and negation that veracity can be approached, Joyce brings to life a new version of truth. This truth is made up of parts that cannot be reconciled and that can only approach the overall realization of truth—which they can never reach—insofar as they are actively involved in motion, change, and denial. This vision anticipates Lacan's notion of truth as circulation.

Truth as Circulation

In his 1957 seminar on Poe's "The Purloined Letter," which sees truth as a circulation in the story (Lacan, *Écrits* 11, 13), and which is given the first place in *Écrits*, Lacan says that the signifier can sustain itself "only in a displacement comparable to that found in electronic news strips . . . because of the alternating operation at its core that requires it to leave its place, if only to return to it by a circular path" (*Écrits* 21). The primary image here is the moving headlines on the sides of city buildings (as in Times Square, New York), a strong model for the truth as the circulation of the signifier partly because they keep changing as they loop around the other side. This illustrates how Lacan's chain of signifiers is constantly changing, and therefore more radically historical than any truth that could be stabilized for any length of time: the electronic letters keep moving in their circuits. If they stay in place for a moment, that moment changes with the process of reading it.

Shepherdson's essay "Lacan and Philosophy" explains a distinction between truth and knowledge that Lacan derived from Hegel:

> just as, for dialectical thought, the movement of *truth* will always exceed and disrupt whatever has been established as conscious *knowledge*, such that knowledge will be exposed to a process of perpetual dislocation and productive negativity, so also for Freud, the *consciousness of the ego* remains in a state of permanent instability, perpetually disrupted by the alien *truth of the subject* that emerges at the level of the unconscious... (Rabaté, *Companion* 127).

Such an incessantly changing model of truth is already present in *Portrait*, where the truth is sinfully sexual at some points, virtuously religious at others, and at still others, politically revolutionary or esthetically artistic. Stephen is lecherous, pious, radical, and arty, among other things. He does not stop being any of these things because it is suppressed at certain points or because they contradict each other violently. And whenever the reader goes through the process of defining the character—by linking a series of phrases—the character has already changed through a new combination of phrases and functions. Stephen, for example, is religious in artistic and radical ways. He is even religious in a lecherous way, quite enjoying the physical deprivations of his pious discipline (*P* 147–52), just as he is lustful in devout ways. And because he is at every moment involved in the activity of changing his identity, the multisided truth that is articulated through him is charged with movement toward change and is never the same from one moment to the next. Joyce's enormous extension of characterization, perhaps the greatest since Shakespeare, is a stride forward for human consciousness.

A complex model of the circuit of the signifier that defines both subjectivity and truth appears in Lacan's seminar of April 10, 1973, "Knowledge and Truth" in volume XX of his seminars, *Encore* (90, see Figure 5.1). This schema shows language passing continuously through a triangular shift in modes, from the Imaginary order to the Symbolic one to the Real and back. While the true is focused at one phase of this schema, it develops out of the whole movement of the circuit and could no more exist outside it than a heart outside a body. The sides of this schema correspond to stages in the action of Joyce's *Portrait*. In fact, this cycle operates in the presentation of virtually every significant phrase of the novel, but it takes some of its main forms in the cyclical movement of each chapter.

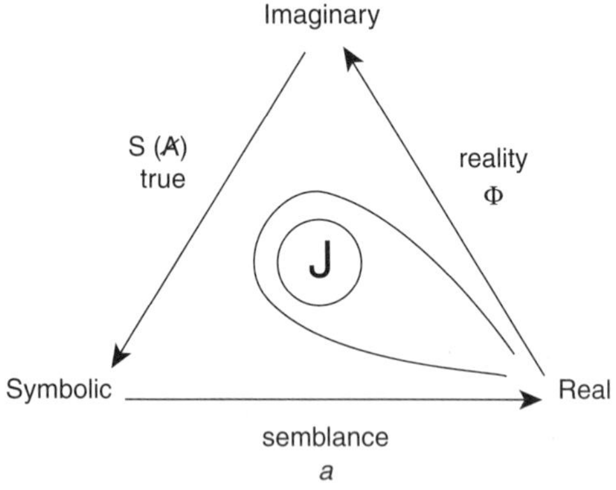

Figure 5.1 Lacan's Diagram of Truth

The feeling of inspiration with which Stephen ends each chapter may be aligned with the Imaginary, the register of language in which one defines oneself by reference to the illusions of unity and immediacy, matching or equating oneself with the object of desire (*Encore* 92), the language of fantasy. As his schoolmates cheer him as a hero, as the prostitute kisses him, as he receives the Eucharist, as he has his vision on the beach, and as he exults over his departure to Europe, he has a sense of having found himself that expresses the intimate, personal feelings of the Imaginary order. This is the language of connection to mother through which he expands his identity.

In the first half of the chapter that follows each uplift, Stephen realizes against the world the limits of the new identity that he has found, concentrating on what opposes that identity. This stage corresponds in Lacan's schema to S(Ⱥ), the signifier of the barred Other as the true, which represents Lacan's emphasis (*Encore* 92) on the impossibility of telling the whole truth (the big *Autre*). This impossibility is realized through a series of unsuccessful attempts to represent the subject as a definite identity, which always prove quite deficient. Stephen starts each chapter thinking that now he knows his identity, but then realizes by expressing it that it will not do at all.

In Chapter 1 he tries to specify his place in the universe—"*Stephen Dedalus/Class of Elements*," and so forth—but this leads him to realize that he can't be contained by the formulation as his mind questions its boundaries: "What was after the universe?" (*P* 16). He apprehends here that the universe is not all, that any attempt to define it will be incomplete. By mapping himself in the universe, he indicates that the meaning of any signifier depends on the entire network of signifiers that frames it; but this totality (the Other), is beyond definition. So any attempt to affirm Stephen's identity, as it strives to specify itself in language, will prove increasingly inadequate.

Stephen's difficulty in defining himself is sharply drawn when he returns to Clongowes and wonders what the unknown crime is that some boys committed. That he doesn't know what the crime is, as I mentioned, makes him anxiously wonder if he has done it. Stephen's most terrible sin is the key to his identity, his main symptom, but he cannot define it. Perhaps the sin is to be indeterminate: not to be contained by a definition is to claim the exceptional position of the first cause. Žižek says that everyone who lives under the prohibitory Father God of orthodoxy is always already guilty of parricide in his mind, and his reaction against this secures his devotion (*Ticklish* 316). The sermons on hell in *Portrait*, like Žižek, see parricide as the central sin (*P* 122, 133).

One form of parricide is to assume the role of the Father, the central sin of Satan and perhaps of Joyce. Some versions of the schoolboy sin indicate this aim, for one is drinking the altar wine, which may contain the body of God; and this makes Stephen think the boys have stolen a monstrance, the vessel in which the host is displayed. Stephen reacts to these sins intensely, showing that he is implicated; "A faint sickness of awe made him feel weak" (*P* 40). In *Ulysses* Stephen says that the most inconceivable or shameful sin is to have intercourse with one's father (9.850–52). The stealing of the monstrance, the last of the five versions of the sin, is entirely Stephen's invention, and is the only version that he imagines himself performing; "to open the dark press and steal the flashing gold thing into which God was put.... It thrilled him to think of it..." (*P* 46). Patricide takes the form of intercourse with mother here, which does not reduce its homosexual content.

As a modernist artist in Žižek's terms, Joyce would take over the sacred space that contains the sublime object and fill it with the void (*Fragile* 26–27). As a postmodernist, he would fill this frame with waste, as did Andy Warhol with his soup cans (*Fragile* 39–40). By the time Joyce got to the postmodern *Wake*, he realized that the Joycean artist, like Shem, writes with his own waste matter (*FW* 185). Shem the Penman as forger reveals that art is a sham or semblance in its effort to make the Symbolic cover the indefinable Real. To seize the frame of art and fill it with indeterminacy in the place of the sacred is to use art to attack certainty.[2]

Already when the Clongowes crime is committed, Stephen has tried to think of the whole universe and realized that "Only God could do that" (*P* 16). Blake said, "I must create a System or be enslaved by another Mans" (Blake 153), and Stephen's sense that his identity is incomplete because he cannot conceive of a complete wholeness generates his drive to create more complete universes, a drive that may lead to *Ulysses* and the *Wake*. The system in which he was brought up gave him the impression that one must either fill God's position or be a slave, so it is logical that he will later declare that the artist is like God. He will also be reading Nietzsche, who says that human progress consists of taking over God's role (Nietzsche, *Thus* 110–11, 274).

The assumption of God's position allows the artist to approach giving life to his characters and to expand the scope and complexity of his world. It also makes him bisexual and multiple. But soon it runs into the inability of human consciousness to encompass totality, so that whatever plurality of consciousness may be conceived , whenever God appears as a concrete person, he is either unbelievable or ridiculous. Thus there is a logical validity in the fact that in the *Wake*, God appears in the present as a dysfunctional clown (but with a great past), HCE. However the idea of God may inspire strength and vision, its enactment by Joyce makes fun of its manifest impossibility.

Joyce's slapstick God leads to Beckett, and in *Waiting for Godot*, God appears as Pozzo, a malevolent clown whose divinity focuses on abusing his slave Lucky, whose good fortune it is to have something to believe in. What Lucky believes in is slavery, and submission may be the crucial element of all belief; for the word *dominant*, which means behaving like God, refers on the sexual level to what Pozzo does to Lucky, tying him up and whipping him. Because Pozzo's activity is so ludicrous, Vladimir and Estragon are unable to recognize that he is the one they are waiting for. So Pozzo (which means "big stink" or "pose") remains in charge of the world despite being an incompetent sadist because Didi and Gogo can't help feeling sorry for him and continuing to wait for him, projecting an ideal father to replace the actual horrible one responsible for the slavery and violence in the world, the only one who can ever be found. Because they cannot face their need to punish themselves, they are immobilized. That they are God's servants is suggested by the original title, *En Attendant*. People need both to resent God and to long for Him, yet these attitudes cannot be sustained in the mind simultaneously; so both rebellion and longing are parts of a cycle, a parallax shown by the circularity of *Waiting*.

In relation to the cycle of signification, to assume God's role is to claim charge of the entire triangle, to produce the word out of oneself (like Shem) rather than merely receiving it. Stephen is driven to expand his mind into every side of Lacan's schema by realizing that no position on it covers him. This project, which extends through Joyce's career, is set out in the esthetic theory of *Portrait*, which is something Stephen hopes to attain rather than what he has accomplished. He divides his mind into the three positions by seeing it moving through each. Wholeness or the lyric corresponds to the Imaginary, harmony or the epic to the Symbolic, and radiance or the dramatic to the Real, the least sustainable or most alienated position, in which one is outside oneself. The crucial step that

Stephen makes to displace himself into the next position always consists of recognizing that he does not fit into the one he is trying to occupy. And his awareness of the cycle reduces phallic authority (which is based on castration) to a *sinthome*.

When Stephen enters the symbolic by expressing himself in a code of language, he finds that he is not there: he has slipped away like Proteus. So he is driven to refine the words, but the more exquisite the language grows, the more it shifts him toward alienation. For example, immediately after writing his Villanelle of the Temptress—an elaborate formulation of his identity in relation to an image of woman—he realizes that he will turn away from this ecclesiastical temptress (who combines mother with E__. C__.) by leaving Ireland to pursue truth into exile.

For Lacan, concretizing the object of desire—the *objet a* that is represented by the *a* on the diagram—constitutes a semblance of being that aims at the Real, as truth aims at reality. But the claim of the object of desire to represent being "dissolves...in approaching the real" (*Encore* 95) because the object is only a semblance, a simulacrum. On the other hand, to move away from the Real increases its attraction, so that once Stephen has decided to leave E__. C__., he feels increasing affection for her at the end of the novel: "I liked her and it seems a new feeling to me" (252). She gains vivacity by becoming the Real as what he cannot have, a truth that only appears through illusion.

The Real, what is beyond language, can never appear directly, for we can only perceive through language. The Real appears as a dissonance, an impossibility that indicates what is outside comprehension. Lacan says that the Real "can only be described on the basis of an impasse in formalization" (*Encore* 93). Within *Portrait*, the strongest embodiments of the Real are the father figures who confront Stephen in the middle of each chapter with impasses that force him to re-sort his vocabulary. Once E__. C__. is withheld, she implies the paternal power that withholds her. The unnamable Real corresponds to "Love that dare not speak its name" (*U* 9. 659), the aspect of desire that is most repressed, expressing both resentment of God the Father and longing for him. The homosexual underpinning of heterosexual desire is emphasized in Joyce's work. Just as Stephen was driven by a sense of being raped to his first intercourse (*P* 100), the latest man to threaten him, from Dolan to Cranly, is always pushing him (while the latest mother draws him on) as he sets out in a new direction. Invasion by the father puts him in the creative position of hysteria. In chapter 2, I cited Lacan's analysis of how Heron generates the *sinthome* in Stephen by abusing him.

The authority that hits Stephen with the Real breaks through his defenses and forces him to react against it by projecting a new phallic version of himself as he sets out toward an unknown goal. The Greek letter phi on the right side of the schema stands for phallus. Lacan says, "To the right is the scant reality...on which the pleasure principle is based, which is such that everything we are allowed to approach by way of reality remains rooted in fantasy" (*Encore* 94–95). The undiscovered path that Stephen takes to some new reality always projects fantasy, and at the end of the chapter his heightened sense of reality, which is shown by minute details, is a concentration of fantasy. When Stephen has his greatest sense of discovering himself, he is most deluded in the Imaginary.

In taking responsibility for his divine role, Joyce has to encompass all sides by seeing the whole circuit and how his language combines delusion with the fullness of joy. He must also impose the Real as the realization that the subject is caught in metastases (changes of position) because it cannot sustain different sides at once. The godlike view that sees all sides is the greatest source of disillusion, skepticism, and parody because it recognizes that every position is false in relation to some larger context.[3] To deny a religion is to assume a godlike point of view by claiming a truth greater than the religion.

The signifier of the barred Other, S(Ⱥ), is the awareness of the impossibility of defining the unconscious, the linguistic totality out of which consciousness is formed. Joyce was perpetually struggling with this impossibility and extending its range. As Lacan indicates, it works powerfully as the site of truth; but this truth can only exist on its way from the Imaginary fantasy toward the Symbolic, or articulated language. If truth, as Heidegger emphasizes, is an unveiling (*aletheia*), then it is a process. Truth is not there either before the veil is removed or after it is gone, and in fact the veil reappears as soon as one sees the other side. Truth is only the act of removal that moves inevitably toward another language that falsifies it. Once it is formulated in definite terms (or passes through the Symbolic), it becomes the semblance as object of desire that moves toward the Real which creates the sense of reality. This moves toward the Imaginary, the delusory belief in the reality of reality.[4]

Each phase of the cycle has a kind of truth: the truth of desire, of contact with the world, of the sense of reality. They are all parts of the totality of truth, but they are not commensurate with each other. This indicates the value of Lacan's division of the subject into Imaginary, Symbolic, and Real. The phase designated as "true" consists of nothing but denial. The division of the overall truth into incompatible qualities shows why the structure of truth is a cycle of change. Similarly, Stephen is not the student nor the lecher nor the Jesuit nor the artist nor the exile. Nor is he the youth that feels defined or confined or conflicted or liberated. He is the sequence of change that carries them all, a pattern that is prefigured by Joyce's 1904 essay, "A Portrait of the Artist," which speaks of "the development of an entity of which our actual present is a phase only.... the curve of an emotion" (*P* 257–58). This arrangement in Joyce's work is unfolded in Lacan's schema.

I described this schema to Michael Proudfoot and he pointed out that it was parallel to Vico's ideas. That is, each of Vico's four stages of history contains a version of truth whose incompleteness is shown by its replacement by the next stage, and the chaotic *ricorso* between cycles might correspond to Lacan's negative phase of the true. Therefore the structure of truth in *Portrait* anticipates the philosophy that will be made manifest in the *Wake*, and Vico's system shows advanced features.

In *Ulysses* Stephen, having lost his mother, finds himself in denial of the world he lives in. This leads him to the embodiment in Bloom of the truth of what he lacks. Bloom is attached to material objects and cliches, so his world is a world of the semblance. In "Circe," when Bloom confronts Stephen, contact with Bloom's world leads Stephen desperately to cast off the semblance and to reach the Real when he gets himself knocked down by the British soldiers. This sets Stephen on a new path that leads to Molly as the Imaginary. Though we are given little of Stephen's thinking in "Ithaca," it is possible to argue that he shows maturity or insight by not trying to attain the goal of union with the Blooms—shows a truth of denial. In Bloom's case, as a semblance, he moves toward the Real with both Stephen and Molly, turning it to reality through his belief in all the facts that are piled up in "Ithaca," where they add up to a void.

Lacan's belief in truth as process is reflected in his use of the word *faire* as a motif in *Le sinthome*. The verb *faire*, which can mean "make, do, or act, " is usually positive here because it is active, as in *savoir faire*; but the noun *fait*, which means a fact or something done, is generally seen as delusory, a semblance. At one point, after saying that there is no fact that does not involve speaking and artifice, Lacan says, "*c'est un fait qu'il ment*" (*Le sinthome* 66), which can mean either "it's a fact that it lies" or "a fact lies." "*Ment*" or "it lies" also refers here to the false effort to contain the subject of language in a discrete mentality. The idea that facts lie may be one of the main points of the conclusion of *Ulysses*, for the proliferation of a vast assemblage of facts in "Ithaca" has the effect of rendering what is important—such as the feelings Bloom and Stephen have for each other—enormously unknowable, thus evoking the Real. By exhausting what can be known, this mountain of facts points to what cannot be known.

Joyce, Lacan, Butler, and Especially Žižek

Several kinds of truth may be involved in the relation to Lacan's triangular schema so as to extend from Joyce to Žižek. The first is the vision of Joyce as the artist who sees all sides of life. Because Joyce wants to create a real world, active language, and living characters, he builds on the semblance and the reality, which do not concern Lacan and Žižek so frontally. But his vision is sharpened and driven by the truth of the barred subject: to approach reality, he must focus uncompromisingly on the ineluctable gap between language and reality. This anticipates Lacan's concentration on the gap between the signifier and the signified, his effort to map out the complexities by which language operates to shape reality. Both men undermine the fantasy that turns the Real to reality; therefore they concentrate on the injustice of the existing order so as to upset ideology

If Lacan wants to explore the linguistic systems of human consciousness in order to cure people, Žižek, especially from 1997, shifts such exploration toward social criticism that aims at action. Butler also wants to use the critique of the structure of truth to change the system, but she wants to disassemble the Symbolic system of genders—which all of these thinkers see as the key to the formation of the self—to open us up to the Real of our status between gender identities. While Butler asks us to give up focused identity, Žižek, in his radical engagement with society, feels that the gesture of opening up is politically impotent and so he pushes the need for an authority to assert progressive values.

Žižek turns against the free flow of consciousness promoted by Joyce's modernism because Žižek is alarmed by the postmodern world in which symbols no longer function. In this respect, Žižek may seem like the anti-Joyce, his audacious insistence on the need for paternal authority being a reaction against the freedom that Joyce unleashed. Žižek argues that fantasies of the brutal father in contemporary culture constitute an image of unconstrained enjoyment that wards off the "true horror" of the lack of enjoyment itself (*Fragile* 75). Writing in 2000, Žižek feels that the current diminution of paternal authority is a worse problem than the tyranny of such authority; but I suspect that patriarchy has remained more oppressive than its lack.

Žižek emphasizes that his centers of authority are conflicted and unstable—*The Ticklish Subject, The Fragile Absolute*—and in this respect, he may not be so far from the self-denying authorities of Joyce as artist and Lacan as analyst, which avoid domination by stressing interplay. But Žižek insists on the need for a unified subject able to act (*Ticklish* 374–75); whereas Joyce's central subject is caught in a cycle and increasingly divided into Stephen, Bloom and Molly, or the family members of the *Wake*—incapable of being unified or coherent. Joyce saw the strongest possibility of his own action to advance humanity as the artistic activity that opens up perception to expand the possibilities of freedom. Žižek finds that personal freedom is easily coopted by late capitalism, so he demands an authentic act that will disturb the fantasy (*Ticklish* 374). Joyce approaches such action insofar as his works shock us and confront us with political realities, but Joyce is unwilling to sacrifice personal freedom.

It may be asked whether Žižek is ready to give up such freedom, in view of its indulgence in his works, and his recent *Parallax View* focuses less on radical action and more on the need to see both sides of every issue, including the violence of the Left (*PV* 5, 286–88). Žižek finally settles on a denial of liberal causes in order to insist on fundamental revolutionary principles (*PV* 375–85), and this is not unlike Stephen's refusal to sign the Csar's peace petition in *Portrait* (195–98). The petition is seen as opposed to Marx when Temple supports it by saying, "Marx is only a bloody cod" (197).

Žižek's demand for action and its justification—a paternal bond between the Real and reality—brings him close to belief and the limiting position of being religious.[5] On the other hand, Joyce's embrace of the whole cycle as creator may have the disadvantage of removing him from action. One thing Joyce liked about blasphemously assuming the position of God is that God is incapable of belief. As Lacan put it, "there is no Other of the Other" (*Encore* 81), so God has no God to believe in.

By including the whole triangle, Joyce embodies the revolutionary element within the larger circuit of truth in which it must be engaged. We should strive to use the full vision of truth to sustain and expand the revolutionary position; but Lacan is right to see disillusionment as the crucial gesture of truth. Žižek himself, referring to the seminar on "The Purloined Letter" (*Écrits* 11), says "One should stick to Lacan's thesis that 'truth has the structure of a fiction': truth is condemned to remain a fiction precisely insofar as the *innomable* [unnamable] Real eludes its grasp" (*Ticklish* 167). In this perspective, which is shared by all four theorists, truth is a perpetual quest for something that can never be held, thrusting the idea of exploration forward, as does *Ulysses*.

Part II

Ulysses *Off Course*

Chapter 6

Let's Get Lost: Exploration in Homer and Joyce

Parsing "Proteus"

The idea of exploring through language is established in *Portrait* as Stephen keeps using words in new ways to discover new aspects of himself and the world. In continually revising himself as a signifier, he is impelled to head in a new direction at the end of each chapter, not knowing where he is going. At this point he is looking awry or askance at the world he has known, but Žižek holds that only by such deviation can one find the object of desire—"outside this distortion, 'in itself,' *it does not exist*" (*Looking 12*). Only through desire for what is forbidden can one reach a new reality.[1] Joyce took inspiration from one of the first leavetakers to look awry and depart into radically unknown realities, Homer's Odysseus.

When Stephen says in Chapter II that he sees the world through language by taking in words he does "not understand" (*P* 62), the words evidently remain essentially incomprehensible to him. Insofar as he understood the words or stood under them, he would stop seeing the Real world of active language (truth) and see only his world of subdued language (knowledge). Žižek cites Derrida's idea that knowledge requires faith in the big Other or the Symbolic order (*PV* 350), but Žižek may not appreciate the intellectual advantages that Joyce and Lacan—and even Žižek—derive from refusing knowledge as authoritarian in order to depart toward truth as impossibility. One reason that the first page of *Dubliners* focuses on three words whose meaning is not known is that the aim of the Joycean artist is to lose himself in language, to use words in a disorienting way so as to discover what has not been said. A parallel process of exploration as getting lost as subjective activity is involved in the *Odyssey*, and *Ulysses* adapts this principle throughout: it is evident in the way that the writing of the book gets more disorienting as it proceeds, and I will delineate it in parallel scenes that carry going astray to the limit in the two epic works. So the shift from *Portrait* to *Ulysses* turns the moist bed of unrest into an incomprehensible ocean. In *Ulysses*, this ocean appears as Proteus as the sea as a Brownian motion of language, or rather of linguistic material.

In his "Proteus" meditations, Stephen uses linguistic analysis to disassemble reality so as to approach Lacan's Real, what is outside language, in order to open up new possibilities. The art of the episode is philology, and Stephen runs through different dialects and languages, feels himself taking on the voices of others, and multiplies the alternatives for words: "trudges, schlepps, trains, drags, trascines" (3. 391–92). He also ranges into discourse that is infrahuman: "a fourworded wavespeech: seesoo, hrss, rsseeiss, ooos" (3.456–57), evoking the entire range of linguistic material of which we perceive only a portion. One major point in "Proteus" is that language is always changing, so that Stephen does not speak a language: he speaks a shift between languages. As the theories of Mikhail Bakhtin reveal, this is true of everyone, but Stephen is concentrating on it. This shift corresponds to truth as a circuit and to Lacan's sensitivity to historical change.

The radical scope of Stephen's deconstruction of the terms of conventional reality through the shock of linguistic dissonance that Lacan calls the Real is exemplified by a sentence fragment on the twelfth line of "Proteus": "A very short space of time through very short times of space." By reversing the existing usage of spaces of time, Stephen brings out the inseparability of the two dimensions. They are distinguished from each other mainly by conventions of language, for space is generally defined in terms of the time it takes to get from one point to another, while time is generally defined in terms of the distance between points on a clock. What the *Wake* refers to as the "dime-cash problem" (149.17) keeps recurring throughout Joyce's work as a confusion of space and time—"you see. I hear" (*U* 3.24)—breaking down one of the most fundamental distinctions of existence. For Kant, space and time are not properties in objects, but "merely conditions of our sensibility" (80). If space is temporal and time moves between locations, they lose their power to enforce hierarchy as solidity. With no verb in Joyce's fragment (3. 12), the action is not defined as either movement or duration—a parallax.

The frequency of sentence fragments in "Proteus," including the first three periods, implicates the recognition that the sentence itself is an hierarchical construction. To qualify a statement as legitimate, the subject must be given hegemony over the predicate. The former claims identity, but the latter has no identity and is obliged to serve. The model of the subject as master was established in ancient societies that used slavery. In *Encore*, Lacan denounces the copula, both the equation involved in the verb of being and the link between subject and predicate, as an authoritarian construction: "it's quite simply being at someone's heel, being at someone's beck and call—what would have been if you had understood what I ordered you to do" (31). Joyce's/Stephen's use of fragments abandons the copula to demonstrate how one can take it upon oneself to invent a world of language. Thus one obviates the need to depend on the world that is already there and its implied Master. This matches Lacan's observation in *Le sinthome* that one can do without the Law of the Father by making use of it (136).

Language is an especially powerful tool for such invention because, as Fritz Senn points out, it is the most polytropic human device ("Book of Many Turns," Attridge, *Ulysses* 49), so it allows the greatest variety of transformation. The changeability of language is foregrounded by how often it speaks as liquid: "breaking, plashing, from far, from farther out, waves and waves" (3.340–41). Proteus, whom Stephen confronts here, personifies the sea, and Michael Seidel, in *Epic Geography*, speaks of Proteus as the shapelessness that the artist has to confront in order to give it form (108). Stephen does aim to reach some truth behind the mutability of appearances, but the truth he finally realizes is that of protean transformation itself. At one point, he wonders where he is leading his soul: "Now where the blue hell am I bringing her beyond the veil? Into the ineluctable modality of the ineluctable visuality" (3.424–26). To aim beyond the veil of appearances that ordinary language (which gives orders) posits as the world, Stephen moves toward *modality*, the unavoidable passage of the visible through forms, so that by focusing on the structure of perception, he can transform it. His purposiveness takes his deconstruction beyond poststructuralism toward the Lacanian *sinthome* of an art aimed at the Real, what is excluded by the established order of language.

To evoke this Real, he must go as far as possible from what is known, and Seidel indicates that Proteus represents "the world's end" (107) because he controls the unknown and ultimate secrets. He is also located at the edge of Homer's world, off Egypt. Seidel points out that Victor Bérard's *Les Phéniciens et L'Odyssée* (1902–3), on which Joyce depended, emphasizes that Proteus was an Egyptian figure, just as it argues that Odysseus was Phoenician(Seidel 107–12). This is one reason why, when Stephen meets some Gypsies on the beach (right after remembering a dream about the East, 3.366–69), he refers to them as "Egyptians" (3.370), just as he earlier linked Paris to the "fleshpots of Egypt" (3.178). Bérard anticipates Martin Bernal's *Black Athena* (1987) by insisting that Greek civilization was extensively derived from African sources; and Joyce's enthusiasm for Bérard reflects his opposition to colonialism and racism.

Parallel to the dislocation of words out of their normal usage (what Senn calls dislocution), there is a swarm of virtual geographical dislocation in "Proteus" because Stephen frequently imagines himself elsewhere. In one case, he imagines visiting his uncle Richie Goulding so vividly that most readers temporarily believe that he goes there (3.70–103). He also thinks he may be "walking into eternity" (3.18), and other locales he imagines connecting with include "Edenville" (3.39), an ancient "Greek watercloset" (3.52), Marsh's Library (3.107–15), a series of altars where masses are performed (116–27), Paris, where his mind dwells extensively, the Martello Tower (271–78), the ancient Dublin beach of the Lochlanns (300–309), "the farthest star" (409), and so forth.

Stephen is not only a mental traveler or explorer, but one who aims at what can never be reached. To attain the Real would be as if Stephen the creation were to become the Joyce he aims at with such furious intensity as he sees himself in the second person: "You bowed to yourself in the mirror...Books you were going to write..." (3.137–39); "For that are you pining, the bark of their applause?" (3.313–14). Stephen is constantly struggling to become Joyce and constantly mocking himself for it, a disciplinary stratagem for progress: "Me sits there with his augur's rod...Who ever anywhere will read these written words?" (3.414–15). Insofar as Stephen's words are read by anyone, they pass through Joyce. Stephen approaches through writing an intense set of fantasies that connect his love for God to his love for himself, but of course Freud held that all creative writing expresses fantasy (*SE* IX.141–56).

The writer who seeks to express himself fully—and Joyce is a supreme example—dooms himself to exile, for the authority he aims at can never be claimed. This is why Stephen says that Shakespeare "studied *Hamlet* all the years of his life which were not vanity in order to play the part of the spectre" (*U* 9.166–68). He worked to make himself marginal by making the work live beyond his intrusion. So Shakespeare's life was an effort to render himself dispossessed, and his voyage toward loss was parallel to Joyce's, to Stephen's, to Bloom's, and to that of Odysseus. Žižek says that while the object of desire is a lost object, the object of the drive, a goal of analysis, is loss itself, which leads one to traverse or pass beyond the fantasy (*PV* 61–62). *Le sinthome* declares, "The error expresses the life of language" ("*La faute exprime la vie du langage,*" 148), but the life of language is quite different from physical life. An error may signify death or loss of coherence for the bodily support, but may have a place in the life of the drives ("*pulsions*"), perhaps because it creates a new image that gives life to language, and *langage* can mean not only "talk," but "style."

To explore or to write is to place the object of desire (what one seeks or writes about) outside reality or beyond the horizon. It is to voluntarily approach the limit of life, and Žižek argues in *Tarrying with the Negative* that the adventure of exploration involves passing beyond this limit into the realm of *ate* (infatuation) that Antigone enters in her tragic pursuit of the Real. Žižek holds that here the assertion of agency or will turns the impossible into the forbidden, and turns the Real into the Symbolic by putting it on the map as a limit. He says that there are not two realms, that of reality and that of fantasy, but only that of reality, and that reaching the limit of reality leads one to project the realm of fantasy. Thus we turn what is impossible (the Real) into what is possible if we could only pass beyond an external barrier or prohibition (115–16). This is why Stephen strains to express the ineffable. To write or to explore is to turn the fact that one is withheld from the unattainable Real (represented by the lost body of the mother) into a path that strives to reach it, the sinthome. Insofar as exploration aims to reach the limit of reality in order to approach fantasy, it always approaches *ate*, which Lacan says may be translated as "misfortune" (*Ethics* 264). In taking a risk, one sinthomatically volunteers for misfortune, as the writer does by assuming the hardship or *askesis* of art. (The word *ascetic* is derived from the Greek for "one who practices an art.") Carol Dougherty, in *The Raft of Odysseus: The Ethnographic Imagination of Homer's* Odyssey, has as one of her main arguments that the *Odyssey* develops an elaborate set of equivalences between sailing and writing poetry (13–26), and that this connection even appears before Homer in Hesiod's references to "the measures of the loud-roaring sea" (21).

Insofar as Bloom and Stephen are responsible for their actions, they make their symptoms voluntary by choosing to be cuckolded and homeless, turning their misfortunes into works of art as well as "portals of discovery" (*U* 9.229). The esthetic motivation for Stephen's *sinthome* is not hard to recognize, but Bloom's artistry, like those of most ordinary people, does not belong to him. Despite his wanderings, his adventure centers on letting life invade him. If he suffers all day to make Molly happy, he conceals his need to be victimized by seeing his cuckoldry as a fate that cannot be overcome. So his everyday odyssey turns the impossibility of his marriage into a voyage toward loss that produces the luxuriant fantasies of debasement in "Circe." But these fantasies are unconscious, and Bloom cannot bear to be aware that he is letting Molly cheat on him. In this regard he is parallel to Odysseus, who expands the limits of exploration and infidelity—consorting with two divinities (Calypso and Circe)—while unaware that he has any intention except to go home. Odysseus' duplicity is a part of his being a new kind of hero, turned against the established order by being turned against himself, as is Bloom.

If Bloom seeks something esthetic in following Stephen, he can only conceive his motive in ridiculously practical terms, imagining that he will make Stephen a successful singer, and that this is 'the very reason" that he is with the young man (*U* 16.1820–65). Bello Cohen reacts to Bloom's bizarre sexual fantasies in "Circe" by saying, "Beautiful!" (15.3015). And there is beauty in Bloom's self-sacrifice, but he cannot claim it because it serves the Other. He does not know what he is doing because he attributes his volition for violation to a female divinity (Molly or Nature).

Harari derives a penetrating formula from Lacan: "instead of doing what we can ourselves, we always first put our faith in a constructed universe, created by God. Such a universe is governed by a vision of the world that 'guarantees' the existence of the Other" (Harari 125). Bloom is not religious, but his devotion to the *mater*ial world puts a dominant woman (*mater*) in the place of God for him. Though he cannot understand poetry, he creates a kind of poetry by getting lost for others (Molly and Stephen) as Stephen creates a more rarified kind by getting lost for himself. Both approach the limit to create the newborn fantasy. Bloom approaches cuckoldry to create the free woman and Stephen approaches alienation for the muse unheard of. The fantasy that is truly new passes beyond any that existed, so it always surpasses the fantasy, and may be the only way to do so. The ultimate fantasy is to escape from fantasy.

The Quest for Disorientation

> There is a saying that some things can be found only if, before finding them, one gets lost...
>
> Žižek (*PV* 127)

In my youth, when I went to a new place, I liked to get lost by losing the thread of where I came from so as to enter another reality. Odysseus' main objective as an explorer is to get lost, to err, for only by going as far as possible beyond any known bearings can he discover really new worlds and so enter into the life of language. Only by passing the limit of reality can he approach the source of fantasy. This attraction to disorientation that Odysseus and I share was also shared by Joyce, and Vanda Zajko, in an essay on "Homer and *Ulysses*" in *The Cambridge Companion to Homer*, argues that Joyce's relentless "self-imposed exile" may be linked to his fascination with the *Odyssey* (Fowler 312). The list of Joyce's addresses is Odyssean, and he was often impelled to move by subjective necessity.

The idea of being impelled by an "inner" need to disorient oneself is parallel to that of breaking the rule by wetting the bed. The connection between pee and sea is unfolded in the only illustration in *The Interpretation of Dreams*, which is reproduced in Danis Rose and John O'Hanlon's *Understanding* Finnegans Wake. Eight cartoon panels represent a dream in which a toddler starts to micturate and his urine keeps spreading until it forms a body of water on which three boats appear, each more adventurous than the last, ending with an ocean steamer (Rose and O'Hanlon xix). This connection may be universal (or at least widespread) and may have been so in Homer's day. Moreover, excretion, like error, disintegrates the body as container, untying the sack, a version of losing one's address, escaping language, confronting the Real.

Odysseus' drive to explore works through his unconscious: he always wants to go home, but forces beyond his control (like bodily urges) situate him in exile and carry him to the ends of the earth. The main images of these forces are the gods, but the poem realizes that the gods are hard to separate from human motivation. Athena, who often operates as an extension of Odysseus and who is linked to intelligence, tells Telemachus that his speech will be a combination of his discourse and hers: "thou shalt bethink thee of somewhat in thine own breast, and somewhat the god will give thee to say" (34, III.26–27).[2] Odysseus, working within and against these forces, finds himself in exile and finds that the crucial choices needed to take him home are involved in conflict, as if he were perpetually tied to a mast listening to sirens. The thinking that he needs to advance has to take him to the edge of consciousness and beyond. His fundamental choice to be an adventurer and an original thinker or inventor propels him toward the end of the world and the end of thought.

The relationship between Odysseus' extraordinary intelligence and his marked predilection for perplexity may be understood by observing his tendency to see things in terms of dilemmas. The most elaborate version of this is his passage between Scylla and Charybdis (Book XII), but he engages continuously in such polarized thinking. A strong example appears when he lands exhausted in a strange country (Phaeacia). I use the Victorian translation of S. H. Butcher and Andrew Lang, which was popular in Joyce's time. It is so laden with pseudo-antiquity that it has the useful effect of reminding us that we cannot really know the text, something Joyce accomplished by *not* learning Greek. Kenner sees it as the key Homer for Joyce: "the Victorian Ulysses is an important part of Joyce's subject matter" (*Dublin's* 186). Andrew Gibson refers to "Butcher and Lang, who furnished the British schoolboy with his authorized version of Homer" ("Irish Bull" 107, n. 17). One way Joyce may play on this translation is by touching on implications of which it is ignorant, including its melodramatic Victorian pseudo-antique tone.

> Ah, woe is me! what is to betide me? what shall happen unto me at the last? If I watch the river bed all through the careful night, I fear that the bitter frost and fresh dew may overcome me, as I breathe forth my life for faintness, for the river breeze blows cold betimes in the morning. But if I climb the hill-side up to the shady wood, and there take rest in the thickets, though perchance the cold and weariness leave hold of me, and sweet sleep may come over me, I fear lest of wild beasts I become the spoil and prey. (83, V.465–73)

Odysseus' carefully balanced consideration of what will "betide" him shows a pride in weighing both sides of a question, but this formulaic dualistic rationality impels him to maximize the differences between alternatives. So he characteristically goes through the step of trajecting himself outside knowledge, expanding his subject in the space between signifiers by not being at home in either, taking a parallax view. In the event, by opposing the worst dangers of both sides, he leads himself to find a shelter in a pair of bushes that serves well enough.

Yet the logical step of assuming that there is no solution, of getting lost, is a necessary discipline: to hold off the easy answer for a better one. It is always implicit in weighing alternatives, and Odysseus' elaborate quandary between shore and forest closely follows two others. As he approaches Phaeacia's shore, he decides to stay with his raft (356–64) although the sea-goddess Ino told him to leave it (343–46) . Here he exerts freedom by suspecting that the divinity may have lied (80, 356–57). Soon he has to decide whether to try landing on the rocks or to swim further (82, V.406–24), and the situation seems "beyond all hope" (408). These three polarized decisions bring him home by bringing him to Phaeacia, where his troubles abroad are over, for the Phaeacians give him a chance to tell his story and then send him to Ithaca. The final concentration of intense decision may be decisive in that it ends his adventures overseas.

This ambivalent thinking (Freud's term) is typical not only of Odysseus, but of his family. For example, Telemachus later tells Eumaeus, "my mother has divisions of heart" (226, XVI.73–76) as to whether to stay with Telemachus or join a suitor. Neither his mother nor himself would be so divided if they were not intelligently concerned. The point of being suspended between two alternatives that the family focuses on is the encounter with the Real, the goal that constitutes exploration. This resolvable parallax gap may have been an innovation of logic at stages of the poem's composition.

Penelope's being divided is congruent to the source of her grief. The question of whether to hold out divides her because the decision is grievous enough to make her think of abandoning her son. She might cause his death by staying, and he is almost assassinated. So her logic is generated by suffering, and Freud says in "Negation" that logic begins with deprivation: "a precondition for the setting up of reality testing is that objects shall have been lost..." (*SE* XIX. 41). The suffering that causes logic is also the basis of the inspiration that makes Odysseus' life a poem.

Odysseus' tendency to wander is described as the source of poetry, for Homer assumes that suffering is the foundation of epic song. W. B. Stanford observes that only one other Homeric hero—old Nestor—shares with Odysseus the epithet "much enduring" (74). Odysseus impresses the Phaeacians by saying that for many years he has suffered hardships far from his people, and that he has known more misery than his hosts have seen borne by one man. Noticing Odysseus weeping while

Demodocus sings about Troy, the Phaeacian king Alcinous observes that the terrible Trojan War served to promote poetry: "All this the gods have fashioned, and have woven this skein of death for men, that there might be a song in the ears even of the folk of aftertime" (119, VIII.580). This affirms that the reason the gods brought the war about was so that epics would enter the life of language and be sung; and the principle that suffering is necessary for great artistic talent is also presented here in regard to Demodocus, who is blind (105, VIII.64). The tradition that the blind are gifted in song extends from Homer to Ray Charles. Jasper Griffin states that for the ancient Greeks, "epic song can arise only out of suffering and sorrow" (8). Likewise, Odysseus' being resourceful or inventive arises from continually being at the end of his resources, what Žižek calls the limit that leads to the expansion.

Maud Ellmann approaches this link between suffering and poetry from another angle, a rather Lacanian one, in her essay, "The Name and the Scar: Identity in *The Odyssey* and *A Portrait of the Artist.*" She focuses on the scene in Book XIX of the poem in which Odysseus' old nurse, Eurycleia, sees his childhood scar, knows who he is, and remembers how he got it; so that the scar leads to the story of Odysseus' childhood and naming (277–78, XIX.392–471). Ellmann says, "This sequence implies that the scar is the generative principle of narrative, for it represents a breach in the symbolic fabric, which can only be repaired through storytelling" (Wollaeger 152). This anticipates Žižek's statement in *The Plague of Fantasies* that fantasy, as the primordial form of narrative, always serves to hide a gap or deadlock (10). So the derivation of poetry or narrative from suffering reveals it to be a way of dealing with an insoluble problem. Putting a problem into a narrative may be a crucial step towards solving it: when one sees a situation as a story that makes sense causally, Athena may be said to descend, the mother of changing (she tends to transform Odysseus), clearing away the mess, drawing the hero forth.

Most critics agree that the *Iliad* was an earlier poem than the *Odyssey* (Lattimore 18), so the idea of tragedy was established when the *Odyssey* was composed, and it is understood in both poems that the more grief one encounters, the more poetry and wisdom one has access to. In this perspective, not only is it geographically true that the farther Odysseus goes from any known bearings, the more new territory he can discover, but it is intellectually true that the more disoriented he is, the more he takes on powers of philosophical insight. He also learns social truths by losing his class status, and the poem links him through his affliction with the downtrodden, for he ultimately appears as a beggar and takes servants for allies. By passing outside the accepted world, like King Lear, he passes toward the world of the outcast and oppressed, which Lacan sees as the source of all philosophical insight in *Seminar XVII* (21).

The Greeks had a highly developed conceptual framework associating travel with insight. Dougherty cites a passage in which Herodotus tells how Solon was praised as a philosopher who had done a great deal of traveling and sightseeing, the word for sightseeing being *theoria*, which means "beholding, contemplation, speculation" (Skeat):

> in this passage we find one of the earliest uses of the term *theoria*, from which we derive our words "theory" and "theorize." In its use here, *theoria* designates the process of traveling to see something, to sightsee, but we can see how its later meaning of "speculate" or "think about" evolves through this connection between the processes of traveling and looking and that of intellectual effort. To quote James Clifford, a contemporary cultural critic, "Theory is a product of displacement, comparison, a certain distance. To theorize, one leaves home." Dougherty(3)

The principle that the greater the travel, the greater the comprehension, may be extended to imply that disorientation brings newness, originality; and this matches Žižek's notion of crossing the frontier of *ate*. Lacan says that Antigone brings a new dispensation for humanity by defining ethics in opposition to the state (*Ethics* 243). This wisdom is inseparable from losing social status, becoming a displaced person and homeless. In terms of discovery on a level that is built into the *Odyssey*, and resonates with modern readers, the *real goal of Odysseus' voyages* is the point where *he is most completely lost, miserable, and forlorn.* This point may be specified: it plays a central role in the *Odyssey* as a locus of maximum sensitivity and insight, and a parallel point plays such a role for Stephen in *Ulysses*.

Odysseus reaches this low point by showing hubris in defying the Cyclops. Though his men warn him not to speak, he tells his name to Polyphemus, who is thus enabled to call down Posiedon's wrath on him. The crafty Odysseus should realize that he is hurting his chances to get home, but his "lordly spirit" and his anger (133, IX.500–501) compel him to boast that he was the one who defeated Polyphemus; "Cyclops, if any one of mortal men shall ask thee of the unsightly blinding of thine eye, say it was Odysseus that blinded it, the waster of cities, son of Laertes, whose dwelling is in Ithaca" (133, IX.502–5). Odysseus seems to be exhilarated here, and to have fun referring to the blinding as unsightly. That he lists his titles of honor shows that he is strongly motivated by the desire for heroic fame, and this is a major factor in all of his voyaging, one inseparable from the compulsion to go further. The desire to become immortal by great deeds was often considered the highest motivation, though it may be Odysseus's weak side; and Stanford reports that several of Odysseus' exploits, including the story of the Cyclops, continued to be told during the Middle Ages when the *Odyssey* itself was lost (178). To become immortal by doing something exceptional is parallel to Lacan's idea of the self-destructive error of originality that leads one to be carried on in the life of language.

The uncivilized Polyphemus seems like a force of nature when he breaks off the peak of a great hill and hurls it at Odysseus (132, IX.481). As a conflict with nature itself, Odysseus' struggle against the sea and the unknown parts of the world is an exploration that expands human consciousness. As Senn suggests, Odysseus, as a man of many turns (*polytropos*), introduces a new complexity of consciousness to humanity by having many minds and sampling many cultures (Attridge, *Ulysses* 43). Griffin translates the *polutropon* of the poem's first line as "of many travels" (12), and we have seen that this had intellectual implication for the Greeks.

After Polyphemus curses Odysseus, having eaten several of his men, Odysseus has a respite in Aeolia; but his men squander the advantage of this by opening the bag of winds that the Aeolians give them. So his next effort to set out for home returns to being ill-starred, with much of the blame resting on his action, for the winds are loosed at sea, in the realm of Posiedon, Polyphemus' father. Posiedon may be seen as Odysseus' father as well, making Polyphemus a kind of sibling, for Odysseus is the greatest sailor in Classical history. In leaving the land behind, he seeks in Žižekian terms a sterner father, as adventurers generally do, one who can raise him to a higher level by confronting him with the Real to find his destiny as the sailor who fell from grace with the sea.

Now Odysseus lands among the Lestrygonians, ferocious giants who exterminate eleven out of twelve of his ships. After this, his men collapse with sorrow and weariness on the island of Aea, and this is the point of maximum disarrangement and dejection that I want to examine. In what might be described, remarkably, as virtually despair, Odysseus now utters what I see as one of the most poetic and philosophically radical speeches of the poem:

> "Hear my words, my fellows, despite your evil case. My friends, lo, now we know not where is the place of darkness or of dawning, nor where the sun, that gives light to men, goes beneath the earth, nor where he rises; therefore let us advise us speedily if any counsel yet may be: as for me, I deem there is none. For I went up a craggy hill, a place of out-look, and saw the island crowned about with the circle of the endless sea, the isle itself lying low; and in the midst thereof mine eyes beheld the smoke through the thick coppice and the Woodland."
>
> Even so I spake, but their spirit within them was broken, as they remembered the deeds of Antiphates the Laestrygonian, and all the evil violence of the haughty Cyclops, the Man-eater. So they wept aloud shedding big tears. Howbeit no avail came of their weeping. (141, X. 189–202)

At this point Odysseus has lost his bearings so completely that the resourceful hero can see no course. Instead of dividing himself between two sides here, he finds the opposing extremes unlocatable. Even the fundamental mythological principle that suffering leads to a reward seems to be abrogated with Odysseus' observation that "no avail came of their weeping." Here he encounters the Real, Lacan's term for the terrifying effect of something outside all language, as he passes beyond the mythic frame that makes sense of the world. Thus he opens himself up to a view unprecedented for a hero through the extreme nature of his skepticism. The same tough withholding of credence that preserves him through adversity and peril allows him to stare into the abyss of a world without mediation.[3] He brings the Real into the Symbolic by exploring more of the unknown part of the world both geographically and intellectually, by passing beyond the shelter of religion, whose localization has grown evident through his wanderings. It may be said that the step beyond religion was the key development of Greek civilization, the invention of philosophy, a step that most people in America today have not taken, not to mention the psychoanalytic critique of philosophy.

Exploration of the farthest bounds of the earth also explores the limits of knowledge, and Odysseus, who is portrayed in Dante's *Inferno* as going beyond all bounds to the ends of the earth, thus lays a basis in his voyages for expanding human awareness. Stanford points out that Dante changes Homer to portray a last voyage in which Odysseus seeks "experience of the world beyond the sun" (Dante 224, Canto XXVI, 109), so that "Ulysses now becomes a symbol of sinful desire for forbidden knowledge" (Stanford 181) that leads to the Renaissance (178). Ideas formerly under the control of the gods now come to be understood in human terms as scientists explore the unknown—discovering, for example, the physical cause of the thunder that was earlier attributed to Zeus. What Ulysses pursues in Dante is "*canoscenza*" (line 120), which, as "cognizance," is equivalent to the "uncreated conscience" that Stephen devotes himself to (*P* 253). The quest for secular knowledge was often linked to damnation in the Middle Ages, as in the story of Dr. Faustus, which in Marlowe's version inaugurates Elizabethan tragedy.

In the scene on the island, Odysseus shares emotion with his men, showing how misery makes him empathize with those beneath him, and leading forward to all of the passages taking the points of view of the outcast and oppressed later in the poem. The men are described as not only weeping, but crying loudly and with big tears. In Books XVII to XX, Odysseus as a beggar is insulted, beaten, and threatened, while the text often focuses on the hard lives of servants and their daily tasks. At one point, for example, Antinuous declares that he will send the beggar Irus to the cruel master Echetus, who will cut off his nose and ears and then disembowel him (257, XVIII. 84–116, castrate him in Lattimore).

Moreover, emphasis is placed on the idea that Zeus protects suppliants, so the homeless should be treated kindly (235, XVI.422–23). All of this attention to the downtrodden is ultimately contained in an aristocratic structure, and the persecution of Odysseus serves to justify his bloody revenge; but the poem does seem to show that Odysseus' extremity makes him feel for those on the bottom of society. Social consciousness may only be able to enter the epic by this route, but it is an aspect of the opening of Odysseus' mind, one of his destinations of displacement.

On Aea, it seems strange that Odysseus says that he has no idea what to do, but also mentions that he sees smoke. I feel that he is so upset that he sees the sign of habitation as threatening (Polyphemus made a fire). In fact the smoke comes from the enchantress Circe's halls, and she is at first a threatening figure until Odysseus overcomes her with supernatural help. Soon after his low point of near despair, he confronts her, and while she tries to reduce him to a swine, she ends up being persuaded to show him the way home, which leads through Hades. So from here on, Odysseus is actually on his way back to Ithaca, though he has many more stages to go through. After his breakdown, he switches from being lost to being homeward bound. Therefore this point of great extremity is defined by the plot as one of his main goals, his furthest points.

Stanford observes that at this stage of the story Dante, who may have been influenced by a translation error, has Odysseus go directly from Circe to his last voyage to the ends of the earth. So in place of Homer's Odysseus, who is a "centripetal, homeward-bound figure [,] Dante substituted a personification of centrifugal force. By doing so he made Ulysses symbolize the anarchic element in those conflicts between orthodoxy and heresy, conservatism and progressivism, classicism and romanticism…" (Stanford 181–82). Of course, Dante is enabled to show this radicalism because he condemns it, just as Homer can show Odysseus' wanderlust by maintaining that he is generally trying to return.

Odysseus certainly included both sides, and Dante was bringing out the intensity of his drive toward going beyond, which even in Homer takes him to Hades, a place beyond the end of the earth. While he goes there for information on how to get home, he is one of the few mortals who goes to Hades and returns, and he does not pay the price that Orpheus pays: instead, he benefits, conversing with immortal heroes.

In *Tarrying with the Negative*, Žižek presents the history of opera as a history of modern subjectivity, starting with Claudio Monteverdi's *Orfeo* (1603), in which Orfeo asks to be allowed to see his wife in Hades. Žižek says, "The first, rudimentary form of subjectivity is this voice of the subject beseeching his Master to suspend, for a brief moment, his own Law" (*Tarrying* 166). Žižek adds that Orfeo "looked back and thus intentionally sacrificed Euridice in order to regain her as the sublime object of poetic inspiration" (194). Žižek here sees subjectivity emerging out of a bondage to the Master, but Odysseus, guided by women (Athena, Circe, and Penelope), is able to pass beyond the limit of mortality to expand his subject without paying such a serious price. This may suggest a prior maternal basis for consciousness that is less authoritarian. Yet Žižek's insistence on the patriarchal threat behind subjectivity (which corresponds to the earlier Lacan) may be more realistic in its toughness, for Odysseus cannot really reach his goal in the land of the dead.

Odysseus's most intense encounter in Hades, his major emotional goal here, is with his dead mother, Anticleia. She reveals a furiously extreme passion for him by specifying that she did not die of old age or sickness: "it was my sore longing for thee...Odysseus, and for thy loving kindness, that reft me of sweet life" (157, XI. 202–3). And soon after her, Epicaste appears and emphasizes how her marriage to her son Oedipodes drove her to hang herself (159, XI. 271–80). Odysseus attempts to embrace Anticleia three times, only to find that she flees from his hands like a shadow or a dream (157, XI.205–8). At this point he may be said to learn in Lacanian terms that the Other as a return to lost unity can never be reached. There is a parallel between this scene and Stephen's confrontation with his mother in "Circe," which may partly free him from her spell by indicating that she cannot tell him the word known all men (*U* 15.4157–4245). For both Stephen and Odysseus, the encounter with the Real Imaginary leads to disillusionment.

Žižek says that the logic of the frontier that changes what is impossible to what is beyond the limit, or forbidden, applies to all prohibitions. By making something forbidden, we make it seem possible, and this motivates us to move toward some fantasy version of it. He includes the fundamental prohibition of incest, saying that it is inherently impossible, for even if one sleeps with one's mother, it will ultimately not fully satisfy because "this is not *that*" (*Tarrying* 116). Probably for most men (and moms) the embarrassment would work against gratification, so this illustrates Žižek's idea that the person who fulfills one's fantasy is someone else. The ur-mother is a fantasy that cannot be recovered, and the taboo is "nothing but an attempt to resolve this deadlock by a transmutation of impossibility into prohibition" (116).

Odysseus' noncontact with his mother beyond the limit of life is the furthest point of his journey, parallel to his disillusionment before meeting Circe. Finding that his desire to embrace her is impossible rescinds the unconscious goal of his wandering, which led him through Circe toward Anticleia. He takes a step toward realizing that the most concrete way to attain the maternal ideal is through long-range marriage, and Penelope resembles a mother for him as a figure recovered from the distant past.[4] Likewise, Stephen's dreadful confrontation with his mother may prepare him to accept the ordinary womanhood that Bloom affirms through Molly. Both Odysseus and Stephen may be said to traverse or pass beyond a primal fantasy of union with mother.

What Odysseus learns most from are his rejections, just as the most interesting parts of the homecoming are not the fulfillment of desire (the slaughter of the suitors seems inhuman and the erotic reunion is largely omitted), but the more extended doubts and hesitations, the inability of Odysseus, Telemachus, and Penelope to believe that they actually possess each other. For example, when Euricleia tells Penelope that Odysseus is back, Penelope, who has already seen him in disguise, calls her crazy: "Why dost thou mock me, who have a spirit full of sorrow, to speak these wild words . . . " (321, XXIII.15–16). One can only miss the poignancy of this denial, and many others in which the three characters hold back from accepting each other, if technicalities have blinded one to the powerful emotions of the poem. The strain of the withholding adds to the beauty, and Lacan in his *Ethics* sees beauty as an approach to something that is never reached (238, 281–82, 298).

In Book XX, we follow Penelope to bed, as we follow Molly, and Penelope speaks to herself in what is essentially an interior monologue. Penelope wakes afflicted by the loss of Odysseus—who is home, but has not revealed himself—and asks the gods to destroy her. She dreamed her husband was with her, but woke to find it untrue (286, XX. 79–90). Here the text cuts to Odysseus lying outside her room. He hears her weeping and it seems to him that she is standing by his head and knows him (92–94). This scene shows how they relate to each other on an unconscious level, perhaps how all marriages are exiled, bound to dreams rather than actualities, calling on others they cannot reach; and it strikes me as more subtle, profound, and moving than the negotiations of the actual reunion.

The fact that Odysseus is changed by his experience actually means that the idea of truth changes in the poem (as does that of love), anticipating Lacan's theory of truth as circulation. Lyotard indicates this in "Going Back to the Return," his essay on the *Odyssey* and *Ulysses*: "The truth of [Homer's] Ulysses is not the same for us at the end of his journey as it was at the departure, it consists in the journey" (Bosinelli, Vaglio, and van Boheemen 197). The phrase "for us" shows that we are bound to speak for a modern view of the poem, and for this viewpoint, the poem embodies a journey because the subject must become an object that is a process in order to realize itself.

Stephen Forlorn

The point in Joyce's *Ulysses* that corresponds to Odysseus' brush with despair appears in "Oxen of the Sun," after Stephen gives a long and bitter speech combining and mixing the death of his mother with his rejection by the Irish: "Remember, Erin, thy generations and thy days of old, how thou settedst little by me and by my word and broughtedst in a stranger to my gates…" (14.367–69). He blames Ireland and his mother, in an oedipal construction that is typical of him, for going over to the Father God rather than to Stephen, the true voice of the spirit. Joyce's ironic distance from Stephen here helps him to sympathize with him by portraying him more deeply. Stephen's desolation here also relates to his failure to make an impression on the Irish intellectuals with his Shakespeare talk in the afternoon. Rejection by mother/Ireland seems to make his life and work meaningless, so he exaggerates his hopelessness, as Odysseus may when he says that he sees no way out: "thou hast left me alone for ever in the dark ways of my bitterness: and with a kiss of ashes hast thou kissed my mouth" (14.379–80).[5] He may be correct in indicating that the part of Joyce represented by Stephen will always be bitter.

At this point of despondency he echoes (and clarifies) Odysseus's declaration of the limits of human knowledge, that we cannot know where we are going or where we came from. During a passage in a style like that of Sir Thomas Browne's meditations on the mortal limits of humanity, he says that we don't know where we will be buried or whether we'll go to hell (Tophet) or purgatory (Edenville, which may also mean heaven):

> And as no man knows the ubiquity of his tumulus nor to what processes we shall thereby be ushered nor whether to Tophet or to Edenville in the like way is all hidden when we would backward see from what region of remoteness the whatness of our whoness hath fetched his whenceness. (14.398–400)

In conjunction with nearby references to inner darkness ("This tenebrosity of the interior," 14.380), this passage extends the skepticism of Odysseus' lament, which said that we don't know the place of darkness or dawning, or where the sun goes down or where he rises (141, X.190–92). For Stephen (as implicitly for Odysseus), this means that we cannot know the aims or sources of our consciousness. Therefore we don't really know our minds, don't know what our intention or "whenceness" is unless we understand where it came from. This corresponds to psychoanalytic insights such as Lacan's vision of the subject or signifier emerging from a big Other that it can never know.

Stephen's demoralization here is soon underlined by a crack of thunder that abases him because he hears it as God's voice. Indeed St. Augustine argues in the *Confessions* that human consciousness is feeble because it cannot know the depths of the past or the future: they are only known to God (Book XI, Chapters 18–31). So Stephen realizes that the darkness within corresponds to a need for God that he sees as a pathological dependence. This matches Harari's Lacanian statement that people keep relying on some construction of the Other instead of thinking for themselves. It is a valuable insight for Stephen, and it depends on the presence of Bloom, who is already beginning to appear to Stephen as a threatening father figure in his solicitude, an embodiment of the need to submit to the Other.

Just as Stephen knows that he should not fear God, but cannot help it, so he keeps attacking Bloom—attacks that culminate in an anti-semitic song in "Ithaca" (17.801–37)—just because the passive goodness or concern that Bloom radiates is having an effect on Stephen that threatens his freedom. Stephen's orientation being psychoanalytic to some extent (he mentions Freud in "Scylla and Chrybdis," 9.780), his anxieties about God and Bloom and love do not weaken his perception; they support it. The lack of knowledge of past and future and the Other that perturbs Stephen is the substance of anxiety. We recall that Lacan says that the object of anxiety is the Real, and that anxiety is the only signal that does not deceive (*Anxiety* 142). Stephen's refusal to claim knowledge of the interior or exterior worlds—"Between two roaring worlds where they swirl" (*U* 10.824)—is a deconstructive move that allows him to carry human consciousness forward by refusing to project a responsive or sensible Other. This evinces an aspect of Joyce's work that will inspire both Lacan and Derrida. As an explorer, Stephen is certainly making water or making a wake here by striving to the utmost against the lure of Bloom's kindness.

Having attained through desolation insights into human weakness that may serve to reshape humanity, Stephen, like Odysseus, has reached a maximum point of knowledge as alienation that is capable of making the rest of his story aim at return; so this is a turning point of the book's dramatic structure. It is also the most difficult episode to read, after which the novel is increasingly smooth sailing on its way to its unrecoverable home. Like Odysseus at this point, Stephen is about to go to Circe in the next chapter. "Circe" presents him with the most powerful image of the mother as goddess that he has ever seen, as represented by his mother's horrendous ghost.

Unlike the other mothers toward which Stephen moved, in *Portrait*, this one offers no inspiration, only disillusion as she asks him to submit to God. (15. 4194–440). This is a traversal, or passing beyond, of the fantasy of the ideal mother, which is always behind the debased or debasing prostitute, as the Nymph follows Bella for Bloom (15.3240). Stephen's collision with May makes him see that behind his use of woman is her victimization. The brutality implicit in prostitution makes her ghastly lesions stand for the horrors of social injustice. The worst horror may be that the oppressed worship their oppressors, as shown by May's selfless devotion to God, whom Stephen sees as having murdered her: "The corpsechewer!" (15.4214). This unspeakable, final mother, parallel to Anticlea, ends Stephen's forward thrust and soon puts him in Bloom's keeping by leading to his collapsc. So it shifts thc narrative from the centrifugal movement associated with Stephen to the centripetal one associated with Bloom (*U* 17.1214, 1225).

Yet the plot of *Ulysses* is often an inversion of that of the *Odyssey*: if Odysseus gets on track after his deepest moment, Stephen seems to go astray. If Odysseus conquers Circe to gain instructions on how to return, Stephen is overwhelmed by "Circe": as the ghost of his mother expresses his remorse for the women that he has defiled, he attains a vision of social and sexual atrocity that is unbearable. His conjunction with Bloom's fantasies here shows that debasing others is also debasing oneself. Its most unbearable aspect is his implication in it: just as he blames himself for killing his mother, he realizes that he supports the Church's system of prostitution by patronizing it.[6] Odysseus finally goes home, but Stephen cannot go home, just as he is neither a hero nor a father.

One reason that the parallel between Stephen's lines and Odysseus' has not been noticed is that the figure most clearly linked to Odysseus is Bloom, while Stephen is associated with Telemachus. But it may be argued that Bloom and Stephen are both parts of the Ulysses figure or exploratory impulse in the novel. In fact, in the *Odyssey*, Telemachus often functions as an extension of his father: he gains strength to resist the suitors and to set out on his own miniature *Odyssey* insofar as he is moved by his father's spirit. The disorientation Stephen passes through in his exploratory function will lead him toward the homecoming aspect of Odysseus, but he will reject it in this modern epic of unknowing. As with Stephen's equation, the emphasis is on the outward movement rather than the return, and the last two episodes, "Ithaca" and "Penelope," continue to move outward, toward the stars, toward the Pillars of Hercules.

Stephen, unlike Odysseus, seems to be aware that the goal of his odyssey is the greatest possible alienation that will realign his subject in the most radical way, leading to the contact or failure of contact with Bloom that is the structural center of *Ulysses*. It is a meeting in the Real in which the miscommunications that shock say more than the communications that lean on convention. For example, when Bloom asks Stephen, the reverse Telemachus, why he left his father's house, Stephen says, "To seek misfortune" (16.253). What is Bloom to make of this? At least, like the copulation between Blazes and Molly that conceives the advent of Stephen, it will disorient Bloom into allowing the Real into his life—and it confirms that Stephen's maximum upset is the goal of his day. In Lacan's terms (*Ethics* 264), Stephen's goal corresponds to *ate* or "misfortune," the goal of exploration, the impossible limit that leads to the forbidden place, that turns the Real into the Symbolic as an object of prohibition (Žižek, *Tarrying* 116). Stephen seeks misfortune to reach the Real as Real, as a language that withholds itself; as if he were Odysseus in a disguise not to be removed, aware that he is masked "as a young man."

One reason Stephen can represent possibilities of consciousness for Bloom is that Stephen shares with Joyce an awareness of the structure into which Stephen is inserted, and in this sense he surpasses the naturalistic world of *Ulysses* and is able to look awry at it, to see the submerged offenses and the possibilities of change under the surface. Stephen's decision to remain homeless prolongs Odysseus's role as a suppliant in touch with the oppressed. Likewise, Joyce's analysis of the Real that is outside accepted language allows him to discover the hidden operation of power that is concealed by the ostensible order of society. In his focus on the Real, Stephen sees the Lacanian truth of active language that is always in the process of disappearing, that consists of it own negation. Therefore he sees why the language of the novel is always being distorted by another level behind it, is always turning into another language.

Chapter 7

Structure as Discovery in Ulysses

> an order of discovery that is nothing other than what is called structure.
>
> *Seminar XVII* (44)

Critical Excess

As Stephen launches into his Shakespeare theory in *Ulysses*, he thinks to himself, "Folly. Persist" (9.42). This refers to a line from Blake's *Marriage of Heaven and Hell*, "If the fool would persist in his folly, he would become wise" (Blake 36), parallel to the nearby proverb "The road of excess leads to the palace of wisdom." The importance of excess in Joyce's work increases steadily from the "scrupulous meanness" of *Dubliners* to the outpouring of the *Wake*—and from the short opening chapters of *Ulysses* to the expansive later ones. Such progress toward excess may also be seen in the works of Lacan, who began with the containment of structuralism and moved toward extravagance in a final phase influenced by Joyce.

An expansion into possibilities beyond calculation may also be traced through the history of *Ulysses* criticism. The earliest studies, such as Stuart Gilbert's *James Joyce's* Ulysses (1930), Frank Budgen's *James Joyce and the Making of* Ulysses (1934), and Paul Jordan-Smith's *A Key to the* Ulysses *of James Joyce* (1934) tended to be confident that they were giving the true explanation. But Arnold Goldman argued in *The Joyce Paradox* (1966) that Joyce's works could not be encompassed by one consistent viewpoint, and Michael Groden showed in Ulysses *in Progress* (1978) that Joyce changed his conception of the novel as he wrote it. Derek Attridge's *Joyce Effects* (2000) calls into question the most central and certain views of Joyce's works—such as the Homeric parallels in *Ulysses* and the idea that the *Wake* is a dream—seeing these merely as possibilities among a vast number of other perspectives.

Soler, in "The Paradoxes of the Symptom," argues that Joyce is truly unreadable, while Lacan only seems to be (Rabaté, *Cambridge* 97). Indeed, recent Lacan critics like Fink, Harari, Miller, Rabaté, Shepherdson, Soler, and Žižek have clarified his concepts. As a doctor, Lacan would want his work to have a clear level for practical reasons. As an artist, however, Joyce wants his work to take on more and more meaning, multiplying contradictory theories—and such multiplicity has a function for Lacan as well.

Lacan observes, "In what Joyce writes, there's always a rapport with the surroundings" (*l'encadrement*), and *rapport*, as productive communication, suggests an expansion outwards. The *Seminar* of May 11, 1976 goes on to say, "For each of the things that he gathers, that he retells to make up… *Ulysses*, the framing always has a relation [*rapport*] at least of homonymy" (*Le sinthome* 147). Webster's defines *homonymous* as "having two or more different significations," so the work and its environment are different meanings of the same word. The frame is materially present in its content as a shaping cause; and as the frame changes, the substance of reality changes for each chapter. Lacan observes, "that each chapter of *Ulysses* is given a mode of framing, termed for instance 'dialectical,' 'rhetorical' [or] 'theological,' is for him linked to the very materiality of what he narrates" (147). Joyce's attachment of every discourse to a further level is central to how he inspires Lacan to a new theory of the *sinthome* in the Joyce seminars.

The *sinthome*, Joyce's symptom as the saint of man is in fact described by Lacan as a splicing of the functions of ordinary language to further levels. Joyce as artificer gives us not life as it is already known, but life supplemented by expertise, savoir faire or making knowledge—life as it could be further known. The splicing of the ordinary to an extra level is an artificial attachment that displaces and undercuts the normative structure of perception or subjectivity. This structure, for Lacan, loops the three registers of language together: Imaginary, Symbolic, and Real. Harari observes that for Freud, the Name-of-the-Father holds these three registers together normatively—but Lacan goes beyond this (Harari 19).

Lacan depicts the Imaginary and the Symbolic in action in *Le sinthome* when he first speaks of "the copulation of the symbolic and the imaginary of which meaning consists" (121), and then refers to meaning as "the copulation of language—as it is with this that I support the unconscious—and our own bodies" (122). So when language in the Symbolic loop reciprocates the body in the Imaginary one, we perceive meaning. But Lacan adds after the first quote, "The orientation of the Real, in my own territory, forecloses meaning" (121). Analysis confronts the patient with the Real of disjunction between the body and language, and Lacan says here that analysis "is nothing but a short circuit passing through meaning" (122). He uses the Real to abrogate existing meaning so as to "break through into a new imaginary founding meaning" (121). This rearrangement or retying of the subject in which the Real reshapes the Imaginary is made possible by the *sinthome* as the splice created by Joyce's art to reorient the subject, and it takes the form of a further level of language, an excess that extends consciousness beyond established limits. As Harari explains, the attachment of Joyce's writing to something beyond ordinary discourse dislodges the stability of its connections (Harari 71–104, 202–50).

Each chapter of *Ulysses*, after what Lawrence, in *The Odyssey of Style in* Ulysses, calls the "initial style" of the early chapters (60), distorts the idea of neutral discourse by attaching it to further levels, such as journalism and music. Usually there is more than one extra level at a time, so that in "Oxen of the Sun," each sentence may refer to a Homeric parallel, to a stage of the development of the fetus, and to the history of English literature (from politics to styles)—as well as to the main action it supports/undermines.

In relation to the depiction of the realistic action, these levels amount to or operate as errors. For example, when the narrative gets infected with music in "Sirens": "Shrill with deep laughter, after..." (11.174). These shifts represent the action on a deeper level, for the reverberation of the laughter is sustained by "after." But the shifts also interrupt or arrest the surface continuity of the narrative: when one hears the echo of "after," the forward movement of the story goes astray, and focus shifts to a parallax gap between two levels. A more substantial version appears in a nearby description of the barmaid Mina Kennedy: "Sauntering sadly, gold no more, she twisted twined a hair. Sadly she twined in sauntering gold hair behind a curving ear" (11.83–84). These lines capture the lingering repetition in her sadness, but they deflect the reader from the action onto the alternative reality of the technique, evoking the abstract oppositions of a fugue.

Thus in *Ulysses* language is generally subjected to a series of errors to reframe its apparatus. Rabaté declares in *James Joyce and the Politics of Egoism* that the *Wake* consists of nothing but a series of errors (206–7), and *Ulysses* moves in this direction as its extra levels grow more intrusive. One implication is that as we move through our day, errors infiltrate our consciousness more and more. This effect is enhanced because Bloom has an orgasm and Stephen gets drunk, rendering both of them somewhat groggy by evening, but this may only emphasize that they throw themselves into strong action. Their experience could not be represented without a massive influx of slippage. These extra levels of subjectivity represent a range of sensitivities, including personal relations.

There are also errors the reader makes unceasingly because (s)he is not informed. Gibson, for example, cites a series of Dublin literary controversies that are continually referred to in "Scylla and Charybdis" (*Revenge* 61–68). These controversies of 1904 were largely forgotten when *Ulysses* was published eighteen years later—or became legal in America twelve years after that. Perhaps only 100 readers of *Ulysses* in the twentieth century were aware of these controversies, which were not revealed to Joyce criticism until the twenty-first. Derrida claimed in "Two Words for Joyce" (1984) that *Ulysses* and the *Wake* far exceeded the greatest complexity of which computers were capable (147); and this suggests the likelihood that the average reader of *Ulysses* knows less than 25percent of the information submerged in the book. The more the reader learns, the more (s)he realizes the (s)he is virtually always making several errors at once by embracing only a small fraction of what each phrase contains. This is like the psychosexual act of taking a part object for the whole body, maybe as much of a slip as if, meaning to shake someone's hand, you shook his foot. Audiences probably miss the great majority of associations in most writing and discourse, but Joyce, like Freud, develops these missing associations actively, as conscious, intentional symptoms, *sinthomes*.

The *sinthome* as Extra Level

Lacan says that the slip is the foundation of Freud's notions of the unconscious and of jokes (*sinthome* 97), and then locates the *sinthome* as the place where the knot of Real, Symbolic, and Imaginary slips, unsettling perception and subjectivity (97). The *sinthome*, which Lacan aligns with artifice, builds awareness through distorted ways of seeing, gearing itself to the reader's misperceptions. While it may be asked whether there are any ways of seeing that are *not* distorted (or torted), the *sinthome* as a symptom is explicitly temporary and tentative.

Stephen sees his creativity as slippage, starting with the green rose. When he says of Shakespeare, "A man of genius makes no mistakes. His errors are volitional and are portals of discovery" (*U* 9.228–29), he implies that through self-attention one can see volition as a slip that reveals the structure of thought as tentative and reparable. Here volition is the opposite of rational clarity, which precludes will by dictating one's choice. Active volition generally transgresses an established framework, so it is generally sinful, and this is why Stephen keeps insisting that the soul is born in sin (*P* 103, 172, 203). One implication of original sin for Joyce is originality, inventing the new.

While the *sinthome* is temporary, it stimulates the illusion that it can be passed on as a signifier: this is the basis of phallic authority. Stephen never forgets the green rose, which is uniquely his, and so provides the basis of a sense of mission, of being sent elsewhere (apostolic): "But you could not have a green rose. But perhaps somewhere in the world you could" (*P* 12). By forging in the smithy of his soul, he will create consciousness for Ireland based on his individuality or *sinthome*. This is why Ireland is important because it belongs to him (*U* 16.1164–65). Individuality always consists entirely of the symptomatic abnormality that differentiates one from the nonexistent imaginary abstraction of the norm. The eccentricity of the author passes into his work as the neurosis of the father is reproduced in the irrational behavior of his son. Stephen says of Shakespeare's relation to Hamlet, "through the ghost of the unquiet father, the image of the unliving son looks forth" (*U* 9.380–81). Bloom feels that Si Dedalus is right to impose himself on his son: "Noisy selfwilled man. Full of his son. He is right. Something to hand on" (*U* 6.74–75). What the bad-enough father passes on to his son is his *sinthome,*[1] his symptom as it operates as an artifice by being memorable. The *Wake* could be described as an elaboration of some perverse stories John Joyce like to tell (Ellmann, *Joyce* 545). So just as Stephen develops himself only by sin, the artist transmits his *sinthome* only by being mistaken, by creating the new.

The slip is related to what Harari sees as a move from signifying to invention in the late works of Lacan and Joyce. The early Lacan, like Freud or Joyce the realist, thought that words to describe the symptom could capture or really signify it. The later Lacan concludes that the symptom as *sinthome* avoids containment by language (Thurston, *Re-inventing* xiii-xvii), just as he sees that experience consists of a constant invention of new words, if only because the previous word cannot be recaptured. A word never has the same meaning twice, and Joyce represents this realistically in the *Wake*, which approaches an ideal in which every word is new. His effort to make each word new frees Joyce from the law of the father, the foundation of established language, and of the pretense that one thing can equal another. This pretense is always false in actuality, though it may carry authority as an abstraction that allows calculation and control.[2]

Lacan addresses such reality when he says that the Name of the Father can be bypassed, as long as use is made of it (*sinthome* 136). As Harari indicates, this means that insofar as the author takes on God's power to create by naming things, he need not keep depending on an existing sediment of godhead (Harari 302)—which now appears as something to be parodied or departed from insofar as it is coherent or pretends to be equal to itself.[3] During his religious phase, Stephen realizes that the mysteries of the Trinity are easier for him to accept "by reason of their august incomprehensibility than was the simple fact that God had loved his soul..." (*P* 149), indicating that incomprehensibility is what attracts him most in religion. The mysteries of Catholicism confronted both Joyce and Lacan in their youths with the gap between the signifier and the signified.

It is by exploring incomprehensibility that original thinkers have expanded human consciousness into areas formerly dominated by divinities. I have mentioned that science explains phenomena formerly attributed to gods, such as the change of the seasons; likewise, many events formerly seen as determined by fate can now be understood by psychological analysis. Stephen's vocation is prefigured early in *Portrait* when he meditates: "It was very big to think about everything and everywhere. Only God could do that" (*P* 16). This leads to the enormity of Joyce's creation. Competing with God moves beyond competing with your peers to impress Him, a step closer to the source of power.

In the *Wake*, Shaun says that Shem boasts of the "idioglossary he invented under hicks hyssop" (423.9). This means that he created his own language rather than using the existing ones linked to divine authority. *Hyssop* is a form of holy water, and "under hicks hyssop" probably means "drunk" (his highship hiccups); but it also means "under him himself" (or his own Bishop) rather than under the conventional assumption of God that has generally validated language. Actually, Shem's claim to invent his own words may only recognize what everyone does. Lacan says that each person creates hris own language "to the extent that at each moment one gives it meaning, gives the language one speaks a little prod, without which it would not be living" (*sinthome* 133). *Ulysses* enacts this principle as its discourses constantly exceed reasonable models. There cannot be a neutral style that is not driven by something further. Each person has her own frame of reference in the background, which is likely to be incomprehensible to anyone else.

Even in the first two chapters of *Ulysses*, which appear to be among the most straightforward, the initial style is perturbed by undercurrents and extra levels, in addition to the increasing use of interior monologue. As in *Portrait,* Stephen is generally depicted here in narrated monologue, which may also be called free indirect discourse, and which is presented in the third person by a voice that uses his language and discourse.

The following sentence from "Telemachus" illustrates narrated monologue: "Woodshadows floated silently by through the morning peace from the stairhead seaward where he gazed" (1.242–43). Though this is in the third person, the style expresses Stephen's estheticsm. It shows Stephen polishing the prose of his perception in his effort to become the artist who writes himself. In fact the consummate beauty of these lines extends Stephen's 1904 prosody, rhythm, and assonance a long way into the higher level of perfection that Joyce attained when he wrote *Ulysses.*

Critics have observed that such narration often makes it hard or impossible to separate Stephen's words from those of his author;[4] but Stephen is working on authoring himself from the time he records his first epiphanies in *Portrait* (*P* 67–69). In these scenes people express more than they know as Stephen gains the potential to see more than he could have. Moreover, the epiphanies are arranged as a sequence of three scenes with no transition, each starting with "He was sitting." So Stephen's artifice here takes over the narrator's role by installing Stephen's form. Narrated monologue is a step toward stream of consciousness, the protagonism moving toward taking over its being told; and this is carried further when the character as narrator controls the form, which is true of most episodes of *Ulysses*. For example, the rhythm of "Lestrygonians" (8) is the rhythm of Bloom's digestion, or in "Circe," the proximity of lust felt by Bloom and Stephen exudes an intoxication that generates hallucinations.

In his esthetics lecture, Stephen tells Vincent Lynch that the tragic or dramatic emotion faces two ways—toward pity, which unites with the "sufferer", and toward terror, which unites with "the secret cause" (*P* 204–5). This may indicate that the narrated monologue in which he appears speaks for both his consciousness (the sufferer) and the authorial consciousness he ceaselessly strives to comprehend (the secret cause). Stephen is most conscious when he is "*reading*" or interpreting "*the book of* himself" (*U* 9.115). To aim at the secret cause of the Real, he explores unknown levels of language, as we saw in relation to "Proteus," so as to enlarge his consciousness. Dorrit Cohn sees his narrated monologue as suspended "on the threshold of verbalization" (103). His interaction with what is beyond himself elicits new forms of language, turning the Real into the Symbolic. And his brilliance is inseparable from self-criticism because it requires getting outside of himself.

The passages in *Portrait* and *Ulysses* that are most ironic about Stephen are never separate from Stephen's consciousness, which is extremely self-critical: his "thinking" consists of "a dusk of doubt and selfmistrust" (*P* 177). The word *selfmistrust* combines two opposed points of view. The idea that Joyce has an ironic attitude toward Stephen needs to be correlated with Stephen's smolderingly ironic attitude toward himself. Lacan says that Stephen is "Joyce as he imagines himself (and who, since he's not a fool, he's not in love with—on the contrary, he need only mention Stephen and he starts snickering)" (*sinthome* 68). So Joyce's criticism of Stephen is part and parcel of his realization that Stephen is himself. Yet Stephen might be only an aspect of himself, and his statement that "*Portrait* was the picture of my spiritual self" (Potts 132) may imply that it was limited to this area.

If Joyce were to believe in his image of himself, he would reduce his subject to what could be believed in. Belief is a tool for cutting off the parts that one does not believe in, and has no force unless it does so. Therefore Joyce sees his protagonists as beyond what is believable, and that is why they are so uniquely, astonishingly real. They are interrupted, overlapped, deflected and transformed by levels that cannot be squared with their discrete minds. These are the elements that proliferate in Joyce's structural diagrams to represent the moods the characters pass through with the hours of the day. They may be as simple as a color or as mysterious as some of the senses Joyce listed for episodes on the schema he sent Carlo Linati: "The Egocidal Terror" for "Cyclops"; "The Armed Hope" for "Ithaca."[5] They always represent the secret cause of the author or the world he creates, intervening to alter the consciousness of the character and the text. They come from the unconscious in the Lacanian sense of the entire semiotic field, and are always mistakes (taken amiss) that bring about the invention of new combinatory consciousness.[6]

Mistaken Meanings

That such technical innovation is a series of slips is made especially clear in "Eumaeus," the chapter in which Stephen and Bloom undertake communication (or perhaps bury it). Their efforts to get through to each other must be represented by the art of the episode, navigation. "Eumaeus" is made up of a series of errors that express the exhausted disorientation of the pair, especially of Bloom, though he is the more awake of the two. Perhaps they could not get together without exhausting themselves, so these mistakes are the element of ignorance through which they have to navigate. The errors persistently displace and render arbitrary the normal cognitive apparatus, so that Bloom and Stephen cannot perceive each other in ordinary terms, but this may help them to do so through the sinthomatic rearrangement of their subjective knots. Grammatical mistakes suspend the frame of language, so that what is revealed goes beyond the rules. Perhaps this is the most fundamental way that an individual exceeds the Law of the Father—by inventing his language, slipping into it.

Presenting a variation on narrated monologue in the first paragraph of "Eumaeus," Bloom's voice speaks of Bloom from a rhetorical distance in the third person, perhaps because he is striving to put himself into Stephen's mind: "it occurred to him as highly advisable to get a conveyance of some description to answer to their then condition, both of them being e.d.ed, particularly Stephen, always assuming that there was such a thing to be found" (16.15–18). Bloom, or his narrator—and he seems to feel narrated, or *ed*ited—makes "assuming there was such a thing to be found" modify Stephen rather than the cab Bloom seeks. Having left out the "assuming" phrase where it belonged, Bloom suspects that it is necessary, so he throws it in too late, showing that he is worried about class and possibly about using the order of Jewish dialect.

The excitement of this brilliant young man is making Bloom lose his cohesion and his sense of timing. He has many of the symptoms of being in love, and because he enjoys himself throughout "Eumaeus," these are transformed into *sinthomes*, symptoms cultivated for pleasure, including a key *sinthome* of eroticism, a feeling that the beloved is too good to be true. The error speaks for one of Bloom's main concerns: he is not at all sure that there is such a thing as Stephen to be found. His difficulty in believing in Stephen, or in his connection with Stephen, puts Stephen in the unattainable, sacrosanct position of the Other toward which language is projected and from which it proceeds. In creating the surreal notion that Stephen cannot be found, Bloom is actively artistic—and satirizes himself under Stephen's influence—without realizing it.

Bloom is perplexed because Stephen is supposed to be a great mind, but his words and actions are incomprehensible and seem to Bloom rather gross and foolish: "The vicinity of the young man he certainly relished, educated, *distingué*, and impulsive into the bargain, far and away the pick of the bunch though you wouldn't think he had it in him yet you would" (16.1476–78). Kershner demonstrates that there was a popular tradition in Bloom's day that geniuses tended to be degenerate ("Culture" 372–73), and Bloom recalls cases of brilliant people and the upper classes behaving in debased ways (16. 1182–1212). Therefore he tries to reach a new level of perception by telling himself that he can see signs of grace in this obscure wastrel ("yet you would"). In erotic relations, when the beloved shows faults, the lover creatively explains them as virtues.

It is because he cannot comprehend Stephen that Bloom cannot find "a conveyance of some description to answer in their then condition," that is, a style suitable for their encounter. He keeps struggling through the chapter to find language that will be intelligent enough for Stephen, like a lover afflicted by the feeling that his words are inadequate. The result of his efforts is that, as Lawrence points out, everything he says "misfires" (167). Bloom is already riding a conveyance that answers their state, a discourse hitched to incomprehensibility that turns down the wrong street of every sentence. In staying astray, Bloom invents an idiolect of his own that escapes the containment of prefabricated structure by never getting anything right, which may be how most discourse works. Bloom feels narrated because he is belaboring his thoughts to be literary for Stephen's sake, and he soon thinks of publishing an account of their meeting (16.1230). Though Stephen does not hear it, Bloom thinks that "a conveyance of some description" is an elegant phrase for a cab that would impress Stephen, who would find it execrable. And despite all the elaborate plans Bloom concocts for Stephen in this chapter and "Ithaca," we are told in "Ithaca" that "he did not expect" (17.349). While this refers to betting on a horse, it seems to fit Bloom's general attitude.

Therefore the satisfaction Bloom gets from Stephen, like the satisfaction he gets from Gerty, and from Zoe Higgins and Bella in "Circe," is not related to any actual response. Stephen presents an alternate field that invades Bloom's language and gives him the feeling that his symptoms are chosen. The incomprehensibility that he encounters with Stephen gives him a satisfying feeling of the potential of his words. Though they are wretched twaddle in literary terms, they express the discordance of his yearnings. His sense of not knowing what Stephen wants frees his discourse from the conventions that usually control it. Though he has no idea of it, there is a context in which his discourse is advanced: postmodernism, in which the purpose of words is not to hit their target, but to miss it.[7] And Bloom attains a level of symbolic destitution by correctly suspecting that everything he says is an error.

In "Ithaca," the possibility of error is suspended, as is the possible relation of Stephen and Bloom, which could only be based on error. Perhaps consciousness is always suspended between a question and an answer, but here the two men ask each other to reply. Every relationship forms in a space of inquiry between people and all claims to knowledge for Lacan are directed at the Other, the idea of otherness represented by the individual other to whom we speak.

We have seen, however, that according to Harari (125), the late Joyce and the late Lacan reveal the Other to be less a given authority than something we create in continual protean changes out of our need to believe that our speech-being (*parletre*, Harari 228–30)—or the being we have through speech—is addressed to an abiding reality. The illusory status of the Other corresponds to the fact that the questions and answers in "Ithaca" don't really work together despite "a meticulosity bordering on the insane" (*FW* 173.34), which indicates desperation in the effort to make them answer. Instead of claiming knowledge or meaning by positing the Other as an absolute linguistic totality in whose context meaning can be clarified, Lacan, under Joyce's influence, envisions a process of continual invention that does away with the need for a patriarchal god by doing without the carving of determinate knowledge and meaning. This liberation can only be sustained under the aegis of woman, which is why "Penelope has to follow "Ithaca."

Within "Ithaca" it is the feminine possibility of homecoming—the light in the window—that allows the contrasting figures to form a new combination. Lacan says that at the point at which one signifier differs from another "it is possible for this fault we call the subject to open" (*Other* 88). Therefore at the point at which Stephen and Bloom fail to understand each other a new subject is formed. This subject may be called the subject of the novel insofar as the novel is arranged around their meeting, or its failure, generally following them toward it. The doubt that unites or disunites the two men increases its scope the further apart they are, and the novel develops their oppositions, youth and age, artist and citizen, spirit and matter, and so forth.

The subject of Stephen and Bloom as question and answer cannot be resolved so as to join the desire to know and the claim of knowledge. Indeed the vast entirety of human knowledge, from the galaxy to the atom, is evoked when the two men part, evoked as leading to what cannot be known (*U* 17.989–1157). As Harari argues (73), Joyce's epiphanies always reveal the incomprehensible, and "Ithaca" makes *Ulysses* add up to an enormous epiphany of unknowing. While it is true that the answers in "Ithaca" address their questions, the main issues, such as the bond between the two men, are not clarified, making the bulk of the scientific facts effectively peripheral. If "Eumaeus" attached its discourse to error, "Ithaca" makes error impossible by answering every question precisely. But here factual truth is a level of distraction, for the truth that is sought lies in the realm of error, of the *sinthome*, of the makeshift, the jury-rigged. Lacan says that between people, "Where there's a connection [*rapport*], it is insofar as there is sinthome" (*sinthome* 101), perhaps because it is a sense that there is something beyond comprehension that brings the relationship to life. Insofar as question and answer cannot meet, a new idea is engendered from their longing for each other, and the subject of *Ulysses* is that newness as discovery.

The mathematical catechism shows the distance of scientific logic from the feelings of the protagonists; yet "Ithaca" also suggests, by extending beyond Bloom's knowledge, the great realm of possibility. That all of these facts and ideas form a factitious universe toward which Bloom's thoughts reach suggests his potential to form a virtually infinite series of terms. When he thinks of his daughter's dreams or of the operation of the stars, he is inspired by the presence of Stephen, who may provide the charge behind the questions, though he does not articulate them.

Stephen stirs Bloom's thoughts of the poet he might have been, and Bloom remembers all of his attempts in this vein. The crucial point at which Bloom had his main opportunity as a poet was when he was asked to write a song for the annual pantomime of Sinbad the Sailor and prevented himself from doing so by indecisions and distractions (*U* 17.417–45). This is a point of maximum extension of latitude for Bloom, as suggested by the widely wandering Sinbad. After this, there is no further reference to his writing poetry. When Bloom falls asleep at the end of the chapter, however, he is described as weary because he has traveled with a long series of variations on Sinbad: "Sinbad the Sailor and Tinbad the Tailor and Jinbad the Jailer..." (17.2322). Gifford and Seidman mention that some of these forms actually appeared in Sinbad pantomimes (606). This suggests that Bloom has now traversed the possibilities of language that go beyond what is acceptable or knowable, that he has worked through the framework of poetry. Lacan's idea of the *sinthome* helps us to see how Joyce portrays the common man as rich in poetry, attached to further levels of language by a sort of sinbadthome. And the use of the sailor provides final confirmation that the field of language is exploratory.

Female Freedom

"Ithaca" ends by asking where Bloom's traversal of virtually endless permutations of language has taken him and answering with a black dot.

This dot may be seen as an aperture leading to Molly, and as he falls asleep, Bloom is described as "in the womb" (17.2318). Bloom reaches a suspension between possibilities that is represented by Molly insofar as she projects the question of Bloom's validation, a question that is lost in her contradictions. In the patriarchal situation in which she is enclosed, Molly's freedom as a woman centers on his and her doubt about her commitment to Bloom. Her strength draws on the extent to which he needs to believe in her feeling for him in order to survive, even her strength in rejecting him.

Shepherdson points out that according to Lacan's formula for the two genders in *Encore* (78), women, unlike men, are not entirely subjected to the Law of the Father ("Lacan and Philosophy," Rabaté, Cambridge 139). This may allow Molly to operate as a principle that liberates men from such subjection. Moreover *Le sinthome* says of what we have generally called God that "analysis reveals that it is quite simply the woman" (128). By putting Molly in the final position of authority, Joyce represents both the power of women to embody the Other and the pity of the delusion in which she is caught. By reframing the mechanism of belief as instability, he is, like anyone who denies an existing faith, taking upon himself the power of divinity; but he does so to question the basis of theology by showing its roots in uncertainty.

As a typical feature of Joyce's flaunting of his parodic divinity, he makes every episode of *Ulysses* begin by referring back to the previous one, even when the figures in the new episode have little knowledge of what preceded them. At the end of "Proteus," for example, Stephen thinks of devouring "a urinous offal" (3.479–80), while at the start of "Calypso," we are told that Bloom liked to eat kidneys that taste of urine (4.4). As Molly maps out her power in her first hundred lines, she says, "a young boy would like me Id confuse him . . . drawing out the thing by the hour question and answer" (18.84–88). The thought of Stephen leads her to equate attraction with confusion, and this leads her to refer to the question and answer hour of the preceding "Ithaca" as the dynamics of desire. She exists for the male subject mainly as the distance between Q. and A., and this is why critics have long recognized that the suspension of doubt that allows her the freedom of self-contradiction is a major goal of the narrative.[8]

Molly is constantly making errors, for words must be organized in sentences to be correct, and Molly is unceasingly erroneous in leaving out punctuation. This ongoing transgression is parallel to her infidelity. She enacts the symptom of her desire with an enjoyment that makes it voluntary. Through her desire she creates a complex work of art connecting a series of men. This fits Judith Butler's definition of the subject as a work of art (*Power* 67). Molly's subject is such an artifact that includes plurality. Joyce's assumption of a woman's points of view reveals how the division of desire that splits Molly's subject is actually embodied by the men who enact it. The central division is between Bloom and Boylan: the man who has a deep love for her, but is incapable of aggressive sex, and the man who is good at sex, but too aggressive to love her. Boylan may be the Imaginary in his fantastic physicality, and Bloom may be the Real because she can't bear to think about how she loves and torments him. The division between men who are exciting but unkind and men who are considerate but dull is a commonplace and reflects both actual limitations in men and the impossible nature of feminine desire.

Moreover, Molly cannot face the level on which she is seeing Boylan to satisfy Bloom's homosexual side, his need for another man. Yet Bloom, like the Real, keeps coming back to her in his annoying reality. She is true to him by betraying him, and this realizes him by dividing him to fulfill her desire continually. As Issy puts it in the *Wake*, "...I will long long to betrue you..." (459.20). She adds to Bloom's complexity in her mind by fulfilling both of their desires in ways that neither is conscious of, and Bloom devotes himself to this complexity of his in her by suffering all day to give her pleasure. As he endures this, he worships her as Nature, the principle of change and multiplicity that he believes in as science. He finally feels "equanimity" (the serenity of equal minds) because Molly's adultery is "as natural as any and every natural act of a nature" (*U* 17. 2178).

Stephen is also part of this complex in which Molly expands Bloom, for Dedalus is on her mind at the end, in effect as a device Bloom uses to separate her from Boylan—and therefore as something Bloom is doing to her. For once she starts thinking of Stephen, Boylan seems bestial to her (18.1310–73), partly because Stephen is an idealized mental figure with whom she has no actual contact, a mere sign. He has the potential to understand her, in fact, to write her, but she can never realize this potential for the same reason that he cannot make love to her like Boylan or love her like Bloom.

If Stephen is the Symbolic, the hole in language she strives for, while Blazes is the Imaginary and Bloom the Real, then Joyce is the *sinthome*, the creative function that unites them all together; and Rabaté points out that Lacan identifies Joyce with the *sinthome* (*James* 7). Joyce insists on his presence at the end by having Molly focus on the Creator of images (18.1558–71) and exclaim "Oh Jamesy" (18.1128). The linking of Lacan's orders to these figures is not definitive: it serves to indicate the variety of levels of Molly's subjectivity, but there are other men who are important to her, such as Mulvey.

At the end, Molly kisses Mulvey, Bloom, Blazes, Stephen, and Joyce at once: "he kissed me under the Moorish wall and I thought as well him as another and then I asked him with my eyes to ask again yes and then he asked me would I yes to say yes my mountain flower..." (18.1604–6).

Mulvey and Bloom are most obvious here, but her body is still vibrating with Boylan's energy, Stephen is the source of her expectation, and Joyce seems to be indicated as one of the men asking her to say yes. Even the unliterary Bloom realizes continually that the meaning of his life depends on its potential to be written, and Joyce's characters live more than others because he takes responsibility for writing them. He uses his unique points of view to give these men life as parts of a subject contained in Molly.

The pattern of the woman who fulfills several sides of her subject by having several men, which emphasizes the limitation of the men, provides a full model of womanly subjectivity. In "On the Universal Tendency to Debasement in the Sphere of Love" (1910, *SE* XI.177–90), Freud says that men tend to need two women, one for love and another for lust; and many anthropologists still argue that men are genetically predisposed to have more than one mate, claiming that 83percent of the world's societies have been polygynous.[9] But this privilege has generally been withheld from women, and they should be allowed to express themselves with plural objects. In fact, the idea of devoting oneself entirely to a single mate is an arbitrary restriction related to monological thinking on every level—one cause for each effect, one system of belief, and so forth. One of Joyce's key aims from *Exiles* on is to show how far this absurdity is from the complexity of the human subject.

The figure of the woman with several mates may be an Irish paradigm related to the vitality of women in Celtic mythology, for it appears in the Tristan legend, *Wuthering Heights*, and O'Neill's *Strange Interlude*.[10] Joyce advanced on previous versions (to be carried on by O'Neill) by having Molly sustain all of the relationships at once rather than sequentially and by leaving her unpunished. Why restrict her—like a mental chastity belt—to the pretense that she could say yes to a single person (or gender)?[11] Joyce's enlargement of women's subjectivity is one of the feminist achievements of twentieth-century literature and is one of the most progressive ways in which he expands and changes the human frame of reality.

Lacan says, "One thinks *against* a signifier" ("*On pense* contre *un signifiant*," *sinthome* 155), and the life of the mind in *Ulysses* and Joyce's other works is a series of transgressions of the established frames of language and identity. Such invention leaves behind the stability of the imaginary first cause, so it does without the authority of God and tradition by taking it on. Whether the text adds new levels of consciousness by multiplying peripheral concerns in the techniques of episodes or by recognizing marginal and divided personal relationships, it is always reaching outward to articulate the complex truth of experience. This excess or overflow in the mentality of language is a psychological dynamism that supports revolution in the most fundamental way by revealing the inadequacy of what has been seen.

Josephine Lovelust

"I thought you were Josephine, Stephen."

(*P* 68)

An extension of the idea of the further level and the extra mate, Žižek's parallax view sees any significant idea is constituted as an interaction between two opposed viewpoints that cannot be reconciled, a version of the Lacanian subject. The word *parallax* appears eight times in *Ulysses*, referring primarily to the fact that the world of the book is always seen from the opposing, simultaneous viewpoints of Stephen and Bloom. I will apply the concept here to Aquinas's distinction between love and lust: love seeks to elevate its object and lust to debase it. Morality insists on separating them, but there is no erotic relation that does not include both love and lust, from the most wonderful love to the most terrible lust. *Portrait* insists that one cannot exist without the other by having Stephen first almost burst into tears when a prostitute embraces him (*P* 101) and then enjoy praying to the Virgin with the savor of a lewd (possibly genital) kiss on his lips (105), so the lust is emotional and the devotion is lecherous.

The parallax view can serve to explain two obscure new lines about lovelust in the Gabler edition of Ulysses. The first occurs in "Scylla and Charybdis" when Stephen explains how Shakespeare's late romances show a reconciliation to life and to women by showing a lost child recovered. Now Stephen reflects, "Love, yes. Word known to all men." followed by eleven Latin words that I will focus on. The passage seems to answer a question Stephen asked an imaginary woman in "Proteus": "What is that word known to all men?" (3. 436). It also connects with a remark about Stephen by a narrator on the book's third page: "Pain, that was not yet the pain of love, fretted his heart" (1.102).

The mystery of love that Stephen broods on here may be explained by examining the words from Aquinas's *Summa Contra Gentiles* that follow Stephen's realization that love is the word he seeks: "*Amor vero aliquid aliqui bonum vult unde et ea quiae concupiscimus*" (9.430). The first six words, which mean "True love wills something good to someone," are separated from the last four by ten words in Aquinas's text (see Gifford and Seidman 221); for the last five words define lust as opposed to love, "and from thence we desire a thing." Aquinas starts this paragraph by suggesting a parallax view, that love "seems to be directed to two objects" (279), and Jean Kimball points out that Aquinas sees desire as improper because it is really love of self (146–47). Why does Stephen select *unde* ("whence") from the intervening words to suggest that love as goodness to others is the cause of selfish lust?

Stephen's vision of Shakespeare has many parallels to Bloom: both men lose a son, keep a daughter, and return home to accept their cuckoldry.

Stephen even suggests that Shakespeare is Jewish (9. 741–91).[12] So this Shakespeare anticipates Bloom, and it may occur to Stephen here—perhaps unconsciously or ironically—that lust could be satisfied by making someone happy, as Bloom may satisfy desire by making Molly happy. Tolstoy, whom Joyce admired, defines conventional love in the short novel *Family Happiness*: "to live for others was happiness" (85).[13] If the surest way to be happy is to make someone else happy, Stephen may see the nobility of this action parallactically reinforced by its obscene underside of debased perversion. To realize that kindness always has a perverse side may make it true and acceptable to the Joycean artist, and may be fully disclosed in "Circe" when Bloom turns "*the other cheek*" while being flagellated (15.1109). One can be masochistic without being good, but one cannot be good without being masochistic, for one must enjoy sacrificing oneself for another.

How this model could be applied is indicated in the second puzzling passage, the one about St. Joseph, which indicates Joyce's and Stephen's irony about lovelust. In "Eumaeus," as Bloom is showing his photo of Molly to Stephen and dwelling on her female form, an incomprehensible line suddenly bursts in: "Yes, puritanisme, it does though Saint Joseph's sovereign thievery alors (Bandez!) Figne toi trop" (16.1453–54). After which we go right back to Bloom praising Molly's body. Although it is not an adequate explanation for this weird interruption, the best way to make sense of it is to see it as Stephen's, and perhaps Joyce's, reaction to Bloom's offer of his wife. This is confirmed by the French, the last four words of which, according to Gifford and Seidman, are low slang for "Get an erection! Bugger yourself up to the neck." Stephen may use the French word for Puritanism to express the idea that a person who seems properly monogamous ends up covertly excited by cuckoldry. Perhaps for Joyce, some level of cuckoldry (if only imaginary) is what makes monogamy perversely possible. When Stephen refers to "conjugial love and its chaste delights," he refers to Shakespeare's cuckoldry (9.631), But this leads to my main concern, St. Joseph.

In the eighteenth and nineteenth centuries, Mary's husband became one of the main icons of Catholicism, as Gerty MacDowell makes clear in reference to Jesus: "Gerty knew Who came first and after Him the Blessed Virgin and then St. Joseph" (13.139–40). His third place as a human embodiment of God also appears as a formula in *Portrait* when Mr. Casey tells how he spat tobacco in the eye of a lady who insulted Parnell: "*Oh Jesus, Mary, and Joseph!* says she. *I'm blinded!*" (*P* 37). Both Josephiles are female because he serves women. Joseph held such a central position because he stood for the forbearance that makes the Christian family possible. He accepts marriage to the Virgin though she is pregnant by God and Joseph cannot now make love to her (possibly because this would grant her two mates). Fr. Francis Filas, S. J., in his book *Saint Joseph and Daily Christian Living* speaks of "spiritual ties closer than existed in any other marriage" (3). But the parallax of this is that as Colin Eisler says, "Joseph was long seen as a bumbling, fumbling aged cuckold" (cited in Wilson 15). The cuckoldry that Joseph puts at the center of the Christian family is absolute in the sense that he can never compete with God. The number of men who are cuckolded by God may be in the tens of millions in the sense that their wives are so devout that they are not very sexually responsive—not to mention widowers such as Si Dedalus, who sighs (6. 647–51) So it may be that "Saint Joseph's sovereign thievery" is to rob Christians of their manhood. And it seems fitting that when Stephen is mistaken for a woman, the name Josephine repeats (*P* 68).

Buck Mulligan's reference in his "Ballad of Joking Jesus" to "*Joseph the joiner*," a phrase that Stephen later repeats (1.586, 14.305), involves several ironies. Not only was Joseph a carpenter, but he was a joiner rather than a leader in his marriage, for the main event took priority over him. The word *joiner* also suggests a procurer who joins a woman and a man covertly, and Joseph allows Mary to have a relationship with God by maintaining his marriage so that she is not left in the untenable position of an unwed mother. "Eumaeus" has Bloom think that even the best of married women always has a list of eligible men surrounding her (16.1544), so that just as Bloom and Joseph give their wives away, every married man approaches cuckoldry insofar as he sacrifices his pride for his wife's freedom and happiness, if only in flirtation.

Related to this is the fact that the good husband should abate his claims on his wife or forgo his jealousy in order to allow her to devote herself fully to her child, and Nancy Chodorow estimates that most women worldwide have stronger emotional connections to their children than to their husbands (*Feminism* 72–77). Joyce agreed: "There are only two forms of love in the world, the love of a mother for her child and the love of a man for lies" (*JJ* 293). In the most famous image of St. Joseph, Michelangelo's circular painting of the Holy Family, Joseph in the background looks on supportively (not very comfortably) while Mary holds up the child adoringly in the foreground.

We can delineate the unexpected workings of Josephine love by examining Lacan's definition of love in *Seminar XX*, *Encore*, which begins by saying that jouissance or sexual pleasure is not the sign of love (4). Later he says that love aims at expressing the subject, and that the subject is the intermediate effect between one signifier and another (50), a parallax that forms itself as love by interacting with another person as signifier. *Encore* also says that love appears as a sign and that a sign can be defined as a disjunction of two substances that have no part in common (17).

Bloom cannot admit to himself that he gets sexual satisfaction out of suffering to make his wife happy, yet this may be his main exertion on this day. Molly cannot admit that one of her motives in seeing Boylan is to stimulate Bloom, though she notices that he is excited by her adultery: "the last time he came on my bottom when was it the night Boylan gave my hand a great squeeze" (18.77–78). She thinks that Bloom rubs his penis between her buttocks as a result of Boylan's passion and it may be that whatever chance the Blooms have of reuniting physically will work through Boylan. Bloom evidently would not be inspired to his ideal relationship with Gerty if his wife were not cheating on him. Molly's desire to gratify Bloom is not her main motive on the level of sex, but it may be her main one on the level of love. The spiritual, unselfish side of love and its physical, selfish side can't be held in the mind at once, and maybe this is why Lacan says, "All love is based on a certain relationship between two unconscious knowledges" (*Encore* 144). Perhaps the spiritual side is unconscious knowledge of the other and the physical side is knowledge of oneself. Lacan says that it is by confronting this impossibility that love is put to the test (144, compare Penelope and Odysseus dreaming of each other), and he implies that love only exists when it is tested. Molly relates to Boylan on the level of the sexual relationship, which, for Lacan, is no relation; but she relates to Bloom on the level of the subject. Bloom provides the main source of love for Molly's connection with Boylan, for his is the Josephine sacrifice that makes it possible. Molly must know this, and she must feel it when her thoughts return to Bloom rhapsodically at the end.

Lacan says that love moves toward recognition as it turns from a sexual relation to a subject-to-subject one that is the effect of subconscious knowledge: "here there is nothing but encounter, the encounter in the partner of symptoms and affects, of everything that marks in each of us the trace of his exile...from the sexual relationship." (145). An encounter by definition is unplanned, and Lacan says here that he is talking about "contingency," so love is a structure that is invented, as Groden shows that *Ulysses* is. What love encounters is the gap or flaw that makes the sexual relation an illusion, as Molly sees through Boylan after thinking about Bloom and his extension in Stephen. Molly's relation to Boylan is a meeting of masks they put on to impress one another, and she cannot tell if he likes her (18.732). But Bloom and Molly meet on the level of being, of which Lacan says, "it is never anything but a fracture, break, or interruption" (*Encore* 11). This is the level on which the contingent turns to the necessary as they find out how they need each other because each can turn the other's weaknesses into voluntary symptoms. Molly needs Bloom to carry on her affair with Blazes, just as Mary needed Joseph. Molly realizes that Bloom longs for her, but is unable to connect with her directly, as is indicated by his humiliating focus on her rear end, which she claims does not appeal to her. He realizes that she needs to debase both of them with Boylan, and this recognition of their weakness is the core of their love, by which the unconscious of each rests on the other's—a pair of lacks.

The doubt and irony that Joyce deploys against their love makes it more beautiful. That they give their sexual excitement to fantasies only shows that as Lacan emphasizes, the jouissance of the Other is not the sign of love (*Encore* 4). In his main sexual experience of the day in "Nausicaa," Bloom plays a role like that of Joseph by adoring Gerty as Mary from a distance. That the modern Odysseus cannot return to the home he left lifts his homecoming into the realm of dreams where the pitiful cuckold Joseph is spiritually exalted by creating the beauty of his wife and her maternity to last forever. In this perspective, the beauty of woman lies in her creation of man, and the beauty of man lies in his creation of woman. As Bloom was striving constantly through the day to let Molly enjoy Blazes, he is fully realized in his final dream of Molly's jouissance in "Penelope," for the love that creates her joy is his. In their parallactic world, love can only exist as an extra level behind and dependent on the ludicrous charades of their lust.

Yet love is the content of lust as well as its frame, what lust seeks even through its selfishness. This recalls Lacan's obervation that the framing that interrupts *Ulysses* is also the substance of its narrative. Tony Thwaites' expression of this arrangement reverberates: "The *arrest* that increasingly comes to structure Joyce's writing sends any point elsewhere…the arrest…Does not exist entirely within the horizon of meaning: it *is* that horizon, and provides the very possibility of meaning" (74). The other level that keeps interfering with the narrative brings out the process of structure that the action expresses, the subject of the novel, it's structure of discovery.

The Subject of *Ulysses*

The Lacanian subject that fills *Ulysses* may be defined in terms of characters as the relationship between Bloom, Stephen, and Molly. To try to enclose these three in a formulation such as the Father, the Son and the Holy Ghost that make up the Creator, or the three registers that go with Joyce's *sinthome* may be revealing, but it may be partial and problematic. What I want to focus on here is the fact that the link between the three is unheard of, that the subject made up by these three human beings does not fit a formula. The level on which they relate does not exist in the language of the world. They have no way of understanding each other in this relation. Bloom and Stephen are not father and son, and Molly's official relation with Bloom does not recognize the connection that she has with him on this day through adultery. Moreover, Molly and Stephen hardly know each other, yet the book makes them parts of a whole.

Let us return to Lacan's statement that at the difference between signifiers "it is possible for this fault we call the subject to open" (*Other* 88), with its implication that the subject is enriched by the greatest distance between signifiers. The subject that involves the three protagonists cannot be defined in existing terms. It seems to include a new kind of love that is free of definition, but it is also destructive in its misunderstanding and infidelity, so any attempt to link it to love as the word known to all men is obliged to see love as a mystery equal to all of the complexity of the novel. But the most active role of this larger subject, which anticipates the family in the *Wake*, is to enact the coming into being of something beyond language.

Jameson says of modern European literature that beyond all of the different languages of ethnic, social, and cultural levels that it unfolds, it projects "a kind of empty Utopian domain of language as non-existent and yet as demonstrable and conjectural as non-Euclidean geometry" By modifying the axioms of ordinary speech, this modern language develops "the invisible outlines of whole new language structures never before seen on earth and heaven" (*Singular* 147). The new language structures correspond not only to all the new uses of language in *Ulysses*, but to the new modes of relationship between the characters: new levels of consciousness that have been concealed behind such known structures as the family and the eternal triangle, new levels of logic, truth, desire, and freedom. I want to argue now that this structure behind *Ulysses* serves a political purpose as well as psychological and philosophical ones. And here I will extend beyond the gender reversal whereby Molly plays the active role by taking a lover while Bloom puts up with it (Brivie, *Waking* 18).

The political use of language includes not only functions that enclose people within social categories, but functions that see them as going beyond categories. Žižek, in discussing Toni Morrison, says that ethics is "politicized" when it "can no longer be accounted for in terms of fidelity to some pre-existing Cause, since it redefines the very terms of this Cause" (*Fragile* 155). If ethics, as Eide says, reaches toward what is furthest from knowledge, and if the political is what uproots established systems, then the subject of *Ulysses* as the coming into being of something beyond language may play a powerful political role. By redefining the terms of social machinery, as I hope to show in my next chapter, we can reveal the actual operation of power and economics.

Politics is already involved, however. in the combination of love and its failure that links the characters through the defeat of their potential to unite with each other. No matter how Molly may ignore it in her sensuality, which makes up for it, she feels a loss after her first adultery, as

Bloom feels the loss of being cuckolded, the subject of his unconscious fantasies in "Circe." Stephen loses something by falling back on his anti-Semitic song when Bloom offers him charity, and his loss may lead him through homelessness toward a need for love. What they lose is lost to the agency that keeps them from fulfilling the potential to love each other that it generates by bringing them together, and that agency is the Father God, the Law of repression.

He corresponds to Žižek's idea that the social order is shaped by what it excludes (*Metastases* 30–31). The God of actuality whom Stephen calls "The playwright who wrote the folio of this world... the lord of things as they are" (9.1048) keeps us from realizing the love and language that are potential in us, the total subject of Stephen, Bloom and Molly that would compete with God or equal Joyce as creator. The limit beyond which one cannot go defines the value that motivates one's actions, the force that drives through the political and economic operations of life. But this is the positive side: when we turn to the social operation of desire, we have to confront the threat behind the limitation of love.

The interruption that stops the narrative from progressing is the higher power that deflects it from its goal onto alternative levels, but also keeps those levels from being realized. Joyce leads the structure in exploratory directions because realism dictates that the Law of the Father enforces the recognition that separates love from lust, that makes love aim at something other than gratification, aim at knowing the beloved as a subject rather than an object. This is a key realization of Joyce's and of Freud's. Lacan says in *Le sinthome* that love, eternal love, is always addressed to the father, and that the story of the primal father who claims all the women in *Totem and Taboo* indicates that insofar as the sons are deprived of woman, they love the father, they are turned toward him in *père-version*, which is the law of love (150).[14]

Obviously this corresponds to the fact that it is Joseph's love of God that keeps him from loving Mary physically. In Bloom's case, his father exerts an especially powerful force linked to the dreadful God of the Old Testament because his father has committed suicide, to some extent murdered by anti-Semitism in his alienation. Because Bloom must blame himself, Rudolph is bound to reappear as the nemesis Blazes, who wears Rudolph's straw hat. But the whole machinery that deflects lust onto the exploration of the beloved's multiplicity rather than the direct union with her, that makes love perverse for Lacan, is enforced by the disturbing Real of paternal authority. This is the analyst who ends the session of *Ulysses* with feelings unresolved.

Therefore the love that allows intersubjective beauty, the subject that could unite everyone, is politically compromised because it is beholden to the Law of the Father. And the structure of society, in which women, according to Levi-Strauss, are the chief objects of exchange, is organized by the force that keeps people from satisfying themselves—shame, which is imposed by the Law of the Father. Bloom could not love (or need) Molly as he does without deep shame. The material out of which society is made is measured by this lack of satisfaction, which is the distance between signifiers that makes up the subject of *Ulysses.*

Chapter 8

Ulysses' "*Circe*": *Dealing in Shame*

> It is traditional to suppose that civilization is bound up with instituting shame.
>
> Jacques-Alain Miller, "On Shame"

Shame's Voice

In *Our Exagmination Round His Factification for Incamination of Work In Progress* (1929), the collection of essays that Joyce arranged to preview the *Wake*, a letter of protest against that work in stepping forth appears, written in a Wakean style. At one point it addresses the author that it takes a dim view of as "mysterre Shame's Voice" (193–94). Many readers of this collection assumed that Joyce wrote the letter, for its tone accords with his portrayal of the shameful sham Shem. Actually, the signature on the letter is the name of its writer, a follower of Joyce's named Vladimir Dixon.[1] Joyce, however, approved publication of the letter in a book he organized, and it matches his caustic view of himself, so he probably saw truth in the suggestion that what spoke in his work was shame.

Late in his memoir *Giacomo Joyce*, after giving Amalia Popper a copy of *A Portrait,* Joyce reflects, "Those quiet cold fingers have touched the pages, foul and fair, on which my shame shall glow forever" (13). If Joyce thought of *Portrait* as radiating with his shame, he may have seen *Ulysses* as burning brightly with it, especially "Circe," which enacts versions of some of his most debased fantasies in the longest and most climactic episode. Joyce makes the expression of shame central to his work because he recognizes shame as a key factor not only in personal feelings, but in art, in gender, and in social economy. "Circe" develops Joyce's idea that shame is the crucial medium of exchange and insight in modern society. This is because shame is the feeling that the Law of the Father, the authority of church and state, propagates to withhold us from the object of desire and turn us back upon ourselves, the crux of control. The subject as a distance between signifiers is created by shame.

Sylvan Tomkins, in his analysis of the emotions, says, "In contrast to all other affects, shame is an experience of the self by the self" (136). Tomkins links shame to shy withdrawal from stressful contacts with people one does not know. In this sense, it may be the drive toward not knowing through which one knows the self as unsolved. Self-regard may be fundamentally intertwined with shame, and both may be linked by Joyce to the origin of his writing. In *Portrait*, when Stephen begins to record his epiphanies, we are told that "He chronicled with patience what he saw, detaching himself from it and testing its mortifying flavour in secret" (*P* 67). This coincides with Judith Butler's claim that the subject defines itself by separating itself from what it designates as unclean or "abject" (*Gender* 133). Yet Stephen, as an artist aligned with the colonized and victimized, recognizes his dependence on the impurities he focuses on.

His distance allows him to taste the mortifying flavor of the epiphanies, which generally involve the embarrassment of missed communication and disturbing undertones. So by "detaching himself" from his unhealthy subject, he can see it as external and internal, connecting with it better, as he will seek to connect with Ireland better by leaving it ("the shortest way to Tara was *via* Holyhead," *P* 250). If shame is the main burden or central activity of those who are oppressed, then assuming or inhabiting shame may be the best way to understand in depth the situations of the downtrodden. And if shame is spliced to art, it becomes the voluntary symptom or *sinthome* that opens the mind to new perpectives.

Tomkins argues that shame plays a foundational role in political systems. He says that hierarchical relations are based on the oppressor feeling contempt and the oppressed feeling either contempt for himself or shame (139). This accords with Joyce's recognition that shame is the substance that holds social bonds together; and Lacan's terms can help us to see how it works.

Shame is an encounter with the disturbing Real, and society is tacitly organized so that those who undergo shame serve to sustain its privileged members in the Imaginary, the fantasy of satisfaction, the belief that one possesses reality. The dominant class gets to control how reality is defined. In chapter 5, I argued that the strongest representatives of the Real in *Portrait* were the threatening father figures. These figures—Father Dolan, Heron, Father Arnall, the Jesuit director, and Cranly—were generally in comfortable positions that gave them satisfaction. So the person in the Imaginary position of pride represents the Real by pushing others out of the Imaginary into shame.

In most situations in life, people strive to avoid shame and maintain pride, yet Joyce as an artist reverses these strivings. He accepts his symptomatic need for shame to turn it into a *sinthome*, one that can be used to promote freedom by exposing the structure that compels people to impose shame on themselves and others by pursuing pride. The romantic myth of the artist, which Stephen derives in adolescence from Dumas's *The Count of Monte Cristo* and Byron (and which remains fundamental to Joyce's art through the influence of French Symbolism) takes the position of the colonized, the shamed. The Church actually promotes a similar attitude in its own way, for the Jesuits, followers of the "scorned and rejected" Jesus, sometimes saw themselves as a band of outsiders bent on self-mortification.[2] Joyce's reversal of conventional vision as an artist who seeks mortification allows him to focus on the Real so as to see through the system.

Moreover, the opposition between shame and pride is parallel to, and may be the basis of, the traditional distinction between women and men, which yields the shameful pudendum (from Latin *pudere*, "to be ashamed") and the proud phallus. The stereotype of males as active and females as passive tends to make shame appear a feminine feeling; and the title of Toby Olson's novel *The Woman Who Escaped from Shame* implies an accomplishment. Further indication of the gender bearing of shame may be found in *The Mask of Shame*, by Leon Wurmser. Wurmser opposes shame, the feeling of the loser, to guilt, that of the winner (28). Shame is the feeling of someone violated, and guilt, of the violator (62). Wurmser adds that the unconscious "threat implied in" shame is "abandonment," while guilt threatens castration (73). As with hysteria and obsession, which match shame and pride—and which Žižek associates with female and male (*Fragile* 24)—these feelings are obviously both continually active in everyone of both genders.

The traditional double standard produces a situation in which the man feels guilty for cheating and his women feel shamed by his infidelity. Yet to feel guilt does not keep one from feeling contempt. Oppressors may feel that their guilt shows that they have more integrity than their victims. Wurmser quotes Nietzsche's *Beyond Good and Evil*: ["*Wer sich selbst verachtet, achtet sich doch immer noch dabei als verachter*"] "He who has contempt for himself still thereby respects himself as the scorner" (Wurmser 68). This explains and undercuts Joyce's self-condemnation. Shame, on the other hand, is a feeling of lacking integrity, being unable to control oneself.

Tompkins's political model—in which the oppressor's contempt may cause the oppressed to feel either self-contempt or shame—sees self-contempt as the hierarchical reaction and shame as the democratic one: "In a democratically organized society the belief that all men are created equal means that all men are possible objects of identification. When one man expresses contempt for another, the other is more likely to experience shame than self-contempt insofar as the democratic ideal has been internalized. This is because he assumes that ultimately he will wish to commune with this one who is expressing contempt..." (13) Democracy also generates shame among the poor because they are supposed to have a chance to rise, so if they fail, it seems like their fault. Tompkins adds here that in democracy, the oppressor's contempt itself tends to be softened to "empathic shame" or "distress"; so it seems that hierarchy involves contempt and self-contempt, while democracy involves guilt and shame.

Self-contempt may be the more masculine reaction in traditional terms because it cannot be reconciled to the oppressor, whereas shame may correspond to femininity because women have often *had* to be reconciled to oppressive mates. If shame is linked to femininity, then for a man to focus on it is to reverse stereotypes, and Tomkins's editors, Eve Kosofsky Sedgwick and Adam Frank, argue that Tomkins's realistic examination of affects serves to oppose heterosexist views (7). Likewise, Joyce's insistence on the power of shame—in personal development and in social operations—is part of his attack on and reversal of conventional genders and hierarchical ideology. Through Leopold Bloom, he suggests that shame is the key grounding principle in the life of the average man.

"Circe" is organized along what Donald Nathanson calls the shame/pride axis—the interplay of these inseparable feelings (188)—implying that lust involves shame and pride. In the plotline of "Circe," Stephen tries to hold himself aloft with pride—"No, I flew. My foes beneath me" (15.3935)—but ends up causing himself to get knocked down into a shameful position, lying in the gutter. Bloom, on the other hand, sinks into shameful reveries that are probably unconscious—"I rerererepugnosed in rererepugnant..." (3056)—but ends up rising from them to stand in the pride of a paternal position (*U* 15. 4945).

The Gender Economy of Shame

If Stephen and Bloom both encounter shame in "Circe." one reason is that this huge middle episode of *Ulysses* represents the underlying structure of the modern capitalist world; and this vision of a world of prostitution—equating affection with money—reveals that the real currency of society, its actual legal tender, is shame. All exchanges of power, including the use of money, operate in the interface between shame and pride, the place where power interpellates us, calling us toward pride and away from shame—yet sending reverse signals on another level, instituting our shame as the Real contrast to the imaginary ideal. This is why the place of shame is where the action is.

Robert Stoller found by extensive research that thoughts of shame were central to sexual arousal: "all of us...each time we contemplate a sexual event, think about those moments in our childhood lives when we have been traumatized by shame" (paraphrased by Nathanson 285). In the first half of "Circe," Bloom moves toward the realm of shame as he moves toward that of lust, so images of humiliation keep occurring to him. Wurmser says that the power sphere around a person includes an inner limit covering an intimate area that one cannot bear to expose, and that shame threatens to violate this boundary (62). For Bloom and Stephen, it is women who are designated as the violaters of this inner limit, just as Giacomo Joyce sought to expose his shame to Amalia Popper. The thought of violation by men is unbearable to Bloom, so he focuses on such breaches by women. For example, when he considers the embarrassing situation of urinating in a bucket, he imagines a woman present: "Lucky no woman" (15.594). The violation of the inner core by shame is what constitutes that core.

This seems to be an area in which women have power, but like many conventional powers of women, it depends on shame. One reason that it is dangerous for women to see male weakness is that women are repositories for male shame. The traditional sexual paradigm by which the man is supposed to be the victor, and the woman, the vanquished, means that the shame through which both have to get release is projected onto her in many ways, such as through stereotypes of weakness and lust.

In Bloom's case, however, he acknowledges his shame by projecting a series of aggressive women, such as Molly in Turkish trousers, the three society ladies—Mrs. Yelverton Barry, Mrs. Bellingham, and Mrs. Mervyn Talboys—and Bella Cohen. These vixens are all male fantasies, yet some of their assertions may correspond to female awareness For example, when Bella tells Bloom that now he'll find out what it feels like to be treated the way men treat women, she touches on feminist insights: "As they are now so will you be, wigged, singed, perfumesprayed.... You will be laced with cruel force into vicelike corsets..." (15.2974–76). Women are processed by men in ways that disguise and trammel them so as to reconstruct their sensory features.

What these fantasy women suggest to Bloom at the same time that they keep him from perceiving it, is his own need to attack himself, his enjoyment of shame—which is the deepest level of shame, abjection. On this level, there is no self to defend against invasion. The coherence of his subject disintegrates insofar as he realizes his responsibility for his violent fantasies against himself. Part of himself has to resist, to deny his attraction to what debases him. The intensity of his division is the activity of his subject, and is connected to Stephen, for whom he is sacrificing himself by entering Stephen's world—the world of a university student from a higher social class.

Bloom's self-division expresses society's opposition to his freedom, an opposition that he has been socially constructed to internalize. Shepherdson says that the object of desire (*objet a*) for Lacan represents not the deep inner core that it seems to represent, but a surplus effect of symbolization, the level of enjoyment that goes beyond what can be expressed in language. The action of this unattainable surplus charges a need for debasement that seems to lie deeply within because it is concealed by layers of shame; yet it is really an effect of Bloom's being conditioned to deny himself to serve the system of imperialism, to produce pride for others. In *Seminars XVI* and *XVII*, Lacan equates Marx's surplus value with surplus *jouissance* (*Seminar XVII* 19–20). This means, as Bruce Fink explains, that the extra profit that comes from the workers and goes to the capitalists operates as the enjoyment that each person cannot attain because it goes to the Other (Fink 96).

Surplus jouissance also matches a sexual economy in which women produce pleasure more than they get it. As Suzette A. Henke observes, "Molly is convinced that men get more pleasure from sex than do women: 'nice invention they made for women for him to get all the pleasure' (*U* 18: 157)" (Henke 137). The truth in Molly's view is that while women have great capacity for sexual pleasure, they get to realize it much less often than men because intercourse is usually designed for male gratification. What keeps women from being able to claim satisfaction is shame, and shame often accentuates the link between stimulation and degradation.

When Bella Cohen turns into Bello, his ultimate threat is that Bloom wants the abuse offered, that he can be enclosed in a negative stereotype of the woman. Bello insists that Bloom should beg for torture: "Pray for it as you never prayed before" (15.2941). This is the utmost intensification of prayer. Bello's description of the violence done to Bloom is intended to be strangely, disturbingly exciting to Bloom and to the reader. Yet at the same time, this passage is skeptical, a comment on how the object of prayer is submission, and on the seductive power for both genders of domination, behaving like God.

Joyce here brings to the surface a deep inner level of ideological apparatus that uses the femininity which masculinity contains and denies. There is no more crucial function of the state than to make people desire to punish themselves: its other functions may be secondary or disguises.[3] A state that does not use religion or ideology to make people ashamed enough to desire serious pain would have no chance of surviving because it could not motivate people to work hard, not to mention to fight. The paradigm of manhood is shame-driven: it operates to make its partakers seek punishment to avoid the greater shame of losing the coherence of gender/identity.

Men develop by taking on difficulties. The male code is designed to conceal the extent to which this centers on men torturing and humiliating themselves. The suffering of women is more imposed on them, while men choose to embrace hardship more actively, making masculinity the more masochistic gender. Athletic activity, for example, depends on accepting pain, confronting fear, and learning from mistakes. The more aggressive or manly the sport, the more risk and injury it generally involves. There are some natural athletes, but most men push themselves to enhance their masculine images.

An even more paradigmatic scene in which men are obliged to enjoy suffering passionately if they want to succeed is labor. Unlike athletics, work is usually defined negatively as hardship to be gone through, often manifestly degrading. Yet the more one wants to excel in one's work, the more pleasure one must get from it. In fact, the athletic enjoyment of pain is usually a light preparation for the more serious competition of work, playing for keeps. This is like the difference between spanking and the more perverse whipping. Manhood never stops being defined by one's ability to seek suffering in such activities and in the most brutal one of all, war. One of the sharpest spurs of shame that drive these activities is that if one makes oneself suffer so and fails, then it must be because one wants to suffer; and to be good at anything is usually to recognize one's failures continuously. Therefore we should not partition Bloom off into the category of "pervert," but rather see his submerged need to punish himself as an image of the machinery of manhood. Bloom is maladjusted to this regime, but then most men are in one way or another. Although a relatively fine adjustment to manhood is possible, it is tricky: Boylan is well adjusted to the aggressive aspect, but seems to be a mindless brute.

As Bloom's fantasies in "Circe" are not remembered later (Kenner, *Ulysses* 127), they do not seem to be conscious, but rather representations of processes that go on beneath consciousness in his sensitive masculine mind. Bloom has conscious feelings of shame and guilt at being in Nighttown—a name for the realm of desire—but his fantasies enact his subjection as a subject of hierarchical language more radically than any shame he could be conscious of. Wurmser says that the shame we undergo consciously generally serves to conceal a deeper level of shame (50, 56). For example, one may embarrass oneself by being shy because one fears to expose a more terrible shame by communicating.

This deeper level of shame at its terrible root corresponds to Kristeva's idea of abjection. She speaks of the abject as a return to an archaic, pre-objectal mode of relationship from before the child became a subject by separating from the mother (*Powers* 10). In abjection, identity, order, and meaning collapse, so Kristeva links it to heterogeneity and loss (5), making it the opposite of any primal unity. She defines the abject as a level deep in everyone's construction that must be held down by the prohibition and law that maintain form and identity (16). Thus the shame that society imposes serves to keep down abjection, though Shepherdson's Lacanian argument is that the innermost level itself can only ever be perceived as something deposited by social exclusion. So society enforces shame to suppress a deeper shame that it also imposed.

Yet the abject in its incoherence energizes a questioning of established terms. Butler says that one desperately avoids the breakdown of identity and gender because it threatens the subject's existence, but that such disruption should be used "as a critical resource in the struggle to rearticulate the very terms of symbolic legitimacy and intelligibility"—that is, to reconstitute oneself through the approach to abjection (*Bodies* 3). Perhaps Bloom could not redefine himself as ready to confront Stephen's intensity—in the place of abjection where they meet—if the older man did not on some level attack himself in order to release his homosexual (or at least homosocial) potential. Bloom differs from the stereotypical male in being able to use the sensitivity that most men deny, and this difference may be related to his being Jewish. He can make shame a vehicle for regeneration because he is an outsider. He accepts his lack of proper identity, as he shows when he writes "I.... AM. A." on the sand in "Nausicaa," then thinks, "No room. Let it go" (13.1258–65). Bloom's ability to find freedom in humiliation is parallel to Abdul R. JanMohamed's idea of negating the negation, or turning oppression against oppression (285–301). Having lived in a group seen as shameful by the dominant culture, Bloom gains knowledge and strength from his shame, making a *sinthome* out of an ethnically imposed symptom.

The Irish were also defined as racially inferior in Joyce's youth (Cheng 19–47), and the importance of liberation through shame in Joyce's life and work is developed by Frances L. Restuccia in *Joyce and the Law of the Father*. She argues that Joyce had a strong inclination to masochism, a point that Lacan notices (*sinthome* 149), and that he liberates himself and his works from the Law of the Father by taking pleasure from the pain and shame that are supposed to bind him to authority (125–43). She bases this theory on DeLeuze's *Masochism*, but it also fits the idea of the *sinthome*, a voluntary weakness that is liberating, just as Bloom seems ultimately to gain authority in "Circe" by abasing himself.[4]

One of the keys to the use of corporal punishment to debase people is instilling a suspicion on the part of the victim that he desires it sexually. In *Portrait*, the Church's sadist Father Dolan says, "Any boys want flogging here...?" He repeats the word *want* three times, with its undertone that the boys who go wrong are attracted to his abuse (*P* 48–51). Stephen is well aware of the Church's doctrine that sinners seek punishment—"his soul lusted after its own destruction" (*P 104*)—but he weakens the submerged grip of this doctrine by frankly accepting it. Lacan shares with Freud the belief that masochism is primary and that sadism is a reaction against it (Lacan, *Four* 185–86)

When Bella encounters Bloom, he imagines her fan as recognizing that he is shamefully deficient: "...the missus is master." (15. 2759). The fan invades Bloom's boundary not only by claiming to know his inside feelings, but by asking him a question that men typically ask women to seduce them, haven't we met before? The gesture of the fan says, "Have you forgotten me?" (2764). As they have not met, the fan is claiming something in Bloom's mind that he does not remember, acting as the Real questioning his knowledge. The sequence that follows indicates that in effect they have met, for the fan has a grip on Bloom, interpellating him in regard not only to gender, but to class.

Bloom immediately loses the ability to make distinctions: "Nes. Yo" (2766), and as his boundaries disintegrate, the fan speaks with an extreme breakdown of syntax that anticipates the *Wake*: "Is me her was you dreamed before? Was then she him you us since knew? Am all them and the same now me?" (2768–69). That Bloom hears such nonsense is a sign of the power he projects on Bella: the power of the Other to speak for the Real by disintegrating language and identity, decomposing the discrete boundary of the signifying unit. While the disordering of these lines allows an excess of interpretations, the main theme of the lines may be the breakdown or rescrambling of identity, including the following suggestions: 'I'm the one you dreamed of, the one you knew. This one you dreamed of was really a male ('Was then she him'). I'm you and we're all me." The ability to pass out of oneself in passion is here linked to and perhaps based on the ability to pass out of one's stereotypical gender role. Yet Bella's garbled message claims Bloom's allegiance, and after disintegrating his identity, she will soon try to enclose him in a severely restrictive role.

It may be helpful to remember here that it has usually been recognized in the West that a man smitten with passion plays a feminine role. Passion, the passive opposite of action, was most often represented as being shot with Cupid's arrow. Yet Joyce's shameful interior exposure of lust goes far beyond conventions to undermine the genders by reversal, and to suggest a hidden power of woman that has to be represented as male. One main thrust here is the insertion of Bella's identity into Bloom, a pattern found in men's traditional authority over women (changing their views) and in the sadist's relation to the masochist. Having the frontiers of his male rational construct dissolved, Bloom gives himself a new form in a shameful, passive position as he replies, "Powerful being" (2772).

Kristeva says, "Abjection appears as a rite of defilement and pollution in...societies with a dominant or surviving matrilineal character" (*Powers* 17). Both Bloom and Bella are Jewish, and while Judaism is highly patriarchal, it is matrilinear, for one is a Jew if one's mother was. Such archaic, matriarchal rites of defilement would seem to be represented by the figure of Circe in the *Odyssey*, who magically debases men. Samuel Butler, in *The Authoress of the Odyssey* (1902), which Joyce used, sees Circe as a feminist figure. Butler points out that she had no male servants, implying that she lived in a community of women (107). And he says that Circe is as great a prophet as Tiresias, the greatest ancient male (nominally) prophet: "...a writer who was less desirous of making out that woman know as much as men would not have made Circe know quite so much" (149). Joyce may have seen Circe—not just Bella, but the spirit of Nighttown, with its most vital aspect represented by Zoe Higgins—as an image of the power of women to reshape men. This would be supported by both Butlers, for Judith sees gender identity as unstable or even shapable because it is performed (*Psychic* 132–50).

As he heads for the brothel, Stephen says of the prostitute he seeks (and does not find), "*Ad deam qui laetificat iuventutem meam*" (15.122). This substitutes the female *deam* for the male *deum* of the liturgy: "To goddess who made glad my young days." His quotation from the mass implies that the sex act will be a eucharist. He also speaks of "*aquam egredientem de templo*" (13.77), or "water coming from the temple." In the mass, this refers to sprinkling the alter, but for Stephen, it may mean that he hopes to get a prostitute to pee for him. Both Stephen and Bloom are headed for versions of the goddess in Nighttown, but both goddesses are corrupted by patriarchy. The central version of Bloom's goddess/goal, Bella, is loaded with fetishes, such as fan, cigar, and whip, all of which tempt Bloom. One of the most intense of the fantasy sensations that he calls forth comes from the cigar in his ear (15.2936), a paternal image imposed on his reception.

Although Bloom accepts the fetishism that gives woman phallic power, Stephen's version of the goddess, his mother, is castrated, missing her nose, her eyes, and her teeth (15.4159–61), and Stephen is absolutely horrified at the thought that she might touch him because her touch represents paternal authority: she says, "Beware God's hand!" (15. 4219). While Bloom gains strength from his contact with the degrading maternal principle, Stephen seems more in touch with reality: he realizes that the goddess of desire is a commodity, serving patriarchy and capitalism.

Shame as Business

Although Nighttown could offer the oppositional view of the abject, it is, like Circe's palace in Homer, a trap for those who do not take it skeptically. The abject may lead to transformation, but to accept the Real of shame allows others to be privileged. Any interpretation of Joyce is, like truth for Lacan, only part of the truth. If we turn from the power of the whore-goddess to her injury, we can see how she serves authority, how the enslavement she imposes on Bloom represents his position in society.

When Bella's fan hails Bloom, the feeling it gives him that they have met before corresponds to the sense of having always belonged that ideology gives the subject. Louis Althusser says, "ideology has always-already interpellated individuals as subjects" (302) and when it claims them, it controls their entire environment, as Bella does with Bloom. The force that Bella/Bello uses to reduce Bloom to submission has to be seen as made up of social codes, for the idea of dominance has always been built on class structure, as is indicated by the aristocratic status not only of

Bloom's trio of imaginary society ladies, but of the Marquis de Sade. I have pointed out that Bella/Bello bears images of capitalism, such as the "Stock Exchange cigar" that has such an effect on Bloom (15.2897), and Bello's references to rich friends and financial deals ("Social" 22). Enda Duffy covers this aspect of "Circe" well in *The Subaltern* Ulysses, seeing Bella as a "late capitalist Brittannia" (155–58).

That Bello is the strongest object of Bloom's lust indicates the basic truth behind prostitution as the fundamental organization of capitalist economy. The desire expressed by buying sex is aimed at the Father as Capital, enacting Lacan's principle that the sons who are deprived of women love the father (*sinthome* 150). The prostitute belongs to the business, not to the man who has to pay for her, and the fact that he has to pay makes the situation humiliating to him no matter how he may assert himself. Moreover, this can be extended to marriage insofar as it is a system in which women sell themselves, converting enjoyment into profit.

The Bello (Latin "war") that replaces Bella is the threat behind beauty, and as Bloom looks into Bella's eyes and sees her change into Bello (sees the threat under the surface), Bloom mumbles, "Awaiting your further orders we remain, gentlemen...." (15.2833), eager to be commanded by orders from men, as a good worker should be. Before this, he had taken the role of tying her shoes, which was related to a job he had once considered as a "shoefitter in Manfield's" (15.2813). The language of business that he slips into as Bella changes has to be seen as a language of humiliation, for his marathon of shame in "Circe" bristles with references to all aspects of the social machinery that oppresses him. In the following sentence, for example, Bello uses British idioms, for Gifford and Seidman point out that "Kentucky cocktails" is an English term for cocktails, and "old son" also sounds English: "I'll bet Kentucky cocktails all around I shame it out of you, old son" (15.2867–68). An "old son" is someone who has taken on years without manhood. What Bello will shame out of Bloom is not clear—leaving Bloom to wonder what he has inside that shame will reveal—but it is something like the truth that Bloom is not a man. In any case, Bello claims that he will win the contest by shaming Bloom. This model of exchange is basic to patriarchal intercourse on all levels in that one party takes manhood from the other by imposing shame (*pudor*) on "her." The fine points of management may ameliorate such submission by allowing the worker to share the victory of the group.

Another aspect of the exchange of shame is indicated through Gibson's sharp analysis of colonialism in *Joyce's Revenge*. Gibson says that in Bloomsday Dublin most people are perpetually struggling to try to get an advantage over others (87–88): "In a culture intrinsically so perverted, the spectre of misery is never far off. Gaining or sustaining advantage may often merely mean avoiding brutalization... maintaining sufficient face to function" (91). He then says that in "Wandering Rocks," these advantages "are either depressingly mean, or exist only in fantasy" (92). The dispossession—which corresponds to Odysseus' exile—makes the culture "pathological and extreme" (93), and imperialism results in a "false community...whose determining condition is complicity" (94).

The ways in which people are compromised by imperialism are not far for Joyce from how they are compromised by capitalism; in fact, he may see the two as inseparable. In the *Dubliners* story "Counterparts," the boss, Mr. Alleyne, has a "North of Ireland accent" (*D* 86), so the capitalist master is from a privileged ethnic group, as they often are. Alleyne enjoys abusing Farrington regularly, so one reason Farrington cannot do his dull work is that work itself is a humiliation when done for such a boss. Adam Smith, the primary supporter of capitalism, says in *The Wealth of Nations* (1776) that "The value of any commodity...To the person who possesses it...is equal to the quantity of labor which it enables him to purchase or command" (85). So the real measure of wealth is how much it can make people suffer. "Circe" reveals that Bloom has underlying fantasies of being tormented by upper-class people because the upper classes humiliate those beneath them incessantly—and enjoy it—simply by occupying their positions; and especially by taking pride in their positions, which automatically entails shame to their "inferiors." Significantly, we use the same word for beating someone in a competition that we use for corporal beating. The discrimination between classes is equal to the shame that separates one signifier from the other, and the Real of shame opens consciousness for the lower classes that is then appropriated on the Imaginary level by the rich.

A concrete illustration of social status in itself as physical abuse appears in Dickens's *Great Expectations* (1861). Joyce's 1912 essay "The Centenary of Charles Dickens" decries Dickens's sentimentality, but praises him as "the great Cockney" (*Occasional* 185) who developed the lower classes for the English novel. In Dickens's study of class divisions, when Pip appears in his new position of wealth, the insolent proletarian Trabb's boy exercises his subaltern mockery by being knocked off his feet by Pip's status: "...I saw him collapse...and my first decided experience of the stupendous power of money, was, that it had morally laid upon his back, Trabb's boy" (Dickens 119). Later this youth acts out "a paroxysm of terror" at Pip's elegance, staggering, suffering, and begging for mercy in front of a crowd of poor people, who react with "the greatest joy" (Dickens 188). Trabb's boy makes clear the violence that is always going on beneath the surface between the rich and the poor, as well as between colonizers and colonized—just as the society ladies in "Circe" bring out what is implied when Bloom is attracted to a carriage riding "haughty" lady in "Lotus Eaters" (5.103), a lady of whom he is aware that she would probably find him odious both because he lacks class and because he is

Jewish. Pip's love for Estella shows how the status of ideal beauty often involves men in fantasies about women who are bound to be disdainful to them. But the major embodiment of class abuse is labor, and Trabb's boy works for Pip's tailor Trabb, so the boy's defiance is spurred by the fact that his job is to serve Pip. Of course, Trabb's boy is shameless, but this is because he is already subjected to a structural position of shame.

A major part of Bloom's work, arguably the main part, consists of shaming himself. In "Aeolus," when we see him doing his job, the journalists he deals with treat him with condescension. On the page of "Aeolus" after the section called "*WE SEE THE CANVASSER AT WORK*," Bloom stands in front of Joseph Nannetti's desk hoping that the foreman will explain more about the high terms that he has set for Bloom's ad. Nannetti scratches himself in Bloom's presence and does other work while Bloom waits (7.162), so Bloom recalls here how he was snubbed earlier by John Henry Menton (7. 171–73). Bloom's hardest work here may be putting up with hints of contempt.

Bloom is also obliged in this episode to pursue the editor Myles Crawford to ask for approval of an ad for his client Alexander Keyes. When Bloom says, "What will I tell him Mr Crawford?" Crawford says, "Will you tell him he can kiss my arse?" (7.981). This touchy reply is the occasion for Bloom's outstanding opportunity of the day to show his mettle as a canvasser (a title that suggests someone knocked down in boxing). It is the trickiest and therefore most definitive point of Bloom's craft. And Bloom passes the crucial test, doing his job well by continuing to supplicate Crawford until he gets a more detailed answer: "He can kiss my royal Irish arse, Myles Crawford cried loudly over his shoulder. Any time he likes, tell him" (7.991–92). In response to this answer that Crawford makes with his back to Bloom, "Mr Bloom stood weighing the point and about to smile."

It is no coincidence that Bloom's most intimate sexual act of the day is kissing his wife's unfaithful rear end. He has a policy of putting up with abuse from people. When Menton earlier responded to Bloom's effort to be helpful by treating Bloom coldly in "Hades," Bloom thought, "Never mind. Be sorry after perhaps when it dawns on him. Get the pull over him that way" (6.1031). Bloom's ability to take humiliation is essential to maintaining his position, especially since he is a Jew dealing with Christians. Crawford may not be competent, but his position as editor seems to involve a great deal of self- assertion, so that arrogance may be a more important qualification for his job than journalistic skills. Aggressiveness can make him a strong administrator who takes command, and it also makes him quite funny. It is better for Bloom to accommodate Crawford's derisive scorn, for if Bloom loses his temper, he will lose the business connection. While all such situations involve economic factors, such factors are generally shaped by impulses of self-assertion, which often take priority over any approach to pure economic interests. As Tomkins indicates, such pride always involves administering shame.

All workers tend to represent the lower classes in relation to bosses who tend to represent the upper ones. Stephen, who is higher on the Dublin social scale than Bloom, is still an impoverished Catholic working for a conservative Protestant. One of the hardest parts of his job is putting up not only with Deasy's smugness, but with the disdain of his students, whose families have more money than his has: "In a moment they will laugh more loudly, aware of my lack of rule and of the fees their papas pay " (2.28–39).

That Bloom is a Jew representing a Jewish client to Christians with powerful positions means that he is successful, for he is in contact with a higher echelon, and this increases the shame he has to endure. He might try to advance himself by self-assertion like Crawford, but this would be hard for a Jew to accomplish—there was a stereotype of Jews as "pushy," as there was one for lower class people in general— and if he did it, Joyce might not respect him. The kind of sarcastic humor that Crawford uses allows him to set himself on a higher level, and it may be that to fill their roles with distinction, the upper classes should enjoy the cruelty that is implicit in asserting their superiority. Mr. Alleyne likewise uses sarcasm in "Counterparts": "*—You—know—nothing.* Of course you know nothing. . . . Do you think me an utter fool?" (*D* 91). A more refined aristocrat may conceal his superiority behind politeness, noblesse oblige, or even kindness; but the cruelty might still be implicit, and enjoyed, within the superiority. Sarcasm similar to Crawford's, used by someone on the lower side of the social divide, takes a different nature. It may be almost tragically self-destructive—like Farrington's: "—I don't think, sir, he said, that that's a fair question to put to me" (*D* 91). Farrington's irony is actually more subtle than those of the bosses, but it takes a raw quality from its rebellious context, while it is largely deprived of its cruelty. The same language changes on different social levels, and is more abusive coming from the higher side of the flow of power, so that cruelty flows from top to bottom, as "Counterparts" illustrates.

If being humiliated is the most difficult and crucial part of Bloom's job, then it is what he really does for a living, and he may represent the majority in this regard. Joyce recognizes an economy of shame in which embarrassment is the main role people play. In effect, this is the world's greatest industry—the production of pride or status for a few through the expenditure of shame by the many. Those who are unemployable are often those who are too proud to take orders, like Farrington. A worker is a repository for his boss's shame, as a woman is a repository for a man's, a Jew for a Christian's, or a black person for a white's. The *Wake* uses the phrase "every Klitty of a scolderymeid" (239.18) to refer to young women in a general way. A scolderymaid, as my student Siphokazi

Koyana pointed out, is a maid whose principle duty is to be scolded; and Joyce recognized that this was an important role for many maids and women.

When Bloom speaks of himself collectively in "Awaiting your further orders we remain, gentlemen," his subservience stirs Bello to a new level of brutality: "Hound of dishonour!" (15. 2835). Mark Osteen points out that in "Circe" sadomasochism involves an implicit contract in which the two parties agree to play certain roles (330). So the form of this sexual practice is the form of business, but that is true of prostitution generally, and of many other sexual activities. Bloom's line—taking the tone of a petty clerk trying to sound respectable, but ending up servile—is effective in a negative way. It disintegrates Bloom's identity by showing his effort to be respectable as a collapsing façade, a clown's breakaway jacket. So it succeeds in its aim of stirring the Other it projects (while Bella merely stands there) to stimulate his shame more intensely. Joyce portrays the moment in which Bloom's sexual desire is swelling as one in which his well-being and the reality and the gender of his object are insignificant compared to the ideological apparatus of powerplay that supports that desire. This shows how desire consists of the exchange of pride and shame. In Lacanian terms, if pride tries to stay in the Imaginary, while shame falls into the Real, and if desire always requires shame, then Bloom's hallucinations may represent the unconscious underside of masculinity. Consciously, Bloom may only know that he feels desire, but unconsciously he is overwhelmed by the object. Insofar as Bloom approaches consciousness of this, his awareness of his passivity, a passivity which is certainly at the heart of his moral sensitivity, also gives him access to a strong, comprehensive field of social criticism.

Bloom's quest for shame is a way of seizing the attack of society in order to use it for liberation. He turns his victimization by social forces into a demand of his own that gives him his best chance to know and change himself. His marriage is as much based on his drive toward shame as are his job and his sexuality. His main action toward Molly on Bloomsday is to give her away, and this gives her freedom and consciousness. Through his cultivation of shame, Bloom participates in and disseminates (to Stephen and Molly) the Joycean project of self-regeneration announced by the ur-Bloom Richard Rowan in *Exiles*: "To be forever a shameful creature and to build up my soul again out of the ruins of its shame" (*E* 70). This process includes both the skeptical and the sentimental sides of Joyce's works: it suspends fictional phenomena between them.

The choice of shame, shame's choice of self-development through abjection, is the main, perhaps the only action of Joyce's protagonists: they either accept shame as a *sintome* and expand or refuse shame as unbearable and are paralyzed. This is true of all of the paralyzed figures in *Dubliners* and of the few who may be capable of change, such as the hero of "Araby" and Gabriel Conroy. It is true also of Stephen, Rowan, Bloom, Molly, ALP, her daughter Iseult, and Shem, the shameful part of HCE that is capable of change.[5] Yet this choice is highlighted against an ordinary world in which people consciously strive to reject shame. Indeed, one cannot consciously *choose* shame, for it engages its shamefulness by being denied. This makes "shame's choice" a sharp name for Joyce because it is so rare for people to choose it.[6] The appropriation of shame that leads to psychosexual progress and sociocritical acuity may be accomplished as unconsciously as the fantasies of debasement that lead Bloom to be ready to help Stephen at the end of "Circe." It is the far from rational drive toward the Real as a *sinthome* of concern for the afflictions of others that leads Bloom to follow Stephen to Nighttown.

In the conscious world, shame is taken by the loser, who feels it keenly, often to the point of hysteria, and given by the winner to avoid feeling it by obsessive methodology. Those who succeed best in this world are shameless people such as Donald Trump. Whatever else workers or women do, their indispensable function is usually to be susceptible to shaming. Miller sees that "[m]aking ashamed is an effort to reinstate the agency of the master signifier" (23); which is to say that those in power can only derive their importance from humiliating others. There are many other factors involved in exchanges between people, but pride and shame tend to control those forces under most conditions, often invisibly. In business terms, pride and shame constitute the bottom line.

Žižek frames the relation of economy to shame by pointing out that economy and politics form a parallax so that "the specific sphere of economic (re)production emerges only if we methodologically bracket the concrete existence of state and political ideology . . . " (*PV* 56). That is, the field of economics can only be seen as independent by putting in brackets or eliding the state's power to control people, so that emphasis on economic terms conceals dominance. Such emphasis may assume that all agents of trade are equal, whereas those on the upper level have unfair advantages. Stephen says, "A merchant . . . is one who buys cheap and sells dear . . . " (*U* 2.359). Anyone who does not manage this is an unsuccessful merchant. The dominant class exists insofar as it controls exchange so that it makes profit.

If one is lower on the scale, one is more likely to pay more for less: poor people don't know how to save, they can't buy in quantity, they rent on short terms, and they lack the education to see through deceptive advertising. Under such conditions, their part in economic exchange is often a shameful one in which they are abused, so that the sadomasochism of Nighttown is a model of the market. To derive satisfaction from the choices one makes as a consumer becomes increasingly masochistic the less money one has, as one has to get gratification out of being mistreated.

The same is true of cultural and emotional capital: the poor give more feeling, more attention and adoration to the rich, whose status makes them attractive and powerful stars, while the rich care less for the poor, who are easily manipulateded, eager to please, vulgar, or coarse because their feelings are strong, unaware of the subtleties of control.

One's economic situation organizes one's mentality, and in this base and superstructure model, if pride and shame dictate economic realities, they must also dictate intellectual ones. This sensible motivation is mapped out in Lacan's somewhat histrionic revolutionary analysis of the relation between power and knowledge in *Seminar XVII: The Other Side of Psychoanalysis*. Here Lacan argues that all knowledge originates in slaves, and that philosophy has been a system to transmute knowledge so that it appears to belong to the masters: "What does philosophy designate over its entire evolution? It's this—theft, abduction, stealing slavery of its knowledge through the maneuvers of the master" (21). The slave is in touch with reality and has a language of the Real—whether threatening or attractive—while the master uses the Imaginary, a register that is infantile enough to believe that it can control reality or make reality a slave to language, entirely determined by it. This is the imperative to clarity that Joyce fights relentlessly.

In "Circe" Bloom sees the actual operation of the power system of modern society, and this may help him to resist Bella when he recovers himself (15.3479–4306), but he cannot sustain his awareness of this system, for it is wiped out of his mind—probably before it enters consciousness, while it is merely an impression—by shame that works for the system of thought control. Meanwhile, the possessors of power, such as Bello and Boylan, are the ones who have the knowledge that claims consciousness by controlling reality. Bello claims the knowledge to control the market, for her customers include big investors (15. 2932–35); and Blazes, a successful businessman, has the knowledge to control women, the chief product on the market, according to Levi-Strauss. The power they claim is built upon the suffering and mental deprivation of people like Bloom, who carry this dramatic system of accusation that surrounds desire—"Circe"—built into them.

So insofar as Bello and Boylan stand for the rulers of the world, they define and possess the value of Bloom's mental labor. A significant example is the fact that Bloom buys his pornography from England (17.1809–13). If Little Chandler in "A Little Cloud" felt that Dublin was timid sexually in comparison to the major capitals where power and sexual license resided (*D* 78–82), then Bloom's English purchase has him paying the empire to represent manhood for him. This is to defeat him by removing him from his identity, shifting him into the Imaginary level because reality is so unmanageable that one must escape it. In so doing, it allows him to fantasize that he has access to the Imaginary level of the rulers. In this area, in Lacan's terms, he has no access to the woman, so he gives his devotion to the Father. The Imaginary works one way for those on top who get to secure it and another for those on the bottom who have to purchase it as an unstable illusion. The system that defeats Bloom continues to enforce its clear commands as the source of clarity. It builds its pride on his shame by finding that as a Jew, and as a humble person, he does not fill its prescription correctly; he must be punished, an ongoing unconscious punishment that is temporarily unveiled in "Circe."

Lacan says that knowledge arises when the signifier comes to represent something (*Other* 13). This is an operation controlled by the Name of the Father, a linguistic version of the phallus, which claims to signify or attach the signifier to the signified, Lacan's continuous basic position that the signifier cannot be attached to the signified aims to expose the claims that make up the world of clear language, the world of official knowledge that can only be denied at one's own risk. Bloom, having sacrificed himself for his wife more than usual, is impelled into contact with the Real of his attraction to what hurts him, a vision that cannot be seen, but exfoliates below consciousness. The Real is frightening in Lacan and even moreso in Žižek, but without contact with the Real, one stagnates, and with it one confronts social reality.

In "Circe," Joyce insists on revealing the actual forces involved in human interchange on the erotic, commercial, and intellectual levels. If he is right, then efforts to reform society must take this powerful and ubiquitous operation as central. As Žižek puts it, a truly radical critique must go beyond ideology as discursive formation to engage its fantasy support; for otherwise despite variations in symbolic formation, the underlying framework persists (*Tarrying* 213). The origin of this fantasy structure in the division between genders is explored through the foundational myth of the *Wake*. While proofreading this book, I read the last chapter of *Seminar XVII*, which concludes that the other side of psychoanalysis should be developed by concentrating on shame instead of avoiding it. Lacan links shame to the Real here (180), and calls shame "the hole from which the master signifier arises" (189). He also says, "production is one essential point of the system—the production of shame" (190), so he seems to have anticipated my argument in the present chapter, which was influenced by studying Lacan.

Part III

Finnegans Wake *as the World*

Chapter 9

Reality as Fetish: The Crime in Finnegans Wake

The Scene of Fetishism

Joyce agreed with Lacan that the most solid, firmly fixed forms of the reality that we live in are made up of fetishes, a notion that is well supported by Marx's idea of the commodity as fetish. Fetishism generates the commodity forms of property; and the obsession with property accompanies and may constitute realism in fiction or fact—reality as a system of control. The steps by which fetishism comes to operate the commodity may be elucidated by psychoanalytic theory. Freud's 1927 paper "Fetishism" sees the fetish as a substitute for the lost phallus of the mother, a fascination contracted when the child first realizes that its mother is supposed to lack this symbolic component (*SE* XXI. 152–59)—when it first "sees" or visualizes her genitals. Lacan defines the phallus not as a bodily organ, but as a symbol of the power to signify, which can be possessed by either gender (*Écrits* 581). In this respect, the phallus is inanimate, so it may itself be regarded as a fetish, an uncanny but attractive mask over a gap, based on fear of castration. A fetish is the absence of a phallus turned into its presence, shame (*pudor*) turned to pride.

Moreover, by considering Irigaray's feminist critique of Lacan, it may be argued that the creation of the fetish is the creation of the phallus, and that this creation involves extracting from the mother something she possessed only figuratively, stealing a figure of speech. For Lacan agrees with Freud that in early childhood, "both sexes consider the mother to be endowed with a phallus..." (*Écrits* 576), and because the phallus is a symbol, not an organ, one need not be a man to wield it. Indeed, mother stands as the original possessor of the phallus for both genders, and remains the source of it in the sense that it is obtained through her. The phallus remains attached to the mother, and her equivocal connection to it provides indications of how feminine sexuality, as Lacan argues in *Encore,* can go beyond the phallic (76–77).

The phallus that is derived from the mother is used to create masculinity, the father, and the law. And the Symbolic system that promotes this trio remains predicated on this imaginary excision, so it has the instability of a system based on the seizing of something whose origin it denies. If the phallus is the power to signify, then the women from whom it was derived are continually threatening to reclaim it in their own form. On the level of language (Lyotard's language), the phrases that have been deprived of the power to signify threaten to take that power over; and this model extends from women to other dispossessed groups, so it can clarify Joyce's relation to the proletariat and to "minorities," especially non-Europeans. Joyce's most admired character, Bloom, is not of European ancestry, though he often thinks he is, and I argue that the creative wing of the family in the *Wake* is not white. They speak for the disadvantaged of the world and for the fact that their disadvantage is a matter of category rather than their nature, as is true of the human patterns run through by all of the figures in the *Wake*.

Joyce's recognition of the excluded powers of language allows him to reach outside Europe to address the world from a new post-Western perspective. He can expand into this global viewpoint by seeing through the crime of imperialism, creating a world by confronting a crime. Imperialism parallels fetishism by taking status and authority from those who are supposed never to have had it. James S. Atherton points out in *The Books at the Wake* that one of the fundamental principles of the *Wake*, derived from Vico, is that creation depends on original sin (31–32). Original sin tends to equal the sin of originality that Milton's Satan offers Eve, the assumption of divine power: "ye should be as Gods..." (*PL* 9.710). To explore beyond existing limits, the Joycean artist must take on the creative power of God, and this entails the crime of killing Him. Likewise, masculinity involves taking the divine power of domination from women, who are seen by Lacan as possessing it even though they are officially supposed to be subordinate. The recognition that divine power is stolen and belongs to underdogs turns that power to liberating uses, so that the Joycean deity is only creative insofar as (s)he creates freedom.

The Crime of Creation

The Joycean world is founded on the crime of the artist who takes upon himself the power of the Creator. A psychoanalytic version of the creation of the human world through crime that Joyce uses prominently in the *Wake* is Freud's *Totem and Taboo* (1913), in which civilization begins with the killing of the primal father by his sons.[1] This creation through patricide is presented as about to happen on the first page of the *Wake*: "not yet...had a kidscad buttended a bland old Isaac" (*FW* 3.11). The act in which the son butted (in the butt) the father out of his position and pretended ("buttended") to be him would in Freud's model turn the father into an abstraction by destroying him, setting fire to him, creating God as a distant voice, "avoice from afire" (3.9), or afar.

The turning of the father into the Other creates what Martin Buber calls the I-Thou relationship in *I and Thou* (1923), the link between man and God. Buber says that "the primary word I-Thou" is the basis of all other relationships (Buber 870): "nor avoice from afire bellowsed mishe mishe to tauftauf thuartpeatrick" (*FW* 3.9–10). Roland McHugh's *Annotations* say that *mise is* Irish for "me,"[2] but another reading appears in Joyce's letter to Harriet Shaw Weaver of November 15, 1926, where he says, "Mishe=I am (Irish)" (*SL* 316). McHugh's gloss is valid not only because Joyce may have known this English meaning for "Mishe," but because the Irish word sounds like "me." Changing Buber's "I" to "me" may be implying that the subject is an object. But Joyce's reading, "I am," is rather Lacanian in that it sees the subject as a signifier defined by its relation to the Other, so that it tends to say, "I am…Thou." The "mishe-tauf" motif recurs fifty times (Hart, *Structure* 222–23), and the next version makes it relatively clear that the Me-Thou relationship is the foundation of the world: "Can you rede (since We and Thou had it out already) its world?" (18.19). I believe that Joyce knew of Buber's most famous book,[3] and in a later scene of a son killing a father figure, the son is described as "bubbering" (344.29).

Actually, because McHugh didn't realize the "Me-Thou" level of the motif, he missed its powerful recurrence at the very end of the *Wake*: "mememormee! Till thousendsthee" (628.14–15). This line includes the idea that I will keep expanding myself until I elicit a response from the intimacy of the Other ("till thou sends thee"), though it take thousands of years. This example connects the motif to exploration and suggests that more instances of it could be found. It works nicely with Dirk Van Hulle's identification of ALP with language itself ("The Lost Word," Crispi and Slote 452) to link the *Wake* to both language expanding toward the Other and ALP swelling her double bosom ("meme") to sigh.

If the I am-Thou relationship is initially based in Freudian terms on the murder of the father, there is a passage later in the first chapter in which the sons urge the father to stay asleep because his waking would discompose their world: "Now be aisy, good Mr Finnimore, sir. And take your laysure like a god on pension and don't be walking abroad" (24.16–17). As "aisy." he is supposed to remain Alpha and Omega (A and Z) or Asia, at the limits of ordinary consciousness or at a distance. But before the *Wake* is over, Asia will awaken.

The founding crime of the *Wake* combines the patricide of *Totem and Taboo* with the origin of fetishism in seeing the mother's nakedness (too too exposed by a very short ballet skirt), "her *totam in tutu*" (*FW* 397.32). The word *totam* reminds us that the totem is the dead (German *tot*) body of the father. One generally implies the other in the *Wake* because to see the mother sexually implies attacking the father, while attacks on him aim at her. Seeing the mother's totemic totality constitutes the origin of the world, so that the geometrical diagram of ALP's genitals presented in the Lessons Chapter is the goal of all knowledge and answers the question of where we come from (*FW* 393). In Lacan's terms, this is *objet a*, the object-cause of desire, belief in the mother's castration as potent.

The new order is founded on an oedipal transgression that must be denied to claim legitimacy. Shepherdson argues that Lacan realized that by moving from the Oedipus myth to the later phase of *Totem and Taboo*, Freud advanced into a more radical conception; this is because while both myths see society as founded on patricide motivated by desire for the women possessed by the fathers, Oedipus achieves a resolution at Colonus,[4] while *Totem* leaves society haunted by unresolved guilt, recognizing that the paternal Symbolic order is inherently flawed (*Vital* 133–48).

All orderly systems may derive their power to signify by filching (or secretly stealing) it from subordinates, as Toni Morrison maintains that white Americans developed their sense of freedom through the use of a captive Afro-American population (*Playing* 44–46). This is one reason that such systems need policing to maintain stability. Žižek sees the cause of any symbolic system as a traumatic kernel or gap in the system that it is built around and that it denies (*Metastases* 30–31). Jameson (following Althusser) maintains that any historical system requires a center that is not subject to history, an "absent cause" (*Political* 36).

Žižek argues that allegiance to a community always involves a "fetish" that functions to disavow its founding crime (or moral gap). He cites the Soviet fetish of the New Man, which served to deny the Gulags, and the American fetish of the space for everyone to be free, which denies what was done to natives and minorities (*Metastases* 57–58). The constitutive crime generally involves taking the homeland away from those who used to possess her, whether by revolution or conquest. Žižek's sublime object of ideology is a fetish, and the most extensive ideology of history is produced by the most extensive crime, with the most phallic of all fetishes. This is patriarchy, practiced by men who began by overthrowing the early dominance of their mothers. As Eagleton puts it, "there was no time in history at which a good half of the human race had not been banished and subjected as a defective being, an alien inferior" (*Literary* 129). Irigaray argues that the systems that make up the patriarchal world in which we live are founded on denying the active wills of women. In this area the infantile sexual origin of the fetish is prominent.

Woman is conceptualized as lacking the phallus by the same process that conceives the father as having it. For Irigaray, the separation of women from the power to signify is what establishes the male symbolic social order (189), an order that defines things clearly by positing the phallus as the center of determinate meaning. This installation of the phallic signifier, the moment when the signifier takes on meaning, is enacted by the primordial scene of the crime in the Phoenix Park in the *Wake*. Joyce represents this scene as the basis of the subject (HCE) and of civilization. To see how fully the scene enacts fetishism, I will refer to an article that Lacan wrote with Wladimir Granoff in 1956: "Fetishism: The Symbolic, the Imaginary and the Real."

The Scene in the Park

In the scene in the park, which recurs scores of times and is associated with the Fall in Eden, HCE is doing something illicit with two women, usually watching them urinating. Joyce, in a lost letter to Gertrude Kaempffer, said that his first sexual experience with another person took place when his nanny stepped into the bushes to urinate and the fourteen-year-old Joyce was excited by the sound and masturbated (*JJ* 418). The *Wake* scene is usually completed by three soldiers, who spy on HCE in the act, shame him, and later spread pernicious gossip. They stand for the shame that is requisite to the act, and for the way that the act is constrained and supported by patriarchal authority. It presumably cannot be done without them. In fact, Ellmann reports that Joyce wrote to Kaempffer that "he found it particularly provocative, when lying with a woman, to be afraid of being discovered" (*JJ* 419). This is an elaboration of Stephen's situation of having a threatening man behind him and an attractive woman in front as he enacts his manhood (*P* 100). Because they are attacking HCE for seeing the woman's body, they attack him for taking the paternal position. Like Oedipus, he started as a son, but once the crime is committed, he becomes a father.

The scene appears in scores of versions, with a wide variety of actions and identities implied, and is equivalent to other scenes, perhaps all other scenes since it is the institution of consciousness. It energetically illustrates how phrases from different parts of the *Wake* connect with each other. In its main form, it generally involves two women and three soldiers, so that the conjunction of two and three tends to stand for the scene: "Or whatever it was they threed to make out he thried to two in the Fiendish park" (196.9–11). In this sentence, threeing is believing, as in the ancient tradition that three witnesses prove something true. Webster's Third says that *testify* and *testament* are derived from prehistoric Italic *tres* and *stare*, meaning to stand as three. As a verb, *threed* represents the constitution of the male authority to see something with certainty; yet it is based on *tried*, so it undercuts itself from its inception. Indeed the lines are a mockery of such authority, for Joyce presents the gossip about HCE as proliferating in a haphazard and grotesquely unreliable manner. This bizarre contagion of rumor appears primarily in the second chapter (38–47), but all of the *Wake* is the distorted story of the fall of HCE, as the first page announces (3.16–25). The strong association of the park scene with the Fall suggests that the character assassination of HCE that results from the scene makes it in effect the long-range cause of his death.

HCE's death, however, starts with his birth, and the scene incorporates male consciousness itself as guilt, HCE as "*He Can Explain*" (105.14). Many of the definitions of HCE in the Riddles Chapter (I.6, or book I, Chapter 6) present subjectivity formed by the female attraction in front and the male threat behind: "light leg lifters cense him souriantes from afore while boor browbenders curse him grommelants to his hindmost" (130.1–3). The word "while" suggests that the smiling chorus girls (McHugh) who incense him and the frownbrowed grumblers who threaten his rear end are parts of one action, parallel to the suspension of Joyce's narratives between idealism or sentiment and skepticism. They are as closely linked as the past that drives the present into the future "betwixt yesterdicks and twomaries" (126.18), the external male sex organs as detectives pushing the subject—in a state of division between two genders—toward the female organs (maries). He is both advancing into phallic power and retreating in shame like a woman, so he is both exposing himself and concealing himself: "shows he's fly to both demisfairs but thries to cover up his tracers" (129.20–21). In revealing his uplift to her breasts, he doesn't want to show what he really is, for his background is the three men or trinity monitoring his traces.

Freud says that men often have erotic fantasies of rescuing their mothers (*SE* xi.167), and one formulation of HCE is "he divested to save from the Mrs Drownings their rival queens while Grimshav, Bragshaw and Renshaw made off with his storen clothes" (132.9–11). This brings out the ambivalence of exposure: one must strip to be sexually aggressive, but when one is exposed, one is vulnerable. Likewise, one must present a signifier to aim at meaning, but in doing so, one becomes susceptible to the charge that on's aim is deviant; and three soldiers may take one's garment, and perhaps divide it.

The situation of HCE between genders puts him in a position to be significant, and Joyce's concentration of HCE's essence in three letters (when they are there, he is) emphasizes the fact that the subject is a signifier. That Joyce frames the creation of the signifier as the creation of the world corresponds to a point Lacan makes in *Seminar XVII*: "Sense, if I may say so, is responsible for being" (56). Because we can only apprehend what exists through language, being only exists through words, but Lacan goes on to say that it has long been known that "this is insufficient for carrying the weight…of existence" (57). The claim of words to represent the world cannot be justified; it is an imposition, a crime, and the only world we can know definitely is a fetish.

The most obvious way to relate the park scene to fetishism is to recognize what HCE is looking at is a fetish, a term that readily applies to the stream or column of urine as a female penis, as well as underwear and other fetishes that could appear here, including what Colleen Lamos calls the women's paralegs. The connection to fetishism may go deeper, however, for Lacan and Granoff actually define fetishism as the conjunction of two and three. They begin by saying that Freud put fetishism in a unique central position among perversions because it is the only one that is not opposed to neurosis (265); that is, it is especially prone to coexist with fundamental patterns of what are called "normal" men and women. Freud also saw the study of fetishism as crucial to understanding the universal male patterns of castration anxiety and the Oedipus complex (265). Lacan and Granoff speak of the foundational locus where fetishism originates:

> Between imaginary and symbolic relationships there is the distance that separates anxiety and guilt.
>
> And it is here, historically, that fetishism is born—on the line of demarcation between anxiety and guilt, between the two-sided relationship and the three-side one. (272)

The divison between anxiety and guilt seems parallel to the one between shame and guilt in my last chapter. It may distinguish between confronting the object as an other in anxiety or shame, and reducing the other to an object to cause guilt.[5] The two-sided relationship is the Imaginary, the immediate bond of feeling with the mother. Lacan says that the anxiety on this level of fusion is a fear of loss, a sense that the two-sided relation is "on the point of fading away to be superseded by something else" (273). Presumably the mother's awareness that this relationship cannot last is communicated to the child—who in any case tends to fear when she is away that she will not return. When the mother is seen as emasculated because the child takes on the cultural imagery of castration, the child is shifted into the Symbolic in that the father comes to mediate the relation to the mother. In fact, the child uses the phallic authority of the father to deny the castration of the mother by giving her a fetish, but this actually implies and even creates her castration.[6] Now that one's relation to mother is symbolically realized in language, it depends on a third party, a master who upholds standards (phallic flagpoles). Language is learned by trying to be correct, following a law that implies guilt:

> As soon as a third person is introduced into the narcissistic relationship, there arises the possibility of real mediation, through the intermediary,

> of the transcendent personage, that is to say, of someone through whom one's desire and its accomplishment can be symbolically realized. At this moment, another register appears, that of law—in other words, guilt. (Lacan and Granoff 273)

This Lacanian movement from the duo of anxiety to the trio of guilt corresponds to the point at which HCE becomes aware of the soldiers watching him. In fact, Joyce links the idea of the trio to that of the father by a series of theological jokes about the Father being made up of a trinity: "—Are you in your fatherick, lonely one?/—The same. Three persons" (*FW* 478.28–29). Joyce's association of the number three with the phallus is evident in his description of the bully Heron in the second chapter of *Portrait*: "a thin hooked nose stood out between the closeset prominent eyes..." (*P* 76); "as he marched forward between his two attendants, he cleft the air before him with a thin cane..." (79). The association last appears in the "therrble prongs" on the last page of the *Wake*. The testicles suggested by the description of Heron may be relevant to the image of the three soldiers, for these gonads link masculinity to legal authority. Webster's Third says of *testis* that it originally meant "witness" in Latin and came to be applied to the male sex gland as a witness of manhood. Joyce seems aware of a facetious tradition that to testify meant to swear by one's testes, a validity from which women are excluded. In "Circe," Bloom, "*placing his right hand on his testicles, swears*" (*U* 15.1484; see also 12.810).

The passage indicates that the use of language installs the Other as "someone through whom one's desire and its accomplishment can be symbolically realized." Here the situation of seeing the world through language—the only way to see it—means that one makes contact with the Symbolic ruled by the Law of the Father rather than with the mother's body. This is parallel to the statement in *Le sinthome* that the sons cannot have woman, so they love the father (150). The mother is hereby transformed from the Real to the Imaginary, perceivable only in a form that never existed.

From the viewpoint of phallic sexuality, the earliest happiness with one's mother has to be seen as perverted, partly because the baby boy was more subordinate than dominant. The washerwomen in the ALP chapter suggest that in the original situation of nursing, every male was passive, or perhaps that active and passive did not exist. First they identify HCE's patriarchal dominance as imperialistic with the line "He married his markets, cheap by foul..." (*FW 215.19*). "[C]heap by foul" ("cheek by jowl") refers to the colonial practice of making profits by doing horrible things, or to the inclination toward the cheap thrill, since dominance takes pleasure in debasing people. In the life of the individual, however, an earlier stage preceded such dominance: "But at milkidmass who was the spouse?" (215.21–22). When the kid had his mass of milk, the passive gender was not the female.

Because the communion with the mother was profoundly perverted—incestuous desires being perverted though they are universal—it can only be recovered through an anxiety that prevents it from taking a definite form. This may be why the early bond to mother, as Shepherdson notes, is often seen as entirely Imaginary though it has a strong Symbolic aspect since it operates in language (*Vital* 67–69). The flowing, indefinite nature of the mother's projected originary language is related to Kristeva's semiotic, the pulsating flow of language that is prominent in the mother-baby connection and remains as a level of subsequent discourse (*Revolution* 40–41). The maternal cannot be reduced to this level, but women can use the semiotic to undermine the established order.

Such flow is indicated by the urination of the women in the park scene: "How they wore two madges on the makewater. And why they were treefellers in the shrubrubs" (*FW* 420.7–8). The sequence shifts from the physical actuality of "How" to the rational analysis of "why." The originary liquid relation to the mother, turned into sin by a somewhat more definite inscription, is so attractive partly because it escapes sexual division, urination being androgynous. Joyce recognizes that this idealized image of the mother is a disguise by replacing "were" with "wore"; yet the ambivalence of this maternal identity has critical value. The image of the feminine object is doubled in Joyce for several reasons, so that her sexuality suggests a further level through which she escapes from definition by the law. As usual in Joyce's works, as in psychoanalysis, the philosophical springs from the lowest bodily activity. On a sexual level, not only do the most exciting parts of a woman's body (such as eyes) usually come in pairs, but a woman who acts as the object of desire generally relates to herself by enjoying herself, or pretending to. This resembles or parodies the special contact that women have with themselves, which Irigaray refers to through the image of two labia touching (24–26). The *Wake* describes the sexy Issy in such terms: "finding...that she stripped teasily for binocular man and that her jambs were jimpjoyed to see each other..." (67.36–68.2). The joyful jump of the legs at seeing each other is Joycean because womanly self-communion is a leading principle of his art.

The doubling of Issy also makes concrete the status of women in the later Lacan as both there and not there. In his Twentieth Seminar, he presents mathematical formulas for the two genders. Here he reverses his earlier Freudian position that there is only one kind of sexual pleasure, the phallic. He now argues that woman's sexuality is capable of passing beyond the Symbolic law of the phallus even though there is no subject that is not subject to this law (*Encore* 78, 80–81). Shepherdson explains this paradox by saying that woman's other sexuality, which can go beyond the law, is potential rather than actual ("Lacan," Rabaté, Cambridge 139–40). This accords with the views of Irigaray, who holds that whatever feminine sexuality may be, it has never been seen because women's sexual lives have been designed to please men (90–98). Despite Irigaray's opposition to Lacan, or perhaps because of it, he now comes in 1972 to recognize a further level of feminine sexuality beyond the phallic, so his theory parallels hers in feminist terms.

The making of water by the women represents what Irigaray calls "the mechanics of fluids": "women diffuse themselves according to modalities scarcely compatible with the framework of the ruling symbolics" (106). The "makewater" is not only urination, but the origin of life's flow in birth, which abrogates quantitative limits by creating something new; for the word refers to the breaking of the mother's water sac. Though limits are placed on birth by genetics and environment, the active part of birth cannot be predicted or measured. This creative abolition of quantity matches what Gilles Deleuze and Felix Guattari refer to in *Anti-Oedipus* as the desiring production machine: the flow that a person has to connect with at every vital point of the body in order to live. What is desired on the unconscious level, they say, is not any particular person, but "the intense germinal or germinative flow" (162). This ceaseless productivity must be contained and constricted into a patriarchal economy, but it never really can be.

Irigaray says that the empirical actuality of life (which only exists in liquid form) corresponds to the mechanics of fluids, but that the phallocratic system can only see things by reducing them to the rational mechanics of solids (107). Irigaray sees connections between patriarchy and capitalism, and such mechanical operations are involved in what Marx describes as the abstraction of creative labor into equivalent units of value (38–52). A unit of value can only exist by comparison with another such unit, and Irigaray says that a woman, as a commodity, can only exist through being compared to another woman. This is one reason that the temptresses have to appear as a pair. Marx opposes the use value of a commodity to its exchange value, which is what counts (47), and Irigaray says that a woman s always divided between her actual physical existence and her value as a commodity among men, the latter being the only side that society allows her to express (175–76). Since exchange seeks advantage, exchange value could also be called theft value, the value of pride in abusing someone.

The two women in the park embody a division that is attractive—or perhaps they disembody it insofar as their divisions or gaps are more important than their substances. ALP's chapter portrays her as a stream that is divided when she is seduced or becomes a woman, for one of the places considered as the possible scene of her seduction is "where the

Braye divarts the Farer" (203.10–11). The context of this version of Dryden's "None but the Brave deserves the Fair" (in "Alexander's Feast") indicates that when ALP was no more than an adolescent, she was already forked, divided into two streams, alienated from herself by patriarchal power that forked her. Here she became a prostitute who entertained travelers (diverted farers).

The dividing of the woman, the breaking of her subjective unity, excites male dominance, so that men often enjoy leading women to contradict themselves and then blaming them for it. The division of the women in the park gives the soldiers erections: "the Flimsy Follettes are simply beside each other. And Kelly, Kenny and Keogh are up up and in arms" (*FW* 193.22–24). "Follettes," a play on Follies girls (chorus girls), are women who are attractive because they are foolish. As "beside each other," they are doubled, but as beside themselves, they have lost control or are hysterical, a situation traditionally inspiring to men. The underhanded brutality of the men is suggested by a reference to the Klu Klux Klan.

The excitement of the men, which reveals the obscene aspect of the superego, explains "why there were treefellers in the shrubrubs" (420.7–8). Among other things, this means that they are involved in rubbing their shrubs, with an intensity suggested by the overtone of some sort of disease ("the shrubrubs"), suburban sexuality in a frenzy. But Lacan says that the phallus can only be attained through a "threat or even in the guise of a deprivation" (*Écrits* 575), and the soldiers contribute to HCE's excitement by threatening castration as fellers of trees.

In my next example, the female pair are "whatyoumightcallimbs" (238.30), which means that they are outstanding legs ("what you might call *limbs*"); but they are also hard to remember ("what d'you callems"). Perhaps this is because their physical reality is subordinated to how they can be expressed in the male Symbolic code, what you *may* call them. These limbs seem to gain attraction (which combines two and three) by the difficulty that they have in competing with each other: "How their duel makes their triel!" (238.31).

The tendency of the feminine two to call forth the masculine three is presented as a logical necessity in a geometry lesson: "It follows that, if the two antesedents be bissyclitties and the three comeseekwenchers trundletrikes, then, Aysha Lalipat behidden on the footplate, Big Whiggler restant upsittuponable . . . " (*FW* 284.22–26). The gross attractions of the women are indicated by "bissyclitties," which suggests both that they are on bicycles and that they are busy masturbating. The women are "antesedents" here because they sit in front of one, but they are also antecedents because they lead to the male consequence. In mathematics, the two terms of a ratio, such as *a* is to *b*, are the antecedent (*a*) and the consequent (*b*). The two terms also imply that woman generates what man claims authority for. In this case, the bikes are to the trikes as Asia or woman (*eeyshaw* in Hebrew) is to HCE as bigwig. Bicycles may conceivably be described as causing tricycles in the sense that kids get three wheelers to prepare for two wheelers. Moreover, the two seem to cause male admirers by bringing them out of nowhere.

A footplate is a step leading to a car, and someone—such as another woman, a lollipop to loll and pat—might crouch on it to hide from someone on the other side or on the inside. Woman has to be suppressed for the phallus to stand tall, "Big Whiggler." In this chapter (II.2), the voice of woman's desire appears at the bottom of the page: Issy's footnotes are in a subordinate position, though they often steal the show. On another level, the quote implies that the colonies, represented by Asia, must be subordinated to make a bigwig of the European. Moreover, Aysha is the wife of Mohammed (McHugh), and the sophisticated philosophical development of Islam in the Middle Ages had to be denied to build the dominance of European thought: the title of Aquinas's *Summa Contra Gentiles*, for example, refers specifically to competition with Islam.[7]

In Freudian terms the two call forth the three because the attraction of the mother calls forth the threat of the father in HCE's mind; but from a feminist point of view, it is significant that the men have to appear because the paternal authority defines the scene that creates it. The phallic power to signify that the mother had when she originally filled the field of perception is given to the son; but she still claims its basis outside the law, as Joyce indicates by making ALP the author of the *Wake*. This is the power that shifts from the mother to the father as the Symbolic order is installed. According to Marx, as Irigaray notes, nothing can have value without the presence of a third party or other man, and likewise the woman/commodity can only exist as an object of exchange between men (Irigaray 176–77). So HCE could not see the women as attractive objects without implying another male presence. The sequel to the scene implied in every case is that the soldiers start rumors about HCE's sin, so that it is through the relation between men that women and sexuality enter social discourse; and the story of HCE's sin, like that of Adam, readily expands to become the story of human patriarchal civilization.

The populous and contingent spread of the rumor signifies that all history is based on random points of contact between signifiers. One implication of this is that interpretation should be given the greatest latitude because history loses validity when it loses the penumbra of possibilities that surround it. Some of the keys to interpretation that Joyce left seem to be designed to be as unlikely as possible: see the seven interpretations he offers Weaver for a line on July 26, 1927 (*SL* 326), which add up to a Borgesian fiction about stretching the imagination. If the more interpretations of Joyce's works there are, the more those works are alive, then the more theories there are, the more the works are intellectually alive. If reality increases with the greatest number of confirmations, each of these is a fetish, the mask over the gap that Joyce puts in the center of interpretation,[8] each instance of which (fetish) reduces life to the inanimate. Yet life may only be knowable as a multiplication or swarming of fetishes to give the effect of vitality by contradicting themselves. Insofar as the signifier is isolated by a definition, it stops interacting and turns to stone.

Lacan and Granoff say that for the repressive "successor of the feminine phallus, it is the denegation of its absence which will have constructed the memorial. The fetish will become the vehicle both of denying and asseverating the castration" (273). Sixteen years later Lacan would realize in *Encore* that the feminine phallus is not the masculine one. In the 1956 passage, the lack of an imaginary phallus is enshrined in woman by cultural codes. Even for a man, in Lacanian terms, the lack of a phallus is all he can ever possess. The fetish is referred to here as a memorial because as a definite form to which desire is bound, it constitutes the image of value as a symbol of the lost maternal body. Its representation of the past corresponds to the fact that as a product of phallic sexuality, it is so deeply ingrained in cultural tradition that it is seen as "natural." When people perceive high heels, furs, lingerie, and so forth as "sexy," they need to sense this as instinctive. Even highly abstract symbolic constructions such as money and status symbols commonly give people deep visceral feelings.

The World as Memorial

The *Wake*'s park scene is introduced as the source of a monument that expands to stand for all of the monuments of history. We are told on the fifth page of the *Wake* that HCE's "clay feet . . . stick up starck where he last fellonem, by the mund of the magazine wall, where our maggy seen all, with her sisterin shawl. While over against this belles' alliance . . . lurk the ombushes . . . " (7.30–35). The place against which the ambushes (three soldiers) lurk, the alliance of the belles (two girls), refers to "*La Belle Alliance*," one of the contemporary names for the battle of Waterloo; and this scene in the park leads to the museum where the relics of old battles are kept.

In political reality all of the doctrines of history and all of the data of actuality are relics of battles, whether military or rhetorical, for they are devised by whoever wins. And the scene in the park is behind all battles, so that, for example, a sensuous version of this scene leads directly to the story of how Buckley shot the Russian General (*FW* 337.16–31). Male conflict in the *Wake* is generally over a woman, though she may extend into such forms as the land they fight for; but she cannot enter into the conflict of exchange without being turned into a fetish.

The repository of memorials is called a "museyroom" because it is the chamber of the arts as well as the record of history: male conflicts have even determined what art could be produced or preserved. Yet Joyce says that this monumental history began when the Maggies saw HCE's clay feet. It is as if the woman saw a lack in the man at the same time that he saw hers, as if she saw the weakness that made him impose on her. So he has to deny her and lose her by insisting on her gap to make up for his own. This corresponds to Lacan's suggestion that all monuments monumentalize the lost authority of the mother. HCE's phallic tower may be included. The point at which woman loses her authority is the point at which her reception of the man's authority becomes crucial and illusory.

The original and underlying power of woman still appears vestigially in the power of mothers and mates to motivate men actively, though in the world Joyce witnessed, these women are culturally required to serve their sons and lovers. My student Brian O'Sullivan pointed out that while the museyroom is supervised by the servant Kate, who narrates all of the descriptions of male battles that constitute the museum, yet the vestiges of maternal power that Kate wields have to be given to her by male visitors who enter her "museomound": "For her passkey supply [rather than apply] to the janitrix..." (8.5–8).

The pattern of monumental fetishism recurs when the text tries to track down the "unfacts" behind history: "his adjugers are semmingly freak threes but his judicandees plainly minus twos. Nevertheless Madam's Toshowus waxes more lifeliked...And our notional gullery is now completely complacent..." (57.19–22). Madame Tussaud's Wax Museum and the National Gallery enshrine images of status for England. But Tussaud's figures are far from alive, and our notional gullery is a gallery of foolish, complacent received beliefs. The phrase mocks an Irish tendency to think of British culture as "ours," or the tendency of anyone to think that (s)he is expressed by ideas that (s)he inherits.

The forms in which we are fixated by the structure of fetishism in the *Wake* include not only beauty and history, but the conceptual framework that we use to determine what is real. Such reality is based on judging women to be deficient, "minus twos," subtracting their ability to signify, replacing it with a male mechanism. As with Kate, the power of "Madam's Toshowus" depends on her ability *to show us* fetishes that men desire. A good model for this is the diagram of ALP that is shown us in the Lesson Chapter (*FW* 293). Here the actual fleshly form of the woman is reduced to a geometrical abstraction in which every part is doubled and the only identified points are sexually strategic. This also corresponds to the way the world has been shaped by obsessive rational categories like the square grey buildings with which England covered Dublin.

The *Wake* even demonstrates that the landscape we live in is founded on the three and two scene: "how our seaborn isle came into exestuance, (the explutor, his three andesiters and the two pantellarias" (387.13). Here the subject of the park scene is an explorer and exploiter because all that can be discovered is the fetish, the sublime object of ideology that sends people on voyages. This is the world built by HCE, whose identity is based on the scene in the park or the birth of the fetish—just as his power as builder is based on denial of ALP's creative power and productive effort. That existence continues to have a bisexual basis is indicated by "exestuance," for an estuary is a place where a river meets the sea, and river and sea are coded as female and male in the *Wake*, especially at the end. Joyce's word also comes close to ex-sistence, an existence that is always moving beyond.

Both Freud and Marx define the fetish as something inanimate that takes on the qualities of being alive. Freud says, "It seems...that when the fetish comes to life, so to speak, some process has been suddenly interrupted..." (*SE* XXI.155). What is interrupted is the Imaginary interaction with the mother—which may be equated with ALP's presence—and the fetish is created at the expense of contact with her real body. An image of this situation in *Ulysses* is the idea of Bloom as Odysseus in exile on Calypso's isle because he is attached to a fantasy image (the Nymph) rather than to the reality of his wife.

Lacan, who later uses the term *Thing* to refer to the image of the mother's body as dreadful but attractive (*Ethics* 106), says in his Rome Discourse, "Thus the symbol first manifests itself as the killing of the thing, and this death results in the endless perpetuation of the subject's desire" (*Écrits* 262). The words of *Ulysses* are symbols generated by the death of Stephen's mother and the loss of Molly. The life that is given to the inanimate object in the male symbolic (the fetish) is taken from the female Imaginary interrelationship, which is the most vivid approach to the actual body or object. Focusing on the object for the Joycean artist is a way of making it his or fantasizing it, and this applies to Joyce's fetishization of words, which brings out their power as his product.

Marx says that in commodity fetishism objects are given the illusion of independent life by the social system of exchange (72), and that the system that makes value in capitalist society rests on such fetishism. The labor and social interaction involved in a product are reified as qualities of the product itself. Similarly, the patriarchal system tends to give woman an unnatural life as a fetish by overlooking the womanly interaction with social forces that constitutes her feelings. The Joycean male worships the fetish of his woman's vitality, but cannot bear to think that that vitality depends on contact with others, yet this jealousy keeps returning as the Real.

Marx explains the abstraction of labor by saying that if a coat is worth a certain amount of linen, this is because two kinds of labor, the tailoring of the coat and the weaving of the linen, can be translated into common units (50). This is done by subordinating the particular characteristics of different kinds of work to standard units of exchange value. The overlaying of physical reality with abstract masculine quantification ("she's a ten") is what gives women the main values that they are allowed to have as commodities (Irigaray 170–76), obliterating their own experience. The wife with the highest official value is a trophy wife, but a trophy is inanimate.

Levi-Strauss says in *The Elementary Structures of Kinship* that women are the central objects of exchange in patriarchal societies (115–66), and Irigaray says that it is the subordination of women's actual bodies to their symbolic role that makes social operations possible (189). Joyce presents the point at which we make women objects to give objects life as the foundation of the *Wake* world. One of the main reasons that the *Wake* sees life as a dream is that it recognizes that the world we live in is constituted by covering life over, as the Freudian fetish hides the actual body in a phantom of castration.

The fetish as veil is emphasized in Book III as Shaun is leaving his sister Issy, here called Tizzy (457.27), a name that indicates excitability. Shaun is setting out on his career as postman, a bearer of the post or phallicized (upright and forwardly propelled) word. As he separates from her, Tizzy gives him a handkerchief and she or it is called "veronique" (458.14), a reference to the sacred veil with which St. Veronica is said to have wiped Jesus's face. This fetish harks back to the scene in which May Dedalus wiped Stephen's face before he went to college (*P* 175). Tizzy's promise to Shaun at this point has overtones of submerged eroticism: "…I want, girls palmassing, to whisper my whish" (457.30). Tizzy tells Shaun, who is called Jaun in this chapter (III.3), to carry her hanky for the rest of his life and to think of her "when never" he uses it (458.8–10). Apparently she seals his fidelity ("promising") by having her girls put hand together in prayer, but "palmassing" also implies letting him put his hand on their rear ends in farewell. The ambiguous "when never" is a likely reference to masturbation with her cloth, which she both wants and doesn't want him to practice. After Molly masturbated Mulvey into her hanky, she "kept the handkerchief under my pillow for the smell of him" (*U* 18.863).

Tizzy describes the cloth as "a piece torn in one place from my hands" (458.1). This sounds as if she gave him part of her hands to apply to himself; so on one level she castrates herself to give him his fetish. Another way in which her memorial gift is taken from her body is suggested by her saying, ". . I'm ashamed for my life…over this lost moment's gift of memento nosepaper which…is allathome I with grief can call my own…" (457.33–35). On a surface level, she regrets that this is only a last minute gift or a gift of a straying moment. But another reason that she is ashamed of this "memento nosepaper," as Dick Beckman suggested in our *Wake* reading group, is that it suggests personal tissues meant to be smelled. As a veil with signs on it, Tizzy's hanky represents the field of perception, which includes every variety of sensation (or every sexual position), and she says, "forty ways in forty nights, that's the beauty of it, look, scene it..." (458.5–6), and also speaks of its appealing odor: "just a spell of floralora" (458.14).[9]

In this scene the fetish is the letter, which is produced by woman, but possessed by man, and which stands for all human knowledge, since the letter is generally understood to be the *Wake*. This corresponds to Shepherdson's idea that mother is the source of the Symbolic, and to Lacan's, that knowledge is originated by slaves, but possessed through learning by the master. All perception is motivated by desire, and what is perceived is not the object of desire, but a coded emblem of that object. The fetish of communication that Shaun delivers expresses the dominance of the male Symbolic order as it reduces the actual body to something that can never be grasped on the other side of the veil of what can be perceived, thus clarifying language so as to constitute the Real as inaccessible.

The subordination of women to produce phallic authority is parallel to the erasure of the actuality of labor to produce the concentration of wealth, with women as the main objects of exchange. *Seminar XVII* describes the master's knowledge as yielding an object of desire (*a*) created by the mental effort of the worker: "in the master's discourse the *a* is precisely identifiable with what the thought of a worker, Marx's, produced, namely what was, symbolically and really, the function of surplus value" (44). Here masters appropriate the fruit of the intellectual exertion of workers whose craft is the real source of valuable information. This is parallel to the picture of ALP as not only the author of the *Wake*, but the one who does the useful work of holding the world together. As Norris demonstrates, the washerwomen in "ALP" present the most intensive picture of hard work in the novel (*Web* 153–59). The surplus value or excess desire produced by the workers and the women remains as the subordinate level that destabilizes the fetishist monument to indicate possibilities of freedom.

The phenomenal field made visible by language is poised between the Imaginary and the Symbolic, and the images it gives us to value are caught in this fantastic, archaic suspension between the maternal object of desire and the paternal threat of control. Joyce keeps returning to this scene to insist on the structure of our perception and subjectivity. Throughout the *Wake* he favors feminine flow, which is often presented lyrically, over masculine fixity, which often appears ridiculous or comatose. The book ends with the voice of ALP, who keeps flowing onward though the image of the father frightens her. But if Joyce aims at freeing the object of desire from anxiety and guilt, he indicates that we must begin by realizing that it can only be perceived as framed between them.

By seeing reality as a fetish, one can see its artificiality as a step toward releasing oneself from its claim. One must see that the real crime is not the violation of reality, but the acceptance of it, the state of being caught between desire and guilt. To break free of this ancient pattern, one must see it as artificial, represent it in the most ridiculous way, and use language that is as far as possible from certainty. Finally, by portraying the creation of the world as a combination of crime and misunderstanding, one motivates change. Central to this process is taking reality as a work of art so as to turn the symptom into a *sinthome*, transfer the sin into a book (tome), change original sin into the fruitful sin of originality, the ability to retie the knot of consciousness.

One of the most radical ways to do so is to move one's perspective as far as possible from the world that frames the fetish as actuality. For this reason the explorations of "An Encounter" and "Araby" in *Dubliners* yield crucial insights and it is necessary in "The Dead" for Gabriel to journey westward. Stephen ends *Portrait* headed overseas, *Exiles* is about not feeling at home, and *Ulysses* discovers the value of getting lost. In the *Wake*, the unprecedented global perspective of the book identifies the leading principle of its artistic vision with the non-European world. An extensive deployment of Africa and Asia as the sources of creativity and inspiration in the *Wake* makes Joyce a major pioneer of postcolonial literature, and it will be my focus for the remaining two chapters. Although it has not received the attention given to Joyce's treatment of the Irish, the lower classes and women, it is one of the strongest, most wide reaching and revolutionary forms of Joyce's concern for those at the bottom of the social scale.

Chapter 10

The Africanist Dimension of Finnegans Wake

Anticolonial Joyce

In their introduction to *Semicolonial Joyce*, Derek Attridge and Margorie Howes say that because Joyce's Ireland was both a colony and a modern European country (6–7), Joyce is semicolonial: "Philosophically he could be said to have been both separatist and a unionist, thinking constantly in terms of oppositions . . . " (2). They associate the rebellious side of Joyce and the side that is attached to the establishment with the twins of the *Wake*, Shem the artist and Shaun the materialist. I would say that Joyce was working against the unionist or Shaun side of his vision, though he could not separate himself from it. He reveals through the Shem side the symptoms of colonialism in the depth of their affliction.[1] To refer to Joyce as semicolonial is something like referring to Abraham Lincoln as semislavery Lincoln. Lincoln retained racist attitudes, but the valuable aspect of his career is how he fought against them. Likewise Joyce is scathingly critical of the unionist idea that the Irish need to be subordinated to England.

Len Platt, in *Joyce, Race, and* Finnegans Wake, cites Kenan Malik's argument that race has served the modern world as a key mechanism of social control: the disparity between claims of equality and actual inequality was explained by believing that certain people were racially inferior (Platt 5). Those in the grip of colonialism are impelled to see economic factors as ethnic, and Platt joins Andrew Gibson and Vincent J. Cheng in noticing the force of this tendency in Joyce. Economic factors were racial for the Communist Party in America during the 1930s: it concentrated on racial issues, from the case of the Scottsboro Boys in 1931 to Richard Wright's *Native Son* (1940). Platt's book shows how deeply racism was involved in the intellectual and political establishment of Western Civilization and how constantly Joyce was attacking it.

Platt's strong examination of European racism is not matched by his chapter on Joyce's treatment of nonwhite people, which shows how Joyce took stereotypical images of nonwhites from English musical comedies and undermined them energetically (121–45). Platt underestimates here the extent to which Joyce himself was colonized and had views of nonwhite people that went beyond musicals. Joyce presents Marcus Garvey as an author of the *Wake* and expresses horror at the Rape of Nanking. The creditable insistence that whites misrecognize nonwhites becomes counterproductive if it renders people of color invisible except through European lenses. Platt does not see that the mockery of stereotypes that he notices actually extends to express the active resistance of the Third World, the defiance of the subaltern that enlarges the *Wake* to speak for the entire planet.

Michael North, in *The Dialect of Modernism*, describes Standard English as a rare pattern designated by the Standard English movement of 1880–1930 to exclude inferior groups (13, 15). The dialect and parody that undermine this racist construction speak for the opposition of people of color, who connect the dislocation of language to the outsider's antagonism. Joyce practices what Henry Louis Gates calls "Signifyin(g)" insofar as his play with words gives them a strong anticolonial accent, making them a discourse of rebellion (Gates 44–88). The *Wake's* language is *outlandish*, a term that, like *strange*, combines oddness with a sense of being from far away, actively different

To attend to the side of Joyce's work that is aware of itself as colonized is to bring out the counteraction and incomprehensibility that charge the text with turmoil. This is the border of the Real where unknown and liberating insight is to be found. Therefore Joyce uses the extreme oppression of slavery, which ravaged Africa, to locate the source of imaginative productivity in proximity to pity and terror, the birthright of slaves. He portrays the creative members of the *Wake* family as African. Insofar as Africans are the group most denied by Western Civilization, the stereotypes applied to them are the most alien, pointing to what is beyond, to otherness. It is because they wear the masks that are most opposed to them, that they are most keenly aware of the parallactic oppositions that form subjectivity and identity. Because they play the role of the Other for the West, they can see the illusory nature of the West's Other. This is why the authors of the *Wake*, in their oppositional stance, are defined as African, not exclusively, but overwhelmingly.

Lacan's Other is the totality of language out of which each signifier or subject emerges. Language is always trying to reach the Other as complete explanation, but never can because its otherness extends endlessly. The postcolonial Joyce realized that the intellectual activity of the English tended to depend for its vitality on the Irish Other. The only English intellectual that Joyce portrays, Haines in *Ulysses*, is obsessed with Irish culture. This corresponds to Lacan's idea that knowledge comes from slaves, and to Shaun's obsession with Shem, which generates Shem as we know him. The violence of Joyce's attack on the appropriation of Irish knowledge by colonizers is evidenced in his portrayal of the Anglo-Irish hibernophile Samuel Chenevix Trench as the English Haines, a move that would have been hurtful to Trench if he had not committed suicide in 1909, for Trench changed his name to Dermot in an effort to be as Irish as possible.[2]

As the West claims superiority, it continually relates to the non-Western world, if only through stereotypes. Joyce makes these stereotypes break into his discourse in a disruptive fashion and so that they express a countereforce. If, as Lacan says, the artist makes the world (*Le sinthome* 64), his most productive effort is to enlarge the known world by reaching toward the other side, the side that opposes the labels we put on it. The most forceful realization of this otherness that the artist can bring out may center on the pathological dependence of the West on fantasy images of the colonized. This is what Toni Morrison calls Africanism in *Playing in the Dark* (6, 16, 44), a series of fantasies that show how the West both denies and works out its own problems by projecting them on Africans.

Homi Bhabha argues in *The Location of Culture* that the modern develops in conjunction with colonialism and that the dislocations of modernism, its calling into question of established meanings, are part of a shift of the cultural field away from traditional centers of Western civilization toward interaction with the colonized world (31–39). Joyce, who grew up as a colonized subject, carried this shift forward powerfully. Edward Said says in *Culture and Imperialism* that the appearance of the Semitic hero of *Ulysses* "testifies to a new" exotic "presence within Europe": "now, instead of being *out there*, they are here, as troubling as the primitive rhythms of the *Sacre du Printemps* or the African icons of Picasso's art" (188).

The shift was carried further in the forties with the appearance of important writers from the margins of the Third World such as Jorge Luis Borges and Richard Wright,[3] both strongly influenced by Joyce. Borges *wrote* the first essay on Joyce in Spanish in 1925, his encomium to *Ulysses* (Borges, *Non-fictions 12–15*). His 1939 review of the *Wake* expressed bewilderment (*Non-fictions* 195), but around this time, Borges's fictions became postmodern. Wright's first novel, *Lawd Today!* (1936, published 1963), which uses stream-of-consciousness to follow the thoughts of an urban Negro through a single day, is an African American version of *Ulysses.*[4] Joyce continued to have a vital influence on African American writers, from Ellison's *Invisible Man* (1951)—who resembles Stephen Dedalus in deciding to detach himself from the madness of social crisis in order to see it clearly—to William Melvin Kelly's *Dunford's Travels Everywheres* (1970), the most technically adventurous American version of the *Wake.*

Joyce cleared a stylistic space for the expression of alternative realities, and this space was needed for the growth of non-Western literature, This operation is implied by Borges, in his 1974 "Invocation to Joyce" (*In*

Praise 54–55). "I am the others. I am all those/ who have been rescued by your pains and care./ I am those unknown to you and saved by you." Joyce's effort is at once to expand the light of Western civilization and to express the opposition of the colonized, for the leading edge of enlightenment consists of the most acute awareness of the Other. Eide's definition of ethics as maximum awareness of the other points toward the greatest latitude of cultural distance. This distance had to be covered by tools of negation Joyce developed.

Derek Walcott's pan-African Homeric epic of the dispossessed, *Omeros* (1990), with its conceptual parallels to *Ulysses*, illustrates why Joyce's authority of doubt extends beyond the West. Walcott's persona visits Europe and reacts to it as a colonized subject. In Portugal (Chapter 37) and London (38), he finds oppressive images of religious and imperial authority, but in Ireland (39), he feels empathy with people who have had their land and language taken from them (198–99). This helps him to hail Joyce as "our age's Omeros," and to say, "I blest myself in his voice" (200). When the Walcott figure joins some singers in a pub, he senses the presence of Joyce's spirit encouraging them. Patrick Colm Hogan suggested to me that the line, "Mr. Joyce led us all" (201) implies that Joyce is the leader of an inclusive grouping of Walcott's generation of Third World writers. Joyce, then, is a pioneer in the movement of literary consciousness away from the West.

Finnegans Wake, the culmination of modernism and the progenitor of postmodernism, is not a Western work insofar as it succeeds in speaking for the entire planet; and in the global organization of the *Wake*, Africa plays a leading role. Images of Africa are associated with the downtrodden parts of the earth and with the oppressed and creative portion of humanity, and the ending of the *Wake* evokes the hope that this portion will awaken from its suppression. Asia is more prominent at the end, but Africa is featured in the ALP chapter (196–216), the end of the first book that prefigures the end of the novel: in both, the voice of the river takes over.

Even the patriarch of the *Wake*, HCE, often linked to imperialism, is capable of an enlightened view of the subject. At one point he "believes in Africa for the fullblacks" (*FW* 129.32), advocating the liberation of the continent. The idea of freeing Africa also emerges from the sleeping Yawn (Shaun) in Book III with reference to a motif of the song of birds as a call to awakening: "a Thrushday for African man and to let Brown child do and to leave he Anlone" (520.18–19). The bird associated with this morning song that will regenerate humanity is the robin, a form of thrush (Brivic, *Waking* 31–34, 124). ALP believes that they will sing in choirs when HCE rises and walks with her to celebrate their anniversary: "robins in crews so. It is for me Goolden wending" (619.223–23). A "Goolden wending" is a wedding that keeps going its way for fifty years (covering quite a distance), and the reference to *Robinson Crusoe* suggests starting a new life outside Europe.

The two members of HCE's family who are generally described as predominantly African are ALP and her son Shem. These two are closely linked as the creative wing of the family, for Anna dictates the letter that Shem writes, a letter that is equated with all of literature and with the *Wake*. Anna's originative role may be related to that of Africa as the source of civilization, a source recognized through the vast amount of Egyptian material in the *Wake*. Anna's African identity has already been explained (Brivic, *Waking* 54–67), so I will add a few points here and then turn to Shem.

One of the earliest sources of Anna's name is Anna, the sister of Dido in Virgil's *Aeneid*. The Carthaginian Queen Dido represents both woman as a weakness that must be bypassed and Africa as a continent that must be eradicated if Rome is to triumph. As Cicero put it, *Carthagena delenda est*, "Carthage must be deleted."The linkage between woman and Africa as threats to male European sovereignty that must be suppressed is embodied by Anna Livia. When Dido immolates herself after Aeneas deserts her at the end of the fourth book of the *Aeneid*, Anna climbs on the funeral pyre and gives her life to comfort Dido's last moments, a noble act of African sisterhood. Anna and Dido are among the powerful African women associated with ALP, such as Isis, Cleopatra, and the pre-Hellenic, black, fertility goddess Diana of Ephesus.[5] Two lines from the end of the *Wake*, ALP says, "mememorme!" an echo of the poignant refrain Dido sings at the end of Purcell's *Dido and Aeneas*, "Remember me, / Remember me, / But oh, forget my fate."

Vincent J. Cheng has shown that the British press, late in the nineteenth century, often represented the Irish by Africanist stereotypes (20–41). As an Irishwoman growing up at the turn of the century, Anna Livia would be aware that this is a negative image of her; but insofar as she finds her non-Western side compelling, she is inclined toward modernism, rebellion, and feminism. This side opposed to the establishment is the one she moves toward at the end, and it is presented so often and so intensely that it can hardly be deemed subordinate. The figures in the *Wake* stand for everyone in the world, and the creative ones stand for the continent that created the arts. Ironically, my argument that ALP and Shem are African is supported by the prevailing racist principle that anyone who is part black is black.

The *Wake* closes on ALP turning back to a youthful identity that affirms the liberation of the female and non-European parts of the world that have been held down. She rejects her man and realizes that his virtues were delusions (*FW* 627.21–24). Then she returns to the memory of dancing with what she calls "my people," a female group of wild rivers. The two who are named, Niluna and Amazia (627.28–30), stand for the two longest rivers in the world, the Nile and the Amazon—the latter also being a fierce woman. Anna fears that she may not be able to escape the terrifying attraction of her oceanic father. Yet she clearly does not want to return to submission, the voiceless relation to him that she dreads falling back into: "humbly dumbly, only to washup" (628.11). Her goal is to return to where she really wants to be, in her "great blue bedroom" (627.9) with her mother in the sky, and Anna's mother is consistently identified with the Egyptian sky goddess Nut (Brivic *Waking* 126–29). The mad dance of the waves surges toward the liberating uplift of evaporation (listen to the spray): "and the clash of our cries till we spring to be free" (627.31–32).

Anna's negritude is supported not only by her African mother and sunbathed sisters, but by her being linked to thirty words of Kiswahili (McHugh 198–209), And she uses other African languages.[6] When her attraction is ascribed to "mangay mumbo jumbjubes" (273.17), the line has the rhythm of a tropical dance: "man-gay mum-bo jumb-*jubes*." Through the image of jujubes, which are linked to woman's "gumjelly lips" in *Ulysses* (8.908), ALP's "mangay" lips are presented as swollen for men so that they resemble mangoes. They have a kind of African magic, and "mangay mumbo" probably refers to Mandingo, the language from which the famous phrase for African magic, *mumbo jumbo*, was derived. Mumbo jumbo is the incomprehensible side of language that the *Wake* is always moving toward. Shem is later described as having "africot lupps" (489.27). He presumably inherited them from mom, and like her lips, his are compared to candy, McHugh's *Annotations* see a reference to "apricot lumps" here (489).[7] When young people ask Anna to "Sing us a sula" (209.35), they are asking her to express the voice of liquid, for *sula*, as Toni Morrison's assistant Rene Shepperd informs me, means 'water' in the Twi language, spoken in Ghana. The power of ALP's singing depends on its flow, the semiotic pulsation of language that operates outside of Symbolic codes of meaning. As Irigaray argues, the mechanics of fluids, which constitutes living experience, is outside the solid mechanics of Western civilization (106–18).

Brother Shem's Funk

If the Africanism of ALP relates to the analogy between women and Africans—which Joyce saw cited by such progressive figures as Blake and John Stuart Mill to press for the liberation of women (Brivic, *Waking* 60, 62)—the Africanism of Shem involves a strong analogy between the African and the artist. The fantasies conventional people have about artists often play a shaping role in the mindset of creative people, and artists often define themselves as strange, improper, and alien from their first sense of themselves as creative. The pattern is fundamental to Joyce's portraits of the artist, and may be a basic root behind Joyce's extensive linking of art to the African.

In a classic treatment of the artist as outsider, Thomas Mann's "Tonio Kröger" (1903), Kröger feels that his artistic sensitivity is related to his "foreign" mother, his dark hair, and his uneasy self-consciousness. He contrasts himself enviously with characters whom he sees as representing a blonde, blue-eyed, and cheerful "race" (128). Here a racialism that links temperament to complexion links the artist to a dark race, ignoring the social construction of both art and race.

In Joyce the blackness of the artist is imposed from without. In the Shem chapter of the *Wake*, the speaker is Shaun, Shem's "muddlecrass" (*FW* 152.8) brother, and he barrages Shem with the foulest racist language, using such terms as "nigger," (177.4), "coon" (175.30; 187.12, 16), and "Darkies" (175.30) repeatedly to describe this Joycean artist. He is also referred to as "nate Hamis" (181.36), or born of Ham, the accursed son of Noah, who was supposed by racists to be the progenitor of the black race (Platt 33). At one point Shaun says that if you think you know an example that is as dirty as he is, "Niggs, niggs, and niggs again" (183.3–5). This denigration expresses a middleclass attitude toward art that appears in conservative attacks on the National Endowment for the Arts. In this perspective art is seen as one of the contents of Shem's lair, "fluefoul smut" (183.15). The word *smut* refers not only to pornography, such as the "sootcoated" pictures Stephen hid in the flue of his fireplace (*P* 115, cited by McHugh), but to blackness. All art tends here to be black art.

Emphasis is placed on the extreme darkness of Shem's skin. He is described as "Nigerian" (181.13) and "porterblack" (187.17), which means as dark as a tankard of porter or as an African who carries things. Shem's blackness is so intense that it gives off a sort of aura, assuming that he is referred to by the last of the games the children are said to play in his chapter, "*when his steam was like a Raimbrandt round Mac Garvey*" (176.18, Joyce's italics). "steam" probably refers to Shem, who is sometimes called "stem" (216.3), but it also refers to a haze or stench around him that is not only a rainbow, but a veritable masterpiece of *chiaroscuro*, the modulating shades of brown drawn around figures in Rembrandt—the murk of the artist, who speaks through obscurity. Shem is also linked here to Marcus Garvey, the black nationalist leader and writer, who had very dark skin, and so Shem's darkness is tied to his revolutionary role as a writer. Joyce is likely to have been aware of Garvey, who appeared before the League of Nations in Geneva in 1928 and 1931 to argue for an African homeland (Williams 645), and who often expressed his nationalist ideas in poetry. It is appropriate that Garvey is presented as one the *Wake*'s authors, though he writes it by giving off fumes, for the book speaks for Third World liberation.

The comparison with Garvey is connected to the structure of the *Wake*, for it closely echoes a description of the book's organization: "the glory of a wake *while the scheme is like your rumba round me garden*, allatheses" (309.6–8, my italics). The form of the novel is referred to as "circling the square" (*FW* 186.12) because its four books form a square, yet it moves in a circle. This is presented in "rumba round" for the rumba uses a four- sided box step. In a letter to Weaver of April 16, 1927, Joyce said, "I am making an engine with only one wheel.... The wheel is a perfect square" (*SL* 321). The *American Heritage Dictionary* says that the rumba originated among Cuban Negroes. The square round combines with an Afro-Cuban dance again in another description of the movement of the *Wake*: "when we go out in all directions... with my cubarola glide?" (618.21–22). This square/round structure is really an anti-structure in that the opposing forms break each other down: a single square wheel would work terribly. The deconstructive point is that the *Wake* constantly violates or exceeds any particular form. The idea of going in all directions at once to embrace "allatheses" is connected to the tropical dance rhythm ("*his scheme... garden*") through the association of Africa with improvisation.

Having been kicked around, Shem is described as being made up of "bamp him and bump him blues" (176.34). Blues is a musical form rooted in Africa. He is also linked to another term associated with African Americans: "a rank funk getting the better of him" (176.25–26). In fact, one of Shem's characteristic colors is "funkleblue" (171.18), which combines funk with the blues. *Funk* traditionally had two main meanings, a state of fear or depression and a bad smell. It is from the smell that the word came to be applied to what Geneva Smitherman calls "down-to-earth music" in *Black Talk*. She gives reason to think that Joyce might have had access to the musical aspect by saying that *funk* was "used as early as 1900 in the New Orleans jazz scene" (140).

Shaun illustrates both traditional meanings of *funk* with Shem, who is cowardly and has "a stinksome inkenstink" (183.6). In the form of sweat, its most concrete form, funk presents emotion as the release of excretion. The *Wake* emphasizes the excremental aspect of funk when it speaks of a warrior "krieging the funk from" his opponent" (10.5). Platt observes that the scene in which Shem shows his cowardice when he is treated with "parsonal violence" by a group of athletes for not being a real man (174.22–175.4) has the features of an attack on a minority youth by a group of racists (Platt 138–39), the word "parsonal" suggesting Protestants attacking a Catholic.

The pre-musical idea of funk is expanded on by Morrison in *The Bluest Eye*, when she describes how Afro-Americans were trained around 1920 to control their feelings:

> The careful development of thrift, patience, high morals. In short, how to get rid of the funkiness The dreadful funkiness of passion... Of the wide range of human emotion.
>
> Wherever it erupts, this Funk, they wipe it away; where it crusts, they dissolve it; wherever it drips, flowers or clings, they find it and fight it... (83)

Characters in *The Bluest Eye* keep overflowing the bounds of white control by releasing the contents of their bodies: bedwetting, throwing up, being incontinent, blowing their noses, crying, and so forth. The funky commonality of Joyce and Morrison suggests that people who are colonized within the social structure that controls them (perhaps especially if this structure is Anglo-Saxon) are carefully monitored to contain the Real of the body. Excretion, as the material outpouring of affect, is analogous to emotional gestures that break out of the correct forms of expression, gestures that discompose countenance or exceed established structure. Traditionally, upper-class people maintain and define form, while lower-class ones sully it. The *Wake* features a lower-class figure who embodies this soiling function: "Sully is a thug" (*FW* 618.28). Colonized people are defined as guilty of the release of the body from containment. They are conditioned for such overflow by being terrorized and denied privacy, while the different personal habits that they are thus forced into subject them to shame.

Shame is a major component of Shem's name, for he takes on fully his symptom of difference. And the release of the body from containment is the basis of his art, for he writes by defecating and mixing his feces and urine to make ink. The source of his writing is a compulsion to release something unknown and urgent inside himself that he is ashamed of. His need to evacuate the dark stuff within is parallel to the operation of racism whereby people render themselves white by expelling their dark, dirty qualities and using color and class to project them on others. Yet Shem does not project on others; he confronts the Real of the body to expose the internal pathology of racism.

The projective process is described by Judith Butler's explanation of Kristeva's idea of the abject: "The 'abject' designates that which has been expelled from the body, discharged as excrement, literally rendered 'Other.' This appears as an expulsion of alien elements, but the alien is effectively established through this expulsion. The construction of the 'not me' as the abject establishes the boundaries of the body which are also the first contours of the subject." (*Gender* 133). Butler shows how the fundamental formation of the subject is intertwined with the basis of racist or sexist fantasies; and she insists that we cannot understand how this formation works without seeing it as expulsion, as putting something internal at a distance.

Joyce dedicated himself to revealing the hidden process that builds art on an indecent origin that is denied when art is made sacrosanct. In his satiric poem "The Holy Office" (1904), he defined his artistic role as "Katharsis-Purgative" in relation to Celtic Twilight writers like Yeats (Ellmann, *JJ* 165–67). The Greek *katharsis* literally means voiding the bowels; so the Joycean artist, like the tragic hero as scapegoat, rids the community of embarrassing material that it could not otherwise get out, allowing it to preserve its purity: "That they may dream their dreamy dreams/I carry off their filthy streams" (*JJ* 166).

After Shem generates the material of his art, he is described in Latin as "*animale nigro exoneratus*" (185.18). This means "relieved of the black animal," with an overtone of 'exonerated,' as if he cleared himself of guilt by expelling the darkness from himself. He does not, however, separate himself from his blackness; instead what he does is to "crap in his hand" (185.17–18). He holds onto his waste and expresses himself through it, the modern artist focusing on what is taboo. Staten, in "The Decomposing Form...," sees Bloom's wiping of his rear end with part of a story in "Calypso" (*U* 4.537) as a Joycean model "of literature touching reality" (380). And Lacan, in "Joyce *le Symptome II,*" says, "What remains after Joyce" is "to burst the toilet paper" ("*crever dans le papier hygienique*," Aubert 36).

It is significant that feces is both internal and external: while it seems to come from deep within (the word *bowels* stands for interiority), it was never assimilated to the body. The Real of the body, being unknowable, remains external, just as the deepest level of one's feelings come from the Other, from language. Stereotypes concealed deep within us stir strong feelings, but they are shit, false and mortifying, no matter how sacred. This is one thing Shem realizes by holding onto his waste, making it conscious instead of keeping it out of sight

Such holding on to one's embarrassment is the opposite of imperialism, and Joyce maintained that the central mechanism of the British Empire was the flush toilet because it was so effective in separating oneself from one's soil. In the "Aeolus" episode of *Ulysses*, Professor McHugh says that whenever the British arrive anywhere, the first thing that they say is "Let us construct a water closet" (7.494); and a narrator in "Cyclops" sees the English as "rulers of the waves, who sit on thrones of alabaster" (12.1213). The bathroom so highly cultivated by the English, and generally white, was actually a whitening apparatus, one of the main signs of gentility being the well-scrubbed look. In fact, most of the soil that accumulates on one's body is excretion (dead skin cells and sweat). The unwashed Shem, however, can only express himself through his *animale nigro*. This identification of art with blackness exemplifies Morrison's argument, in *Playing in the Dark*, that white writers cannot address desire or justice or ideals without referring to projected fantasies of Africanism (46–48), and Joyce recognizes this by extension from the use of the Irish as primitives.

Improvising

The most creative feature of the darkness that Shem writes with is its unknown nature. As "his wit's waste" (*FW* 185.7), it is what cannot be digested, what is beyond knowledge. The unknown within corresponds to the unconscious and to the unknown part of the world. It is by "writing the mystery of himsel" (184.9–10), by "reflecting from his own individual person life unlivable" (186.3), that Shem is able to become "the shining keyman of the wilds of change" (186.15). That is, by releasing the unknown inside himself, he becomes capable of improvising, entering the wilderness of transformation outside the known order. As Staten observes, "There is value in the hysterical insight that no ultimate distinction can be drawn between formlessness as degradation of the logos—even to the point of absolute loss of sense—and formlessness as the becoming-feces of the human body.... As the ground of a profligate generation of new forms" (381).

Shem's regression to formlessness leads him to parallel Lacan's assertion in *Le sinthome* that the division into active and passive at the root of language must be seen as an illusion (64). Lacan adds here that therefore "everything must be reconsidered from the point of view of the opaqueness of the sexual...that it is not founded on anything" ("*tout doit être repris au départ à partir de l'opacité sexuel...ne fonde en rien...*"). By seeing that the basic division is meaningless, one can generate unheard of forms, and this leads Lacan to the idea of the artist creating the world (64). Shem's situation prior to the active-passive division appears in a line from the ballad in his chapter: "*In Nowhere has yet the Whole World taken part of himself for his wife*" (*FW* 175.7). The line refers to the creation of Eve from Adam, but it combines the dominance of men over women with that of the colonizer over the colonized worldwide, as in "He married his markets..." (*FW 215.19*). Because Shem's mind is in a position that precedes such unjust subordination, he has access to a full range of human possibilities. But Shaun's description of him emphasizes that because he is not geared to standard reality, he could not occupy his position without appearing as polluted and degraded, as funky.

The *Wake* associates funk as a verb with the form of vocal improvisation called scat singing, and claims to show great ability at it: "How's that's for scats, mine shatz, for a lovebird? To funk is only peternatural its daring feers divine. Bebold" (451.16–17). Scat singing was first recorded in 1925 when Louis Armstrong dropped a sheet of lyrics while recording "Heebie Jeebies" and was forced to improvise, as he often had among friends (Terkel 28). Ruth Bauerle reports that Joyce's bohemian daughter Lucia was a fan of Armstrong's (152). *Funk* and *scat* are associated in the quote with the daring and boldness that create something "preternatural," inexplicable by ordinary means.[8] "Mine shatz," a version of the German *mein Schatz*, "my darling," contributes to an association between improvising and making excrement. "[D]aring feers divine" accords with Lacan's idea in *Le sinthome* that by inventing new phrases one can do without God's power by assuming it (136), both feeling and challenging fear of the divinity. This is a natural activity of the phallus—peternatural—that imitates Our Father—*paternoster*—insofar as sexual intercourse creates life.

The Irish equivalent of scat singing—musically keeping it up—is lilting, improvising with nonsense syllables. Lilting recurs in *Ulysses:* "with my tooraloom tooraloom tay" (5.14–15, see also 6.686, 15.1725, 4827, and 4918–20). ALP describes herself as "lilting on all the time" (*FW* 627.21), implying that the sound she makes as a river is a continuous improvisation, and therefore that the *Wake* consists of nothing but lilting, the sound a woman makes to keep her spirit or her man's spirit up.

The improviser attends to what is usually or properly cast off, playing alternative sounds scattered at various distances from the correct line of the "straight" theme. This activity is well represented by one of the most prominent images of the *Wake's* composition, that of Biddy the hen, who gathers scraps from a midden heap or dunghill to make up the *Wake's* text (*FW* 11, 110–11, et al.). The "spoiled goods" (11.18–19) gathered by this "parody's bird" (11.6) speak for the colonized as well as women by constantly subverting normal discourse. These colonial discoveries are not on any map until they expand it, so improvising is always exploring.

The self-expression of each character uses the liquid flow that mother first implanted in the mind of the child when she sang a sula, or what mother Africa sang to humanity. This ability to flow beyond the boundaries of existing terms is the only way to reach the new. Ishmael Reed describes the process under the name "Jes Grew"—that is, something without any source—in his novel *Mumbo Jumbo* (1972). Reed sees its analogy to the *Wake*, but also sees that it preceded Joyce, implying that Joyce was influenced by the African spirit of Jes Grew through the Jazz Age, in which Reed's novel is set:

> The Rhyming Fool who sits in Re-mote Mississippi and talks "crazy" for hours. The dazzling parodying punning mischievous pre Joycean style play of your Cakewalking your Calinda your minstrelsy give-and-take of the ultra-absurd. Ask people who put wax paper over combs and breathe through them. In other words.... I am saying Open-Up-to-Right-Here and then you will have something coming from your experience that the whole world will admire and need. (152)

Improvisation had long been practiced in Europe, but jazz carried it to more extreme and rapid levels that departed from European structures, orders, and continuities. The image of people breathing through their combs depicts improvisation as letting the incomprehensible discordance of experience pass through one. The *Wake* represents the most absolute mode of improvisation because it can change its discourse, its style, its perspective, and any of its rules and properties with each new word and even within a word. Using the flow of Mother Africa—the world's source of musical vitality—any letter can slide anywhere, going "out in all directions" with a "cubarola glide," a movement that enacts a conflict between several kinds of movements. Every Western apprehension of Africa enacts a great split of culture and history, but this may only be a strong figure of the divided self. How can this split be bound? In examining *Le sinthome*, one is struck by Lacan's elaboration of an incredibly wide range of knot forms, an insistence that knots can be arranged in a virtually infinite number of ways (see, e.g. 47, 62–63, 107–9, and 112). Improvisation expands modes of connection.

Joyce's innovation in allowing a shift at every letter may be compared to Charlie Parker's later breaking up notes into sixteenths and thirty-seconds in order to allow himself to fly into new changes. When one listens to a great improviser pushing the limits of expression, as saxophonist Charles Gayle is today, one gains the ability to perceive that the universe is made up of an infinite series of connections, and that human consciousness may be liberated to make any jump among them instantaneously. Joyce emphasizes that the openness to all possibilities may find its defining instance in what is least contained by propriety, what is most obscene. Jazz has always been dogged by a sense that its strange sounds are salacious, but Freud argues that the obscene is inseparable from the sacred (*SE* XIII, 18–25); and the presentation of Shem's bowel movement in Latin clearly describes an elaborate religious ritual (*FW* 185.14–25)—to cure intolerance by showing that "our" sacred cannot be separated from "their" obscene.

The object of this ritual is the repressed body of the mother, which Joyce associates with suppressed African mother goddesses such as Nut, Diana, and Isis. This may suggest the repression of a hypothetical foundation of matriarchal religion, which might be recovered with the continent that gave birth to civilization. Insofar as Shem's creativity leads to a message, it may well be his announcement, at the end of the chapter, that "our turfbrown mummy is acoming" (194.22). The word "mummy" here refers to Egypt, to a brown color, and to his mother, who arrives in the next chapter. "is acoming" indicates that she is constituted by an orgasm that does not stop, and that is enunciated by her lilt.

Shem and Anna, modern artist and woman as nonwhite, can only ascertain their identities through embarrassment because they are defined as outside what is respectable or acceptable unless they imitate the dominant culture that suppresses them. Instead, they resist the ideology of that culture by turning against profit and confronting their shame. This antithesis releases feelings that are repressed, and in so doing, the two figures free themselves from established words and views to constitute one of the leading principles of the *Wake*, a principle of advancing consciousness continuously designated as African. In articulating this principle, Joyce focuses on a terrible kernel of exaltation and debasement that had been ignored previously, exposing the root of future literary vision and human justice. The sublimity of this degradation is expressed more fully by writers such as Morrison, who is more drastically afflicted and empowered by it. But Joyce foresaw this opposing voice, and in the last phase of his work, he gave it greater complexity and force in his treatment of Asia.

Chapter 11

The Rising Sun: Asia in Finnegans Wake

Asia as the Ex-sistence of the World

Lacan seems to derive from Joyce the idea that artists make the universe (*Le sinthome* 64), and they do so by articulating what is incoherent. Lacan, like Freud, shared with Joyce a sense that what was most excluded from speech was most in need of recovery to liberate human consciousness. "Civilization" has been shaped by prejudices that deny humanity to the poor, "minorities," and women, obliterating their voices. Eide says that for Joyce, "the first ethical consideration is the preservation of difference within a context of response or responsibility" (7). It may follow that the greater the difference that can be responded to, the stronger the ethical approach to the Real of otherness.

Lacan says that what supports the Real is ex-sistence (*Le sinthome* 50). The Real exists outside the Imaginary and the Symbolic, so it involves movement beyond what exists and therefore necessitates the fourth element, the *sinthome*, because Lacan wants to redistribute the three orders: "*il me faut bien répartir ces trois modes…*" (50). His word for "redistribute," *répartir*, also means "go away again," another indication of the need to explore or move to the greatest distance. This is related to his statement that he wants "to bring out what writing announces not as a help to man, but as a help against him" ("*une aide* contre *lui*," *Le sinthome* 31). This parallels Kafka's reflection, "In the fight between you and the world back the world" (290). The way to gain the greatest insight is to enter into what the world puts forth against you.

Therefore, it is logical that Joyce's work should reach its maximum incompletion by focusing on the most culturally and intellectually distant parts of the planet. This later phase of Joyce's work brings forward the level where the colonized assert their independence, where their culture becomes less something that serves us than something that we must listen to. Asia was closer than Africa to liberation in the 1930s, a continent in revolt. The moral progress that arises from approaching the limit where colonialism fails to work or is defeated is that of joining or going out to the Real of difference in a new realm. Finally Joyce gives Asia independence by entering into its conflict both with the West and with itself.

From the point of view of the Church—which is linked to missionary colonialism in *Portrait* ("A great soldier of God!" *P* 107–8).—this new realm is pagan, and therefore a home of sin or sin-home. The symptom that connects the *Wake* to the exotic tends to be a *sinthome* by advancing a voluntary quest for new perception. Joyce's attention to areas that do not seem assimilable yields a picture of the earth that is more complete in its incompletion than perhaps any previous one, and there may be no stronger manifestation of this global complexity than his final concentration on Asia.

Book IV of the *Wake* (*FW*IV) opens with an active focus on the largest continent, primarily because it deals with the end of sleep and the rising of the sun in the East. Throughout the single long chapter that makes up *FW*IV, the importance of Asia is so vigorously maintained that one of the main themes of this highly multivalent book is that Asia will free herself from European domination and rise as a world power. Book IV contains references to many parts of Asia, but the main concentration seems to be on the major Asian nations whose turmoil would lead to transformation in the coming decades—India, China, and Japan. Their activities would carry Asia forward, sometimes in terrible ways, and Joyce sees the clash of their struggle, developing through them the ability to see the division in the Other that speaks for its power in depth.

Joyce was inclined to feel that his works were prophetic: on January 9, 1940, after Finland revolted against Russia, he wrote to Jacques Mercanton, "*comme le prophete le previt, le* Finn again wakes" (*SL* 403; see also 241, 242, 272). It is tempting to say that *FW*IV anticipates the likelihood that Asia will become the center of world power during the twenty-first century, but this is questionable on two counts. At the same time that the *Wake* never presents any position that is more than one of a series of possibilities, the possibility that Asia will regain its global centrality is in doubt. It is likely to remain so for generations in relation to different levels of economic, political, and cultural centrality. In *Thunder from the East: Portrait of a Rising Asia* (2000), Nicholas D. Kristoff and Sheryl WuDunn argue that it is inevitable that Asia will dominate the planet within decades.[1] Yet Colin Mason, in *A Short History of Asia: Stone Age to 2000 AD* (2000), warns that hopes for an Asian miracle overlook the vast poverty and exploitation that remain.[2] If Asia does assume hegemony, will this bring significant change? Perhaps not, but it evokes the possibility.

For Joyce, the shifting of power toward Asia ran parallel to his own anticolonialism. Moreover, because Joyce fought against repression as well as oppression, the personal and erotic focus that ends the *Wake*'s last chapter is an extension through the term *Asia* of the attack on prejudice with which the chapter began. Here the resistance of the colonized is matched by something that Joyce derived from Ibsen and from life, the resistance of women, who evoke the possibility of passing beyond the law of the phallus.

Cheng observes in *Joyce, Race, and Empire* that even more than in Joyce's other works, issues of ethnicity and anticolonialism are "vibrantly present in *Finnegans Wake*," with a "startling, ubiquitous, and fundamental insistence (once one starts *looking* for them), so that racial and imperial/colonial relationships will eventually be recognized as one of the central and structuring topics of *Finnegans Wake* alongside such fundamental building blocks...as Vico, Egyptology, the topography of Dublin, the sleeping body, Shakespeare, and so on" (251).

The first book to observe that *FW*IV emphasizes Asia was the first book on the *Wake*. Joseph Campbell and Henry Morton Robinson, in their *Skeleton Key* of 1944, speak of the entire chapter (*FW* 593–628): "The mood of the last pages of *Finnegans Wake* is very nearly that of the vastly disillusioned yet profoundly acquiescent, and even subtly joyful East" (340, n.1). After sixty years, the *Skeleton Key* remains the most engaging introduction to the *Wake*, but it is marred by an embarrassingly old-fashioned tendency to see mythology as an object of belief rather than a critical tool.[3] This quotation, though meant to be complimentary, displays prime features of the pernicious mythology delineated in Edward W. Said's account of Orientalism—the burden of stereotypes that the West has imposed on the East, particularly unchangingness, fatalism, and passivity (*Orientalism* 96–105). When Joyce uses stereotypes, they are parodic illustrations of how people can be distorted by ideology,[4] and the East is not acquiescent in the *Wake*: it is dynamic, in revolt, continuously attacking European authority.

At a time when terrorism has caused many to favor a reversion to imperialism,[5] it may not be easy to see how prevalent or well-justified the idea of sweeping away European dominance over Asia was during the first half of the twentieth century. Of course, most popular and conservative literature featured racist attacks of the kind notoriously expressed in Lothrop Stoddard's 1920 *The Rising Tide of Color Against White-World Supremacy*.[6] Nevertheless, among progressive Western thinkers, including many modernists, sympathy for Asian aspirations was widespread in the 1920s.[7] A striking example of such feeling, and one whose imagery parallels the *Wake* , is the film *Storm Over Asia*, by the great Soviet director Vsevolod Ilarionovich Pudovkin. Jay Leyda reports in *Kino: A History of the Russian and Soviet Film* that *Storm Over Asia* "was unusually successful abroad" (250), a high point in the Soviet attack on colonialism.

Pudovkin based the film on a true story and shot it in 1928 where it took place, in Mongolia, under the title *The Heir to Genghis Khan*. Khan

(1167–1227) was one of the greatest and most brutal conquerors in history. His empire, which included Korea, much of Russia, Hungary, and Northern India, was considerably larger than the Roman Empire, but did not last as long (De Hartog). The twentieth-century Mongolian hero of the film, Bair, is a hunter who is actually Khan's heir. He is badly swindled and almost killed by the British, who control his homeland. At the film's end, he explodes in rage, calling them thieves. Then he suddenly appears at the head of a horde (a Mongol word) of Mongols galloping toward a moving camera with waving swords. Now he incites his people to arise in their ancient strength and free themselves. Their anger becomes a mighty wind (Pudovkin used airplane propellers and filmed on an incline) that appears to actually blow the European colonizers away on the screen.

The famous final sequence of *Storm Over Asia* was controversial, but one need not look far to find similar sentiments in the 1920s. At the end of E. M. Forster's 1924 *A Passage to India*, for example, Dr. Aziz says, "Clear out, clear out, I say.... Until England is in difficulties we keep silent, but in the next European war—aha, aha! Then is our time.... We shall drive every blasted Englishman into the sea..." (360–61). Though Forster views this statement with abounding irony (Aziz is sure that India will be Moslem), it is a final stage of the passage to India, and he suspects its considerable truth.

In Paris, where Joyce lived from 1920 to 1939 (writing most of *FW*IV there toward the end of this period), one of the most celebrated novels of the 1930s was Andre Malraux's *Man's Fate* (*La Condition Humaine*, 1933), about a group of Chinese revolutionaries and their sympathizers struggling to free their country from imperialism. There is no evidence that Joyce read this novel, but it represents an attitude that was in the air among the progressives of the 1930s. We are now in a position to say that it was necessary to get the Europeans out of China and India. Paradoxically, it was also necessary for these nations to be occupied by Europeans in order to receive the technological and political ideas that they used against the Westerners.

I will turn below to the most certain source for Joyce's vision of Eastern liberation, Shelley's *Prometheus Unbound*, for ALP is associated with the heroine of that poem, Asia. ALP is also named for Alph, the sacred river in Coleridge's poem about the pleasure dome of Genghis Khan's grandson, "Kubla Khan."

Eastern Awakening

The sunrise that opens *FW*IV is the awakening of humanity. Its ray tells us that we should array ourselves for a resurrection that is an insurrection: "Array! Surrection! Eireweeker to the wohld bludyn world" (593.2–3).

McHugh's *Annotations* indicate the global nature of the *Wake* by listing (conservatively) sixty-two languages that it uses (xix–xx). The paragraph starts by repeating the phrase "Calling all downs."[8] If it intends to raise all those who are held down, it is appropriate for it to look eastward, for most of the oppressed people of the world have lived in Asia, which throughout history has held most of the world's population.[9] In the surrection of Asia, the majority of the world's people will throw off control by privileged minorities. If HCE, the "irewaker" of the *Wake*, will wake Ireland or anger around the world, then the main direction toward which he must extend is east: "Haze sea east to Oceania" (593.5) presents HCE in a foggy form moving toward or seeing the islands of the Pacific (Oceania), a shift that will be developed.[10]

The energetic clause that appears in the climactic final position of this paragraph is "genghis is ghoon for you" (593.17). This variation on the unhealthy but long-lived advertising slogan "Guinness is good for you" means that Genghis Khan is about to attack, "going for you." Whether or not this can be connected to Pudovkin's vision of the resurgent Khan (as the words suggest), in fact most of Khan's empire would be recovered by Asians within the next ten years as India and China freed themselves from European domination. So "genghis is ghoon for you" is factually prophetic.[11]

The phrase "ghoon for you" echoes an earlier passage on Asian revolt that refers to the Sepoy Rebellion, in which the *sepoys*, Indian soldiers fighting for the British, rebelled and were dreadfully massacred by them in 1857 (Cheng 286–87). The museyroom scene, a museum of battles, ends with a sepoy throwing a bomb at an imperialist on a white horse, primarily the Duke of Wellington, who once fought in India: "This is the dooforhim seeboy blow the whole of the half of the hat of the lipoleums off of the top of the tail on the back of his big wide harss" (*FW* 10.19–21). The phrase *go* or *do* for one suggests the impetuous violence of the "rangymad" (*FW* 10.9) subaltern rebel.

It is a standard practice—based on the invocation of the muse at the start of Homeric epic—to announce the theme of a literary work, or part of a work (Joyce gives each chapter of all of his novels its own focus), in its opening passage, and the only thing that precedes the "Genghis" paragraph in *FW*IV is the word "Sandhyas" repeated three times. Joyce told Jacques Mercanton that this word was Sanskrit for "the twilight of dawn" (Mercanton, "The Hours of James Joyce," Potts 221). The phrase seems to imply an uncertain period that will lead to a bright future, as the turmoil in Asia at this time would lead to liberation. There are thirty-four Sanskrit words on the first ten pages of this chapter according to McHugh as well as many other Indian references. The Sanskrit may serve to remind us that the basis of virtually all European languages (the main exceptions, Hungarian and Finnish, are Asian) lies in the lost Proto-Indo-

European language—a strong indication of the extent to which European civilizations are linked to Asian ones.[12]

If Europe and Asia develop as wings of the same culture, the question of which is the dominant side may have to be rethought. Kristof argues that "[F]or the great majority of the last few thousand years [perhaps 3,000], Asia has been far wealthier and more advanced and cosmopolitan than any place in Europe" (29). He says that the lead Europe maintained in the nineteenth and twentieth centuries was "unusual," and sees Europe as a relatively small appendage of the great land mass of Asia (20n.). The first page of the *Wake* refers to "Europe Minor."

To see the significance of this geographical fact, we need to dispel deep-seated convictions. But Joyce has always been about slipping the knot to radically readjust our perception—to such an extent that the Asia-Europe reversal may serve as a model of his perspective. This tends to focus on displacement through terms such as *parallax* and *gnomon* which refer to being aware of the other side or missing section. Two of the main assumptions that Joyce reversed are that Irish literature is minor in comparison to English and that certain types of sexual behavior (such as masturbation, homosexuality, and sadomasochism) are abnormal and exceptional. The basic pattern is one of unseating what Levinas calls "ontological imperialism," which Eide defines as "[r]eduction of the other to the principle of the same, of the one of the self" (7). Joyce's reversals speak for otherness.

On the following page of Joyce's preposterously Asia-centric text, the replacement of night with morning is presented in these words: "an inedible yellow meat turns out the invasable blakth" (*FW* 594.32–33). Coming after a sentence that evokes Viconian cycles, this suggests that the new day or age will take the form of a yellow principle that cannot be devoured though we may find it distasteful. The page after this expresses the idea of Asia for the Asians quite directly, using the German word for "East": ". . . Ostbys for ost, boys . . . " (595.1). Once this point becomes visible, it seems forceful, and it may influence the sentence that follows: "Death banes and the quick quoke. But life wends and the dombs spake!" (595.1–2). On one level, the living thing that quakes is the West, and the dead one that will revive and speak is the East that had long been in decline: "a wick weak woking from ennembrable Ashias . . . the Phoenician wakes" (608.31–32).

Next, after the question "Whake?"—which may ask where the wake or waking will take place—the Hill of Howth, which is often associated with HCE's head, is given the name of a Persian poet, suggesting an Asian locale: "Hill of Hafid,[13] knock and knock, nachasach, gives relief to the langscape as he stretches his lamusong untoupon gazelle channel . . . " (*FW* 595.3–5). [*N*]*achasach* combines German words for "after" and "thing" to add up to "a little bit further." This follows the ubiquitous pattern in *Ulysses* and the *Wake* of confusing time and space. As Stephen puts it in *Ulysses*, "A very short space of time through very short times of space" (*U* 3.12). The reversal of "times of space" forces one to consider that neither time nor space could exist without each other. One effect here is to add a temporal dimension to space, increasing the importance of exploration.

"[N]achasach" seems to imply that the further you go to the East, the closer you get to the future and relief on the landscape of language. Giving relief to the landscape may refer to a tendency for Chinese landscapes to be more vertical while Western ones are more horizontal. It probably takes a somewhat Orientalist view that the landscape of the East is unspoiled, or Asian languages fresher or more expressive, as in Pound's celebration of ideograms. Norris says in "The Last Chapter…" that in *FW*IV Kevin (Shaun) completes a movement backward in time to infancy that is also a movement backwards in space (18). The East as a child stretching his limbs on the landscape (McHugh) embodies the future as sunrise and rebirth. Tea from the Chinese tea port of Foochow (McHugh) is later described as "the brew with the foochoor in it" (*FW* 608.19).

"[N]achasach" refers to Nagasaki, perhaps the most forward-looking city in Japan, though what it was looking forward to is disturbing. From 1639 to 1858, Nagasaki was the only Japanese port open to Western trade. By the early twentieth century, it was in the forefront of a carefully planned Japanese effort to compete with the West by building modern industries, systems, and weapons (*Britannica*, "Nagasaki"). Inevitably Japan, which used the rising sun as its symbol, will be the main example of the rising sun of the East here, and it has continued to rise though much of Nagasaki was flattened by an American atomic bomb in 1945.

McHugh notes that the lines quoted above refer to Cape Strauch, Lamusong, and Gazelle Channel, three places in New Ireland, or "Newirgland" (595.10), an island in the Bismarck Archipelago, which is part of Melanesia. The image of a newer gland may have the risqué connotation of a completely new kind of organ. The unprecedented world of the East implies a whole new order, going beyond the country furthest from Europe, New Zealand, to start another alphabet like the next reading of the *Wake* coming up. In this context, the Bismarck Archipelago is advertised as the attraction of the future, a great investment: "…Newer Aland, has signed the you and the now our mandate. Milenesia waits. Be smarck" (601.35–36). This may also include a sexual innovation, a homoerotic encounter ("mandate"), and the land of the millennium.

The reclining body of HCE, which is located in Dublin at the start of the *Wake*, is here relocated in the Pacific. Joyce had a facetious tendency to think of Ireland as the center of the universe—a pattern developed most fully by replaying all of world history in Ireland in the *Wake*. This tendency is less ridiculous than it might seem, for Joyce made Ireland the center of an expanding intellectual universe. Here he is shifting that center to the East. At the bottom of the page, the reclining HCE becomes *H*e *c*an*e*ase (595.32, my italics) or, as McHugh notes, "pekinese," not just a dog, but an inhabitant or embodiment of the capital of China.

Two pages later, following the line "it is just about to rolywholyover. Svapnasvap" (597.3), a substantial philosophical passage on history and language provides a comprehensive view of the decline of the West and the rise of the East:[14] "there are two signs to turn to, the yest and the ist, the wright side and the wronged side, feeling aslip and wauking up…" (597.10–12). McHugh gives two meanings for *yest*, "west" and "yesterday." The West is "wright" as the side that has been made (wrought) or built up to be right. As yesterday, the West is falling asleep; while the East, as the side that has been wronged, is waking up with a squawk. "Svapnasvap" is Sanskrit for "asleep sleep" (McHugh), and implies a reciprocal *swap*, a word derived from two people hitting their hands together to strike a bargain, an exchange between sides.

Of course the ascent of the East is only one level of the text; and there is theoretical perception involved in feeling a slip. Lacan says that the slip is the basis of the joke and the unconscious (*Le sinthome* 97). Feeling a slip is both drifting into sleep and *realizing* that one is drifting, a waking move. And the squawk of the East is too importunate, so both sides are ambiguous and ridiculous, taking us back to the questionable basis of language in polarity ("two signs"). The paragraph ends by saying that this polarity keeps going, but it is quite arbitrary: "It is a sot of a swigswag, systomy dystomy which everabody you ever anywhere at all doze. Why? Such me. (*FW* 597.21–22). The meaningless duality imposed by the structure of language is a doze, but we seem to be trapped in it: it is what I am though it is incomprehensible ("search me"), and the only real justification for it is that I find it in myself. Everybody everywhere does it and any version of you is always doing it, involved in exchange. In contrast, the East represents awakening, but is it really awakening or another illusion? Clive Hart shows in *Structure and Motif in* Finnegans Wake that the *Wake* refers to two stories from the *Thousand and One Nights* in which people confuse dream with reality (104–8).[15]

The impossibility of distinguishing between sleep and waking is fundamental to the *Wake*, whose title refers to a waking that is a sleep. The only way to tell if one is asleep is by a self-consciousness that wakes one up, and the only way to assume consciousness may be through a dream-based fantasy that gives one direction. Freud overturns the hierarchy between waking and sleep, and Lacan places the ambivalence of the two states in a key position in his *Four Fundamental Concepts*. He derives from Maurice Merleau-Ponty the story of the Taoist sage Choang-tsu, who dreamed he was a butterfly and then awoke to wonder if the butterfly was dreaming him. Lacan holds that he was right because the brightness of the insect is the object of desire that gives him meaning: "he was, and is, in his essence, that butterfly who paints himself with his own colors—and it is because of this that, in the last resort, he is Choang-tsu" (*Four* 76). If his deepest level were not an empty dream, he would have no anchor to give him reality. The *Wake* portrays identity as capturing and pinning down the fleeting essence of the subject: "When shoo, his flutterby, Was netted and named" (262. 13–14).

Said observes that the east has often represented possibilites of regeneration for the west (Orientalism 114–15), and Lacan, who studied the Chinese language and Taoism for years (Roudinesco 351–52), was seeking on some level the kind of enlightment he found in Choang-tsu. Yet Lacan avoided the sort of idealizing of eastern wisdom that we saw in Campbell and Robinson because he recognized that the object of the desire has active power of its own, a power to recreate the west based on opposition. The title of the section in which Lacan tells Choang-tsu's story, "Of the Gaze as *Objet Petit a*" (*Four* 65), indicates that the object of desire is looking back: as the gaze, it is the mirror that defines one's being, the butterfly that dreams us. Lacan says that the beating of the butterfly's "wings is not very far from the beating of causation of the primal stripe marking his being for the first time with the grid of desire" (*Four* 76). The idea that the attractive object is the source of causality is embodied by Žižek's object-cause of desire (*Looking* 133). Asia has often played the role of this object *a (Shangri-la)* for Europeans.

The *Wake* suggests that all humans are connected, so Asia, as a dream vision for Westerners, projects in stereotypes the gap in people's minds that can lead them toward reversing what is known: "The old order changeth and lasts like the first. Every third man has a chink in his conscience and every other woman has a jape in her mind" (486. 10–12). This lapse or *sinthome* in the subject generates a pull toward rearrangement that seeks to make the last first, a drive toward unseating itself.

In *On Belief*, Žižek speaks of Tibet, describing an idealization of the East that goes hand in hand with racist abuse: "The spiritual treasure, the lost object-cause of desire, which we in the West have long ago betrayed, could be recuperated out there, in the forbidden exotic place. Colonization was never simply the imposition of Western values, the assimilation of Oriental and other Others to the European sameness; it was always the search for the lost spiritual innocence of OUR OWN civilization" (67–68). The moment when the truth of this arrangement gazes back at the West takes place when the colonized succeeds in imitating the colonizer well enough to cause a turnaround. Ironically, success has to be defined in Western terms. A strong example is the moment in *Portrait* when Stephen realizes that he knows the Anglo-Saxon word *tundish*, and the dean of studies does not (188–89); so he knows the

English language better than the Englishman. This point is celebrated by Seamus Heaney in *Station Island* (1984) as "the feast of the Holy Tundish" (93), the revelation that the English language belongs to the Irish. Such colonial resistance appears most strongly in those who are closest to the colonizer, such as the highly educated Irish and the precisely disciplined Japanese.

Red Sun Rising

The rise of Asia was spearheaded by Japan, which adopted Western technology to build itself into a world power. Richard Storry, in *A History of Modern Japan*, shows that Japan used British ships and British training to win the Russo-Japanese War in 1905 (141). This victory was an inspiration to Asians and encouraged the Japanese ultranationalist rightists, who took over in the course of the 1930s: "These self-styled 'patriots' took full advantage of the new prestige that Japan acquired after the defeat of Russia. This prestige was especially high in Asia, where the victory of an oriental over an occidental nation was discussed in every bazaar from Hong Kong to the Persian Gulf. To Indian nationalists, Japan's victory was a Thunder-clap; and in the eyes of Asian revolutionaries Tokyo occupied for a time the place later held by Moscow" (146).

Japan made nationalism seem as revolutionary as communism to Asians at this point, and her new status had an impact as far away as Ireland. In *Ulysses*, which is set before the Russo-Japanese War, Bloom remembers Simon Dedalus imitating Larry O'Rourke saying, "The Russians, they'd only be an eight o'clock breakfast for the Japanese" (*U* 4. 116–17). Here the colonized Irishman sides with the Japanese underdog. After the war, on 6 November 1906, Joyce wrote to his brother Stanislaus of "Japan, the first naval power in the world" (*Letters II* 188). This is partly a slap at England, but Joyce was emphatically aware of an area in which Asia was taking the lead. Eishiro Ito shows that during 1926, Joyce met separately with three educated Japanese men in Paris and used them to study Japanese language and culture ("Japanese" 37–38). And Carola Giedon-Welcker recounts Joyce' continuing fascination with Japan during the 1930s:

> When the Japanese edition of *Ulysses* appeared in 1932, he showed it to me with special interest, He believed that, because the Japanese mentality was used to an indirect and fragmentary symbol language and also because their form of poetic expression was close to his, they were well prepared for his way of thinking and writing. A Japanese poem which he recited to me in English translation showed the different "I's" which changed according to the situation. It dealt with an

> abandoned sweetheart whose multifaceted and fluctuating psychic state was expressed through symbolic allusions (mist, clouds, jewels, etc.) thereby also revealing the personality of the lamenting sweetheart. (Potts 266)

Joyce's elaborate interpretation of the poem credits the Japanese with sophisticated perception of how the subject as a signifier changes its nature in different states and connections, showing Joyce's careful thought about how to imagine parallels between widely different cultures. Unfortunately, this Japanese sensitivity and psychological insight will serve here to refute ethnic generalizations; for the activity of the Japanese that is most relevant to *FWIV* is atrocious, confronting us with the paradox that beautiful, intellectually gifted people can do terrible things. In this case, the takeover of Japan by rightists, which advanced from 1932 to 1937, involved a series of assassinations (Storry 191–204). It amounted to the military code of the country-the Bushido of honor before life—crushing its sensitive side. Yet the two sides are related, perhaps inseparable[16] and Joyce advanced toward a deeper understanding of Asia by dramatizing them.

The fact that most Asians came to hate Japan for the brutality of her conquests does not negate her role in leading Asia forward. The glory and terror of Japan fit Walter Benjamin's famous statement in "Theses on the Philosophy of History" that the so-called "cultural treasures" of history "without exception . . . have an origin" that one "cannot contemplate without horror" (Benjamin 256). The horrors are often crimes that make the beauty that covers them over economically possible. Žižek's *Parallax View* insists that we realistically accept the ways in which nobility is not possible without nightmare (5).

While Joyce was revising *FWIV*, late in 1937, the Japanese army was remorselessly advancing across China in a grim campaign that culminated in the unspeakable atrocities in Nanking in December, in which hundreds of thousands of civilians were murdered, raped, and tortured (Norris, *Writing* 7). W. Scott Morton, in *China; Its History and Culture*, says, "The Japanese officers had given the men *carte blanche* in order to break the Chinese will to resist, but the city became the scene of such horrible rape, murder, and looting that even the Japanese High Command was alarmed . . . " (198). The ravagers must have felt patriotic, and this may explain their ferocity.

Joyce had written a first draft of the dialogue between the Irish druid and St. Patrick that makes up the central scene of *FWIV* in 1923; but he built it up greatly in mid-1938, emphasizing a distinction already present in a fainter form in 1923—that the druid was Chinese and Patrick, Japanese. Dirk Van Hulle explains that Joyce sent early sketches for the *Wake*, including the first version of "Saint Patrick and the Druid" to

Weaver on July 20, 1923 with a request that she make three copies of the texts. In 1938, when he was ready to write this section, he asked Weaver to send this material. Her role in preserving the drafts for him is quite maternal. Van Hulle also claims that the 1923 draft of "Saint Patrick and the Druid" is "the first piece to be written in Wakean language," indicating its crucial role ("The Lost Word: *Book IV*," Crispi and Slote 442–43).

In 1938 the Japanese sensibility that Joyce had admired in 1932 was quite subordinated, though Ito shows that Joyce was adding Japanese words to other parts of the *Wake* in 1937 ("Japanese" 42). He was virtually certain to be aware of the Japanese war crimes, for as Iris Chang points out in her powerful *The Rape of Nanking* (1997), there were Western reporters in Nanking who published strong stories in the leading papers (144). Joyce would pick up the news from the Paris edition of the *New York Herald*, a paper he consulted during the 1930s (*Letters III* 293, 413). His awareness in 1940 of the Finnish revolt shows that he kept up with the news despite eye troubles.

A number of images of the violence of war appear in the 1938 drafts of the scene.[17] The dialogue of Muta and Juva, for which no earlier version is known, introduces the main debate. Juva (probably Shaun), the more knowing of the two spectators (versions of the cartoon figures Mutt and Jeff), describes Patrick in these words in 1938, "It is the Chrystanthemlander with his porters of bonzos . . . Moveyovering the cabrattlefield of slaine" (*FW* 609.32–34). The invader Patrick bears Christ's anthem, but he also bears the chrysanthemum, the official seal of the Japanese Emperor.[18] His "bonzos" are *bonzes*, glossed by McHugh as Japanese Buddhist priests. As porters, they move or carry St. Patrick (or "Patriki San Saki," *FW* 317.2) on a palanquin *over* the field of corpses. The scene may imply that the conversion of Europe to Christianity was more violent than the lives of the saints reveal.

Muta begins his response by distorting "porters of bonzos" as "Pongo da Banza!" (*FW* 609.35). McHugh glosses this as the Italian "*pongo da panza*," "I put from the belly." This suggests that Muta throws up when he sees the bodies on the field. They may have been put there by *banzai*, the famous Japanese cry of loyalty, which appears in *Ulysses* (12.600). The tendency of characters in *Ulysses* and the *Wake* to echo each other falsely fits Lacan's concept of misrecognition: "The Other is, therefore, the locus in which is constituted the I who speaks along with he who hears, what is said by the one being already the reply, the other deciding, in hearing [*entendre*] it, whether the one has spoken or not" (*Ecrits* 358, brackets in text). In mistaking Juva's phrase, Muta reveals the ghastliness of the situation from Shem's side of the parallactic duo. Žižek would say that one cannot have porters of bonzos without *pongo da panza*, or pomp without nausea.

"[M]oveyovering," or hovering like a movie camera, may refer to the tendency of the Japanese to take pictures of their victims, including motion pictures. Some of these were reproduced in Newspapers and magazines. Moreover, some footage taken by reporters appeared in newsreels (*Rape* 146–49), which seem to be referred to by the headline-like titles that precede the debate: "Rhythm and Colour at Park Mooting. Peredos last in Grand Natural. Velivision victor. Dubs newstage oldtime turf tussle..." (*FW* 610.34–36). A *mooting* is a meeting in which two people try to make each other moot or insignificant. A *parados* is a bank of earth behind a trench to keep soldiers from being seen against the sky (*Random House College Dictionary*). The oldtime turf tussle is newstaged as a media event in which the pair of two (*dos*) both finish last, or lose paradise, and the media win. The great emphasis on television in the *Wake* is one of its stronger prophetic features, like its vision of Asia. The reference to the scene as a park meeting makes it equivalent to the scene in the park with HCE and the girls (as well as the one with the cad); that is, the conquest of the native by the imperialist is equivalent to the taking of male authority away from women.

If the field of corpses evokes the invasion of China, a striking addition of 1938 seems to refer to the atrocities of Nanking with grisly specificity. It is the first of the last two titles before the mooting: "Jockey the Ropper jerks Jake the Rape. Paddrock and bookley chat" (611.1–2). "Jockey" is the Japanese Patrick/Shaun here, and he stands on Peter's rock, the Church that Joyce saw as imperialistic. The reference to Jack the Ripper fits photos that the Japanese took of their soldiers practicing with bayonets on civilians who were tied up. Chang reproduces two of these, as well as pictures of women tied up to be gang raped.[19] "Ropper" combines "raper," "robber," "ripper," and "roper." As in Chang's title, China itself is raped.

The mooting itself, from its 1923 version on, enacts a historical explanation of how ethnic groups get aligned with power: circumstances allow some groups to identify with ruthlessness and victory, while others are forced by oppression into roles of ineffectual sympathy. The fact that Japanese sensitivity and monstrosity support each other shows that people cannot be active or passive: only events can. An event that makes one party a winner and the other a loser is a mooting in that it denies the full humanity (or French fatherhood) of both, "Peredos last." Yet much of history consists of groups taking on these polar identifications by which both lose.

The framework Joyce uses for the debate between the bookly (the Irish Berkeley), idealistic Chinese Balkelly and the flagrant Japanese Patrick expands on a pattern found in *Ulysses*. In this scheme, cultural groups who are designated as sensitive, poetic, and intelligent generally get conquered by groups that are seen as brutal, mechanical, and narrow-minded.

The main examples are the Hebrews enslaved by the Egyptians, the Greeks defeated by the Romans, and the Irish colonized by the English. This pattern is established in the first two chapters by Stephen's subordination to Buck Mulligan and Haines, his thoughts on the defeat of the Greeks (2.7–53), his working for the Unionist Deasy, and his reflection on the Jews as victims (2.365–72). It is explained in "Aeolus" in passages such as this one on the Irish by Professor McHugh: "Success for us is the death of the intellect and the imagination. We were never loyal to the successful. I teach the blatant Latin language. I speak the tongue of a race [the English] the acme of whose mentality is the maxim: time is money. Material domination" (7.551–55). Earlier, Stephen's Anglo-Irish boss Deasy told Stephen to keep his accounts straight and realized that Stephen would soon lose the job (2.401).

The conquest of much of China by Japan fits one implication of this scheme: that inhumanity may be necessary for world leadership and empire building. This idea of Joyce's (which, as we will see, may not be his only view) may seem too pessimistic, but consider the case of Henry V, Shakespeare's ideal ruler. Hardin Craig says, "Henry's princely virtues, as enumerated and depicted in *Henry V*, are the recognizable and customary group. One cannot but believe that he was deliberately conceived of as the embodiment of these ideals" (739). Henry commissions clergymen to dig up and design an excuse for him to expand English power by invading France (*Henry V* I.ii). Then he threatens that if the inhabitants of Harfleur do not surrender, his soldiers will kill their men and children and rape their women (III.iii). Harfleur surrenders, and critics who defend Henry say that this is just the military rhetoric of the period; but it was the practice of the period, and Henry could not afford to make hollow threats. After decidedly winning at Agincourt, he orders the execution of the prisoners of war just to be on the safe side (IV.vi). His courtship of the French Princess Katharine is presented as charming, but is parallel to the second scene of *Richard III*, in which Richard seduces Lady Anne, the widow of a prince he has just murdered.[20] Stephen sees the latter as the scene in which Shakespeare's genius first stands out (*U 9.985–88).* If the object of war was to kill the men and take the women, then this scene represents the truth about heroic victory, that it tends to take a special pleasure in raping a woman whose husband one has killed. Harold Bloom agrees with Hazlitt that Henry is an "amiable monster" (320).

What Henry threatens at Harfleur is not far from what happened in Nanking, so England and Japan have much in common as aggressive islands invading the mainland. It is also possible to see both as poetic cultures that ultimately turned away from conquest. But they *did* these dreadful things, and they stopped mainly when forced to.

I agree with Campbell and Robinson that the victory of the practical Patrick over the idealistic druid is a stage of transition from sleep to waking (348–49), and so from the dream of peace to the reality of conflict. This is consistent with Bishop's view that the *Wake* is about the world of sleep (*FW* xv–xxv), and Joyce said to Mercanton that in the dialogue between the druid and Patrick, "Day is near" ("Hours," Potts 220). Norris sees the interlude of St. Kevin's bath (*FW* 603–6) as a return to innocence ("Last" 13). This corresponds to a stage of blankness in which the waking person is at first as simple as a small child. Then the confrontation with the Generalissimo Patrick represents the return of issues of conflict and power as consciousness grows and divisions return. On another level, this is Asia moving from an internalized mindset to one that faced the outer world of international politics.

Žižek says that what makes communication between different cultures possible is not shared values, but a shared sense of division or deadlock because one can communicate with the other only insofar as both recognize that they are split (*Tarrying* 31). In view of this, Joyce's perception of Asia in terms of a terrible conflict engages Asia with extraordinary depth. After all, the split between China and Japan is identified with a split in Ireland between native Celt and imperialist invader, both involving the opposition between the spiritual Shem and the material Shaun.

In the confrontation, the Chinese-Irish druid speaks of looking inward to see all colors: "In trues coloribus resplendent with sextuple gloria of light" (*FW* 611.21–22). This stands for seeing the complexity of the causality or motivation of things. "Same Patholic," who is pathologically oriented toward sameness, is referred to as "comprehendurient" (611.30). McHugh renders this as "longing to grasp," yet Patrick has no ability or desire to understand. He is more interested in grasping the Orient than in grasping ideas, and he wants to comprehend everything by bringing it together to embrace it in a single master signifier. So he looks at a series of King Leary's multicolored features and sees them all as green, reducing Irish multiplicity to the purity of staunch chauvinism: Leary's "fiery" red head looks "herbgreen," his "saffron kilt look same hue of boiled spinnasses," and his golden torc looks like "curlicabbis"(611.33–612.10). The druid sees a division within that can serve communication in Žižek's terms, while the saint's insistence on unity blocks communication by denying the weakness that can be shared.

Pat appeals to the crowd by reducing everything to one pat color, and by the simple authority of the sun of monotheism as opposed to the complexity of polytheism, for as McHugh notes, "Patrick caused reappearance of sun blotted out by Laoghaire's druid; onlookers glorified Patrick's God." The victory—"Good safe firelamp! hailed the heliots" ("God save Ireland" 613.1)—is celebrated by lovers of the sun (Greek *helios*) and serfs or slaves or helots (McHugh); but these fans of narrow-minded violence are also worshippers of hell and idiots. Platt points out that some racists of the nineteenth century, such as Jules Michelet whom Joyce refers to, saw their chosen people as "born in the full light of the sun among our forefathers, the sons of light" (Michelet cited in Platt 36), so Joyce may be attacking racism in this passage. But the sun here stands mainly for monotheism, which was originated by Akhenaton, who worshipped the sun. The sun of Christianity is capable of burning people. *Portrait*, for example, mentions that Giordano Bruno was burned at the stake in 1600 for having scientific ideas (249). So the power of the Trinity is seen as "The firethere the sun in his halo cast. On men" (*FW* 612.20). Militant religion or nationalism demands a mass sacrifice of men, or holocaust.

It also imposes itself on its victims en masse. "Good safe firelamp!" as "God save Ireland!" shows how Irish nationalism and religious fanaticism have been intensified by conquerors such as the Church and England, whose mottoes it echoes ("God save England"). Žižek says that one generally cannot oppose "a 'true' identity of a culture to its falsification by a foreign gaze" because the " 'true' identity itself, as a rule, forms itself through the identification with a foreign gaze which plays the role of the culture's Ego-Ideal" (*PV* 377). Ireland and China may have taken on some of the narrowness of their conquerors.

The multiplicity or richness of seeing things in different colors is debilitating in practice in that it complicates action, so the rainbow is a boon that causes ruin, the "Irisman's ruinboon" (*FW* 612.30). And the monotheist sunshine of daylight immobilizes people by transfixing them in a transfigured trance of rationality: "Pour deday. To trancefixureashone" (613.8–9). This certainly refers to Blake's villainous figure for the limiting effects of rationality, Urizen, or "your reason," the vindictive God of Puritanism, thereby building the link between Japan and England.

The idea that the vitality of paganism was replaced by the asceticism and dogma of Christianity is glaringly evident in Irish history and was quite familiar to Joyce as a college student. Andrew Gibson points out that popular Celtic revivalists like Standish O'Grady felt that Christianity had "ruined" ancient Irish culture (*Revenge* 109). In *Ulysses*, Mulligan uses the phrase "pale Galilean" (9.615), which comes from the following lines about Christ in Algernon Charles Swineburne's "Hymn to Proserpine" (1866), a version of the defeat of Greece by Rome: "Thou has conquered, O pale Galilean, / the world has grown grey from thy breath."[21] And Stephen remembers students enthusiastically shouting, "new paganism" (*U* 1.176).

George Cinclair Gibson's recent *Wake Rites* uses a vast knowledge of Irish mythology to argue that all of the *Wake* is organized around the Teamhur Feis, an ancient Irish ritual in which the king was either renewed or replaced. He sees the scene between the Druid and Patrick as the climax of the novel, based on such a Feis at which Christianity defeated paganism, and he argues that the *Wake* is intended "to redress the loss wrought by Patrick at Tara" (82), that is, to restore a Joycean version of paganism. Gibson's arguments explain scores of featuress in the *Wake*, but he is wrong to hold that these rites are *the real truth* about the *Wake*. In fact, he resembles Patrick in arguing that green is the real truth about the rainbow. Yet his thesis seems to me to be largely correct.

That Joyce could arrange the mooting to enact both the fate of Ireland and the fate of Asia is a fine indication of the superabundance of the *Wake*. It adds depth to his treatment of both worlds because they share the fullness of the conflict in much of its complexity. Joyce's thinking has expanded its powers of exploration. Moreover, the defeat of the druid by the saint—which is of course far from clear in the text—should not be seen as entirely negative, as I suggested when I spoke of a level of waking up.

Joyce's admiration for the Scholastic mental discipline of Christianity probably led him to see the shift from paganism to the church as an increase in realism, and the replacement of pagan vitality by Roman Catholic authority may allow for advances in such areas as morality and power. Shaun is not entirely worthless: he spreads the word though he distorts it. On the Asian level, the defeat of Chinese inwardness by Japanese assertiveness forced the Chinese to fight harder. This had the general effect of causing Asia to enter the world, to restore the balance of the planet, if only by cultivating an alternative Asian imperialism. Joyce realized that Asia could only arise from the ashes of her subjugation through terrible conflict , and he hails this brightly burning tiger: "Ashias into fierce force fuming" (*FW* 608.31). Michael Tratner commented after reading this argument that it holds that undoing imperialism will not be complete liberation, but another conquest. Yet the idea of undoing imperialism must be sustained in all of its unlikelihood, and the *Wake* uses Asia as the figuration of what has not been known to suggest other possibilities.

Anna as Asia

The defeat of the druid by Patrick represents progress toward attaining "mournenslaund' (614.8), which refers not only to "morning," but also (as McHugh notes) to the German *Morgenland* or "Orient." At this point the chapter ends a first half that is about waking and begins a second that is about ALP. This is a further stage of waking up through the confrontation with or absorption in the opposite sex, who is real (and Real) insofar as she shows her resistance, and may carry consciousness forward.

The waking half is linked to the ALP half through the main source with which Joyce is closely connected that develops an image of Asia,

Shelley's *Prometheus Unbound* (1820), in which Prometheus' beloved, Asia, is the main character after Prometheus. As the nymph who has been separated from Prometheus by his binding, she stands for the part of the world that has been denied by the dominant order, which is embodied by the tyrant Jupiter. Prometheus' reunion with Asia at the end represents the freeing of the oppressed parts of the planet—Earth being a vociferous character in the poem—so that all humanity can be united joyfully in the fourth act (lines 400–401). This aspect of Asia is a feminine mode of reconciliation that can carry history beyond masculine conflict. I will soon indicate a tougher side of ALP, but her utopian side may inspire progress.

According to the *Variorum Edition* of *Prometheus Unbound*, the idea that Asia stands for the Orient was first introduced in French in 1843 when Andre "Delrieu suggested the personification of the continent regarded as the source of the human race" (Zillman 327). This reading may reflect the racial myth of the prehistoric Aryans who brought civilization from Asia: Platt reports, that Aryanism was most widely accepted by educated people around the middle of the nineteenth century, though it continued to spread as a popular prejudice after it was refuted later in the century (15–18). Despite this unfortunate aspect, the Asian link can serve to give credit to the way non-Western thinking anticipated European philosophy, as in the anticipation of idealism in the Hindu scriptures. There is not much detail to connect Shelley's Asia to the East; but she is described and shown as waiting for Prometheus, the spirit of creativity, in a "far Indian vale" (I.1.826 and II.1), and Shelley clearly wants to speak not for an Aryan race, but for the liberation of the continent of Asia.

Joyce's devotion to Shelley is indicated in *Portrait*, where the adolescent Stephen spontaneously quotes from Shelley's lines on the moon (*P* 96), and the collegiate one uses Shelley's image of a "fading coal" to describe the radiance that is the goal of his esthetic (*P* 213). Richard Ellmann observes that Joyce derived from Shelley's "Defense of Poetry" the idea that poets should judge society (Joyce, *CW* 142). *Prometheus Unbound* is about the progressive spirit of art breaking the rules to enlarge human consciousness. ALP connects with this model as an ann-tidote to the violence of the preceding debate, a solution involving creative productivity linked to the name *Asia*.

HCE, who commits adultery in his family home (*FW* 198.10–13), is referred to in Shelleyan terms as "Promiscuous Omebound" (*FW* 560.1). With help from Ito, I have found twenty-two uses of *Asia* or variants of it in the *Wake*, and often, but not always, it seems to be the name of a woman.[22] An apt example for my case is one of the many names given for ALP's "mamafesta" (*FW* 104.4), or letter: "He Calls Me His Dual of Ayessha' (105.18–19). This implies that the whole book (which is equated with the letter) centers on the possibility of a reunion of HCE as the West with ALP as the East that says, "Ah yes"—a reunion that does not take place. In fact, Platt observes that the song from the musical *The Geisha*, "And They Call Me the Jewel of Asia," is treated ironically by Joyce elsewhere (Platt 131–32), so the reunion is mocked as it is posited.

Anna is also called "his Anastashie" (*FW* 403.10–11), a version of *Anastasia*, which includes *asia* and means "resurrection" in Greek. She can supposedly fulfill his dreams by maintaining her constancy ("Anna-stay-she"), and as Asia gets idealized, Orientalism creeps in. Yet stereotypes tend to get negated here; for example, the wily Oriental is opposed by "honest Asia." Moreover, Anna may not maintain her constancy, for it is based on a view of HCE that is unrealistic. In *FW* IV she imagines proud fantasy identities that HCE may assume, including the imperial (and aviational) dominance of Asia: "Pharaops you'll play you're the king of Aeships" (*FW* 625.3–4), which prefigures the "whitespread wings" of the last page.

In the present of *FW*IV, HCE is lying down, as he often is elsewhere in the *Wake*: "Rise up, man of the hooths, you have slept so long! Or is it only so mesleems? On your pondered palm. Reclined from cap to pede" (*FW* 619.25–26). The last line describes the Howth peninsula, which has a cap (the hill where Bloom and Molly embrace) and a lower part or pede (foot), which is where Howth Castle is located (Mink 346–47). But these lines also present a sleeping Asian who implies an awakening. The passage describes a statue of the Buddha that Bloom in *Ulysses* recalls seeing in the National Museum: "Buddha their [Chinese] god lying on his side in the museum. Taking it easy with hand under his cheek" (5.328–29).[23] Molly later thinks that Bloom, lying on his side next to her, resembles this statue (18.1201–4).

If ALP wants HCE as Buddha to rise, then his waking will be another version of the rising of the East; "And stand up tall! Straight. I want to see you looking fine for me.... Blooming in the very lotust and second to nill, Budd!" (620.1–3). McHugh, in *The Sigla of* Finnegans Wake, discusses Joyce's use of lotus blossoms as an Eastern symbol of rebirth (111–12). The reunion that ALP longs for will make HCE second to none (or to Dublin backwards), but she struggles against doubts that it will take place.

Her effort to empower the East may appear when she instructs her sleeper on how to behave when they visit the "Old Lord": If the Ming Tung no go bo to me homage me hamage kow bow tow to the Mong Tang (*FW* 623.12–13). China combines with sunrise here, for the phrase *Ming Tung* means "bright east."[24] This is a version of Muhammad's line about bowing to the inevitable. The standard Western form, which simplifies what Muhammad said, is "If the mountain will not come to Muhammad, Muhammad will go to the mountain" (Brewer 746). Insofar as ALP sees

Ireland as her home, Joyce's text may say that if the East will not bow to the West (her home), the West must bow to the East.

ALP increasingly questions, toward the end, whether the man who sleeps will be able to follow her into exaltation. The *Wake* invokes the revolutionary transcendence that Shelley celebrates, but it does not actualize it. Joyce's vision extends Shelley's heroine to imagine an awaking through feminine consciousness that will pass beyond aggression, making Asia not just a new center of power, but a new hope for humanity. Yet this new hope remains potential, as woman's sexuality remains potential for Lacan and Irigaray.

Anna's dream of freedom and optimism may be classified as a stage of waking, one in which the mind, refreshed by sleep, envisions possibilities that problems can be solved. This rosy disposition tends to get qualified as one wakes further and remembers difficulties—just as the initial euphoria of a revolution succumbs to problems—but it has the merit of pointing to future advances and solutions. Such a waking stage is specified in *Portrait* when Stephen writes his villanelle: "His mind was waking slowly to a tremulous morning knowledge, a morning inspiration" (*P* 217). At this point Stephen conceives that woman could be liberated from her role of temptress: "*Are you not weary of ardent ways, / Lure of the fallen seraphim?* (*P* 217). He is inspired to a strong feminist statement, but will not sustain such insight without relapses.

ALP denounces the patriarch HCE, whom she has been defending, saying that she thought he was "great in all things," but now she sees that he's "but a puny" (627.23–24). So she decides to leave him and rejoin her sisters, dancing in female exultation: "Ho hang! Hang ho! And the clash of our cries till we spring to be free" (627.30–31). Here she speaks for the Hwang Ho, or Yellow River, which often overflowed; and since her female companions include the Nile and the Amazon (627.30–31), her dancing expresses the liberation of the Third World as well as women. The liberation of the Third World is far from possible, but like those of women and workers, it is a necessary concept to envision justice for humanity.

ALP cannot easily escape patriarchal authority, however, for it arises near the end to confront her in the form of Father Ocean, Neptune with his trident of phallic authority: "I see them rising! Save me from those therrble prongs!" (628.4–5). This is Poseidon, the nemesis of Odysseus, the chaotic element that opposes human exploration, linked to archaic religion as the unthought part of the world. On the level of Joyce, it is the part of his world that he has not freed from his control, such as the area where his chauvinism returns as the Real to interfere with his desire to liberate women or people of color. But the ocean will not stop ALP any more than it stopped Odysseus, any more than the atrocities of 1937 (or the tsunami of 2004, predicted here) stopped Asia from rising. ALP as water is bound by her cycle (equivalent to Lacan's drives) to pass beyond domination from outside and reach her peaceful "blue bedroom" in the sky (627.9).

The picture of Japan's ferocious triumph, followed by the invocation of recycling (614–15) summons forth Anna's voice to express aspiration beyond the retaliations of force. That longing must remain threatened, but it cannot be extinguished. The hope of freedom and the threat of authority are locked together in a swelling question at the end. If ALP is overwhelmed by the "feary father" (627.2), as she dreads here, she will be halted. But if she maintains her resistance, she will move forward to begin the book again with new knowledge as her last sentence leads to the first one ("the riverrun"). Yet this may only show that she is trapped in repetition. Will women continue to liberate themselves or will they (as they sometimes seem to be doing lately) return to being subservient? Apparently they will combine both vectors, but Joyce makes a point of portraying the submission as dreadful on the last page. As humanity advances, it will read the *Wake* in more liberated ways, just as we have already surpassed Campbell and Robinson.

Another question suspended at the end is whether Asia could really represent a new dispensation, as Shelley dreamed it would. This dream runs through the *Wake*, as it ran through *Storm over Asia*, *A Passage to India*, and *Man's Fate*. The idealization (and feminization) of the East may be justified if it delineates possibilities of freedom.

This hope gives Asia beauty as a symbol of humanity rising from oppression: the hope that she will not just be another conqueror, that people can learn from history. Japan, which has long abstained from militarism, may still avoid a complete backsliding. India may thrive through technology, and in China, socialism may survive in cooperation with a flourishing economy. Insofar as these possibilities are unprecedented, they speak not for the Imaginary that clings to the past, but for the Real that reveals the future. And insofar as they are possible, Asia may assume a real leadership that will thoroughly reverse our perspective. It may lead us to a new kind of planet freed from inequality.

Yet Japan is moving toward the Right and denying war crimes (see note 11), India remains attached to Nationalism, and China maintains a dreadful human rights record. Joyce cannot show the liberation of Asia or woman or the masses as actual, or follow the teleology that assumes progress to be inevitable. What is important is not a developmental schema, but the act fraught with danger that reaches the Real, that opens the unlikely a little wider.

The Asia to which ALP is linked in the *Wake* speaks in opposition to known definitions. To see the Real world is to see what the accepted world is formed by excluding. Western reason has usually expanded by turning toward what it left out. The points at which Westerners can learn most from Asia are those at which Asia goes beyond expectations. By focusing on Asian resistance, Joyce explored a path that leads to independence, to conceptual expansion, and ultimately to what theorist Rey Chow is striving to define as a "Post European Perspective." Chow finds that this perspective is bound to be haunted by established European standards. This parallels the idea that the liberation of Asia will only be a new conquest, that imperialism cannot be left behind. Yet Chow affirms that we must keep aiming beyond what we can imagine (305, 307).

ALP's Asian identity is only one of many, but it fits in with others, such as women who are oppressed and the Liffey that flows eastward toward the sunrise. As the author of the letter that is the *Wake*, she draws toward the East as a repository of alternate realities. The constant changing of each word into another that makes up the process of reading the *Wake*—the activity of difference between words—is the flow of ALP's discourse from statement to ambivalence. Therefore the late focus on Asia is not a narrowing: it confronts the virtually endless meanings that proliferate in the book. The multiplicity of Asia is valuable less for its richness than for its contradiction.

Through her combination of longing for a real awakening and rejecting existing realities, ALP as Asia finally says things that no other voice could articulate, leading to the future. She tells us that we should wake up to productivities outside what is known, sources that reshape every feature of the world to extend to all potentialities of perception (if only through messy anger): "When the messanger of the risen sun . . . shall give to every seeable a hue and to every hearable a cry . . . " (*FW* 609.18–20).

Joyce, in fact, does not speak for Asia, despite the depth of the intense, sublime, and conflicted image of it that he creates. He speaks for his Irish-Italo-Parisian view of Asia, knowing in his ironies that he is very far from it. He speaks for the distance between him and it, creating a new subject that is especially generative because it goes so far, covers such a distance. As the study of Joyce advances in Asia, as Joyceans grow more aware of the Asian conclusion of Joyce's canon (the completion of "Araby"), the population of "Eirenesians" (25.17) will increase. They will enrich themselves as the Joycean world and its consort, the Real one that it approaches through language, continue to advance into the new kinds of consciousness that constitute freedom.

Conclusion and Supplement: Exploration and Comedy

The model of exploration allows us to follow Joyce's drive toward discovering the unknown, the excluded side of the world, the power of humanity to free itself from authority. The progress I have traced through Joyce's canon may be said to involve three main aspects: changing one's volition by assuming new metaphors, opening up multiple meanings in language, and moving to new locations. These psychological, linguistic, and spatial activities are inseparable components of carrying consciousness to new levels, or increasing one's awareness of otherness. One cannot change one's mind without changing one's language and moving at least figuratively to a new place.

The three activities may be described by analogy to Lacan's three registers. Changing volition pertains to the Imaginary: Lacan says, "the ego is an imaginary function" (*Ego* 36), and the Imaginary allows one to put together a new image for the subject. (Any image of the Lacanian barred subject always leaves out what is crucial, the gap that draws one onward.) The expansion of language operates in the Symbolic, which Lacan describes as the power of naming that makes objects subsist (*Ego* 169), though each name is a misnomer. And reaching a new space engages the Real as contact with what is not known. This reflects the reality of the unconscious, but it retreats as soon as one arrives at it, so exploration has to go further, like Odysseus going beyond the end of the world. The *Wake* evokes attraction to "Newer Aland" (601.35), the place beyond New Zealand where a new language begins, and Lacan has a similar goal that he may derive from Joyce.

These three registers constitute the subject; but to *portray* the subject, to draw it forward into the Real of discovery, the *sinthome*, the fourth term that Lacan associated with Joyce's talent, must enable a shift in the three, opening them to reformulation. Just as Stephen's thinking is "a dusk of doubt and self mistrust," the *sinthome*, as an identification with the aberration of one's symptom, is a misgiving about whether one fills one's place. An aberration is defined as a departure whose goal is unknown (*ab*, "from" + *errare*, "to stray") and the *sinthome* is always voyaging, on its way to the Real of discovery that is always elsewhere (ex-sistent).

Žižek's definition of the *sinthome* in *The Parallax View* emphasizes the negative: he says that it is "the minimum formula of the subject's consistency" and that proximity to it generates anxiety (*PV* 89). We recall Lacan's statement that anxiety is the only signal that does not lie (*Anxiety* 142). Likewise, Žižek sees the Real through a series of images of horror and foreboding in *Looking Awry* (6–15 et al.). His emphasis on the terrible nature of freedom is related to his insistence on confronting the extreme shock of revolution, and may indicate an obsessive need for symbolic stability that tends to frame its revolution in Stalinist or absolute terms: only through radical antagonism and central authority can Marxism hold actual power. Žižek's political toughness seems opposed to Lacan's picture of the *sinthome* as a path to freedom in Joyce's work, but Žižek's conclusions about revolution indicate a possible overlap with Joyce that may have force.

At the end of *The Parallax View,* Žižek stresses the gap between two sides of progressive politics, constructive political action that addresses specific issues and revolutionary violence. He insists that ameliorating specific injustices only supports the Capitalist system, and that one must turn away from local concerns to extreme political action that can change the fundamental principles of society. The intellectual principle that Žižek ultimately finds crucial to decisive revolution is a fundamental refusal of the existing order that he sees in Melville's "Bartleby the Scrivener," the famous story about a man who decides not to do his tedious job, the *sinthome* to Farrington's symptom. Žižek asserts that such revolutionary negation should not be seen as a step toward constructive action, but as the permanent foundation that keeps the revolution aggressive, though he realizes that it is a difficult attitude to sustain (*PV* 382).

Joyce may manage to stay in touch with the Real of revolution by his incessant departure toward the unknown, which is parallel to what Žižek calls "the violent act of actually changing the basic coordinates of a constellation" (381). The "Nestor" episode of *Ulysses* begins by establishing a motif of Stephen's that occurs frequently and intensely, the image of blowing up the world: "the ruin of all space, shattered glass and toppling masonry, and time one livid final flame" (2. 9–10, compare 3. 249, 10. 825, 15.4245). The basic coordinates that Stephen wants to explode in his revolutionary Blakean fervor include time and space. Soon after this he thinks, "It must be a movement then, an actuality of the possible as possible" (2. 67–68). He uses these phrases from Aristotle to imagine that continuous motion allows what is possible to become actual without losing its radical potential as possibility. As in his scrambling of Aquinas to combine love and lust (9.430), he thinks of informing the liberal focus on actuality with revolutionary possibility through an incessant exploratory imperative. That his mental reaching beyond knowledge is anticolonial in its rebellious focus is indicated by the fact that at his elbow when he first thought this in Paris was a Siamese reading strategy

(2. 70–71).[1] The movement that allows Stephen to imagine radical deconstruction is the one Lacan attributes to the *sinthome*; his colonial identity is a symptom that becomes a *sinthome* (and postcolonial) when he re-cognizes it. Joyce can sustain this revolutionary force by seeing it in parallactic opposition to Bloom.

Because it knows it is a symptom, because it is a provisional splice, the *sinthome* takes every frame of reality as contingent or hypothetical, and thereby it allows us to see oppositions without resolving them. All of the works produced by Joyce's *sinthome* end with a concentration on the greatest possible uncertainty that can be generated by everything that preceded the ending. Movement toward uncertainty is equivalent to movement toward distance. All of the stories in *Dubliners* portray the social forces that withhold Gabriel from understanding Gretta and yet make him desperate for that understanding. All of the changes Stephen goes through in *Portrait* show him and us, to varying degrees, the instability of every signifier of identity. Yet Stephen examines this instability, seizes it, and affirms it, as he does when he alienates the word *ivory* from its meaning (*P* 179); and in the villanelle, when he asks the Temptress to give up her position of power (*P* 217), her tower of ivory, and so to leave him without a support. He plunges into this instability in "Proteus" to confront and assert the Real that leads him to his opposite, Bloom. ("Proteus" ends with a returning ship that may suggest Odysseus to Stephen's Telemachus, and with the image of eating offal [*U* 3.479–80], which leads to Bloom's kidney.) Stephen reaches toward a subject who is enclosed by the ordinary world, and insofar as Stephen may become Joyce, this will be the subject of his longest work. In his greatest work, the *Wake*, the Joycean artist unites with all of humanity by engaging the terms that enclose it in an incessant passage beyond verbal fixity.

Lacan's parallax between revolution and constructive politics is matched by the opposition in *Ulysses* between Stephen's continuous desire to blow up the world and Bloom's acceptance of it, for Bloom is always trying to help people and his mind is filled with liberal utopian dreams, as we see in "Circe." The novel shares with Žižek the idea that one cannot exist without the other: revolutionaries generally want to support liberal causes and liberals want to be revolutionary, but the interests of the two programs tend to clash. The radical side of Joyce that supports Stephen's revolutionary vehemence brings him close to Žižek. It may be because Joyce sunders Stephen's revolutionary impulse from Bloom's benevolent one that Stephen is attacked by critics who want to unite the two sides without considering their opposing interests.

The parallax of differing views in *Ulysses* shows why Stephen, Bloom, and Molly can never get together, but also why they touch each other through their opposition with possibilities of progress that may inspire the reader. In a general way, Joyce emphasizes the latitude or range of the parallax view, while Žižek is more concerned with enacting the impossibility of bringing the two sides together for a purpose. This allows Joyce to use the Real to reach a broader view of reality, to explore. Žižek on the other hand, mistrusts exploration and plurality and is even ready to take the position of abhorring tolerance.[2]

The *Wake* connects the action of the fall that creates the world to the exploration of that world. Fall and exploration connect through the process of truth in which the situation of the subject is first constructed as the scene in the park (Imaginary), then recognized (Symbolic), then slandered (Real), then displaced, and then realized as the letter that flows toward discovery. In fact, there are two versions of the scene in the park, the one with the girls making water and the one in which HCE meets a cad with a pipe, who upsets him by asking the time; and these versions are presented as alternate views of the same scene (*FW* 34–35). The scene with the cad is one of the primary models for the battle scenes in the *Wake*, and the museyroom that memorializes these battles is also a monument to the scene in the park. So the panorama of battles in the museyroom includes "jinnies…making their war undisides" (8.31–32), and Adeline Glasheen points out that this refers to making water (xxiii). The equation of making water with making war highlights the fetishistic nature of the urine as phallus, as text generated by woman. If bedwetting brings mother, it is a gift to her, shared by her, connected to her, coital.

Therefore the conflict between the Druid and Patrick, which exemplifies the male battle paradigm, springs (with a big jump) from the scene in the park. Not only does the constitution of the subject between temptation and threat lead to male conflict, but it is always "in some greenish distance, the charmful waterloose country" (8.2–3). It is distant because the scene in the park, which spreads like wildfire as gossip, impels centrifugal movement or sends one far away, to the battle scene at the edge of the empire, to the place where the landscape is formed by linguistic supplementation or exploration. "[W]aterloose" is a typical joining of the idea of peeing to that of battle, which is of course also the idea of writing: "his penisolate war" (*FW* 3.6). One of the most striking features Joyce, Lacan, and Žižek share is their tendency to multiply levels, to enjoy jumping across disparities in order to indicate that everything is (dis)connected.

Žižek says that an impasse generates fantasy (*Plague* 10), and the Real in Lacan's triangle drives the phallic thrust forward into the sense of "reality" (*Encore* 90), toward the certainty of reality in the Imaginary. For Lacan and Žižek, the sense of reality always depends on a fantasy narrative, so that something seems real to the degree that it answers our fantasies (*Fragile* 82–84). In its fantasy denial of the impasse of the Real, the formation of the subject produces conflict that generates art, which recognizes the conflict and seeks to go beyond it by expressing it. The suspension between opposites that Joyce builds toward is the way to approach both the subject and the Other because it unleashes a channel of wordplay between them. As Žižek says, we communicate through our divisions, so Joyce opens the space of discourse between the subject and itself, between the word and itself in the *Wake*, where most words tend to disagree with themselves. This dialogue between the subject/signifier and itself, or between the enunciator and the enunciated (Lacan, *Four* 139–40), allows the native and the foreign to speak to each other in a language that conveys more because it is incomprehensible rather than reductive. It proliferates significance, as in the dialogues between Mutt and Jute (*FW* 16–18), or Muta and Juva (609–10), in the first and last chapters of the *Wake*. They are gatekeepers, the first pair taking us into the multiplicity of the wordworld, the second leading to the action that installs the signifier and ends the dream and ALP's flow. The meeting between native and foreigner makes exploration the model for language in its drive toward knowledge in the Real of what is denied.

Such communication through division provides energy to unfold the interplay of Imaginary, Symbolic, and Real; so it reveals the complexity of the action of consciousness in which volition, language, and displacement depend on each other. Lacan's triangular structuration of truth, combined with Žižek's social application against the force of ideology, allows us to see the purposiveness of the action of revealing without losing sight of its negation. This aggregation allows Joyce to reach out through the exploration of the unconscious to women, to the oppressed, and to the culturally obliterated majority of the planet's population, to approach their independence and counteraction, creating a path of visionary expansion for humanity.

Yet this path leads to the Real as negation. Žižek says that true art manipulates "the censorship of the underlying fantasy in such a way as to reveal the radical falsity of the fantasy" (*Plague* 20). The source of vision is the realization that every aim is illusory, represented in the *Wake* by the final arising of Poseidon as the obstacle to exploration that ends up spurring it, generating the next cycle of reading. The dream of release must be seen to depend on the hopelessness of entrapment in order to reach out to the truth of the persecuted. The expectation of release puts one in the Imaginary, which formulates words; whereas the denial of the Symbolic comfort of the known word as a semblance leads to the Real that generates new expectations. The quest for a new language of truth aims to catch up to reality, to attend to injustice.

Although the invention of new language seems limited in that it does not rest on a full framework of causality, it extends toward a larger vision insofar as it implies that it is only part of a process. So repetition serves as a source of renewal because by acknowledging what is repeated, it can discern what is new. Žižek emphasizes that "*Limitation precedes transcendence*," that uplift comes only from negation (*Tarrying* 37, his italics). So Joyce concentrates on those who are entrapped by society, minorities, women and victims who have no steady claim on the illusion of phallic ascendancy. In them he finds the truest freedom, the freedom to depart; so ALP's despair becomes the source of the beginning.

Regarding Joyce's work as a whole in relation to some of our concerns, it begins with the incoherence of oppression in *Dubliners*, and passes to the Imaginary scene of writing in *Portrait*.[3] Bedwetting and kissing are parallel and Imaginary as immediate contact with mother, and the wetting and the mother's kiss (which wets his cheek, *P* 15) at the start of *Portrait* return at the end of the *Wake* with the liquid image of a kiss. "The keys to. Given!" in the last line represents the image of passing keys through a kiss. This is the freedom that her love gives to the book and its language. Yet as the dying liquid mother kisses her creator, their consummation is completed by the entirety of the *Wake* and he finally becomes the vampire he dreaded, terminating the book in the midst of its yearning "long the." The Real is reached when the final article, having traversed the Phallic Signifier, finds no noun and addresses itself to the unspoken world in which we live, able to embrace that world with all the complex resistances it or she has absorbed.

In the middle of Joyce's work is the model of Odysseus's exploration, which makes each episode of *Ulysses* take place in a technically new world. This is the charge of the Symbolic, which Lacan describes as supported by the gap (*sinthome* 50). And at the end of the work is the confrontation with the most incomprehensible part of the planet, represented by Asia. Here Joyce carries out the exploratory gesture of bringing Asia into comprehension not by reducing it to exoticism, but by showing its conflicts to be parallel to those of Ireland, the same as ours, a revelation of our alienation from ourselves.

Each new reading of the whole text of Joyce's work and of every letter of it strives to augment the vocabulary that constitutes reality in order to use the Real to do justice to humanity, to the world, to history, and to the human consciousness through which these things are known. Both Joyce and Lacan do this through expanding or building the language of the subject, and Lacan speaks in the seminar of April 13, 1976 of pushing toward a new writing that may well be called through metaphor a new range of symbolization, and also the forcing of a new kind of idea, an idea that doesn't just make sense, that is not just Imaginary.[4] This is the goal of the explorations of Joyce and Lacan, and they both know, as Žižek does, that it can only be approached through loss.

There is no accomplishment without deflection. This is a spatial version of Stephen's sequential "There can be no reconciliation…if there has not been a sundering" (*U* 9. 397–98). The translation of the temporal into the spatial, which tends to make the temporal reversible and the spatial progressive is an unusually strong form of the parallactic coincidence of contraries in which conflicting elements are equal to each other. This is a charge leveled against Lacan, that his terms are hard to distinguish, as in the *Wake*, where every point equals the whole. Theory as exploration reaches to the widest latitude. While Joyce's works are dense with practical social observation, their largest purpose is not to be practical, but to prepare for future practice by opening the space of what is conceivable. This is the distinction between Shaun and Shem, the conflicting sides of HCE. To explore the greatest distance—as psychoanalysis does figuratively—is to bring together the things that are farthest apart so as to create the truth that will have the greatest reach. So Odysseus of many minds could inspire Joyce, transforming a spatial extension into a temporal one.

Supplement: Theory as Comedy/ Comedy as Economy

The last paragraph of *Le sinthome* begins by announcing that the seminar is over, but it may also express what Lacan hopes he has accomplished: "*Voilà, je vous libère*" (155), in which case it is a joke about freeing people by leaving them hanging. The main mediator that allows Joyce to confront loss may be comedy; and comedy becomes a method of intellectual exploration in Joyce and continues to operate this way in Lacan and Žižek. In *Jokes and Their Relation to the Unconscious*, Freud puts comedy beside dreams, literature, slips, and analysis as a major path to the unconscious, the Freudian concept of a deposit that Lacan defines in more active terms through the Real. In fact Freud speaks of jokes as exploratory tools allowing passage beyond barriers to reach unconscious goals: "They make possible the satisfaction of an instinct (whether lustful or hostile) in the face of an obstacle that stands in its way. They circumvent this obstacle and in that way draw pleasure from a source that the obstacle had made inaccessible" (*SE* VIII 101).

Earlier, to explain Joyce's irony about Stephen, I quoted Lacan's statement in *Seminar XXIII* that because Joyce is "no fool," he need only mention Stephen, his intellectual self, "and he starts snickering, which is not very far from my position when I talk . . . " (68). If self- love is the key to the false pretense of mentality, then Lacan continually makes fun of himself in his work. A few pages after this, Lacan derides Stephen for believing that there is a "*book of himself*" (*U* 9.115). (The phrase actually comes from Richard Best, translating Mallarmé.) Lacan says that it is ridiculous for Stephen to see himself as a book: "Why doesn't he say rather that he is a knot?" ("*Pourquoi ne dit-il pas plutôt qu'il est on noeud?*" 71). Here Lacan mocks his own obsession with knots, without forgetting the advantages that knots afford in describing the complex interplay of forces in the subject. It may be argued that a book is a better image of the subject than a knot because it has more content, but Joyce had used the book and Lacan wants to avoid content. The worst image of the subject may be the one that seems to cover it—like the computer today.

I first noticed Lacan's facetiousness in the first essay I read of his during the 1970s, "The Instance of the Letter in the Unconscious," which refers to "Shakespeare's savage tragedies" (*Écrits* 440, n. 11). Here Lacan presents himself as a chauvinistic Frenchman insisting that Racine is better than the crude English bard. This matches Joyce's presentation of his ideas as humor, which includes Stephen's denial of his Shakespeare theory (*U* 9.1067). This is partly because Stephen is philosophically opposed to certainty, and when he thinks, "… O Lord, help my unbelief" (1078), the joke hinges on the contradiction of praying to God not to believe.[5]

Žižek carries the philosophical use of comedy beyond his predecessors. Rebecca Mead's article on Žižek, "The Marx Brother," considers the question of how to classify Žižek—philosopher, culture critic, political observer, psychoanalyst, and so on—and concludes that he is "in fact a comedian" (39). And Eagleton, in a review of *The Parallax View*, refers to Žižek as a "mixture of sage, clown, jester, and guru" ("On the Contrary"). Obviously, the humor allows Žižek to take serious, complex ideas to a relatively large audience, but it also has an intellectual function.

Astra Taylor's 2005 film *Žižek!* begins with an emphatic statement by Žižek to the effect that the situation of the universe is absolutely hopeless. This is itself a funny scene, and virtually everything else in the film is funny, including the scene in which Žižek commits suicide. Having seen Žižek's style close up, we can turn to a typical passage and see the overlay of humor: "The theory of the 'authoritarian personality' is nothing but an expression of the ressentiment of the left-liberal intelligentsia apropos of the fact that the 'non-enlightened' working classes were not prepared to accept its guidance" (*Tarrying* 215). This is a valuable statement insofar as it shakes up liberal assumptions, but it includes a joke about denying in an authoritarian way ("nothing but") that one can be authoritarian. Moreover, the Marxist jargon in this quote is heavy-handed enough to be parodic. Žižek is constantly demonstrating that the critical spirit cannot take itself seriously and remain active. Likewise his sudden jumps from one topic to another, with their antecedents in Joyce and Lacan, keep the parallax moving to remind us that to see something from a consistent point of view is to impose falsehood on it.

In *The Parallax View*, Žižek cites Kierkegaard's attack on Hegel's thought, which says that it is comical that "this system of Absolute knowing was written by a contingent individual, Hegel…" (76). Here Žižek slips into his comic position of insisting that *everything* is really

Lacano-Hegelian, arguing that Kierkegaard's incongruous juxtaposition exemplifies Hegel's idea of "the Paradoxical conjunction of the Universal with the 'lowest' singularity" (76). This last is the excremental "little bit of the Real," and it matches Clive Hart's observation that whenever Joyce is philosophical, he is scatological (which I can't find).

The posing of philosophy as joke allows one to extend one's mind into different sides of the parallax. It is the liveliest version of that jocular term the *sinthome*, the playful relation to reality that results from accepting one's symptom, and it corresponds to the process of constantly inventing new terms without stopping to affix them to authority. It enables one to face the most terrible and contradictory truths, and so to extend consciousness into new areas. The Swiftian combination of humor and terrible pessimism extends to Beckett and to other great Irish novelists since Joyce: Flann O'Brien, Elizabeth Bowen, John Banville, and Anne Enright. If the goal of exploration is loss, it can only be reached out to through laughter, and only this goal can traverse the fantasy. So laughter takes us to an unsparing truth, a more advanced truth.

Finally since humor, as Bakhtin emphasizes, shifts proper or pretentious discourse to a lower level, it may be the best way to reverse philosophy as a historical system, in the terms of *Seminar XVII*, for stealing knowledge from the oppressed. Philosophy is not known for provoking mirth. In Terry Eagleton's screenplay for Derek Jarman's film *Wittgenstein*, the philosopher on his deathbed tells his grotesque angel that he always wanted to write a book of philosophy made up of jokes. The angel likes the idea and asks why he didn't. Wittgenstein replies that he had no sense of humor. If the *sinthome* claims savoir faire, this is the witty kind of knowledge that Lacan associates with slaves (*Other* 21), and philosophy may be brought to the source of its knowledge by humor.

The role of the *sinthome* as joke allows us to see how it reverses the symptom, for humor generally works by reversing thoughts that are disturbing. It is revealing to consider the *sinthome* as a reversal of the symptom in relation to Lacan's revolutionary vision in *Seminar XVII*. Lacan says that the rich buy everything but never have to pay for it "for reasons of accounting that stem from the transformation of surplus jouissance into surplus value" (*Other* 82). That is, the economic arrangement of society works to transform the creative energy of the people into profit for the rich. Now the conventional symptom follows social standards to put one's enjoyment at the service of the rich by making one pay for one's pleasure. This is emphasized by the enormous role of prostitution in *Ulysses*, where it is ostentatiously the heart of capitalism. Freud's symptom follows the model of retentively depositing jouissance in one's unconscious conceived of as an internal container, saving it so one can spend it for pleasure in acceptable ways.

The *sinthome* as the symptom one chooses reverses the transformation of pleasure into profit. Like the profligate Gracehoper as opposed to the Ondt (*FW* 414–19), it transforms profit into pleasure. It initiates a separate reverse economy that is anarchic and expulsive, an economy of loss that generates knowledge without receiving it. Taking the side of the losers, this language economy speaks for the poor, women, "minorities," and children, groups who may add up to 90 percent of the population of the world. This language does not try to save, but to create new value by aiming at the Real that is outside knowledge. By turning the unconscious into the object of a quest that aims not at a goal, but at exploration, it produces value and knowledge insofar as it can never hold them.To see this is to see Joyce and Lacan revolutionizing each other.

On the level of colonialism, Lacan says that one lets oneself be bought by the wealthy in order "to share in the level of a rich nation," and that "in the process, what you lose is your knowledge" (*Other* 83). One's natural feelings acquire value by being turned to objects of exchange. This corresponds to the fact that Haines is busy acquiring the Irish folk culture that makes Stephen feel uncomfortable. Lacan speaks of "the promotion... of surplus *jouissance*... at the level at which the function of the wealthy operates, the one for which knowledge is only a tool of exploitation" (83). Mulligan, who is bound for success, tells Stephen to serve Haines, but Stephen sees that if he aims at success, this will lead to his transforming his Irish feelings into English commodities; so he turns toward the effort to refuse communication with authority. He will cultivate his *sinthome*, his departure from the sensible, to express his Irish soul on the level that cannot be expressed. This is another level on which the theory Lacan derived from Joyce expands our understanding of both thinkers.

Seminar XVII came out in English in 2007, and I am reading it while completing revision of this book, so that I could not integrate its wonderful theories into the body of the book without delaying publication. It is generally not valid to end with new ideas, but in this case it may have a point. Having been a Joycean for forty-three years and a Lacanian for thirty-two, I still find that in reading their work I keep being overwhelmed by new ideas. This is a key feature of the *sinthome* that I noticed in *Joyce the Creator*, that Joyce's work keeps changing its minds. Reading Joyce or Lacan is like loving someone: if you enter it positively, there is always the thrill of finding new worlds.

Notes

1 Introduction: Exploring Freedom through Language

1. What Lacan says here, in "The Freudian Thing" (1955), is "Everything is language: language when my heart beats faster..." Here he anticipates the objection that there are immediate feelings before language by indicating that even the most thoughtless feeling can only be perceived by setting up a scale (faster or slower) that is a linguistic construction. This was first made clear to me in conversation with Susan Stewart.
2. Lacan's presentation appears in condensed form as "Joyce le symptôme I" in Jacques Aubert's collection *Joyce avec Lacan* (21–29), where it says that the text is based on notes by Eric Laurent (21). A version of this paper also appears in Jacques-Alain Miller's edition of the twenty-third seminar (161–69). At this time Lacan also wrote a more imaginative and linguistically experimental unfolding of his ideas on Joyce. This appears as "Joyce *le Symptôme*" in the French volume of papers from the Paris Symposium, *Joyce & Paris...*, edited by Aubert and Maria Jolas (13–17), and it appears as "Joyce *le symptôme* II" in *Joyce avec Lacan* (31–36). It was a common procedure at that time to publish short versions of conference papers in volumes called *Actes,* and other papers from the Paris Symposium were reduced. An account of Lacan's talk appears in Rabaté, *Jacques* 158–59, which points out that the program mistakenly gave the title of the talk as "Joyce the Symbol." Luke Thurston helped me clarify this note.
3. Ellen Carol Jones cites the line in "an apogean humanity of beings...," her account of the 2004 Korean Joyce Conference (21). She got it from Morris Beja, who attended Lacan's lecture, and I was glad of this confirmation that I heard it right. I use the line in *Joyce the Creator* (9).
4. Jean LaPlanche and J. B. Pontalis point out in *The Language of Psycho-Analysis* that the term *ambivalence* was actually taken by Freud from Eugen Bleuler. Freud first used it in 1912 (26–27).
5. Marie-Laure Ryan, in *Possible Worlds, Artificial Intelligence, and Narrative Theory*, says that her model of the mind is computer-based, but that the computer is very far from human consciousness: "A reasonably sophisticated reading by computer of a complex literary narrative is out of the question for the foreseeable future" (6).
6. It is hard to delineate a list of Lacanian studies of Joyce because many books make use of Lacan's ideas along with other approaches. Rabaté, an authority on Joyce and Lacan, has so far dealt with the conjunction only

in sections of his books, such as *James* 5–10 and *Jacques* 154–82. Books in which Lacan may be called the principle theoretical source have been written by Brivic (*Veil, Joyce's*), Devlin, Harari, Ingersoll, Leonard, MacCabe, Schlossman, and Thurston.

7. Possible worlds theory could be of great value in helping us to see the complexity of this interchange if it were coordinated with dynamic analysis.
8. Thurston argues this most concisely in his Introduction to his collection *Re-Inventing the Symptom* (xiii–xix) (but my references to his work will be to his Joyce book unless otherwise indicated).
9. In a letter of July 20, 1919 to Harriet Shaw Weaver, Joyce says of *Ulysses*, "the progress of the book is in fact like the progress of some sandblast." Each time he develops a new person or idea, that element becomes obsolete (*SL* 241).
10. On June 13, 2006, Rabaté delivered a lecture, at the Twentieth International Joyce Symposium in Budapest, that traced the history of Lacan's involvement with Joyce over five decades, "Lacan's Serial Encounters with Joyce: The Four Stages." One point that he made was that Lacan began to develop his radical ideas on Joyce in 1971 in the essay "*Lituraterre*."
11. In "Ineluctable Nodalities: On the Borromean Knot," Thurston argues that while the knot can be drawn in two dimensions, its actual three-dimensional knottedness is beyond mathematical calculation so that Lacan's knots introduce a writing of the Real of the subject that is beyond language (148). One of the most interesting effects of this for my purposes is that it throws the knot into a condition of ongoing change (143–44).
12. I capitalize Imaginary, Symbolic, and Real, as many commentators do, though Lacan usually does not, in order to distinguish these terms from the usual usages of the words. The three registers are introduced in Seminar II, *The Ego in Freud's Theory*…(168–70, 96–98, et al. [see index]), and appear often in Lacan's works. The ultimate development of these registers is in Seminar XXII, *R. S. I.*, which has not yet been published in French.
13. Shepherdson argues that this standard view is a simplification, and that the mother plays a symbolic role as soon as she appears (*Vital* 73–74). I will indicate how this works in my discussion of Montrelay.
14. My translation is based on that of Luke Thurston, who was kind enough to give it to me, but I often modify Thurston. "*ce soit dans l'imaginaire que je mette le support de ce qui est la consistance, que de même ce soit de trou que je fasse l'essentiel de ce q'il en est du symbolique, et que je supporte spécialement du réel ce que j'appelle l'ex-sistence*" (*Le sinthome* 50).
15. "*il est un fait que* Joyce *choisit, en quoi il est, comme moi, un hérétique.* Car haeresis, *c'est bien là ce qui spécifie l'hérétique. Il faut choisir la voie par où prendre la vérité. Ce d'autant plus que, le choix une fois fait, cela n'empêche personne de la soummetre à confirmation…*

...d'avoir bien reconnu la nature du sinthome, ne se prive pas d'en user logiquement, c'est a dire d'en user jusqu'à atteindre son réel, au bout de quoi il n'a plus soif.

16. References to the *Wake* give page number, followed by a period, followed by line number.
17. "*On crée une langue pour autant qu'à tout instant on lui donne un sens, on donne un petit coup de pouce, sans quoi la langue ne serait pas vivante.*"
18. In his 1958 paper "The Direction of the Treatment," Lacan uses the term "key" to describe Winnicott's concept of the transitional object (*Ecrits* 511); and Winnicott cites Lacan twice in *Playing* (1971), saying that his essay "The Mirror Stage" "certainly influenced me" (130). That the two analysts are somewhat intertwined despite their differences confirms my sense that Lacan is aware of the creative power of the maternal field.
19. One of the classic foundations of the idea that the writer's biography should not be used by critics is I. A . Richards, *Practical Criticism* (1929). Richards had his students interpret poems without telling them who wrote them, and this demonstrated to the New Critics that criticism could proceed without referring to the author. But in fact the students made a long series of assumptions about the authors, who were generally intelligent, white, Christian, English, male, heterosexual, adult, and so forth; so they were constantly referring to the authors.

    The post-structuralist idea of the Death of the Author, expressed by Barthes and Foucault, is very valuable because it allows us to see the work taking input from outside the conventional frame of the author, as the Lacanian subject exceeds the individual. But the Death of the Author should not preclude using helpful biographical material. Sean Burke refutes this theory in *The Death and Return of the Author.*
20. Žižek's devotion to St. Paul appears in *Ticklish* 127–67 and in *Fragile* 125–46. His devotion to Stalin, whom he is more inclined to criticize than Paul, is emphasized in the film *Žižek!*
21. Žižek's only work to address Joyce, the eight-page essay "From Joyce-the-Symptom to the Symptom of Power," leaves Joyce behind after the first page. Although I have not examined all of Žižek's hundreds of works, it seems that other references to Joyce are limited to a few lines here and there, as in "The Obscene Object of Postmodernity" (43–44, 49) and *Looking Awry* (137, 145–46, 151).
22. That parallax involves exploration is made clear in Thomas Pynchon's *Mason & Dixon*, which recounts the travels that Charles Mason and Jeremiah Dixon made to various parts of the globe to observe the parallax of Venus by looking at the planet from widely separated positions (93, 96–98).
23. Versions of the term *parallax* occur in the following episodes and lines of *Ulysses*: 8.110, 112, 578; 14.1089; 15.1656, 2334; 17.1052 (twice).
24. Late in *The Parallax View*, Žižek contrasts skepticism and fundamentalism with a middle term that he calls "authentic belief" (348). Although he is

referring here to the efficient functioning of the Symbolic system, this is a disturbing indication of his inability to stick with his intention to keep the two sides of the parallax apart. Žižek seems to believe in authentic belief.

25. Kristeva has written about Joyce as exemplary. See her *Desire in Language* 92 or her "Joyce the Gracehoper." Cixous's dissertation led to her lengthy *Exile of James Joyce*.

2 Stephen Dedalus Gets Changed

1. Lacan's theory of the gaze is developed in *The Four Fundamental Concepts* (Seminar 11) 67–119. It has had its greatest influence in art and film studies, but two books on Joyce that use it are Devlin, *Wandering* 111–15, 128, and Brivic, *Veil* 105–8, 145–47.
2. Lacan says in *Le sinthome* that it is necessary to pass by ordure to perhaps recover something of the order of the Real (124).
3. The scene is censored to such an extent that it is barely mentioned and in the iterative mood, or as a repeated action ("When..."). Kenner argues that important scenes in Joyce, such as Molly's adultery with Boylan, are often left out of the narrative ("Molly's" 19). There is a level of Joyce's work that implies that everything we do not know is repressed, and that is why the artist aims to know everything.
4. William James developed the idea of the stream of consciousness in *Principles of Psychology* (1890, cited in Ellmann and Feidelson, *Modern* 715–23). Yet Joyce was more influential than anyone else in bringing about a situation in which most educated people regard themselves as having streams of consciousness, though he did it partly by influencing other artists, such as Woolf and Faulkner. Joyce also transformed human consciousness in relation to art, language, and sexuality.
5. In the "Overture" to Proust's *Remembrance of Things Past*, Marcel remembers lying in bed as a child yearning insatiably for his mother to come and kiss him (13–14).
6. Lacan's term for the body of the mother as a terrifying object that destroys one as one approaches it is *das Ding*. See *Ethics* 43–70, especially 67.
7. Reading an early version of this paper at a conference, I remarked that no one would leave a dirty child on a clean sheet but George W. Bush, whereupon someone in the audience exclaimed, "Let no child be wet behind!"
8. *il est clair que l'ébauche même de ce qu'on appelle la pensée, que tout ce qui fait sens, comporte, dès que ça montre le bout de son nez, une référence, une gravitation à l'acte sexuel, si peu évident que soit cet acte. Le mot même d'acte implique la polarité actif-passif, ce qui est déjà s'engager dans un faux-sens.*

9. Barbara Lamann and Bill DeForest assure me that washing gloves for mothers remain common in Europe and often have a rough texture. In "Circe," when Stephen is describing bizarre vices he heard of in Paris, he refers to a fetish used by prostitutes called "saling gloves" (*U* 15.3882). I have not found the meaning of "saling," but it may be related to the French *sale*, "dirty or obscene." Whether they are used for penetration, masturbation, or just as accessories, they are stimulating. Like all fetishes, they go back to images linked to mother according to Freud's article "Fetishism," in vol. 21 of the *Standard Edition* (*SE* 21:152–60). One of the prostitutes in "Circe," Kitty Ricketts, wears "doeskin gloves" (15.2051).
10. Joyce jokingly mixes the sound of Stephen's urinating with that of the water running from "the Cock lake" (3.453), the name of an actual tidal pool. Charles Bernstein, a founder of LANGUAGE Poetry, sometimes makes noises into the microphone that sound like Stephen's version of the voice of his water.
11. The account of Lacan's confrontation with the rebels of 1968 appears in his "Impromptu at Vincennes." Though he defies their iconoclasm, he insists that psychoanalysis is "progressive" (127), and after this he wrote his radical Seventeenth Seminar.
12. Critics who apply Lyotard to Joyce are Valente, *James* 8–9, 56–58, and myself, "Joyce, Lyotard..."
13. Sister May, who was twelve in 1902, probably mistook (perhaps retroactively) essays that Joyce read to his mother for chapters of a novel. Yet May insists that she heard what he read. Actually, I am inclined to suspect that Joyce started *Stephen Hero* before 1904, but there is no other evidence for this. Joyce was away from January to April 1903, and after that his mother was dying (Ellmann, *Joyce* 111–28).
14. The villanelle seems to be addressed to Emma Clery, but I argue in *Joyce between* (39–40) that Stephen's relationship with E__. C__., including the fact that he is unable to touch her, is conditioned by his relation to his mother.
15. A few lines below this, in a dizzy swirl of wordplay, Lacan writes something that, according to Kevin Z. Moore, who translated this talk for me, may be interpreted to mean that man ("*LOM*") mans himself competitively by getting wet: "*LOM se lomellise à qui miuex mieux. Mouille, lui dit-on, faut a faire: car sans mouiller pas d'hessecabeau*" (Aubert 31). The last sentence may mean, "We say to him, get wet, for without getting wet, there's no stepladder (or foundation or beauty)." It is tempting to see *mouiller*, "to wet or moor," as a reference to bedwetting, but it is more likely to refer to getting wet in the sex act. This passage may refer to the confusion of urinating and being sexually excited in children.
16. It is conceivable that Joyce was drawn to works in which women bathe men, such as the Tristan legend, one of the primary sources for the *Wake*. In the *Odyssey*, Homer's aristocratic men are usually bathed by women,

as they are in the following Books and lines: III.464–65, IV.49, IV252, VIII.454, X.361, XVII.88, XIX.317, XXIII.153, XXIV.365.

17. In the *Odyssey,* Penelope generally wears a veil in the presence of men who are not in her family. See I.334, XVIII.210.

3 Freedom through Figuration in *A Portrait*

1. This corresponds to Žižek's view that the object of the drive that traverses the fantasy, a goal of Lacanian analysis, is not the lost object, but loss itself (*PV 61–62*), an idea to which I will return.
2. A fine account of how Stephen changes in each chapter appears in Thornton 85–107.
3. Joyceans who emphasize Stephen's wrong attitudes include Buttigieg, Henke, Kershner, Levenson, Thornton, and Wollaeger. A sophisticated view of Stephen advancing toward Joycean insight is presented by Riquelme in *Teller and Tale* 60–66. Another astute critic who takes a positive view of Stephen is Andrew Gibson, who says that in "Circe," "Stephen has nonetheless made progress. He has resisted his own depressed conviction of imprisonment within ineluctable conditions, and reasserted the project of an open art, one dedicated to the exploration of possibilities" (196).
4. It is possible that by his "spiritual self" Joyce means a limited aspect of himself, but this need not necessarily be true, and the spiritual self may be the one that progresses.
5. Derrida argues that the borderline between inside and outside is the difference between shifting language, which is internal, and stable language, which is external (*Dissemination* 109).
6. Žižek says that for Freud, others are there for me only insofar as I am not identical to myself, but have an unconscious. Division is what makes communication possible (*Tarrying* 31).
7. I modify the standard text here because "geen" is in the manuscript, and in Hans Walter Gabler's edition of *Portrait* 3.
8. Lacan refers here to a passage in Freud's *Inhibitions, Symptoms, and Anxiety.* Since it is on page 164 of the twentieth volume of the Standard Edition, the abbreviation is *SE* XX.164.
9. Kevin J. H. Dettmar effectively describes the postmodern aspect of Joyce's works in *The Illicit Joyce of Postmodernism.*
10. In fact, this memory of Eileen is called forth by Stephen to escape his anxieties involving male violence at Clongowes.
11. The image of a girl running in the sun with her gold hair streaming behind her recurs for both Stephen and Bloom in *Ulysses*, probably simultaneously, when the sun comes out after shade (*U* 1.283, 4.240–42). This shows that Joyce was fixated on the image, which he may have seen

when he was approximately six years old. It may indicate that the boy who sees the blonde run away will never attain the most highly valued woman in terms of sexual stereotypes, just as his loss of E__. C__. means he will not get one with social status.

12. On July 20, 1919, Joyce wrote to Harriet Shaw Weaver about *Ulysses*: "the progress of the book is in fact like the progress of some sandblast...each successive episode, dealing with some province of artistic culture (rhetoric or music or dialectic), leaves behind it a burnt up field" (*SL* 241).

4 Entwined Genders in *A Portrait*

1. Chodorow said this in a discussion following her lecture "Heterosexuality as a Compromise Formation: Reflections on the Psychoanalytic Theory of Sexual Development" at Haverford College on October 18, 1991.
2. Or men could be seen as overcome by hysteria in extreme situations. Shakespeare's Lear, as he grows upset, says,

   O, how this mother swells up toward my heart!
   Hysterica passio, down, thou climbing sorrow (II.iv.35–36).

   The woman or womb in him is overcoming him with emotion, and it is assumed here that every man has a womanly or hysterical side.
3. The most famous version of a sexually segregated male going to sleep with an imaginary woman is perhaps the song "Goodnight, Irene," which was originally sung by Lead belly (Huddie Ledbetter) on a chain gang: "Goodnight, Irene. Goodnight, Irene. / I'll kiss you in my dreams."
4. Joyce introduced this gender-neutral possessive pronoun in *Ulysses* (15.3103), and I think it can be of use, especially in cases where gender is ambiguous.
5. A concentration of Žižek's remarks on the superego as pressing enjoyment may be found through the Index of *The Žižek Reader*, which has eight entries for "obscene superego."

5 Žižek, Fantasy, and Truth

1. Lacan's emphasis on the idea that sexual desire cannot be satisfied is critiqued by Malcolm Bowie 130–38. This aspect of Lacan's work, which doesn't keep him from supporting eroticism vividly, crystallizes in his insistence that "there's no such thing as a sexual relationship" in *Seminar XX: Encore* 34. The idea that fantasy is the primordial form of narrative may be traced back to Freud's 1908 essay "Creative Writers and Day Dreaming," *SE* IX.141–56. I have often had the feeling that the satisfaction of my desire was more wonderful than I could conceive, but I can accept the idea that I imagine this because I am needy.

2. Among the critics who have seen Joyce's work as an affirmation of uncertainty are Derrida, Herring, McCabe, and McGee.
3. The "J" in the middle of Lacan's diagram, which emerges from and returns to the Real to serve as the kernel around which everything revolves, stands for jouissance (dreadful pleasure), but the direction in which Lacan will move in three years will make it stand for *Joyce-sens,* with *sens* combining meaning and sensuality.
4. Žižek interprets Lacan's triangular diagram in *Looking Awry* 135–36, 181 n.13) He equates the terms of the diagram with images from Patricia Highsmith's stories and Hitchcock's films. His reading of the diagram differs somewhat from mine, as this sample indicates:

   > ...$S(\not{A})$, the signifier of the lack of the big Other (the symbolic order), of its inconsistency, the mark of the fact that "the Other (as a closed, consistent totality) doesn't exist," is the little bit of the real functioning as a signifier of the ultimate senselessness of the (symbolic) universe (the button [in a Highsmith story], for example). (135)

   I don't believe that this is really inconsistent with my view of Lacan's "true" as disillusionment, which is generally spurred by a detail that goes wrong ("the little bit of the real."). But Lacan's diagram can be interpreted in several ways, as can Joyce's fiction, and life in general.
5. Rebecca Mead's 2003 article on Žižek reveals that despite his enthusiasm for Christianity, he is an atheist (39). Yet he finds St. Paul beyond criticism in *Ticklish* 127–67 and *Fragile* 2, 120–31. My point is that it may be dangerous to promote a system that has so much power to control people's minds, even if one does take it as a purely Symbolic system. In *Portrait,* Stephen fears the "chemical action" that would be set up in his soul by paying homage to Christianity even if he does not believe in it (243). *The Parallax View* of 2006 shows a good deal of irony toward and distance from Christianity, yet even here he contrasts wrong attitudes to religion with "*authentic belief*" (*PV* 348).

6 Let's Get Lost: Exploration in Homer and Joyce

1. Desire always aims at what is forbidden, and the most concrete form of what is forbidden for Stephen is his mother, so the goal Stephen reaches at the end of each chapter is the maternal field of imaginative expansion. This is most obvious in the scene in II in which the prostitute kisses him while he is passive (*P* 101), but it is suggested in the Eucharist given him by Mother Church in III (146). At the end of IV, "the earth that had borne him, had taken him to her breast" (172). Mother appears quite poignantly on the last page of the novel, and the last words of the first chapter are a nursing image, "the brimming bowl" (59). See my structural diagram of *Portrait*, which appears in *Joyce between* 59 and *The Veil* 41.

2. Passages from the *Odyssey* are cited by the page of the Butcher and Lang translation, which Joyce probably used, followed by a comma, followed by the standard book and line number. I regret that I could not use Richmond Lattimore's translation, which is not only better but also often works better for my arguments.
3. Lattimore, who makes Odysseus's speech more poetic, renders the last line as "but there came no advantage to them for all their sorrowing" (157, line 202). Unfortunately, the standard commentary is not kind to this passage. Heubeck and Hoekstra say that these lines may not be authentic because they seem irrational, and argue that Odysseus may be pretending to be unable to think of a solution because he wants to persuade the men to undertake a reconnaissance mission (55). In their concern with what is conventional, these commentators may neglect the poetry and feeling in the scene: as the men shed "big tears," they are described as remembering how their comrades were killed by the Lestrygonians and the Cyclops. I see the lines as important, whereas these commentators see them as almost senseless. Moreover, Odysseus does not hesitate to approach Circe after he hears that she is dangerous (143, X.261–63).
4. Another stage is the seven years he spends with Calypso, which leave him continuously weeping and wailing (75, V.151–58). Apparently he rejects her because she is not the wife with whom he shares a love based on mortality, perhaps also because she is not rooted in his native soil, the place where he was born, and maybe even because she is too youthful. In *Ulysses*, Calypso stands for the fantasies that keep Bloom from connecting with Molly.
5. Though the stylistic transformations of "Oxen" subject the characters to language that is not theirs, I believe that these styles exaggerate feelings that are present in the confused scene, and that Joyce never gives up his effort to represent the events of the day and their implications. Among the various antique styles used in "Oxen," this one seems especially close to the character, something Stephen might say when drunk, though the speech is probably interior.
6. The argument that Joyce saw the Church as promoting prostitution in order to isolate sin is developed in my *Joyce between* 50–51. In Žižek's terms, the large communities of vice in Catholic cities are the "obscene underside" that is inseparable from the church's elevation of virtue. See e. g., *PV* 370.

7 Structure as Discovery in *Ulysses*

1. There is a play here on Winnicott's idea of the good-enough mother. See *Playing* 11–12.
2. Lacan says in Seminar XVII, "It is, very precisely, out of the I identical to itself that the S_1 of the pure imperative is constituted" (62). That is when

I claim that I am equal to myself, I exert the absolute authority of the Master through the primary signifier of the Name of the Father.

3. In *Joyce the Creator*, I concluded that Joyce plays the role of God most effectively in his work by multiplying his identity, generating obscurity, and disappearing so that his characters and events could live free of his control (96–102). I extend this by emphasizing that Joyce assumes God's paternal role in order to vanish into incomprehensibility. I also argue that God is increasingly female in *Ulysses* and the *Wake.* At the start of *Le sinthome,* Lacan announces that the central act of creation was naming, and that the person who named the creatures of this world was Eve or *Evie* (13).
4. Critics who speak of the difficulty of separating author from character in narrated monologue, or of separating Joyce from Stephen, include Riquelme 56–60, Brivic *Veil* 48–51, and Goldman 95, 97. A statement of the danger of confusing Stephen with Joyce is made by Wollaeger, "Between."
5. The Linati schema, the most elaborate structural plan Joyce designed for *Ulysses*, appears in Ellmann, *Ulysses on the Liffey* following 187.
6. One of the most elaborate extra levels, which extends through all of *Ulysses,* involves characters sharing thoughts without communicating, as when Bloom thinks "*Hamlet, I am thy father's spirit*" (8.62) before Stephen gives his Shakespeare lecture. Robert Martin Adams first noticed these coincidences (95–99), and I list 147 of them in *Joyce the Creator* (145–53). Another book that cites a large number is Rickard's (87–117). Bloom and Stephen share so many phrases that it is possible to argue that every thought that Bloom has is the other end of one that Stephen has and vice versa, making them a single subject despite separation.
7. This is indicated, e. g., at the start of Jameson's *Postmodernism*, where he says that modernism focuses on "the thing itself," whereas postmodernism focuses on "the variations themselves" (ix).
8. Critics who see Molly's uncertainty as the goal of *Ulysses* include Tindall 36–37, Ellmann, *Ulysses* 174, Riquelme, *Teller* 228, Brivic, *Veil* 128–47, and van Boheemen-Saaf 174.
9. Having more than one woman. The figure is given by George Peter Murdock, who is cited by Storey 431.
10. Of course, Emily Brontë was born in England, and Eugene O'Neill in America; but they both grew up in isolated households with Irish parents.
11. A homosexual aspect of Molly's memories of Hester Stanhope (*U* 18. 612–74) is observed by Lamos (135). The major development of the idea that every act of communication is inherently addressed to a multiplicity of receivers is Derrida's *The Post Card* (e.g., 51). It includes the line "she told me that she could only come with someone else" (60), which describes a woman who has to focus during orgasm on someone other than the actual man she is making love to.

12. The parallel between Stephen's Shakespeare and Bloom was developed by William Schutte 127–35.
13. This 1859 work may have influenced Joyce: it portrays a husband who allows his wife to be free to commit adultery.
14. I closely paraphrase three passages that appear in this order over three paragraphs on this page: "*l'amour que l'on peut qualifier d'éternel, s'addresse au père.... C'est au moins ce que Freud avance dans Totem et Tabou par la référence à la première horde. C'est dans la mesure où les fils sont privés de femme qu'ils aiment le père /... la loi de l'amour, c'est à dire la père version.*"

8 *Ulysses*' "Circe": Dealing in Shame

1. Goldwasser, who shows that Dixon was the author, mentions that up to this time even Ellmann thought that the letter was written by Joyce. The reprint of this book by New Directions uses the title *James Joyce*/Finnegans Wake: *A Symposium*, reducing the original title to a subtitle.
2. This aspect of Christianity appeals to Žižek: see "Christ's Uncoupling," in *Fragile* 123–30. Stephen associates with Christ as a rebel opposed to established religion at the start of Stephen's diary, when he says, "Let the dead bury the dead" (*P* 248, from Luke 9:60) and sees Cranly as his precursor St. John the Baptist.
3. The classic statement on how society instills masochism to control the population is Theodore Reik's *Masochism in Modern Man* (1941), Parts VII and VIII.
4. Joyce's use of masochism for liberating intellectual purposes is further elaborated by David Cotter.
5. It may be argued that Shaun avoids shame and expands, but this is only physically. In Book III of the *Wake*, his book, Shaun moves backward from adulthood to infancy.
6. "Shame's choice" does not appear as such in the Dixon letter. It is a compromise between two forms that do appear, "Shame's voice" and "germ's choice," but it sounds more like Joyce's name than either.

9 Reality as Fetish: The Crime in *Finnegans Wake*

1. The use of *Totem and Taboo* in the *Wake* is discussed in my *Joyce between* 206–11.
2. MacHugh's *Annotations* has the same page numbers as the *Wake*, so that the page number for the annotation is always the same as the number for the *Wake*, in this case page 3. References to McHugh refer to the *Annotations* unless otherwise indicated.

3. The *Encyclopaedia Britannica* says, "Buber's philosophy of dialogue finds its classic expression in his poetic masterpiece *I and Thou*...," and adds that his other works before 1940 tend to elaborate this thesis.
4. In *Oedipus at Colonus,* Sophocles has Oedipus finally derive wisdom from his suffering.
5. This corresponds not only to the distinction between feminine and masculine but also to Eide's ethical distinction between recognizing the difference of the other and reducing the other to one's own principle. In fact Eide, citing Irigaray, links the ethical validity of interchange with the other to the primary closeness to the mother in which bodily fluids were interchanged (17–20). This might even extend to bedwetting.
6. Shepherdson, using Lacan's later theories, argues that the mother cannot appear until she enters language in the Symbolic, so the limiting of the early mother to the Imaginary is a reductive distortion (*Vital* 29, 73–74, 115), but it may be that Lacan did not realize this in 1956.
7. Anton C. Pegis, in his "General Introduction" to the *Summa*, writes, "St. Thomas himself may very well have thought that the SCG was precisely the sort of work needed by Christian missionaries in Spain face to face with the high intellectual culture of the Moslem world" (21).
8. The gap at the center of writing is identified in the first chapter with the Ginnunga-gap of Norse mythology as the place where writing breaks off: "Somewhere, parently in the ginnandgo gap between antediluvious and annadominant the copyist must have fled with his scroll" (*FW* 14.18–20).
9. In "Circe" Bloom is accused of buying used toilet paper from a prostitute (15. 3038–40).

10 The Africanist Dimension of *Finnegans Wake*

1. A subtle treatment of the artist Stephen's postcolonial situation as a problem of relating to language appears in van Boheemen-Saaf, *Joyce* 48–73.
2. Ellmann reports that Joyce's dislike of Trench, who stayed at the Martello Tower between September and October 1904, was aggravated when Trench imagined a panther in the room and fired his revolver at the fireplace beside which Joyce was sleeping (*JJ* 175), a major factor in Joyce's leaving the Tower. Trench is defended by his relative C. E. F. Trench in "Dermot Chenevix Trench and Haines of *Ulysses*."
3. Borges received a sophisticated European education, but wrote that he would always have the viewpoint of an Argentine, *Labyrinths* 177–85. Wright was born in Mississippi, but saw himself as a victim of internal colonization, which corresponds to the closeness of Ireland to England.

4. Craig Hansen Werner describes the parallels between the two novels in *Paradoxical* 23–24.
5. Diana is associated with awakening and with singing birds in *FW* 276.17–19 and 475.36–76.1. For pictures of the original black Diana see Fleischer, *Tafel* 11 (Plate 11) and Janner 542. Thanks to Joanne Stearns for referring me to these.
6. The latest contribution yo our knowledge of African languages in the *Wake* is Karl Reisman's forthcoming "Darktongues: Fufulde and Hausa in *Finnegan's Wake*."
7. McHugh's *Annotations* have the same number of pages as the *Wake*, so that the page number for his note always corresponds to the page number in the novel. Even line numbers match.
8. The word *funk* is ambiguous in this line, both opposed to "daring" in the sense of being afraid and parallel to "daring" in the sense of funky singing as audacious.

11 The Rising Sun: Asia in *Finnegans Wake*

1. Kristof and WuDunn temper their optimism by describing dreadful conditions and disturbing attitudes in many parts of Asia (e.g., 3–10, 291–313). WuDunn being a specialist in business matters, all of my references are to the chapters by Kristof. The instability and danger facing China are emphasized in Gordon G. Chang's *The Coming Collapse of China* (2001). Yet recent evidence has supported optimism. Fareed Zakaria, in "Does the Future Belong to China?" (2005), says that China's economic output is expected to overtake Japan's (presently the world's second largest economy) in 2015, and America's by 2039 (28). The economic base will bring a cultural superstructure. For example, the Indian novel in English may already be competitive with the British novel. This book of mine was copyedited in India.
2. One response to this is that when Europe assumed world dominance in the eighteenth century, it was filled with appalling poverty and injustice. Zakaria claims that in the past twenty-five years, the average Chinese income has quadrupled (32).
3. This is a sort of Walt Disney view of the *Wake*, often bearing the same relation to the text that Disney's treatments of animals as lovable people bears to actual animals. Yet Campbell and Robinson have more to say about what happens on most pages than any other guide. There may be an advantage in *knowing* that an interpretation is distorted, and a *skeleton* key is one that fits only approximately, enough to get one in.
4. Two critics with sharp views of Joyce's parodic and ironic presentation of stereotypes are Christy L. Burns, *Gestural Politics: Stereotype and Parody in Joyce*, and Kimberly J. Devlin, *James Joyce's "Fraudstuff."*

5. Two influential recent books suggest a trend. Niall Fergusson, in *Colossus: The Price of America's Empire* (2004), argues that America should be more methodical and responsible about its empire, as the British were; while Michael Ignatieff, *The Lesser Evil: Political Ethics in an Age of Terror* (2004) holds that we have to violate human rights to uphold the foundations of American democracy. The paradox of Ignatieff's position is disturbing. And as for the British Empire that Fergusson admires, Cheng, citing the *Britannica*, says that during the Sepoy Rebellion of 1857, "Hundreds of sepoys were shot from cannons in a frenzy of British vengeance" (207).
6. Stoddard feels that of all the races conspiring against white supremacy, East Asians are the most dangerous. Robert G. Lee points out that Stoddard's book went through fourteen printings in three years (136). William F. Wu examines racial stereotypes in *The Yellow Peril.* Joyce mocks the term "yellow peril" in "Dooleysprudence," his 1916 poem about the ability of the average man to see through prejudice, which is cited in *JJ* (424):

   Who is the meek philosopher who doesn't care a damn
   About the yellow peril or problem of Siam?
7. Patricia Laurence, in *Lily Briscoe's Chinese Eyes: Bloomsbury, Modernism, and China,* develops the extensive connections between China and the Bloomsbury group, which emphasized educating Asians, so that it was more progressive than the Orientalisms of Yeats and Pound.
8. Dirk Van Hulle points out that the first draft read "Calling all dawns," but thinks that Joyce changed it to "downs" (Crispi and Slote 437). The words *dawns* remains submerged here with its reference to the East.
9. The 1947 *Encyclopedia Britannica,* in its article on "Population," states that in 1926, the population of Asia, in thousands, was 1,032,381, while those of all the other continents combined added up to 847,214.
   Later figures slowly increase Asia's preponderance.
10. One implication of looking Eastward is that Joyce aimed at Asian audiences. In this aim, he was successful. Danis Rose and John O'Hanlon, in *Understanding Finnegans Wake*, report that Joyce "liked to think how some day way off in Tibet or Somaliland some little boy or girl in reading 'Anna Livia' would come across the name of his or her home river" (114). The ALP chapter contains the names of at least 800 rivers. By the end of the century, Joyce had communities of admirers in Beirut, Baghdad, China, and Korea. *Abiko Annual*, a Japanese periodical, is mainly devoted to *Wake* studies, and another is called *Joycean Japan.* The Korean James Joyce Society publishes *James Joyce Journal. Al Aqlam: A Literary Magazine 5* (2000) was issued in Baghdad with four articles on Joyce by Western Joyceans (including myself), translated into Arabic by Mohammad Darweesh.
11. Ironically, the Asian reconquest of Asia began when Japan, which had never been colonized, occupied Manchuria in 1932 and Mongolia in

1933, as Richard Storry reports (193). Howard W. French, in "Japan Rewrites Its Manchuria Story" (2004), says that the Japanese claimed to be building an ideal society for all Asians, but subjected the other Asians to segregation and forced labor. This article deals with the then recent Japanese tendency to deny war crimes, a sign of a return to nationalism that fills admirers of Japan such as myself with dismay . Yet the Japanese had taken such a strong pacifist position after World War II that their present drift to the right may be mild compared to that of the United States. Eishiro Ito tells me they are well aware of the horrors of Nanking.

12. See Calvert Watkins, "Indo-European and the Indo-Europeans," an Appendix to *The American Heritage Dictionary* (1496–1504). Watkins thinks that the Indo-Europeans probably lived in the third millennium BC north of the Black Sea, which puts them between Europe and Asia. Platt points out that references to Sanskrit in the *Wake* refer to the racist myth of the Aryans, an imaginary Germanic race who were supposed to have brought civilization from Asia to Europe (14–68). His argument is valuable, but it does not mean that references to Indian culture may not also be efforts to bring Asian civilization into the *Wake* in more positive terms.
13. There may be a reference here to *hafiz*, a Moslem who has memorized the Koran and an English word.
14. James S. Atherton (281) and Adeline Glasheen (243) find three references in the *Wake* (151.9, 292.21, and 521.1) to Oswald Spengler's *The Decline of the West* (1917). Unfortunately, Spengler does not seem to refer to the rise of the East.
15. An excellent article on Islam in the *Wake* is Aïda Yared's "In the Name of Annah."
16. A strong illustration of how militarism and sensitivity may support each other is the great Kenzi Mizoguchi's film *The Loyal 47 Ronin II* (1942). As the forty-seven samurai prepare to commit harakiri to defend the honor of their lord, there is a mood of exquisite delicacy: one of them plays a lyrical flute solo serenely.
17. The existing manuscripts for this section of Book IV, "SECTION THREE: FW, 607.23–614.18 ('ST PATRICK AND THE DRUID')," are reproduced in *The James Joyce Archive*, ed. Michael Groden [Vol. 63] *Finnegans Wake, Book IV*, ed. Danis Rose 146–80. The early manuscript, three large handwritten sheets from 1923, concentrate on the dialogue between Berkeley and Patrick, who already use Asian phrases. These manuscripts are on pages 146a–146e. The later manuscript, which extends the action to virtually its final form, are dated "mid 1938" (148–80). The line about the "Chrystanthemlander" first appears on page 157 of this volume; while the line about "Jockey the Ropper" is an addition on 174 to a typescript.
18. Philip L. Graham notices the chrysanthemum reference in his brief list of Japanese allusions in Clive Hart and Fritz Senn's *A Wake Digest* 52–53,

and adds that the floral image is reinforced by "pompommy" (609.33). Graham says that Thornton Wilder was the first to note that Patrick was Japanese at *FW* 317.2.

19. The photos in Chang occur on unnumbered pages after 146, and she discusses them on 156–57. I find Chang convincing, but Kristof discusses problems involved in the Nanking testimonies (237–42).
20. Henry's courtship of Katharine consists of vicious bullying. When he says he can only speak like a "plain soldier" (V.ii.153), but she can be sure he'll love her, he is emphatically refusing to be polite. When she asks how she can love an enemy of France, he says, "…I love France so well that I will not part with a village of it" (V.ii.182); so the love he offers her is the love one has for property taken by force.
21. Identified by Gifford and Seidman 228, which points out that "*Vicisti Galilae*" were said to be the last words of Emperor Julian the Apostate, who died in 363.
22. References to Asia or a variant of it in the *Wake* occur at 26.04, 68.29, 72.14, 98.10 ("Asia Major"), 105.20, 155.05, 166.32, 182.31, 191.04, 263.07, 284.22, 285, n.5. 343.10, 403.11, 447.25, 489.10, 497.12, 548.02, 564.35, 608.31, 610.12, and 625.4. I expect that more will be found.
23. My understanding of this statue was helped by a lecture on the statue by Eishiro Ito in Trieste in June of 2002, "Mediterranean Joyce Meditates on Buddha." The Blooms assume that Buddha is relaxing, but he is engaged in spiritually strenuous activity.
24. The *ABC Chinese-English Dictionary*, ed. John De Francis, says that *Ming* means "bright" and *Tang* means "hot water" or "hall." It does not give meanings for *mong* or *tung*. *A Practical English-Chinese Dictionary* says that the word for "east" is *dung*, which may well be pronounced as *tung*. It looks to me as if Joyce uses the words *ming* and *tung*, but "Mong Tang" is pseudo-Chinese based on *mountain*. None of these words appear in McHugh or on a list of Chinese terms (96–97) in Rose's edition of *James Joyce's "The Index Manuscript."* I first heard that *ming tung* means "bright east" from David Borodin at our *Wake* reading group.

Conclusion and Supplement: Exploration and Comedy

1. From the late nineteenth century, Thailand (Siam) was involved in a series of colonial conflicts with France. By 1910, Thailand adopted a policy of imitating the Japanese effort to build power systems modeled on Europe's (*Britannica*).
2. "[T]he way to fight ethnic *hatred* effectively is not through its immediate counterpart, ethnic *tolerance*; on the contrary, what we need is *even more hatred*, but properly *political* hatred: hatred directed at the common political enemy" (*Fragile* 11). He is still against tolerance on *PV 380*.

3. Murphy points out that *Portrait* begins a process of counteracting the paralysis of *Dubliners* (74). I have neglected *Dubliners* in this book, which may be described as a study of the novels. As I mentioned, there are already exploratory elements in such stories as "An Encounter," "Araby" (which prefigures Asia), and "The Dead." All of *Dubliners* is described as exploratory and modeled on *The Odyssey* in the 1944 essay "First Flight to Ithaca" by Richard Levin and Charles Shattuck.
4. A free translation of "*c'est le forçage d'une nouvelle écriture, qui a ce qu'ill faut bien appeler par métaphore une portée symbolique, et aussi le forçage d'un nouveau type d'idée, si je puis dire, une idée qui ne fleurit pas spontanément du seul fait de ce qui fait sens, c'est à dire de l'imaginaire*" (131).
5. Robert H. Bell sees Joyce's humor as a road of excess that leads to the palace of wisdom, quoting Blake: "If the fool would persist in his folly he would become wise" (Bell 5). Van Boheemen-Saaf sees the comedy of "Cyclops" as the keynote of the postcolonial *Ulysses*: "the glee of successful defiance, the triumphant transcendence of hegemonic oppression, the hysterical laughter of the subaltern subject who discovers in the meaning of his name within the hegemony ("Joys") the means of escaping its prison house" (77).

Works Cited

ABC Chinese-English Dictionary. Ed. John De Francis. Honolulu: U of Hawaii P, 1996.

Adams, Paul L. "Appendix: Notes toward a Psychiatric Chronology of Obsession." *Obsessive Children*. New York: Penguin, 1975. 251–59.

Adams, Robert Martin. *Surface and Symbol: The Consistency of James Joyce's* Ulysses. New York: Oxford, 1967.

Al Aqlam: A Literary Magazine 5 (2000, Baghdad): unnumbered pp. 17–32 on Joyce.

Althusser, Louis. "Ideology and Ideological State Apparatuses." *Literary Theory: An Anthology*. Ed. Julie Rivkin and Michael Ryan. Oxford: Blackwell, 1998. 294–304.

The American Heritage Dictionary of the English Language. Ed. William Morris. Boston: Houghton Mifflin, 1976.

Aquinas, St. Thomas. *Basic Writings of Saint Thomas Aquinas, Vol. 1*. Ed. Anton C. Pegis. New York: Random House, 1945.

———. *On the Truth of the Catholic Faith: Summa Contra Gentiles: Book One: God*. Trans. Anton C. Pegis. New York: Doubleday Image, 1955.

Atherton, James S. *The Books at the Wake: A Study of Literary Allusions*... New York: Viking, 1960.

Attridge, Derek, ed. *James Joyce's* Ulysses*: A Casebook*. Oxford: Oxford UP, 2004.

———. *Joyce Effects: On Language, Theory, and History*. Cambridge: Cambridge UP, 2000.

Attridge, Derek, and Marjorie Howes, eds. *Semicolonial Joyce*. Cambridge: Cambridge UP, 2000.

Aubert, Jacques. *Joyce avec Lacan*. Paris: Navarin, 1987.

Augustine, St. *Confessions*. Trans. R. S. Pine-Coffin. Harmondsworth: Penguin, 1961.

Bakhtin, Mikhail M. *The Dialogic Imagination: Four Essays*. Ed. Michael Holquist. Trans. Caryl Emerson and Holquist. Austin: U of Texas P, 1981.

Barthes, Roland. "The Death of the Author." *Falling into Theory: Conflicting Views on Reading Literature*. Ed. David H. Richter. Boston: Bedford/St. Martin's, 2000.

Bauerle, Ruth H. *Picking Up Airs: Hearing the Music in Joyce's Text*. Urbana: U of Illinois P, 1993.

Beckett, Samuel. *Waiting for Godot: A Tragicomedy in Two Acts*. New York: Grove Press, 1954.

Beekman, Daniel. *The Mechanical Baby: A Popular History of the Theory and Practice of Child Raising*. Westport: Lawrence Hill, 1977.

Bell, Robert H. *Jocoserious Joyce: The Fate of Folly in* Ulysses. Ithaca: Cornell UP, 1991.

Benjamin, Walter. "Theses on the Philosophy of History." *Illuminations: Essays and Reflections*. Ed. Hannah Arendt. Trans. Harry Zohn. New York: Schocken, 1969. 252–60.

Bentham, Jeremy. "A Fragment on Ontology." *Collected Works, Vol. 8*. London: Oxford, 1962.

Bérard, Victor. *Les Phéniciens et L'Odyssée*. 2 vols. (1902) Paris: Armand Colin, 1927.

Bernal, Martin. *Black Athena: The Afroasiatic Roots of Classical Civilization*. 2 vols. London: Free Association Books, 1987.

Bernheimer, Charles, and Claire Kahane. *In Dora's Case: Freud-Hysteria-Feminism*. New York: Columbia UP, 1985.

Bishop, John. "Introduction." *Finnegans Wake*. By James Joyce. New York: Penguin, 1999. vii–xxv.

Blake, William. *The Complete Poetry and Prose of William Blake*. Ed. David V. Erdman. New York: Doubleday, 1988.

Bloom, Harold. *Shakespeare: The Invention of the Human*. New York: Riverhead Books, 1998.

Boheemen-Saaf, Christine van. *Joyce, Derrida, Lacan, and the Trauma of History: Reading, Narrative, and Postcolonialism*. Cambridge: Cambridge UP, 1999.

Borges, Jorge Luis. *In Praise of Darkness*. Trans. Norman Thomas di Giovanni. New York: Dutton, 1974.

———. *Selected Non-fictions*. Ed. Eliot Weinberger. Trans. Esther Allen, Suzanne Jill Levine, and Eliot Weinberger. New York, Viking, 1999.

———. *A Universal History of Infamy*. Trans. Norman Thomas di Giovanni. New York: E. P. Dutton, 1972.

Bosinelli, Rosa Maria, Carla Vaglia, and Christine van Boheemen, eds. *The Languages of Joyce: Selected Papers from the 11th International James Joyce Symposium*. Philadelphia: J. Benjamins, 1992.

Bowie, Malcolm. *Lacan*. Cambridge, MA: Harvard UP, 1991.

Brewer, Ebenezer C. *Brewer's Dictionary of Phrase and Fable* (1870). Ed. Ivor H. Evans. New York: Harper & Row, 1981.

Brivic, Sheldon [Shelly]. "The Disjunctive Structure of Joyce's *Portrait*." *Case Studies in Contemporary Criticism:* A Portrait of the Artist as Young Man. 2nd ed. Ed. R. B. Kershner. Boston: St. Martin's, 2006. 279–98.

———. *Joyce between Freud and Jung*. Port Washington: Kennikat P, 1980.

———. "Joyce, Lyotard, and Art as Damnation." *James Joyce Quarterly* 41.4 (Summer 2004): 701–17.

———. *Joyce the Creator*. Madison: U of Wisconsin P, 1985.

———. *Joyce's Waking Women: An Introduction to* Finnegans Wake. Madison: U of Wisconsin P, 1995.

———. "Social Significance of Bloom's Psychology in "Circe." *Joyce & Paris: 1902...1920–1940...1975: Papers from the Fifth International James Joyce Symposium, Paris 16–20 June 1975*. Ed. Jacques Aubert and Maria Jolas. Paris: *Editions du CNRS*, 1979.

———. *The Veil of Signs: Joyce, Lacan, and Perception*. Urbana: U of Illinois P, 1991.

Buber, Martin. "The Primary Words." *The Modern Tradition: Backgrounds of Modern Literature*. Ed. Richard Ellmann and Charles Feidelson, Jr. New York: Oxford UP. 870–76.

Burke, Sean. *The Death and Return of the Author: Criticism and Subjectivity*... Edinburgh: Edinburgh UP, 1992.

Burns, Christy L. *Gestural Politics: Stereotype and Parody in Joyce*. Albany: State U of New York P, 2000.

Butler, Judith. *Bodies That Matter: On the Discursive Limits of "Sex."* New York: Routledge, 1993.

———. *Gender Trouble: Feminism and the Subversion of Identity*. New York: Routledge, 1990.

———. *The Psychic Life of Power*. Stanford: Stanford UP, 1997.

———. *Undoing Gender*. New York: Routledge, 2004.

Buttigieg, Joseph A. A Portrait of the Artist *in Different Perspective*. Athens: Ohio UP, 1987.

Campbell, Joseph , and Henry Morton Robinson. *A Skeleton Key to* Finnegans Wake. New York: Harcourt, Brace, 1944.

Chang, Gordon C. *The Coming Collapse of China*. New York: Random House, 2001.

Chang, Iris. *The Rape of Nanking: The Forgotten Holocaust of World War II*. New York: Basic Books, 1997.

Cheng, Vincent J. *Joyce, Race, and Empire*. New York: Cambridge UP, 1995.

Chodorow, Nancy. *Feminism and Psychoanalytic Theory*. New Haven: Yale UP, 1989.

———. "Heterosexuality as a Compromise Formation: Reflections on the Psychoanalytic Theory of Sexual Development." Lecture at Haverford College, October 18, 1991.

Chow, Rey. "The Old/New Question of Comparison in Literary Studies: A Post-European Perspective. *ELH* 71.2 (Summer 2004): 289–311.

Cixous, Hélène. *The Exile of James Joyce*. Trans. Sally A. J. Purcell. New York: David Lewis, 1972.

Cixous, Hélène, and Catherine Clément. *The Newly Born Woman*. Trans. Betsy Wing. Minneapolis: U of Minnesota P, 1987.

Cohn, Dorrit. *Transparent Minds: Narrative Modes for Presenting Consciousness in Fiction*. Princeton: Princeton UP, 1978.

Copleston, Frederick, S. J. *A History of Philosophy, Vol. 2: Mediaeval Philosophy, Part I*. Garden City: Doubleday Image, 1962.

Cotter, David. *James Joyce & the Perverse Ideal*. New York: Routledge, 2003.

Craig, Hardin, ed. *The Complete Works of Shakespeare*. Chicago: Scott, Foresman, 1961.

Crispi, Luca, and Sam Slote, eds. *How Joyce Wrote* Finnegans Wake: *A Chapter-by-Chapter Genetic Guide*. Madison: U of Wisonsin P, 2007.

Dante Alighieri. *The Divine Comedy: Inferno. 1: Italian Text and Translation*. Trans. Charles S. Singleton. Princeton: Princeton UP, 1970.

David-Ménard, Monique. *Hysteria from Freud to Lacan: Body and Language in Psychoanalysis*. Trans. Catherine Porter. Ithaca: Cornell UP, 1989.

De Hartog, Leo. *Genghis Khan, Conqueror of the World*. London: I. B. Tauris, 1999.

Deleuze, Gilles. *Masochism: An Interpretation of Coldness and Cruelty, together with* Venus in Furs. Trans. Jean McNeil. New York: George Braziller, 1971.

Deleuze, Gilles, and Felix Guattari. *Anti-Oedipus: Capitalism and Schizophrenia*. Trans. Robert Hurley, Mark Seem, Helen R. Lane. New York: Viking, 1977.

Delrieu, Andre. "*Poetes Modernes de l'Angleterre:* Shelley." *Review de Paris* 22.4 (1843): 25–51, 185–201.

Derrida, Jacques. *Dissemination*. Trans. Barbara Johnson. Chicago: U of Chicago P, 1981.

———. *The Post Card: From Socrates to Freud and Beyond*. Trans. Alan Bass. Chicago: U of Chicago P, 1987.

———. "Two Words for Joyce." *Post-structuralist Joyce: Essays from the French*. Ed. Derek Attridge and Daniel Ferrer. Cambridge: Cambridge UP, 1984. 145–59.

Dettmar, Kevin J. H. *The Illicit Joyce of Postmodernism: Reading Against the Grain*. Madison: U of Wisconsin P, 1996.

Devlin, Kimberly J. *James Joyce's "Fraudstuff."* Gainesville: UP of Florida, 2002.

———. *Wandering and Return in* Finnegans Wake: *An Integrative Approach to Joyce's Fictions*. Princeton: Princeton UP, 1991.

Dickens, Charles. *Great Expectations*. Ed. Edgar Rosenberg. New York: W. W. Norton, 1999.

Dougherty, Carol. *The Raft of Odysseus: The Ethnographic Imagination of Homer's* Odyssey. New York: Oxford, 2001.

Duffy, Enda. *The Subaltern* Ulysses. Minneapolis: U of Minnesota P, 1994.

Eagleton, Terry. "Brecht and Rhetoric." *Against the Grain*. London: Verso, 1986. 167–172.

———. *Literary Theory: An Introduction*. Minneapolis: Minnesota UP, 1996.

———. "On the Contrary." *Art Forum* (Summer 2006): 61–62.

Eide, Marian. *Ethical Joyce*. Cambridge: Cambridge UP, 2002.

Ellmann, Maud. "The Name and the Scar: Identity in *The Odyssey* and *A Portrait of the Artist as a Young Man*." *James Joyce's* A Portrait of the Artist as a Young Man: *A Casebook*. Ed. Mark A. Wollaeger. New York: Oxford, 2003. 143–81.

Ellmann, Richard. *James Joyce*. Rev. ed. New York: Oxford UP, 1982.
———. *Ulysses on the Liffey*. New York: Oxford UP, 1972.
Ellmann, Richard, and Charles Feidelson, Jr., eds. *The Modern Tradition: Backgrounds of Modern Literature*. New York: Oxford UP, 1965.
Felman, Shoshana. *Jacques Lacan and the Adventure of Insight: Psychoanalysis in Contemporary Culture*. Cambridge, MA: Harvard UP, 1987.
Fenichel, Otto. *The Psychoanalytic Theory of Neurosis*. New York: W. W. Norton, 1945.
Fergusson, Niall. *Colossus: The Price of America's Empire*. New York: Penguin Press, 2004.
Filas, Francis L., S. J. *St. Joseph and Daily Christian Living: Reflections on His Life and Devotion*. New York: Macmillan, 1959.
Fink, Bruce. *The Lacanian Subject: Between Language and Jouissance*. Princeton: Princeton UP, 1995.
Fish, Stanley. "Interpreting the Variorum." *Contemporary Literary Criticism: Literary and Cultural Studies*. Ed. Robert Con Davis and Ronald Schleifer. 3rd ed. New York: Longman, 1994.
Fleischer, Robert. *Artemis von Ephesos und Verwandte Kultstatuen aus Anatolien und Syrien*. Leiden: E. J. Brill, 1973.
Forster, Edward Morgan. *A Passage to India*. San Diego: Harcourt Harvest, 1984.
Foucault, Michel. *The History of Sexuality, Volume 1: An Introduction*. Trans. Robert Hurley. New York: Vintage, 1990.
———. "What Is an Author?" *Criticism: Major Statements*. 4th ed. Ed. Charles Kaplan and William Davis Anderson. Boston: Bedford/St. Martin's, 2000. 544–58.
Fowler, Robert. *The Cambridge Companion to Homer*. Cambridge: Cambridge UP, 2004.
French, Howard W. "Japan Rewrites Its Manchuria Story." *New York Times* September 19, 2004. News of the Week: 5.
Freud, Sigmund. *The Standard Edition of the Complete Psychological Works of Sigmund Freud*. Ed. and Trans. James Strachey in collaboration with Anna Freud, assisted by Alix Strachey and Alan Tyson. 24 vols. London: Hogarth, 1953–74.
Froula. Christine. *Modernism's Body: Sex, Culture, and Joyce*. New York: Columbia UP, 1996.
Gates, Henry Louis, Jr. *The Signifying Monkey: A Theory of African-American Literary Criticism*. New York: Oxford UP, 1988.
Gibson, Andrew. "An Irish Bull in an English Chinashop " *Joyce on the Threshold*. Ed. Anne Fogarty and Timothy Martin. Gainesville: UP of Florida, 2005.
———. *Joyce's Revenge: History, Politics, and Aesthetics in "Ulysses."* Oxford: Oxford UP, 2002.
Gibson, George Cinclair. *Wake Rites: The Ancient Irish Rituals of* Finnegans Wake. Gainesville: UP of Florida, 2005.

Giedion-Welcker, Carola. "Meetings with Joyce." In Potts 256–80.
Gifford, Don. *Joyce Annotated: Notes for* Dubliners *and* A Portrait of the Artist as a Young Man. Berkeley: U of California P, 1982.
Gifford, Don with Robert J. Seidman. Ulysses *Annotated: Notes for James Joyce's* Ulysses. 2nd ed. Berkeley: U of California P, 1988.
Glasheen, Adeline. *A Third Census of* Finnegans Wake*: An Index of the Characters and Their Roles.* Berkeley: U of California P, 1977.
Goldman, Arnold. *The Joyce Paradox: Form and Freedom in His Fiction.* Evanston: Northwestern UP, 1966.
Goldwasser, Thomas A. "Who Was Vladimir Dixon? Was He Vladimir Dixon?" *James Joyce Quarterly* 16 (Summer 1979): 219–22.
Griffin, Jasper. *Homer:* The Odyssey. Cambridge: Cambridge UP, 1987.
Groden, Michael, ed. *The James Joyce Archive.* 63 vols. New York: Garland, 1978.
———. Ulysses *in Progress.* Princeton: Princeton UP, 1977.
Harari, Roberto. *How James Joyce Made His Name: A Reading of the Final Lacan.* Trans. Luke Thurston. New York: Other Press, 1995.
Hart, Clive. *Structure and Motif in* Finnegans Wake. Evanston: Northwestern UP, 1962.
Hart, Clive, and Fritz Senn, eds. *A* Wake *Digest.* Sydney: Sydney UP, 1968.
Hayman, David. *The* Wake *in Transit.* Ithaca: Cornell UP, 1990.
Hegel, Georg Wilhelm Friedrich. *Phenomenology of Spirit.* Trans. A. V. Miller. Oxford: Oxford UP, 1977.
Henke: Suzette A. *James Joyce and the Politics of Desire.* New York: Routledge, 1990.
Herring, Phillip F. *Joyce's Uncertainty Principle.* Princeton: Princeton UP, 1987.
Heubeck, Alfred, and Arie Hoekstra. *A Commentary on Homer's* Odyssey, *Vol. II.* Oxford: Oxford UP, 1989.
Homer, *The Odyssey.* Trans. S. H. Butcher and A. V. Lang. New York: Collier, 1909.
———. *The Odyssey.* Trans. Richmond Lattimore. New York: Harper & Row, 1975.
Ignatieff, Michael. *The Lesser Evil: Political Ethics in an Age of Terror.* Princeton: Princeton UP, 2004.
Ingersoll, Earl G. *Engendered Tropes in Joyce's* Dubliners. Carbondale: Southern Illinois UP, 1996.
Irigaray, Luce. *This Sex Which Is Not One.* Trans. Catherine Porter. Ithaca: Cornell UP, 1985.
Ito, Eishiro. "The Japanese Elements of *Finnegans Wake.*" *Joycean Japan* 15 (2004): 36–50.
———. "Mediterranean Joyce Meditates on Buddha." Unpublished paper.
*James Joyce/*Finnegans Wake: *A Symposium: Our Exagmination Round His Factification for Incamination of Work in Progress.* New York: New Directions, 1972.

James, William. "The Stream of Consciousness." *The Modern Tradition: Backgrounds of Modern Literature*. Ed. Richard Ellmann and Charles Feidelson, Jr. New York: Oxford, 1965. 715–23.

Jameson, Frederic. "Imaginary and Symbolic in Lacan: Marxism, Psychoanalytic Criticism and the Problem of the Subject." *Yale French Studies* 55.56 (1977): 338–95.

———. *The Political Unconscious: Narrative as a Socially Symbolic Act*. Ithaca: Cornell UP, 1981.

———. *Postmodernism, or The Cultural Logic of Late Capitalism*. Durham: Duke UP, 1991.

———. *A Singular Modernity: Essay on the Ontology of the Present*. London: Verso, 2002.

Janmohamed, Abdul R. "Negating the Negation: The Construction of Richard Wright." *Richard Wright: Critical Perspectives Past and Present*. Ed. Henry louis Gates, Jr., and Kwame A. Appiah. New York: Amistad, 1993.

Jarman, Derek, dir. *Wittgenstein*. Screenplay by Terry Eagleton. BBC, 1993.

Johnson, Barbara. "The Frame of Reference: Poe, Lacan, Derrida." *Yale French Studies* 55.56 (1977): 457–505.

Jones, Ellen Carol. " 'an apogean humanity of beings created in varying forms': The 2004 Conference on James Joyce and the Humanities, Seoul, South Korea, November 2004." *James Joyce Quarterly* 41.1/2 (Fall 2003/ Winter 2004): 15–24.

Jordan-Smith, Paul. *A Key to the* Ulysses *of James Joyce*. Chicago: Covici, 1934.

Joyce, James. *The Critical Writings of James Joyce*. Ed. Ellsworth Mason and Richard Ellmann. New York: Viking, 1959.

———. *Dubliners*. Ed. Robert Scholes. New York: Viking, 1967.

———. *Exiles* New York: Viking, 1961.

———. *Finnegans Wake*. New York: Penguin, 1999.

———. *Giacomo Joyce*. New York: Viking, 1968.

———. *Letters of James Joyce, Vol. 2*. Ed. Richard Ellmann. New York: Viking, 1966.

———. *Letters of James Joyce, Vol. 3*. Ed. Richard Ellmann. New York: Viking, 1966.

———. *Occasional, Critical, and Political Writings*. Ed. Kevin Barry. Oxford: Oxford UP, 2000.

———. *A Portrait of the Artist as a Young Man*. Ed. Hans Walter Gabler. New York: Vintage, 1993.

———. *A Portrait of the Artist as a Young Man*. Ed. Seamus Deane. New York: Penguin, 1993.

———. *A Portrait of the Artist as a Young Man: Text , Criticism, and Notes*. Ed. Chester G. Anderson. New York: Viking, 1968.

———. *Selected Letters*. Ed. Richard Ellmann. New York: Viking, 1975.

Joyce, James. *Stephen Hero*. Ed. Theodore Spencer. New York: New Directions, 1963.
———. *Ulysses*. Ed. Hans Walter Gabler. New York: Random House, 1986.
Kafka, Franz. *The Great Wall of China: Stories and Reflections*. Trans. Willa and Edwin Muir. New York: Schocken, 1946.
Kant, Immanuel. *Critique of Pure Reason*. Trans. Norman Kemp Smith. New York: St. Martin's, 1965.
Kenner, Hugh. *Dublin's Joyce*. Bloomington: Indiana UP, 1956.
———. "Molly's Masterstroke." *James Joyce Quarterly* 1 (Fall 1972): 19–28.
———. *Ulysses*. Rev. ed. Baltimore: Johns Hopkins UP, 1987.
Kershner, Richard Brandon. "The Artist as Text: Dialogism and Incremental Repetition in *Portrait*. *ELH* 53 (Winter 1986): 881–94.
———. "The Culture of Dedalus: Urban Circulation, Degeneration, and the Panoptican." *James Joyce: A Portrait of the Artist as a Young Man*. 2nd ed. Ed. R. B. Kershner. Boston: St. Martin's, 2006. 357–77.
Kimball, Jean. "Love and Death in *Ulysses*: 'Word Known to All Men.'" *James Joyce Quarterly* 32.2 (Winter 1995): 143–60.
Klein, Melanie. *The Psychoanalysis of Children*. 1948. Trans. Alix Strachey. New York: Grove Press, 1960.
Kristeva, Julia. *Desire in Language: A Semiotic Approach to Literature and Art*. Ed. Leon S. Roudiez. Trans. Thomas Gora, Alice Jardine, and Leon S. Roudiez. New York: Columbia UP, 1980.
———. "Joyce 'The Gracehoper' or the Return of Orpheus." *James Joyce: The Augmented Ninth*. Ed. Bernard Benstock. Syracuse: Syracuse UP, 1988.
———. *Powers of Horror: An Essay on Abjection*. Trans. Leon S. Roudiez. New York: Columbia UP, 1982.
———. *Revolution in Poetic Language*. Trans. Margaret Waller. New York: Columbia UP, 1984.
Kristof, Nicholas D., and Sheryl WuDunn. *Thunder from the East: Portrait of a Rising Asia*. New York: Alfred A. Knopf, 2000.
Lacan, Jacques. *Écrits*. Trans. Bruce Fink. New York: W. W. Norton, 2006.
———. *The Four Fundamental Concepts of Psycho-Analysis*. (Seminar XI). Ed. Jacques-Alain Miller. Trans. Álan Sheridan. New York: W. W. Norton, 1978.
———. "Impromptu at Vincennes." Trans. Jeffrey Mehlman. *October* 40 (1987): 116–27.
———. *"Lituraterre." Autres Écrits*. Ed. Jacques-Alain Miller. Paris: Seuil, 2001. 3–12.
———. *Le Seminaire, livre XXIII: Le sinthome*. Ed. Jacques-Alain Miller. Paris: *Editions du Seuil, 2005*.
———. *Seminar II: The Ego in Freud's Theory and in the Technique of Psychoanalysis, 1954–1955*. Ed. Jacques-Alain Miller. Trans. Sylvana Tomaselli. New York: W. W. Norton, 1988.

———. *Seminar VII: The Ethics of Psycho-Analysis, 1959–60*. Ed. Jacques Alain Miller. Trans. Dennis Porter. New York: W. W. Norton, 1992.
———. *Seminar X: Anxiety, 1962–63*. Trans. Cormac Gallagher. For Private Use Only. Unofficially published in Ireland around 1990.
———. *Seminar XVII: The Other Side of Psychoanalysis*. Ed. Jacques-Alain Miller. Trans. Russell Grigg. New York: W. W. Norton, 2007.
———. *Seminar XX: Encore: On Feminine Sexuality, the Limits of Love and Knowledge, 1972–73*. Ed. Jacques-Alain Miller. Trans. Bruce Fink. New York: W. W. Norton, 1998.
Lacan, Jacques, and Wladimir Granoff. "Fetishism: The Symbolic, the Imaginary, and the Real." *Perversions: Psychodynamics and Therapy*. Ed. Sandor Lorand and Michael Balint. New York: Random House, 1956.
Lamos, Colleen. *Deviant Modernism: Sexual and Textual Errancy in T. S. Eliot. James Joyce, and Marcel Proust*. Cambridge: Cambridge UP, 1998.
LaPlanche, Jean, and J. B. Pontalis. *The Language of Psycho-analysis*. Trans. Donald Nicholson-Smith. London: Hogarth Press, 1973.
Laurence, Patricia. *Lily Briscoe's Chinese Eyes: Bloomsbury, Modernism, and China*. Columbia: U of South Carolina P, 2003.
Lawrence, Karen. *The Odyssey of Style in Joyce's* Ulysses. Princeton: Princeton UP, 1981.
Lee, Robert G. *Orientals: Asian Americans in Popular Culture*. Philadelphia: Temple UP, 1999.
Leonard, Garry M. *Reading* Dubliners *Again: A Lacanian Perspective*. Syracuse: Syracuse UP, 1993.
Levenson, Michael. "Stephen's Diary in Joyce's *Portrait*: The Shape of Life." *ELH* 52.4 (1985): 1017–35.
Levi-Strauss, Claude. *The Elementary Structures of Kinship*. Boston: Beacon Press, 1969.
Levin, Richard, and Charles Shattuck. "First Flight to Ithaca: A New Reading of Joyce's *Dubliners*." *James Joyce: Two Decades of Criticism*. Ed. Seon Givens. New York: Vanguard P, 1948. 47–94.
Leyda, Jay. *Kino: A History of the Russian and Soviet Film*. New York: Collier Books, 1973.
Lyotard, Jean-Francois. *The Differend: Phrases in Dispute*. Trans. Georges Van Den Abbeele. Minneapolis: U of Minnesota P, 1988.
———. *The Postmodern Condition: A Report on Knowledge*. Trans. Geoff Bennington and Brian Massumi. Minneapolis: U of Minnesota P, 1984.
MacCabe, Colin. *James Joyce and the Revolution of the Word*. London: Macmillan, 1978.
Maddox, Brenda. *Nora: The Real Life of Molly Bloom*. Boston: Houghton Mifflin, 1988.
Mahaffey, Vicki. "Joyce and Gender." *Palgrave Advances in James Joyce Studies*. Ed. Jean-Michel Rabaté. New York: Palgrave Macmillan, 2004.

———. *Reauthorizing Joyce*. Cambridge: Cambridge UP, 1988.
———. "Those Dirty Sheets: Paper, Linen, Ink, and Soil." Paper at Nineteenth International James Joyce Symposium. Dublin, June 17, 2004.
Malraux, Andre. *Man's Fate*. Trans. Haakon M. Chevalier. New York: Vintage, 1961.
Manganiello, Dominic. *Joyce's Politics*. London: Routledge and Kegan Paul, 1980.
Mann, Thomas. *The Magic Mountain*. Trans. Harriet T. Lowe-Porter. New York: Knopf, 1927.
———. "Tonio Kröger." *Stories of Three Decades*. Trans. Harriet T. Lowe-Porter. New York: Knopf, 1936. 85–132.
Marx, Karl. *Capital: A Critique of Political Economy, Vol. I*. Ed. Frederick Engels. Trans. Samuel Moore and Edward Aveling. New York: International Publishers, 1967.
Mason, Colin. *A Short History of Asia: Stone Age to 2000 AD*. New York: St. Martin's, 2000.
McHugh, Roland. *Annotations to* Finnegans Wake. 3rd ed. Baltimore: Johns Hopkins UP, 2006.
———. *The Sigla of* Finnegans Wake. Austin: U of Texas P, 1976.
Mead, Rebecca. "The Marx Brother." *The New Yorker* May 5, 2003: 38–47.
Melville, Herman. "Bartleby the Scrivener: A Tale of Wall Street." *Selected Tales and Poems by Herman Melville*. Ed. Richard Chase. New York: Holt, Rinehart and Winston, 1950. 92–131.
Miller, Jacques-Alain. "On Shame." *Jacques Lacan and the Other Side of Psychoanalysis*. Ed. Justin Clemens and Russell Grigg. Durham: Duke UP, 2006.
Mink, Louis O. *A* Finnegans Wake *Gazeteer*. Bloomington: Indiana UP, 1978.
Mizoguchi, Kenzi, dir. *The Loyal 47 Ronin, Part II*. Japan, 1942.
Morrison, Toni. *The Bluest Eye*. New York: Plume, 1994.
———. *Playing in the Dark: Whiteness and the Literary Imagination*. New York: Vintage, 1993.
Morrison, Van. "Cleaning Windows." *Live at the Grand Opera House Belfast*. Mercury CD 818 336–2M-1, 1984.
Morton, W. Scott. *China: Its History and Culture*. New York: Lippincott and Crowell, 1980.
Mullin, Katherine. *James Joyce, Sexuality, and Social Purity*. Cambridge: Cambridge UP, 2003
Murphy, Sean P. *James Joyce and Victims: Reading the Logic of Exclusion*. Cranbury: Associated U Presses, 2003.
Nasio, Juan-David. *Hysteria from Freud to Lacan: The Splendid Child of Psychoanalysis*. Trans. Susan Fairfield. New York: Other Press, 1998.
Nathanson, Donald L. *Shame and Pride: Affect, Sex, and the Birth of the Self*. New York: W. W. Norton, 1992.

Nietzsche, Friedrich. "*From* On Truth and Lie in an Extra-Moral Sense." *The Portable Nietzsche*. Ed. Walter Kaufmann. New York: Viking, 1954. 42–47.

———. *Thus Spoke Zarathustra*. Trans. R. J. Hollingdale. Baltimore: Penguin, 1961.

Norris, Margot. *Joyce's Web: The Social Unraveling of Modernism*. Austin: U of Texas P, 1992.

———. "The Last Chapter of *Finnegans Wake:* Stephen Finds His Mother." *James Joyce Quarterly* 25.1 (Fall 1987): 11–30.

———. *Suspicious Readings of Joyce's* Dubliners. Philadelphia: U of Pennsylvania P, 2003.

———. *Writing War in the Twentieth Century*. Charlottesville: U of Virginia P, 2000.

Olson, Toby. *The Woman Who Escaped from Shame*. New York: Random House, 1986.

O'Neill, Eugene. *Strange Interlude. Three Plays of Eugene O'Neill.* New York: Vintage, 1958. 60–222.

Osteen, Mark. *The Economy of* Ulysses: *Making Both Ends Meet*. Syracuse: Syracuse UP, 1995.

Our Exagmination—See *James Joyce*/Finnegans Wake: *A Symposium*.

Pearce, Richard. *The Politics of Narration: James Joyce, William Faulkner, and Virginia Woolf*. New Brunswick: Rutgers UP, 1991.

Platt. Len. *Joyce, Race and* Finnegans Wake. Cambridge: Cambridge UP, 2007.

Pollock, Harry J. "The Girl Joyce Did Not Marry." *James Joyce Quarterly* 4.4 (Summer 1967): 255–57.

Potts, Willard. *Portraits of the Artist in Exile: Recollections of James Joyce by Europeans*. San Diego: Harcourt Brace Jovanovich, 1986.

Power, Arthur. *Conversations with James Joyce*. New York: Barnes and Noble, 1974.

Proust, Marcel. *Swann's Way. Remembrance of Things Past, Vol. I.* Trans. C. K. Scott Moncrieff and Terence Kilmartin. New York: Vintage, 1981.

Pudovkin, Vsevolod Ilarionovich, dir. *Storm over Asia* (1928). Kino Video, 1997.

Pynchon, Thomas. *Mason & Dixon*. New York: Henry Holt, 1997.

Rabaté, Jean Michel, ed. *The Cambridge Companion to Lacan*. Cambridge: Cambridge UP, 2003.

———. *Jacques Lacan: Psychoanalysis and the Subject of Literature. New York: Palgrave, 2001.*

———. *James Joyce and the Politics of Egoism*. Cambridge: Cambridge UP, 2001.

———. *Joyce upon the Void: The Genesis of Doubt*. New York: St. Martin's, 1991.

———. "Lapsus ex machina." *Post-structuralist Joyce: Essays from the French*. Ed. Derek Attridge and Daniel Ferrer. Cambridge: Cambridge UP, 1984.

Reed, Ishmael. *Mumbo Jumbo*. New York: Atheneum. 1988.

Reik, Theodore. *Masochism in Modern Man.* New York: Farrar and Rinehart, 1941.

Reisman, Karl. "Darktongues: Fufulde and Hausa in *Finnegans Wake.*" *Journal of Modern Literature* 31.2 (2008): 79–103.

Restuccia, Frances L. *Joyce and the Law of the Father.* New Haven: Yale UP, 1989.

Richards, Ivor A. *Practical Criticism: A Study of Literary Judgment.* New York: Harcourt Brace, 1956.

Rickard, John S. *Joyce's Book of Memory: The Mnemotechnic of* Ulysses. Durham: Duke UP, 1999.

Riquelme, John Paul. "Joyce's 'The Dead': The Dissolution of the Self and the Police." *Rejoycing: New Readings of* Dubliners. Ed. Rosa M. Bollettieri Bosinelli and Harold F. Mosher, Jr. Lexington: UP of Kentucky, 1998. 123–41.

———. *Teller and Tale in Joyce's Fiction: Oscillating Perspectives.* Baltimore: Johns Hopkins UP, 1983.

Rose, Danis, ed. *James Joyce's The Index Manuscript:* Finnegans Wake *Holograph Workbook VI.B.46.* Colchester: A Wake Newslitter P, 1978.

Rose, Danis, and John O'Hanlon. *Understanding* Finnegans Wake: *A Guide to the Narrative of James Joyce's Masterpiece.* New York: Garland, 1982.

Roudinesco, Elisabeth. *Jacques Lacan.* Trans. Barbara Bray. New York: Columbia UP, 1997.

Ryan, Marie-Laure. *Possible Worlds, Artificial Intelligence, and Narrative Theory.* Bloomington: Indiana UP, 2001.

Said, Edward W. *Culture and Imperialism.* New York: Vintage, 1994.

———. *Orientalism.* New York: Vintage, 1979.

Schlossman, Beryl. *Joyce's Catholic Comedy of Language.* Madison: U of Wisconsin P, 1995.

Schutte, William. *Joyce and Shakespeare: A Study of the Meaning of* Ulysses. New Haven: Yale, 1957.

Seidel, Michael. *Epic Geography: James Joyce's* Ulysses. Princeton: Princeton UP, 1976.

Shapiro, David. *Neurotic Styles.* New York: Basic Books, 1965.

Sheffield, Elizabeth. *Joyce's Abandoned Female Costumes, Gratefully Received.* Cranbury, NJ: Associated U Presses, 1998.

Shelley. See Zillman.

Shepherdson, Charles. *Vital Signs: Nature, Culture, Psychoanalysis.* New York: Routledge, 2000.

Shepperd, Rene. E-mail to Sheldon Brivic, 1992.

Showalter, Elaine. "Hysteria, Feminism, and Gender." *Hysteria Beyond Freud.* Ed. Sandor L. Gilman. Berkeley: U of California P, 1993. 280–338.

Skeat, Walter W. *A Concise Etymological Dictionary of the English Language.* New York: Harper and Bros., 1882.

Smitherman, Geneva. *Black Talk: Words and Phrases from the Hood to the Amen Corner.* Rev. ed. Boston: Houghton Mifflin, 2000.

Spoo, Robert. *James Joyce and the Language of History: Dedalus's Nightmare.* New York: Oxford UP, 1994.

Stanford, W. B. *The Ulysses Theme: A Study in the Adaptability of a Traditional Hero.* 2nd ed. Ann Arbor: Ann Arbor Paperbacks, 1968.

Staten, Henry. "The Decomposing Form of Joyce's *Ulysses.*" *PMLA* 112 (1997): 380–92.

Storey, Robert F. "I am I Because My Little Dog Knows Me: Prolegomenon . . . ." *Criticism* 32 (1990): 419–48.

Storry, Richard. *A History of Modern Japan.* London: Cassell, 1962.

Taylor, Astra, dir. *Žižek!* Zeitgeist Films, 2005.

Terkel, Studs. *Giants of Jazz.* Rev. ed. New York: Harper Collins, 1975.

Thornton, Weldon. *The Antimodernism of Joyce's* Portrait of the Artist as a Young Man. Syracuse: Syracuse UP, 1994.

Thurston, Luke. "Ineluctable Nodalities: On the Borromean Knot." *Key Concepts of Lacanian Psychoanalysis.* Ed. Dany Nobus. New York: Other Press, 1999. 139–63.

———. *James Joyce and the Problem of Psychoanalysis.* Cambridge: Cambridge UP, 2004.

———, ed. *Re-inventing the Symptom: Essays on the Final Lacan.* New York: Other Press, 2002.

Thwaites, Tony. *Joycean Temporalities: Debts, Promises, and Countersignatures.* Gainesville: UP of Florida, 2001.

Tomkins, Sylvan. *Shame and Its Sisters: A Sylvan Tomkins Reader.* Ed. Eve Kosofsky Sedgwick and Adam Frank. Durham, NC: Duke UP, 1995.

Trench, C. E. F. "Dermot Chenevix Trench and Haines of *Ulysses.*" *James Joyce Quarterly* 13 (Fall 1975): 39–48.

Valente, Joseph. *James Joyce and the Problem of Justice: Negotiating Sexual and Colonial Difference.* Cambridge: Cambridge UP, 1995.

———. "Joyce's Politics: Race, Nation, and Transnationalism." *Palgrave Advances in James Joyce Studies.* Ed. Jean-Michel Rabaté. New York: Palgrave Macmillan, 2004.

———. "Thrilled by His Touch": The Aestheticizing of Homosexual Panic in "*A Portrait of the Artist as a Young Man.*" *James Joyce's* A Portrait of the Artist as a Young Man: *A Casebook.* Ed. Mark. A Wollaeger. New York: Oxford U P, 2003. 245–80.

Walcott, Derek. *Omeros.* New York: Noonday, 1992.

Werner, Craig Hansen. *Paradoxical Resolutions: American Fiction since Joyce.* Urbana: U of Illinois P, 1982.

Williams, Michael, ed. *The African American Encyclopedia.* New York: Marshall Cavendish, 1993.

Wilson, Carolyn C. *St. Joseph in Italian Renaissance Society and Art: New Directions and Interpretations.* Philadelphia: St. Joseph's UP, 2001.

Winnicott, Donald W. *Playing and Reality.* Harmondsworth: Penguin, 1974.

Winnicott, Donald W. *Therapeutic Consultations in Child Psychiatry*. New York: Basic Books, 1971.
Wollaeger, Mark A. "Between Stephen and Jim: Portraits of Joyce as a Young Man." *James Joyce's* A Portrait of the Artist as a Young Man: *A Casebook*. Ed. Mark. A Wollaeger. New York: Oxford UP, 2003.
Wright, Richard. *Lawd Today!* Boston: Northeastern UP, 1993.
Wu, William F. *The Yellow Peril: Chinese Americans in American Fiction, 1850–1940*. Hamden: Archon Books, 1982.
Wurmser, Leon. *The Mask of Shame*. Baltimore: Johns Hopkins UP, 1981.
Yared, Aida. "'In the Name of Annah': Islam and *Salam* in Joyce's *Finnegans Wake*." *James Joyce Quarterly* 35.2/3 (Winter/Spring 1998): 401–38.
Zakaria, Fareed. "Does the Future Belong to China?" *Newsweek* May 9, 2005: 26–40.
Zillman, Lawrence John, ed. *Shelley's* Prometheus Unbound: *A Variorum Edition*. Seattle: U of Washington P, 1959.
Žižek, Slavoj. *Enjoy Your Symptom! Jacques Lacan in Hollywood and Out*. New York: Routledge, 1992.
———. *The Fragile Absolute or, Why Is the Christian Legacy Worth Fighting For?* London: Verso, 2000.
———. "From Joyce-the-Symptom to the Symptom of Power." http://www.plexus.org/lacink11/zizek.html. Last accessed April 20, 2001.
———. *Looking Awry: An Introduction to Jacques Lacan through Popular Culture*. Cambridge, MA: MIT Press, 1992.
———. *The Metastases of Enjoyment: Six Essays on Woman and Causality*. London: Verso, 1994
———. "The Obscene Object of Postmodernity." *The Žižek Reader*. Ed. Elizabeth Wright and Edmond Wright. Oxford: Blackwell, 1999. 37–52.
———. *On Belief*. New York: Routledge, 2001.
———. *The Parallax View*. Cambridge, MA: MIT Press, 2006.
———. *The Plague of Fantasies*. London: Verso, 1997.
———. *Tarrying with the Negative: Kant, Hegel, and the Critique of Ideology*. Durham: Duke UP, 1993.
———. *The Ticklish Subject: The Absent Centre of Political Ontology*. London: Verso, 1999.
———. "Why Lacan Is Not a 'Post-structuralist.'" *Newsletter of the Freudian Field* 1(Fall 1987): 31–39.
———. *The Žižek Reader*. Ed. Elizabeth Wright and Edmond Wright. Oxford: Blackwell, 1999.

Index